BEYOND
NEANDERTHAL

BEYOND
NEANDERTHAL

by
Brian Bloom

citrus press

First published in 2008

Citrus Press
66/89 Jones Street
Ultimo NSW 2007
Australia

National Library of Australia Cataloguing-in-Publication entry:

Author: Bloom, Brian
Title: Beyond Neanderthal / Brian Bloom
Publisher: Ultimo, NSW: Citrus Press
ISBN 978 0 9775356 1 3 (pbk)
Notes: Bibliography
Dewey Number: A823.4

Access to the ancient maps referred to in this novel can be gained by going to
www.beyondneanderthal.com and entering the Personal Identification Number
18000 in the section marked 'Research'.

Designed by saso content & design
Typeset by 1000 Monkeys Typesetting Services
Printed by Ligare

'The only way of discovering the limits of the possible
is to venture a little way past them into the impossible.'
Sir Arthur C Clarke, *Profiles of the Future*

To my late parents, Mildred and Joseph Bloom, who made me.
To my wife, Denise, who made me whole.

ACKNOWLEDGEMENTS

The assistance of the following people is gratefully acknowledged.

Andrea Bloom for words of encouragement when they were needed;

Anselmo Pedroni for challenging my unorthodox views on science in general, the climate in particular, and trying his best to stop me from making a fool of myself;

Alec Corday (www.ambarazul.com) for his generous help with blue amber and Dominican Republic related information;

Captain Meryl Getline, United Airlines (retired) (www.fromthecockpit.com) for her lifesaving assistance with the Boeing's approach into Las Americas Airport;

Catharine Retter for an *amazing* job of editing a manuscript that ended up looking nothing like it started off. Surprisingly, she had apparently never heard the adage about the silk purse out of a sow's ear;

Denise Bloom, thank you for your energy healing concepts, and thirty-seven years (and counting) of life education;

Dennis Polivnick and Warren Polivnick, for their assistance with the B200 flight instrumentation and pilot terminology;

Evan Soulé Jr, for your patience in explaining the principles that underlie Joseph Newman's Energy Machine;

Father Peter McGrath for his advice on the *New Testament* and Love;

Jenna Bloom for a young person's perspective, and for inventing the word 'pubbly';

Ken Biegeleisen, (www.Ark-Of-Salvation.org) for sharing his radically alternative view of the meaning of Genesis 16:12;

Mick Marjan and Karl Marjan for their revelations on Islamic culture over a period of nearly nine years of warm-hearted friendship;

Patrick Grellier for Samana Peninsular related information;

Rabbi David Freedman for his counsel on the *Old Testament*;

Rabbi Nochum Schapiro, for his wisdom, also on the *Old Testament*;

Rabbi Shmuel Kopel for enlightenment on the *Kabbalah*;

Richard Duncan, PhD and originator of the Olduvai Theory;

Steve Kurtz for constantly challenging my thought paradigms and providing me with clues on where to look;

Terence Bloom for his sage advice on various engineering concepts.

Brian Bloom

CHAPTER 1

THE PHONE CALL had come through two hours before the email
arrived.

'Samantha? Bill Tempest here in New York.'

'Hi Bill. Long time no see or hear. How are things going mate?'

'Sorry Samba. No time to chat. We've got an issue building. It needs
your attention.'

'What kind of issue?'

'Need to know basis—Chinese Walls.'

That was yesterday. Now, Samantha's mind was numbed by the enormity of what she had read in the email. It had taken her several hours to
discover the true extent of the problem and, almost certainly, it had been
caused by some dishonest bastard motivated by the myopia of a fat bonus.
He or she had very likely chosen to camouflage a blemish on the loan
portfolio and present it instead as a beauty spot. Almost certainly, the ratings
agencies—the arms length third parties that should have seen through the
cosmetic camouflage—had turned a blind eye. Why? Damn them. Where
were the checks and balances that should have been in place? Were they
too scared of the implications if they were wrong, or maybe … if they were
right? For now, it was just speculation of course. But how could anyone
with even a smidgeon of training have been fooled by such intellectual
dishonesty? Does no one give a damn anymore about ethics and morality?

'Deep, deep doodoo,' Samantha heard herself mutter. At best, and
given the realities of the financial implications, she couldn't see how it
could possibly be resolved with any semblance of integrity. It would
require a master of lies, obfuscation and bullshit artistry to muddle
through this one. But then again, maybe the power mongrels—the smoke
and mirrors experts—in the world's corridors of power could pull it off.

Whatever happened to that 'kinder, gentler nation' that George Bush the elder had been promoting all those years ago?

'We're breaking the problem down into pieces,' Bill Tempest had said to her, 'so that each section works only on its piece. Only two people will have the total picture, the chairman and I. Your piece happens to be the most sensitive. That's why we want you to handle it personally.' She could hear his breath at the other end of the phone. It was short and shallow. He'd either been running or this issue was bothering him even more than he let on. 'With you in Oz, you're far from the action in our time zone, and we don't want the guys in the US or the UK to get a whiff of what you're doing.'

'Sounds serious.'

'It is. And that's also why it's for your eyes only and no questions. No one gets to hear about this.'

'Not even Larry?'

'No one. Larry is Asia-Pacific region. This is Global. You are doing it for us. You talk to me and only me. Are we clear on that?'

'Clear. But I have one question.'

'Shoot.'

'I'm booked to go on holiday for a week to the Barrier Reef, with a friend who's coming half way across the world to join me. Should I cancel?'

'When are you scheduled to leave?'

'Friday. Day after tomorrow.'

'How long in total?'

'A week. Maybe ten days.'

'Don't cancel. Go. There should be no changes in anyone's routine. I'll be sending you an encoded email. It'll be self-explanatory. Read it, work on the attachment, send it back to me when you're finished and delete it from your system. I need it by sparrow fart Thursday morning my time. Okay?'

'Do you want me to keep myself available for follow up?'

'No. Frankly, it suits me that you'll be away on vacation. If you're not around, no one will be able to ask you questions. Just go about your normal business when you get back. Hopefully we can contain this thing to keep it out of the public eye.'

The phone line had gone dead. No goodbye. No nothing.

The email was marked 'high priority' for her personal attention. The attachment had been zipped closed, and required a twelve character alphanumeric code to be opened. Samantha Alexander was one of only three people in the Sydney Office of The Union Banking Corporation who had access to that code.

There was no question now as to its importance. Her heart, fuelled by adrenalin, pounded in her chest. Soft, shallow breaths hissed slowly in and out through her slightly parted lips. Her mouth felt dry. Her brow was furrowed from hours of uninterrupted concentration as she stared in disbelief at the numbers that glared mutely back at her. Alarmingly, some of the numbers which, under normal circumstances, would have been black were red—as red as the blood rushing through her veins. And they were very large numbers. Way too large! She ran her finger across one of the cells in the spreadsheet, manually re-counting the zeroes that appeared after the first comma.

'One, two ... ten, eleven, twelve ...'

The glow of the computer screen contrasted against the midnight sky beyond the windows of her corner office. She was on the fifteenth floor, overlooking Circular Quay in the foreground and Sydney's famous Opera House beyond. Right now, Samantha could have been sitting in a basement cell for all the attention she paid her multi-million dollar view. She had triple checked every formula in every cell, and every linkage between the cells. There was no mistake. Potentially, there could be trillions of dollars of losses. The spreadsheet on her computer was an attempt to quantify the potential fallout from the collapse of yet another US originated market for packaged loans. The single offending number—the 'bottom line'—was a multiple of the size of Australia's total annual $750 billion income.

'Oh my God ...'

The knock on her closed door caused Samantha to jump in heart-stopping fright. 'What the ....?'

As she swivelled in her chair to face the intruder, she managed a reflexive glance at the bottom right hand corner of her computer screen. Years of fighting deadlines had trained her.

12.48 a.m.

'Crean orifice?'

She swallowed. Unable to speak for the moment, she shook her head. Standing at the now half-open door was a worker employed by the bank's contract cleaning company. Ostensibly. But why so late?

The cleaner didn't move. He just stood there, apparently awaiting instructions; one hand on the door handle, the other clutching something behind his back. There was the hint of an expectant smile on his lips, but his eyes showed no expression. Samantha was momentarily paralysed, still locked in the world of sabotage and deceit, until she spotted the feather duster protruding from behind his back. Then, as with the descending curtain at the end of Act One in a murder mystery, reality unfurled itself. Invariably, a cleaner is just a cleaner.

She leant down, picked up the waste paper basket and carried it to the door.

'Just empty this for me please. You can leave my office until tomorrow night.'

'You wait. I bling back stlaight way.'

Instead of seating herself once more, she eased her stiffened back, stretched and took the few steps to the window. She plucked a tissue from its gaudy floral box and absent-mindedly dried her damp hands. Her nerves were certainly on edge. The main question she had been so far unable to fathom was, why me? Why not Larry? Was it a guy thing? Larry was Bill Tempest's mate. Was she being set up as a patsy, a fall-guy, to be let go? She leant her head against the cool of the window to clear her mind from the fog of unreality. Her eyes panned aimlessly across the harbour beyond the darkened glass until arrested by the movement of a water taxi approaching from beneath the Harbour Bridge. It skipped along the water's rippled surface—like one of those flat stones she and her brother Pete, and his mate Patrick, used to throw when they were kids. It didn't make a right hand turn into the Quay. Perhaps it was headed for one of the eastern suburbs? Rose Bay? Maybe even Manly, if the water-taxi driver was lucky. Or do you call them water-taxi captains?

Her eyes moved again to follow the craft's progress for a few more seconds, then stopped as the V of its wake stretched outwards, almost stroking the shoreline below Kirribilli House, the official Sydney residence of Australia's Prime Minister. She lifted her line of sight and stared at the structure on the hill on the opposite side of the harbour.

'He must know,' she muttered. 'Surely, he must be in the loop on this one.'

But Kirribilli House was in total darkness. Could the Prime Minister of Australia also be in the dark? Highly unlikely. Not with the numbers so large, and not given the incestuous relationships that now existed at the intersection of the global corridors of power in banking, politics and industry.

There was a time when the various power camps were separated, and when each camp treated the other two with deferential respect. The Central Bankers ran the economy, the democratically elected politicians ran the country, and the industrialists minded their own businesses and were accountable to their shareholders. No longer. Nowadays, everyone was in everyone else's pockets. Scratch that. Even the term had changed. Everyone was inside everyone else's pants. Business had grown to become the economy, and the economy had evolved to become the country. The demarcation lines between authority and responsibility had blurred. There was no longer any meaningful accountability in any walk of life.

Samantha shook her head to clear the radiating thought-webs and turned back to her desk. The figures that glared out at her were not so much related to how many loans might go into default, or how big the dollar value of these loans might be. It had to do with the so-called insurance policies—the derivative contracts—that hung off these loans. If this problem could not be contained, there would very likely be a catastrophic domino effect. The entire $500 trillion derivatives industry could be at risk. The previous sub-prime stumbles were child's play in comparison.

Of course, the theory was that even if a bank was heavily involved in such contracts, so long as it balanced its portfolio by having a roughly equal value of buy contracts and sell contracts to offset one another, the probability of something going wrong could be kept very low.

That was the theory. The facts—as her spreadsheet was now showing—were that something had gone horribly wrong, and that The Union Banking Corporation Inc. was one of the counterparty banks that would be affected. It was not a problem Union alone would be capable of solving. There was even some doubt in her mind as to whether the world's Central Banks acting in concert could solve it.

Samantha pursed her lips. Suddenly, she couldn't wait for the following day when she and Patrick would be flying out for their island resort holiday. Her brother's old school friend. The one long-standing relationship in her life …

After drafting her email reply to Bill Tempest, she hit 'send' and deleted all traces of both the email and its attachment. Her reply was devoid of any expression of her personal opinion. Satisfied that she had followed his instructions to the letter, and mindful of the energy effi-ciency memos that Admin liked to send around, she switched off her computer and the lights on her way out.

CHAPTER 2

THE DELTA AIRLINES Boeing 757-200, flight 207, had taken off right on time from JFK in New York at 8.45 a.m. It was now 11.45 and Captain Tara Geoffrey was thinking of starting her descent routine as they jetted towards Santo Domingo in the Dominican Republic. The flight had been as smooth as. Visibility was crystal clear. She could see clear across to the edge of the Earth—where Columbus would have fallen off if his world had turned out to be flat.

One of only a handful of women commercial airline pilots world-wide, Tara Geoffrey had been flying for as long as she could remember. At thirty-three years of age, she could hardly be called old, but she had certainly logged an unusually large number of flying hours.

When people asked her why she had chosen to become a pilot, she had to stop herself from smiling. The question always gave rise to the fond memory of a joke her late father used to tell, which went something like, 'How did the artist Toulouse Lautrec get his name?' Then, when no answer was forthcoming because the question was such a dumb question anyway, 'Isn't it obvious?' he would ask. 'He was born Toulouse,' and then could not stop himself from spluttering with laughter.

She must have heard him tell that joke a hundred times. Every time she had laughed with him, but not because she thought the joke was funny—it was such a 'dad' joke. It was just that his enjoyment was incurably infectious.

The true answer to the pilot question would have been 'because I was born to fly' but, because of that stupid Toulouse joke, she could never bring herself to answer in this way with a straight face. Instead, sometimes she responded with, 'I guess I was a bit of a tomboy at heart. I liked the idea of shattering glass ceilings', or at other times with, 'someone had to show those men how it's supposed to be done.' Her heart wasn't really in it, though. The truth was that she loved flying. It gave her a sense of wonder that she never got used to, never took for granted.

Her somewhat unflattering pilot's uniform unsuccessfully hid the fact that Tara was a stunner. She'd cut her copper coloured hair short and it was usually hidden beneath her pilot's cap. But she was unable to camouflage her sapphire eyes. Sometimes, it seemed that flames danced behind them. They lit up when she laughed and it was as if a party animal was held captive inside her, like the genie inside the lamp. Tara was not interested in liaisons with her fellow pilots so she was careful to compartmentalise her life, and those who saw the sparkle saw it only fleetingly. She was an exceptionally competent pilot and, most of the time, that was all her associates saw.

Any socialising on stopovers was usually with one of the gay stewards. She could count on them for good light-hearted company. They were non-judgemental, non-threatening and when she was with them Tara felt she could let her professional pilot persona slip a little.

The Boeing, still cruising at 40,000 feet, was about a hundred nautical miles from its destination. Captain Geoffrey turned to the flight steward who had been chatting to the co-pilot. 'David, I'm about to start our descent down to 18,000 feet. I wouldn't mind a quick cup of coffee before the cockpit goes sterile. Think you can get me one in two minutes flat?'

'Sure thing, Cap'n' he responded and returned seconds later with a freshly poured cup.

'I still can't work out *why* there are no buses from the airport to the city in Santo Domingo,' he said as he placed the cup into the cup holder next to her. Then, expelling an exaggerated sigh, 'Oh well! I suppose I can *learn* to enjoy the comfort of a cab for a change. Are we still OK to share one to the hotel?'

She smiled. Although her attention had been focussed on the various instruments in front of her, her antenna received his thespian message loud and clear.

'Absolutely. We still need to make arrangements for that dinner I promised you, and I'm working up a great appetite over here. Now, why don't you piss off and close the door behind you?' Her tone was cheeky, light-hearted. 'Paul and I have work to do.'

As David closed the door behind him, the co-pilot turned to face her. 'I've lost count of the number of times I've asked you out to dinner on a stopover. How come I get a zero batting average and he has no problems?'

'Come on Paul, there's a big difference between you and David.' She raised one eyebrow as if challenging him to contradict her. 'When I decided to get into the corporate world, my old man told me to never shit in my own nest. It was sound advice. I'm not prepared to mix business with pleasure. It's nothing personal.'

Paul Carthage turned his gaze back to the instruments. He wasn't fooled by her propensity to use four letter words in the cockpit. Tara Geoffrey had about as much chance of being seen as macho, as the recently departed David had of winning a spitting contest at a bikey convention. Whatever she might say, however much her mouth might talk the talk, her pheromones sure walked the walk. There was no way this particular female was going to talk any red-blooded male into accepting her as just one of the boys. Reluctantly, he turned his attention back to his work.

At 18,000 feet Tara fastened her shoulder harness, reduced power for a 1,000 feet per minute descent, and called for the Approach/Descent checklist. In the background there had been an intermittent stream of communications from air traffic control that would ultimately result in her intercepting the Instrument Landing System on runway two.

After a few minutes, she clicked off the autopilot and took over manually, allowing the nose of the plane to dip as she took hold of the yoke and simultaneously reduced the power all the way to idle. Finally, after being switched first to Approach Control and then to the airport tower, they received their landing instructions

'Delta 207. Wind 020 at 14. Cleared to land runway two.'

She called, 'Gear down,' and Paul responded, putting the gear handle in the 'down' position.

The runway came into sight. The on-board recorded warning system kept her informed of her height above the ground, '400 feet' … '300 feet' … '200 feet' …

Just before the wheels came into contact with the runway, she pulled back gently on the yoke to lift the Boeing's nose slightly. The engines roared as she put the plane into reverse thrust, all in one smooth series of practised actions.

Paul couldn't help himself. 'Well that didn't wake any babies.'

Tara moved her feet from the steering rudder to the brake pedals, and transferred her hand from the yoke to the steering tiller after coming out of reverse just as the tower controller said, 'Delta 207 exit next taxiway and contact Ground.'

Tara taxied, slowed the plane down to twenty knots, and then slowed down even further as she manoeuvred the now ungainly flying passenger bus into its position alongside the designated landing gate, her eyes fixed on the ground crewman guiding her in. When he finally crossed his hands above his head, she called 'Let's shut 'em down,' and set the parking brake.

Paul moved the fuel levers to 'off' to shut down the engines.

Then, with irreverent disregard for company protocol, she reached for the intercom and announced, 'Ladies and gentlemen. This is Captain Tara Geoffrey speaking. We have arrived safely at Las Americas airport in Santo Domingo, in the sun drenched Dominican Republic, home of merengue dancing. On behalf of my co-pilot Paul Carthage and our flight crew, we hope you had a great flight and that you will enjoy your stay here. We realise you had a choice of which bankrupt airline to fly, and we thank you for flying Delta today.'

Not long after the last passenger had disembarked, she was on her way from the plane to Customs and Immigration. 'Do you think we can ask the cab driver to give us *each* a receipt for thirty bucks?' David asked her as they walked the long corridor together. 'After all, we could have made our ways separately to our hotel.'

Tara didn't respond immediately. Her attention had been drawn to a group of workmen who had been struggling in vain to erect a large banner. 'Santo Domingo. Host to the 2011 World Energy Congress,' it said, in both English and Spanish.

A workman stood at either end holding the corners in place but the banner ballooned in the middle, entangling a third workman who tried to fight his way out of the voluminous cloth. A fourth man tried to direct proceedings but the banner seemed to take on a mind of its own. Two more workmen strolled over to watch the goings on. They didn't attempt to help. Instead, they shouted suggestions which, by the look of the grins on their faces, did little other than intensify the mayhem.

It reminded Tara of the clowns who used to erect the tents when the circus came to town. They let sections collapse, tripped over each other, and ducked or were acrobatically felled by their fellow clowns carrying long poles over their shoulders. She grinned at the image of comic chaos that had been the circus management's way of getting the local kids to pitch in and help. But there were no kids to join in here and an airport was too busy and impersonal a place to expect help from passers by ... or even other workmen, it seemed.

Belatedly, Tara focussed on what David had said. He was being theatrical again, his voice pitched about half an octave above where it should have been, and his right hand fluttering up to touch his right cheek. He knew that she knew it was all an act. His eyes gleamed like those of a naughty child.

The question of the cab receipt wasn't even a real question. It was just a sound that supported his perpetual pantomime, like the piano music that accompanied the silent movies. She admonished him in a motherly voice, her brow furrowed severely and her nose wrinkled like an angry rabbit.

'Listen, Mr Village People, don't waste your flim-flam act on me. We both know that you're a charming and highly intelligent person.'

'That's why I love spending time with you on these stopovers,' David responded in a more normal voice. 'You see right through me. For a pilot, you're so down to earth. But you must admit, it's fun to challenge the establishment now and then. Especially the oh-so straight establishment.'

'I wouldn't know about that, but I'll take your word for it. Why don't we both quit the act, just be ourselves for the evening and enjoy our time together?'

Their conversation was interrupted for the time it took the two of them to bypass the formalities of Immigration and to negotiate their way through the chaos of people milling around.

At the cab rank David leaned over to murmur in her ear just as the cab arrived. 'Message received my captain,' he said, in a totally normal voice. He opened the kerbside backseat passenger door for her with a flourish; closed it again, just like the gentlemen he really was, then skirted around the driver who was heaving both their bags into the trunk.

As the cab drew away, Tara leaned forward to give the driver instructions. 'Please take us to the Hotel Conde de Penalba in the Zona Colonial.'

'Si señora.'

' "Señora!" I'm not that old, am I?' she whispered defiantly at David.

'It's the cap.'

She took it off, placing in on the seat between them.

'Wheel nauw, Dayvid, me boyo,' she said in her best mock Irish accent. 'Just wheer didya huv a hunkering to huv dinna on this foin evening?'

He laughed out loud. 'To be shoor oim tortally at yer dispoosal and oil foller yerr t'thee ends of the earrth' if that be yerr will.'

Their banter continued for a while, spiralling downwards from that point until the novelty wore off.

She patted his knee in a sisterly fashion and they lapsed into a comfortable silence until she said, as much to herself as to David, 'I've just now taken a decision. I'm going to take my three-week vacation here, starting next week. I want to know what this city has to offer. And, if the hotel has a concierge, let's ask him where to go for dinner tonight, you know, where the locals eat—a genuine Creole meal.'

'Whhat? Why would you want to spend three weeks here all on your own? And why now, suddenly?'

'When I saw that group of workmen erecting that banner at the airport I realised if I leave it for much longer the old Dominican Republic will be completely gone. This whole country is going to change: the Energy Congress, infrastructure changes …'

'So? Why on earth would you want to come here at all, and why on your own?'

'To start with, I'm sure I'll meet a few people while I'm over here. It doesn't really matter. I'm comfortable in my own skin.' She swung around to face him, uncoiling from the seat as though she had been asleep until now. 'This country interests me. Every time we've stopped over during the past few months I've found myself looking at the blue amber jewellery and carved ornaments in the souvenir shops. Why is this the only place in the world where blue amber is found? I think I'd like to see one of the mines, and maybe travel around a bit and take some photographs of the countryside. The scuba diving off the coast here is supposed to be incredible. Did you know that Christopher Columbus landed on this island before he went on to discover America? The waters in this part of the world have shipwrecks that are …'

David broke in. 'And the cockfights? It's the national pastime … might be exciting if you have the stomach for blood and gore.'

The cab arrived outside the hotel. 'And merengue dancing.' Tara held her hands at eye level and jiggled her knees left, then right. 'Let's not forget that this is where it was invented. I wouldn't mind letting my hair down for an evening or two. It'll make a great change. What do you say?'

CHAPTER 3

THE DE HAVILLAND Beaver seaplane was a sixty-year-old rattle-trap that seemed to be held together with bits of wire and duct tape. Its pilot wore a short-sleeved white shirt, navy shorts and a peaked pilot's cap—probably more to keep the sun out of his eyes than to flaunt his status. He'd flown barefooted and now sat contentedly on one of the seaplane's floats with his feet dangling in the water while he waited for his two passengers to resurface from their dive. The water was as clear as a glass windowpane, affording him visibility all the way to the bottom about thirty feet below.

The turquoise blue of the Great Barrier Reef waters shimmered in the sunlight, and beneath the regular flow of air bubbles that rose to the surface, two divers hovered silently, occasionally signalling to each other. An anemone suddenly convulsed for no apparent reason. A crab flexed its claws making itself suddenly visible to the divers. A lone grouper lazily flicked its tail as though bored by a school of tiddlers that darted by.

The female of the human pair, her long brown hair waving with the current, managed to make eye contact with the grouper. With its curiosity piqued, the blimpesque, freckle-skinned creature swam closer. The two beings faced each other from a distance of less than a metre. The human was the more brightly clad of the two species. She wore a large, blue-rimmed pair of goggles, and an iridescent yellow oxygen bottle was strapped to her back by means of a bright purple harness. She blended quite happily with her colourful surroundings.

Below, on the sea bed, a lilac coloured slug with protruding blue eyes and pink stripes on its back slithered by, while not two metres away a giant turtle drifted a couple of centimetres above the seabed. Occasionally, its almond shaped, alien eyes blinked at the intruders while a small school of fish with zebra markings explored a bed of bluish sea-cousins of the terrestrial lilac plant.

The divers had been submerged for nearly an hour when the male diver checked his air and signalled to his female companion that it was time to surface. She formed a circle with her right thumb and forefinger. Slowly, the pair made their way upwards following the twin rising streams of bubbles that escaped from their mouthpieces. They rested a few metres below the starboard float of the seaplane that had been anchored a little way from the coral below. The plane would take them back to the resort on Lindeman Island where they had been holidaying this past week.

As they surfaced, they undid the vests that held their tanks, slipped off their fins and handed the heavy gear to the pilot who stowed it on board. Samantha hoisted herself onto the float, climbed inside the plane and seated herself on one of the tattered seats on the right hand side of the aircraft. Patrick Gallagher followed her, lowering his six-foot frame into a seat one row in front and across the aisle from her. He began mentally preparing himself for what he knew from their earlier short flight would be a noisy return journey. Noisy? Hell, a rock band playing at maximum amplifier volume not ten feet away would be gentler on their eardrums.

Patrick and Samantha had known one another since childhood and had been dating in a desultory fashion for three years. Nevertheless, Patrick found himself studying her features as she gazed out of the window at the water below. She had a good figure and was not unattractive. Still in her early thirties, she had risen to the lofty level of Deputy Country Head at the Sydney branch of The Union Banking Corporation, a 150-year-old financial institution whose footprint spanned the globe. The bank was world renowned for its mega-dollar multinational deals but its name had been linked to the high-risk mortgage problems that had begun to emerge in the United States some months earlier. As a result, its blue chip status had come under question.

The stress lines that had been visible at the corners of Samantha's mouth a week ago had faded, and her pale skin had taken on a berry brown colour. But now Patrick's gaze saw something had changed. He reached across the aisle and tapped her gently on the shoulder.

'Hey sister! Whatsamatta you?' he bellowed over the cacophony of roaring aeroplane engine, whistling wind, and rattling windows. It was an old private joke between them dating back to a song that had been a hit when they were around twelve years old and, more often than not, invited to the same birthday parties.

She turned to face him. 'I'm starting to focus on the fact that this is our last day of holiday,' she shouted back. 'I'm not sure if I'm ready to go back to the bank tomorrow. In fact, I'm sure that I'm not ready.'

'Tell you what.' He stroked the soft skin on the back of her hand with his forefinger. 'Why don't we get wasted when we get back, and you can tell Uncle Patrick about it then?'

In answer, she leaned towards him and planted a slightly open mouthed kiss solidly on his lips before turning back to continue staring down at the ocean's surface. The exchange communicated more to him about her feelings of inner disquiet than of her affection towards him. What was going on at Union?

An hour later, Patrick and Samantha were comfortably seated in the beachside restaurant of their hotel. Their chairs faced the beach and the darkening blue of the sea beyond. They had the area almost to themselves, the sun was setting behind them and each sipped a Pimm's heavily topped with sliced pineapple, a chunk of cucumber that straddled the rim of the glass, and a thin wedge of orange pinned with a toothpick to a spray of mint leaves. Now on her second drink, Samantha was looking somewhat more relaxed, if still a bit pensive.

'You know, I think I like these drinks for their sheer practicality.' Samantha waved her hand over her glass. 'It's the Christmas tree decorations on top. You could live on the fruit salad and if you drank enough of them, you could probably get shade under the little paper thingies.' She held up the four little umbrellas they had collected so far and shaded her eyes from the setting sun.

'Do you want to talk about it yet?' Patrick asked.

'Not sure.'

A couple of minutes passed, Samantha said nothing, lost in her thoughts. Then she gave a long, shuddering sigh. 'You know me too well.' She placed her hand affectionately on his forearm. 'And I think I've started to think more about you lately. Maybe it's because I'm becoming more and more concerned about where the world is going … where the whole financial–political mess is going to land up.'

'Well thanks very much. It's so gratifying to know I've risen to the level of your fall-back position.'

'Doesn't that work both ways? … Not that I'm agreeing with you that you're my fall-back. Far from it. I know that ours has been a relationship based on affection and friendship and maybe a touch of convenience. It's also clear to me that I have stronger feelings for you than you have for me. But, I've always been able to handle it on the basis that I wasn't ready to settle down anyway. I'm not complaining. You're my one sane rock.'

She drummed her fingers absently on his arm, realised what she was doing and smiled up at him. 'On the plane trip back, I started to think about our relationship over the last three years, and, well, one thing led to another and it went downhill from there.'

'How so?'

'We've been together here for a week, and this is the first time I've seen you in six months. I don't want to whinge about it, but hell, where's this all heading? There's no future in this relationship. Three years ago you were commuting between that gold mine in Kalgoorlie and Sydney. I saw you three times in that year. Then, two years ago I saw you once every couple of months when you took the mining engineer job at that silver mine in Twin Hills in southern Queensland. Now you're working in a goddamned nickel mine in the Dominican Republic, for God's sake.'

'C'mon Sam, we both know this relationship wasn't heading anywhere. We've been good friends for ever; we enjoy each other's company … and a bit more. In any event, you specifically told me you were dedicated to your banking career—that you weren't ready to settle down. What's changed? What's really going on here? Are you starting to go all mumsie on me? Is the biological clock ticking?'

'No. It has more to do with how happy and secure I feel with you when we're together … and the lack of moral integrity that I'm uncovering as I move higher up in the rarefied circles of finance and politics.' She spiralled a finger melodramatically into the air. 'The deals I am doing nowadays are getting bigger and bigger, and they're starting to bring me closer and closer to the coalface of power where all the crap is really happening.'

'What do you mean?'

The waiter broke into their conversation to take their order. Samantha ordered the flame grilled barramundi with mashed kumara and green beans; and Patrick, the fried snapper because it came with French fries and Greek salad. 'A double order of fries please,' he said, knowing Samantha would steal most of them.

'Which reminds me,' Patrick said as the waiter left, 'of a Greek holiday I had on Skiathos.'

Samantha knew he was trying to lighten her mood. She also knew she was in for one of his long, drawn out but usually entertaining stories and leant back in her chair.

'I was on this little island swimming and sun-baking in the late summer. It was September and everywhere you went there were swarms of wasps across the island.'

'Sounds like hell,' Samantha said. 'I can't imagine what you and your girlfriend were doing on a wasp infested lump of rock.'

'Who said I was with a girlfriend?' Patrick feigned indignation. 'And my God, you bankers are a breed apart. I say the word "hot". You hear the word "hell". I say the word "island". You hear the word "rock".' He paused, momentarily lost for words. 'Let me try again.' He picked up a spoon and held it in front of his mouth like a microphone, cleared his throat, then continued in a melodramatically hushed voice. 'The island was ablaze with bougainvillea, contrasting magnificently with the muted tones of the verdant olive trees.' His hand swept panoramically through the air.

'The sun shimmered off the roughly plastered white walls of the sleepy villas. And below them, the sea sparkled like a rippled mirror. On the hilltop, the domed roof of the little church was a blue so bright that it seemed the whole sky had been squeezed from it to form the background of God's canvas. There was music in the air ... a sense of magic was interrupted only by ... the buzz of wasps.' Then, Humphrey Bogart style, he said, 'Got the picture sweetheart?'

Samantha could not help but smile back at him with affection. How could she not help but like him so much. 'Okay' she said leaning towards him. 'But wasps? What should I be thinking when I hear the word "wasp"? White Anglo Saxon Protestant?'

'Aarrgh!' Patrick struck his forehead with the flat of his hand. 'I'm not going to answer that.'

'What's the matter darling? Wasp get you?'

'Okay. You asked for it. The barefaced, unadulterated version ...'

Patrick gave her a wicked look as he took a swig from the glass of wine the waiter had poured for him to taste.

Samantha looked at him in mock disgust. 'You cretin. You're supposed to discreetly swirl that around in your mouth and taste it like a sophisticated gentleman of the world. I can't take you anywhere. Give you a billycan of tea, a loaf of damper bread and a lump of meat and you'd be as happy as Larry.'

He ignored her outburst and winked at the waiter. 'It's great,' he said. 'The lady doesn't drink, so you can just fill my glass.'

'Ignore him,' Samantha said quickly before the waiter had time to respond. 'He hasn't been allowed out for a while. And yes, I will have some wine, thank you.'

Patrick fixed his green-eyed gaze on her as though he was about to pin a butterfly to a corkboard. 'Get you Gertrude,' he said. 'This is my story, and I'm on a roll here. And like I said, the bare facts ma'am, nothing but the facts.'

'Okay,' she said. 'I'm having fun. Keep going.'

He took her hand that had been lying innocently on the table near the stem of her wine glass and squeezed it playfully.

'Here's where it gets interesting,' he said. 'The island is so small that tourists hire these Vespa scooters for a few bucks a day to travel from one end of the island to the other. You know, the Italian scooters with the splashboard in front where you put your feet. It's like driving around on a slow armchair with one wheel front and back.'

'Uh oh.' Samantha laughed, her hand flying to her mouth. 'I'm starting to see where this is headed. Tell me, what were you wearing after your swim?'

'You got it in one, sister,' Patrick said with a laugh. 'The answer is that I was wearing a pair of wide legged shorts with nothing on underneath, and this bloody wasp flies straight up my pants leg.'

'No way!'

'Wait! There's more.' he said, shifting mental gears to verbally project another scene. 'I told you that Skiathos is a small island. We had just passed a guy with a donkey laden with whatever, and we were coming into the outskirts of the town. There were a few people walking around on the street. Some other locals were sitting on the verandas of their villas taking in the view of the sea.'

'So give already. What the hell did you do?'

'What could I do?' He answered. 'I brought the Vespa to a screaming full stop. I jumped off and pulled my daks down to my ankles. In the meantime, my … err … pillion passenger was thrown off the back of the bike when it fell over, and she lost her sarong in the process.'

'What!'

'No kidding. There I am hopping around in a panic, with my hands waving around my whatsit that's now flapping in the wind. And there on her hands and knees, is a dazed and stark raving naked woman looking around for her sarong.'

'And?'

'And the guy with the donkey walks up and picks up the sarong and hands it to her like he does this every day of his life for the mad tourists who come to his island.'

'Wasn't she embarrassed?'

'What do *you* think? But hang on! It doesn't end there.'

'Come on. How much worse could it get?' She saw the waiter approaching with their meals but was powerless to stop Patrick.

'Well, I wasn't about to pull my pants back up again without checking them. For all I knew the wasp was still stuck inside the trouser leg,' he continued, his arms flailing theatrically in the air.

The waiter hovered, waiting for the opportunity to put the dishes down. Patrick, in the meantime, was fully immersed in his story. The waiter could wait. She had to hear the end of this one.

'I took my pants all the way off to inspect them,' he gasped. 'But by this time, my friend was so embarrassed that she couldn't stand it anymore. She had managed to drape the sarong around herself. She grabbed my pants out of my hands, and she threw them on the front of the Vespa and screamed at me to start the scooter up again. Now! She wasn't waiting one more second.'

'What did you do?' Samantha asked even though she wasn't sure it would all be too much information.

'I got back onto the scooter and kick-started it again.' He rose slightly in his seat as though kick-starting the chair. 'But as I sat down again I felt this searing pain, because the crown jewels landed on the Vespa's seat that was now boiling hot from the sun. I don't know how the hell I stopped myself from jumping off again, but I managed to stay on, and we hightailed it out of there. Of course a crowd had gathered by then, but I was past caring. As soon as we were out of sight of the crowd I stopped to put my pants on again.'

The waiter, his face inscrutable, saw his opportunity and put the plates down before Patrick could say anything more.

CHAPTER 4

WITH THE ARRIVAL of the food, Samantha was pleased to see that Patrick calmly sipped from his now nearly empty wine glass.

'Listen you,' she said, 'there are two things you didn't mention in your story, and I want the answers. First, did your girlfriend get hurt when she fell off the scooter?'

His eyes crinkled in amusement at the corners. She wished he wouldn't do that, it made him look so enticingly, impishly desirable.

'No. We had come to a virtual standstill when it toppled over. She fell onto a ridge of soft grass on the side of the road. My guess is she must have flung her arms out to cushion the impact.'

'Uh huh. And am I right in assuming that you learned your lesson about the risks associated with bare-assed driving and never did it again?'

Now his green gaze danced with wicked humour. 'Don't be ridiculous.' He chuckled. 'We did it every day. It's a bare-assed kinda place. Hey, I've got this beaut story to tell you about a topless female windsurfer who lost control of her board. You wanna hear it?'

'Listen sport,' she said, fixing him with a deliberate stare in order to emphasize her point. 'Please do *not* tell me any more of your stories until we have at least finished our coffee. I want to be able to eat without choking.'

Samantha tasted the steaming fish in front of her. She didn't think she had ever experienced anything more mouth-wateringly-meltingly wonderful. It was stuffed with green leafy herbs she couldn't identify … something local and delicate.

'Mmmm delicious,' she managed.

He dipped his chin towards his chest and looked back up at her with his mouth pursed. It was that boyish look again that she couldn't resist. 'Stop it,' she said.

They both lapsed into silence as the meal devoured their attention.

'More wine?'

'Please.'

Patrick pushed his chair back and stood up. He draped the serviette over his arm, picked up the wine bottle and walked around to her side of the table—where he topped up her glass as if he was the waiter. She wasn't sure whether to laugh or to admonish him, given that his actions had caught the attention of their real waiter who was scurrying towards them.

She compromised and smiled. 'Nutcase,' she said, picking up her now filled glass to avoid the waiter's gaze.

'And you sir? he asked of the empty chair where he had been sitting, and poured his own glass. He replaced the bottle in its cooler, sat down again then said, as if nothing untoward had happened, 'I've been giving some thought to what you told me earlier about the lack of moral integrity in your rarefied circles. What's gotten you so freaked out? I've never seen you like this before.'

She did not answer immediately. Instead, she looked at him for a long, lingering moment, the expression in her eyes morphing from humorous to more serious. 'It's a long story. I'm not really sure where to begin.' She sighed quietly and turned her attention back to her food.

'Well, I guess you could begin at the top or … how about at the grass roots level?'

This time the silence was more protracted. The seconds ticked slowly by, broken only by the noise of the other diners. Samantha didn't seem to notice but Patrick glanced at her expectantly each time she put her fork down on her plate.

'I'm going to regret this,' she said at last. 'I know it.'

'I asked, remember?'

'It's not a simple question to answer, and I probably need to give you the entire potted history of western banking.'

'Educate me.'

'Well, it's to do with the price of gold and the price of money.'

'A subject dear to my heart.'

'No, really, this is serious. I guess it all goes back to the question I get asked the most by people who want to know about how banking works: how does the Reserve Bank know how much money to put into circulation? I don't think I've ever met a non-banking person who understands how a country manages its money supply and, frankly, I've met very few bankers who fully understand it.'

'Well, your batting average is safe with me,' Patrick responded. 'I wouldn't have a clue either. Why's it important, and who cares anyway?'

Samantha looked at him blankly. 'Have you ever heard the expression, "He who owns the gold makes the rules"?' she asked.

'Of course.' He wasn't sure that he had, but it was obviously so important to her that he wasn't about to admit his total ignorance.

'Well if you want to know who really makes the rules in this world, then you have to understand who holds the purse strings. *That's* why you should care. Nowadays, it's not as obvious as it might seem, because the world is no longer on a gold standard.' She paused to look into his eyes to see whether he was still interested in hearing more. 'Most people would be surprised to know that Great Britain went onto a gold standard way back in 1717, just before the Industrial Revolution. It was orchestrated at the time by Sir Isaac Newton, who had left his day job as the world's leading physicist a few years earlier to become Master of the Royal Mint. And it's very important to understand what was meant by a gold standard. Am I being too basic?'

'Not at all,' Patrick replied. 'I'm an engineer. The world of money is a mystery to me.'

He placed his knife and fork together on the empty plate and leaned back in his chair. He stretched his legs under the table, resting a trousered leg comfortably against her ankle. The actions were deliberate. His body language was encouraging. She had his full attention.

'Under the gold standard in England, a British pound was a certificate issued by the Bank in return for a deposit of gold. So a pound note was "as good as gold".'

He nodded, just to show he was following, and clasped his hands comfortably behind his head.

'The amount of gold in storage at the Bank of England governed how many pounds could be printed,' she continued. 'If too many were printed, the price of gold would rise to compensate, and you would get less gold for your pound when you cashed it in.'

Patrick unclasped his hands, uncrossed his legs and leant forward. 'That would have seriously pissed off the depositors.'

'You bet, but it didn't really matter because Great Britain was rich and the Bank of England could play it straight. Right up until World War I it owned most of the world's gold. Great Britain had the gold; she made the rules.'

'Are you trying to tell me that there is some sort of a linkage between what was happening in the 1700s and the lack of ethics in today's world? That seems to be one hell of a long bow that you're drawing.'

Samantha looked at him and continued eating. She chewed slowly, staring directly into his eyes all the while.

Patrick tried to read the look on her face. It hadn't seemed like an unreasonable question. He leant back awkwardly to retrieve the wine bottle from the ice bucket that had been left just out of reach. The absent waiter was suddenly at his side brushing his hand away and setting him back in his chair with the ruffled indignation of a mother hen.

'Sir, sir, allow me.'

Samantha chose that moment to continue her story.

'Have you ever heard of a Scotsman by the name of Adam Smith?'

'The name sounds vaguely familiar.'

'He was to economics what Isaac Newton was to physics. He published a book, *The Wealth of Nations*, in 1776. He wrote about capital being a fancy name for the ultimate ownership of gold, because if you had capital you could cash it in for pounds, and then cash the pounds in for gold.'

'Yes … so?'

'Well … first of all, does the year the book was published—1776— ring any bells?'

'American independence?'

'Okay! Go to the top of the class. Amongst other things, on the last page of his book, Adam Smith said that Great Britain would save herself the bucket-loads of money she had been spending on her armies abroad if she cut loose the "great empire on the west side of the Atlantic". By implication, if America became less of a financial drain on Great Britain, then Great Britain could preserve its capital and its store of gold. In turn, this would give it *more* financial power relative to its former colony. It didn't really matter who was nominally in political power.'

Patrick wrinkled his nose. 'I'm starting to smell conspiracy theories.'

'No conspiracies. It was done in broad daylight, in full view of the whole world. Smith understood that despite its so-called political independence, the United States would still be dependent on Britain for capital. And so did the British bankers ... many of whom eventually opened offices in New York when that city became the financial hub of the US.'

Patrick nodded in encouragement. 'Okaaay.'

'That same understanding regarding the linkage of political power and money was why the US Constitution is still, to this day, very explicit about who should control the money, and how.' Samantha swept the hair away from her face, tucking it in place behind her ears in an unconscious gesture. It was the way she wore it in the office. 'Thomas Jefferson wanted the money in circulation in the US to be backed by American-owned gold and silver. Secondly, he wanted to ensure that Congress should be in ultimate control of both the amount and value of money.'

Patrick nodded. 'I got it. But what's that to do with England and the gold standard?'

She held up her hand. 'The loophole was in borrowings from abroad. They could still borrow money from England, and Congress couldn't exercise absolute control over what the private bankers were doing. It all worked very well for nearly 150 years until the Federal Reserve Act was signed into law by President Wilson on December 23, 1913.'

'What would the Fed do that wasn't already being done by Congress?'

'Good question. Ostensibly it was to streamline the banking system, to make it more efficient. But the reality was that British banking interests had a huge influence on how that Act was drafted because the privately owned banks, which sponsored the Federal Reserve Act, had commercial links and were partly owned by banks in England. The Bank of England itself also played a big role, and the establishment of the Fed was the first chink in the armour of the 200-year-old gold standard. The UK established its ability to have a powerful influence over the US money supply, without *either* country having to be constrained by a gold standard.'

Patrick twirled the stem of his wineglass, looking into the swirling reflections. 'You've lost me there.'

'It's quite simple really. In 1900, all the currency reserves in the entire world added up to around $11.6 billion, and Britain owned most of that. But the actions of any government are constrained by how much money is available to it. There was a bank panic in the USA in 1906, and the bankers of the day believed that it could have been avoided if they had had access to more money. The problem was that the existence of the gold standard restricted their access to more money, so they had to figure out a way of bypassing it. Remember that in those days Britannia ruled the waves; the US economy was not yet mature. Following the establishment of the US Federal Reserve, if Britain ever found she needed more money than she could create herself because *she* was still constrained by a gold standard, she could borrow dollars from the US, which could just print them.

'Shit, Sam, you're starting to sound like some Hollywood movie plot. In practical terms, how could that be achieved? Surely the Fed can't just print money.'

'You're quite right. In very simple terms, the process is this: The US Federal Government needs cash. It goes to the Federal Reserve and it issues an IOU. That IOU is called a Treasury Bond, which the Fed on-sells to investors, and the US Government pays interest on it. But, if there are no investors immediately available, the Fed effectively creates the money out of thin air—it just prints it or creates an electronic bookkeeping entry—and deposits it at one of the twelve Federal Reserve Banks. Voila! The Government had access to however much cash it wanted.'

Patrick raised his eyebrows. 'You can't mean that the US Federal Reserve was originally established mainly as a means of allowing Great Britain access to more money?'

Samantha left the question unanswered for the time being. 'World War I broke out nine months later. Interesting coincidence, huh? That War, and the post-war reparations, cost Britain a lot of gold, but it didn't really matter any more because the Fed allowed the US to just print most of the $10 billion or so that the Allies lent to European nations to pay for the post-war reparations.'

'So that's why there was the post-war inflation …'

'Exactly. The US inflated *its* money supply to pay for the war reparations for which Britain was responsible. Then of course the inflationary boom was followed by a bust in the early 1920s, as Central Banks took steps to restrict credit and to drive up interest rates. But on the other side of the pond, so to speak, you may remember that Germany was suffering from hyperinflation. Germany was printing its own money like it was going out of fashion. Over a period of three months in 1923, the German mark jumped from 4.6 million marks to the dollar to 4.2 trillion marks to the dollar. That's what can happen when a country doesn't have any constraints to how much money it can print.'

Patrick said nothing, trying to take it all in, trying to fathom the consequences.

'So there you have it, mate,' Samantha finished. 'That's how the modern world was introduced to the so-called benefits of Central Banking. Since those days, between them—the US Fed, aided and abetted by the UK—have become the Masters of the Universe. But now the system is running out of control and their universe is in danger of imploding. That's why you've never seen me like this before.'

'Tell you what,' Patrick said. I'll order us some coffee … and a little something I know you'll love.'

'I wonder what that could be.' Samantha smiled provocatively at him, stood up and kissed him on the cheek. Without saying another word, she turned on her heel and walked towards the far back corner of the restaurant.

When she returned there were two espressos and a silver bowl of dark chocolates on the table.

'We couldn't just have coffee,' Patrick said looking up at her. 'I wanted to end on a sweet note, so I ordered these. They're handmade and I happen to know the owner of the business. His chocolates must have won thirty awards over the past few years. They're to die for.'

'Well let's just hope they're not to die *from*.'

'Trust me. They're out of this world. Are you feeling any better?'

'Mmm. Oh wow! I am now … that's delicious.'

'Fattening you up for the kill, is what I'm doing. Want to go?'

CHAPTER 5

THE FIFTH FLOOR New York apartment was on East 73rd Street, a couple of blocks from Central Park. Although its double-glazed windows could not completely cut out the drone of the traffic below, to those inside the sounds had become faint background noise, much like crashing waves fade into the background for people living close to the ocean.

The apartment was decorated in pale pastel colours of green, blue and sand with splashes of bright sunflower yellow. Woven grass mats covered the beige wall-to-wall sisal weave carpets. A softly illuminated aquarium—with exotic tropical fish against a background of corals—was the central feature of the apartment, dividing the lounge from the dining area.

'One of my clients sent me a gift of a case of this Nederberg Riesling,' Carol Gartner called out to her flatmate in the kitchen. 'It comes from the Stellenbosch–Paarl region near Cape Town in South Africa.'

Carol was in her late twenties and single. She was the owner of a business that earned its living as corporate event planners. She was always at the office long before anyone else had arrived, and long after everyone else had left for the day. It left her little time for a meaningful social life.

She forced herself to make time to see a hairdresser once a week, and once a month put aside two hours or more for Antoine to freshen her blonde highlights. He had become used to her ever-present cell phone, and then her laptop, and had given up trying to ply her with gossip.

The arrangement with her flatmate suited her just fine. She and Tara Geoffrey were like ships passing in the night. Their jobs allowed them considerable freedom of individual action within the apartment and, when they saw each other, they got on well.

Right now, Tara was in the kitchen preparing them a light dinner. Carol was sprawled comfortably on the sofa, her eyes mesmerised by the comings and goings in the world of the fish tank. She sipped her client's chilled white wine. It had a fruity taste, very smooth and pleasant on the palate.

Tara walked into the dining room carrying two plates aloft. 'Ta daa! We will be partaking of spaghetti marinara tonight. I bought a fresh fish of dubious origin from a guy wearing a brown raincoat, a hat and sunglasses. He told me that his fake-brand watch business was under pressure, and he wanted to diversify into something that customers would see as being less fishy. He had a shipment of two of these flown in from Tangiers just this morning. I was his first customer. He also gave me a discount. What more could a girl ask for?'

Carol laughed. 'You're incorrigible, you know that? Where do you come up with all this crap?'

'What would you prefer me to say? That I stood in line at the fish shop for half an hour, and eventually had to elbow my way to the front where the shop assistant took my money and spoke to me like she was doing me a favour? I prefer to see the bright side of life. And if it isn't there at that particular moment, well madam, I will just follow the lead of Mr Lewis Carroll's young heroine. I will just dream it all up in my head. Life can be a ball that way.'

'Yeah, provided no one slaps you in a straight-jacket before hauling you off to the funny farm.'

Tara flounced back into the kitchen, returning with the wineglass in her hand. 'A toast,' she said, 'to my upcoming vacation. May I meet a tall, dark, handsome and mysterious stranger.'

'Stranger than you?' Carol teased. 'So! I take it you've decided on where you're going?'

'Yup. I'm going to spend three weeks in the sunny Dominican Republic. Monday morning, bright and early, I'm going to take myself off to that photographic shop on West 34th to buy a camera that can take both underwater shots and scenery shots.'

'Dominican Republic! Are you crazy?

'Why? What's wrong with the Dominican Republic?'

'Don't you read the newspapers? The place is like the Wild West. A couple of years ago there was a $2 billion bank fraud, and when it came to light there was rioting in the streets.'

'That was in 2003. There was a change of government in 2004. The place is a seething cauldron of peace and tranquillity nowadays. It's a playground for vacationing US citizens.'

'Oh is that so? What about the fact that there are a couple of hundred thousand Dominican refugees living just a cab ride away from this apartment in Washington Heights? What about the fact that the Dominican Republic happens to border directly onto Haiti, which is probably the most unstable country in the region? My understanding is that Haiti is a halfway house for Islamic terrorists targeting to infiltrate the USA. I read an article the other day about how the Hezbollah uses unstable Latin American countries as launching points for their US targeted terrorist activities. They go to Paraguay, and from there to Venezuela, Haiti and Miami or up through Mexico.'

'Listen here Miss Darkness and Despair, if we're looking for reasons not to go, why stop there? Why not drag up the old argument that it borders on the Bermuda Triangle?' Tara said, creeping around the room intoning, 'Boodoo, boodoo, boodoo, boodoo, dooooooo.'

Carol nearly choked on her wine. 'And what is that supposed to be?'

'Theme music from *Jaws*, of course.'

'Of course ... brought to you by my musical friend.'

Tara ignored her. 'On December 5, 1945, Naval Air Flight 19 left Fort Lauderdale on a practice bombing run to Hen and Chicken shoals. Mayday! Mayday! We're encountering bad weather. My compass is spinning. I don't know where we are. We must have got lost after that last turn ... crackle ... hisssss ... silence.'

Carol laughed. 'Do your employers at Delta have any idea who they have entrusted their $85 million Boeing to?'

Tara lifted her face so she looked exaggeratedly down her nose at her flatmate. 'My competence as an airline pilot should not be confused with my well developed sense of humour. Now, tell me ... why did your client give you a case of this fine wine? What did he want in return, and does he have a brother?'

'First of all, the guy is nearly sixty years old. Second of all, he brought several cases across for a wine tasting expo and there were a couple of cases left over. They wrote a few million dollars business. It was his way of saying thank you for being such a brilliant event organizer. Thirdly, he wanted to spread the word that South Africa is amongst the oldest producers of wine in the Southern Hemisphere.'

'I thought wine came mainly from Europe and California.'

'Ah, so little you know! Besides South Africa, they also grow sophisticated wine cultivars in Chile and New Zealand and Australia. All of those countries have become big wine exporters.'

'New Zealand, huh? Maybe I'll take a vacation there one day. I understand its one of God's last unspoiled countries.'

'It's still not too late. You don't pay for airline tickets anyway. Why don't you give away this crazy idea of going to the Dominican Republic? Better you should go somewhere peaceful.'

'Oh, so you would rather I spend a holiday in a country that is floating on a bed of molten lava waiting to erupt, than in a country where the most violent thing that happens nowadays is that two roosters hack each other to death with their beaks?'

'Yuk! Remind me never to approach you for help in drafting my advertisements.'

'Seriously Carol. There's something mystical about the fact that the Dominican Republic is the only location on the face of the planet where blue amber is found. I've been visiting the souvenir shops over the past few months, and it's made me curiouser and curiouser. Did you know, for example, that even though diamonds are rare, they are found in several parts of the world? Same goes for lapis lazuli, or emeralds or rubies or blue topaz. From what I've been able to discover, there are only two semi-precious stones that occur in almost unique locations across the planet. One is opal; ninety-seven percent of the world's opals are found in Australia. The other is blue amber, which comes exclusively from the Dominican Republic.'

'All the others are minerals,' Carol gently chided. 'Amber is not a semi-precious stone. It's a petrified organic substance formed from resin that wept from wounds in the bark of trees millions of years ago.'

'Yes, I know that. But tree resin has a translucent golden orange colour, right? This particular tree resin has a fluorescent bluish tinge to it. I've got a … hang on.' Tara put down her wineglass and ran barefooted to her bedroom. Her empty shoes pointed silently at Carol. She was back in a moment with a coffee table book that she opened unerringly at a section on Dominican amber.

'It's beautiful,' agreed Carol looking at the exquisite photographs, 'and—I grant you—unusual.'

'There's something mystical about it, don't you think? That's what I want to investigate. Maybe it has something to do with the Bermuda Triangle. Strange things happen there. Did you know, for example, that the lost city of Atlantis is supposed to have sunk into the sea some-where near the Triangle? I read recently that an underwater archaeological team found evidence that the so-called Bimini Road they found under the ocean between Florida and the Bahamas was actually the remains of a breakwater that formed an ancient harbour. It was apparently built long before Columbus was even a glint in his daddy's eye.'

'Yeah, I heard about that so-called breakwater wall, but what's that got to do with blue amber? It's the same pile of rocks that most sensible people believe was caused by nothing other than ballast stones dropped by transport ships returning empty after bringing supplies to the Confederates in the Civil War. You're nothing but a romantic at heart Tara, you know that? But I do love you for it.'

Tara snapped shut the coffee table book and curled her feet under her on the sofa. 'It strikes me that you're the gullible one here,' she said. 'Do you seriously believe these ballast stones of yours—neatly cut and shaped into blocks, by the way—would fall so precisely, one on top of the other, three deep, onto much larger foundation stones which weighed several tons, and to do so in a straight line?'

Carol raised her glass, acknowledging defeat.

'Maybe I am a romantic at heart,' Tara conceded. 'But my logical mind still seems to function quite effectively, and I want to find the scientific reason why the amber has a bluish tinge. I also want to find out what legends surround the blue amber. Should I apologise for that?'

'No, but how would my romantic friend like some freshly brewed coffee to round off this delicious meal, the remains of which we were just a few minutes ago scraping off the plates? I've been on the go all week and my book and I are going to hit the sack early.'

'Coffee with cream will do me,' Tara called to Carol's back.

'You really are an anachronism in this modern world. You know that?' Carol called from the kitchen. 'It's like you've been caught in some sort of time warp.'

'Maybe you're right about that, but wouldn't you agree that we laugh a lot when we're together? It's the laughter that keeps me sane.'

'When are you planning to leave?'

Tara followed her flatmate into the kitchen. 'Monday. I've got my annual medical check-up in the morning, so I'll be catching the 3.45 to Atlanta, with an overnight layover for Santo Domingo. I think I'll just take it easy tomorrow. Maybe take a walk in the park and do a bit of washing and ironing.'

'Speaking of which,' Carol said. 'I can't help thinking about all those refugees living in Washington Heights. And I can't help thinking about Haiti being a halfway house for Islamic terrorists. I just hope for your sake that the Dominican Republic doesn't fall short of your lofty expectations and that you're not just flirting with danger.'

CHAPTER 6

IMPLODING? SAMANTHA'S LAST statement before the arrival of the chocolates still filled Patrick's mind as he paid the bill. They walked out of the restaurant along the beach.

'How the hell did we get from a rock solid gold standard in 1913 to this "danger of imploding" as you so delicately put it? C'mon Sam. You're a senior executive in one of the world's major banks. You're not supposed to be talking in hyperbole.'

'Look mate, you asked me what was bothering me and I told you. I work in a world where facts trump opinions. If you want, I can give you the facts so that you can arrive at your own conclusions.'

'Okay. I guess we might as well see this through.' He took the shoes she was carrying, placed them neatly next to his on the grass at the edge of the beach and put his arm across her shoulders.

'You're such a romantic bastard,' she said snuggling up to him to make her point. 'Look how yellow the moon is, how soft the sand is, and here we are talking money. But, hey, we're well matched.' She moved away from him slightly, then took his hand before continuing their walk.

'So, where were we?' Patrick asked.

'Well, I could dazzle you with detail relating to the structure of the Fed, but all you really need to understand is that the very establishment of the US Federal Reserve System took control of the money supply *out* of the hands of Congress. The reason Jefferson wanted Congress to be in control was that he expected it would apply its collective mind to protecting and furthering the interests of the community as a whole.

'Yeah, I got that, but surely the new system was designed to have checks and balances too? Despite the way you're telling it, I can't see how any conspiracy is possible.'

Samantha gave him a penetrating stare before responding. 'Patrick, you have to get the thought of conspiracy out of your head. There is no conspiracy. There never has been. We are talking about *a state of mind* that comes with vested interests, with power … control … through these legally sanctioned operating systems.'

'Okay.'

'Think about this. For nearly a hundred years, world currency reserves have been growing at more than four times the rate of population growth because it suits the bankers who make profits by lending money at a higher price than they pay for it. There are no conspiracies. The bankers are hungry for more and more money, so they push for more and more money to be generated.

Today, around sixty-five percent of the world's currency reserve is in paper US dollars printed by the Federal Reserve. Since 1913, the printing of US money has been under the control of a group of individuals who largely represent or identify with profit oriented private enterprise—in particular, commercial banks and the oil lobby.'

'Well, I think I'd rather have successful bankers looking after the money supply than some government bureaucrats who don't operate in the real world. But, whoa. Where does the oil lobby suddenly come in?'

She did a little skip along the sand. 'Ha! … Keep your eye on the ball, mate. He who controls the purse strings makes the rules. The oil lobby has extraordinary political influence because of the depth of its purse.'

'Okay. Of course. But surely, if the US Constitution still says that the US should be on a gold standard, then all this you've described would have been unconstitutional.'

'Oh, it was all done very subtly. The UK and the US—and in fact the whole world—continued to pay lip service to the gold standard while they were manipulating it for their own ends—all the way up to the end of 1944. That was the year of the Bretton Woods conference.'

'Come on … are you telling me that while the USA and Great Britain were talking about a gold standard, they were actually lying about it?' Patrick cocked his head to the side in disbelief. 'And yet you claim there are no conspiracies?'

'Moral bankruptcy does not necessarily equate to conspiracy. It's all about power. To us it's heinous. To them it's just a game of power. You do what you gotta do to win. Even if you have to slant the playing field in your favour, you do it. Just let me go on, and all will be revealed.'

'I can't believe what's coming out of your mouth but, okay, keep going.'

'At the Bretton Woods conference, all forty-four Allied nations agreed that countries could, from then on, pay their debts to other countries in their own currencies which, in turn, would have fixed exchange rates expressed in gold-backed US dollars. So countries bought dollars with their currencies and paid their debts in US dollars, not gold. That's how the stage was set for the US dollar to become the world's dominant currency. The two main architects of Bretton Woods were John Maynard Keynes of Great Britain and Harry Dexter White of the USA. Do you think those two guys were looking after the interests of France … or any of the other forty-two Allied Nations, for that matter? Pure and simple, it was an Anglo–American power play, and it worked.'

Samantha paused, they had reached the end of the beach. They turned to retrace their steps. 'Hey, the rising tide's already wiped out all trace of our existence.'

'Nature has a way of doing that,' Patrick responded as he bent to roll up his trouser legs. 'So that was just before the end of World War II. What happened after that?'

'Okay, so by the end of the War, the US owned roughly $26 billion worth of gold—that was around two-thirds of the world's entire store of gold. After the War, the US gave western European nations $17 billion in grants to facilitate reparations. Remember that her total gold reserves were only $26 billion to start with, so that was not exactly spare gold lying around, and that implied that the paper dollars she was sending overseas were no longer backed a hundred percent by gold. In fact the ratio fell to around fifty-five percent. You could probably measure the time between the signing of Bretton Woods and that particular act in weeks. Proof positive that it was never about a gold standard and it was always about control by the Anglo–American alliance over the world economy.'

'I'm starting to see a pattern here. It's like the frog in the pot of water. The water needs to heat up slowly or the frog jumps out.'

'Now you understand how it works. Remind me to count the silver after you've gone.' She grinned lopsidedly at him. 'From then on, it was more of the same: Korean war, Vietnam war, and the Fed just kept right on printing dollars, until President Nixon just announced one day that the US would no longer honour its debts in gold.'

'Just like that?'

'Effectively. What was the rest of the world gonna do about it? Declare war on the US? How would they have paid for that war? With US dollars? Right now, the world's currency reserve dollars are backed by less than 2.5 percent gold, and that's assuming the gold is still in Fort Knox ... there's been no official audit there since 1959.'

Patrick stopped in his tracks, oblivious of the fact that the waves were washing over his feet and wetting his pants up to his knees. He just looked at Samantha. 'You're kidding about all this, right?'

Samantha, stopped walking too, but kept out of range of the waves. 'The reality is that the US dollar has a value that is nothing other than what the US Government says it is. The same goes for the currencies of all countries, which are no longer fixed in price relative to each other.'

'Owe the bank $1,000 and it's your problem. Owe the bank a billion and it's the bank's problem,' Patrick said, shaking his head in disbelief.

He waded out of the shallow water at last, out of the reach of the waves and took both her hands in his. He stood there, staring at her. 'I gotta tell you that I'm finding this all a bit surreal. From what you've just told me, it's clear that the world has been run by vested interests—people who just don't care about anything except their own personal or commercial agendas. And yet you also tell me there's no conspiracy, that it's all natural Neanderthal behaviour—just men grabbing for power. Well, maybe you're right. But I want to see where this particular story ends. Let's get back to the original question: without a gold standard, how do the Central Banks decide how much money to print?'

'The short answer is that we've reached a point in history where the entire world's money supply is a function, ultimately, of what the US

Government wants to spend. And there is a massive cloud of political obfuscation and confusion which has been deliberately contrived to hide that simple fact. How do you think the US paid for its war in Afghanistan and its war in Iraq?'

With her gaze fixed at a point on the wet sand just ahead, Samantha walked on, dragging her toes in the wet sand, leaving little gullies behind her that rapidly filled with seawater. Patrick kept pace beside her. He picked up a shell and tried unsuccessfully to skim it along the surface of the water.

Samantha turned her face to him. 'It's all about paper money and paper profits now. And the whole system's about as vulnerable as the three little pigs' paper house with the big bad wolf huffing and puffing at the door. Debt continues to build and the banks get greedier.'

'House of straw actually ... but I get the picture.'

'What's happened is that the banks started dealing seriously in paper currencies and selling futures contracts and options and whatever other financially engineered pieces of paper their spreadsheet jockeys could invent. At the end of 2007, some people estimated that the size of the derivatives industry was $500 trillion—that's around ten times the size of all the income generated in one year across the entire planet.'

Patrick whistled. 'Holy shit. So the US economy sneezes and the UK, Europe, Japan, Australia ... they all catch cold.'

'Or pneumonia,' Samantha said with a slight shiver that could have been from the sea breeze or from a more sinister ill wind. 'The problem is that, in the last few years, the chickens have been coming home to roost. At the end of the day, financial solvency revolves around your ability to pay your bills as and when they fall due. When you cut through all the bullshit and obfuscation and political positioning, you discover that the US Government is insolvent.'

'But this isn't new,' Patrick said. 'What in this ... this mess ... has suddenly made you so glum?'

'Because money has been made so freely available by the Fed, the law-making process has also careened out of control ... purse strings ... rule makers. It doesn't matter which political party gets into power. The problems will still remain while the privately owned banks, the oil lobby and big business between them control the purse strings of the country.'

Patrick whistled again. They were coming within range of the lights from the restaurant, and he was able to see on her face that she really was affected—saddened—by the state of the world.

'If the US Government continues to borrow to pay the interest on its existing debt,' she offered, 'its nine trillion dollar debt will double every sixteen years or so. Eventually it will be offset by a bookkeeping entry. At some point in the far future—if the private sector debt mountain doesn't implode by then, and the derivatives industry doesn't collapse before then—the entire world will come under the control of a single globalised monetary giant … with power of control of a global government.'

'The end of the world as we know it … so globalisation might really be as threatening as the street marchers and banner bearers proclaim?'

'Almost right, but not quite. There are some subtleties and nuances.'

Patrick stopped walking and pulled Samantha gently around to face him. 'Tell, me something Sam. When did it start to go off the rails? Can you pinpoint it?' There was a forcefulness to his voice, as if he already knew the answer to the question but wanted confirmation.

She looked at him in surprise. 'As a matter of fact, it's quite easy to pinpoint the timing. Western markets for oil based technologies, like motorcars, began to saturate in the mid 1970s and the world economy began to slow around that time. By the early '80s, the US started spending more than it earned. You might remember that the '80s was when the Berlin wall came down, and roughly when China began to become economically active. With the opening up of these eastern markets, the demand for energy grew just when the oil supply was starting to peak. The oil price started to rise from about 1999, and it's been rising ever since. In hindsight, the bankers made a serious strategic mistake. The Fed's decision to flood the markets with money was a kiss of death. They forgot that wealth comes from Mother Nature. They thought that they could create it artificially with money. Now there's barely enough oil to keep all the existing cars running, let alone those that China and India are going to be manufacturing or will be buying for their large markets.'

'We're running on empty.'

Samantha nodded. 'It's even more serious than that. The terrorists and the oil producing cartel have been sensing a weakening of the Anglo–American hold over their previous power base. The alliance is running out of wriggle room. The Fed can't solve the energy problem with money. At the end of the day, there's not enough energy to keep the world economic gyroscope spinning. And the CO_2 problem is just making it worse. There's an economic imperative to *expand* energy consumption, and there's an ecological imperative to *reduce* fossil fuel consumption. We're too dependent on dwindling fossil fuels and we don't yet have practical alternatives. We're sitting between a rock and a hard place ... to quote a mining phrase.'

Patrick's response was to smile. He grasped her lightly on her upper arms and stroked the chill he felt there, but his attention seemed to be focussed elsewhere.

Samantha mistook the expression on his face for amusement. 'What are you smiling about?' A note of irritation crept into her voice. 'I can't see anything funny in any of this. In fact, I was so worried that it was going to ruin our holiday that I wasn't going to talk about it at all.'

Patrick shifted his gaze to stare into her hazel eyes. It was a warm and confident stare. 'Have you ever stopped to wonder why I chose to work in the Dominican Republic?' he asked, shifting his hands from her upper arms to his hips, his head to one side, and his smile broadening. He did a little one-two jig with his feet on the sand but fell short of clicking his heels in mid air.

'My guess is that you were running away from a permanent relation-ship with me, but I never really thought too deeply about it.' A wave, stronger than the previous ones, swept around their ankles. Samantha kicked at it playfully, showering Patrick's trousers.

'Well bless my wet cotton socks, and bless you also for that vote of confidence in my character, ma'am.' He belatedly leapt out of her way feigning deep hurt, but the look in his eyes belied his words. 'As a matter of fact, I wasn't running *away* from anything, I was running *to* something.'

Samantha bent, as though to splash him again. 'Oh?'

He grabbed her, swooped her up in his arms to stop her action. It was some minutes before he let her go. They walked on, arms around each other.

'As it happens, the Dominican Republic sits on the edge of the Bermuda Triangle, which is notorious for its electromagnetic anomalies,' he continued as though uninterrupted. 'As an engineer, I wanted to explore those anomalies first hand. My gut is telling me that the solution to the fossil fuel problem lies in environmentally sourced energy.'

Samantha peered at him through the night air. With his wet trousers he looked like a little boy who'd been running through the surf. The focus on her own problems had been diverted at last. 'I hate to burst your bubble, mate, but wouldn't it be a bit less Don Quixote and a bit more practical and down-to-earth to start off by researching what alternatives there are to fossil fuels before you go rushing off into the wide blue yonder?'

'Oh, ouch. Thankfully, my sozzled ego is impervious to that broadside. I'm way ahead of you sister. When I get back to the mine next Tuesday, I will be walking straight into a conference on oil and energy alternatives. As a mining engineer, it's not just idle curiosity on my part.'

The last dregs of her sombreness evaporated in her laughter. 'Sorry … should have known you're not as dumb as you look.'

'Well thanks again,' he said, this time with a wicked grin. 'So now can I tell you my story about the buck-naked female wind surfer with the built in pneumatic life preservers?'

'If you insist' she answered. 'But if you're leaving for the Dominican Republic on tomorrow's flight, I'm sure we can think of better things to do with our time tonight.'

CHAPTER 7

TARA EMERGED FROM the front door of her apartment block and looked up into the bright sunshine. It was Monday morning. Should she take a brisk walk through Central Park then flag a passing cab on the other side, or catch a cab here and now? She had just decided to walk when she spotted an empty taxi standing at the corner. Its driver looked at her expectantly. She raised a finger in acknowledgement, and he drove up alongside her.

'Ninth avenue, please, corner of West 34th,' she said as she climbed into the back seat. 'I want to go to that photographic store. I think it's called B & H Photo.'

'Yes ma'am,' the cabbie answered, as he pulled into the traffic stream. 'I know the one. A lot of out-of-town visitors go there. So, you're interested in photography?'

'Not until a week ago,' she answered. 'I'm leaving on vacation later this afternoon. It seemed like a good idea to take a few souvenir photographs while I'm away.'

She was rummaging in her bag to double check that she had not left her personal credit card in the drawer where she normally kept it when, unexpectedly, she heard his voice again.

'If you don't mind my asking ma'am, where're you going on your vacation?'

The question struck her as unusually forward, and she hesitated before answering. Why would he ask such a question? Her eyes flicked to the cab driver's licence on display in all New York cabs. 'Ali Ibn Said,' she read. She felt her pulse quicken and a cold prickle as the skin on her upper arms raised in goose bumps.

'I'm keeping my options open for the moment,' she responded

vaguely, expecting that it would discourage further conversation. 'I'm flying to Atlanta this afternoon and I'll see how it goes from there.'

'You okay for a ride to the airport?' he asked. 'Need a cab?'

Suddenly she felt foolish. 'If you're available this afternoon, I'll meet you at the same place where I just flagged you. My flight leaves at 15.30 hours—3.30 p.m.—so I need to get to JFK by the latest … 2.45. Maybe you can pick me up at around two o'clock just to allow for traffic.'

'That'll be fine by me, ma'am,' he answered, handing her his business card. 'Here's my number. You can call me anytime. I'll be at the same spot you found me … two o'clock sharp.'

Her nervous reaction had been ridiculous. This is New York City. The guy earns his living driving a cab. All he was doing was fishing for a passenger. Oddly, however, the rationalisation had no effect on her emotional state. It was only thirty-six hours ago that Carol had been talking to her about terrorists. Enough! She was being ridiculous. Consciously, she steeled herself to block the train of thought. Not everyone with a Middle Eastern sounding name is a terrorist. Imagine what he has to go through on a day-to-day basis.

When they reached their destination, she handed him a twenty-dollar bill. 'Keep the change,' she said as she stepped onto the sidewalk. Then, just before she closed the door again, she poked her head back inside. 'See you at two.'

She walked into the B & H camera store and looked around. Where to begin?

'Good morning madam. Can I be of assistance?' said a voice behind her. She turned. He seemed to be some sort of indoor traffic cop. He had on a skullcap, and curls down the sides of his face where most men have sideburns, a Chassidic Jew. He must have been in his late teens.

'I hope so. I'm looking for a digital camera that can take regular photos and underwater pictures.'

'Stills or movie?'

'I think … stills.'

'Why don't you stand in this line here?' he suggested. 'It will take maybe a minute or two and any one of the assistants behind that counter over there will be able to help you.' He pointed to the row of assistants about twenty feet away.

The line moved quickly. The place was like a railway station. It was just past 9.30 and there must have been at least fifty customers milling around. There was one area within the store that displayed video cameras connected by wires to the counters. There were maybe five male assistants, all with the same anachronistic look about them, all wore skullcaps—all talking to customers. Behind them were racks of accessories. Another area was set aside for packaging and despatch. Oddly, there were no female assistants to be seen.

Bemused by her surroundings, Tara inched her way forward in the line, until she got to a point where another traffic cop pointed her to counter No. 6, which had just been freed up by a departing customer. She had never seen such conveyor belt efficiency in a retail store.

'Hi,' the sales assistant at counter No. 6 said, with a broad smile.

Somehow, the single word managed to convey a tone that was both warmly welcoming and boyishly friendly. She felt instantly at ease. It was conspicuously the opposite of the emotion she had felt in the cab. 'How can I help you this fine New York morning?' he asked.

'Hi' she answered, and repeated what she'd told the traffic cop.

'Have you got a budget, or some other starting point?'

'I'd like to keep it under $1,000 if possible. I'm a neophyte, but all the adverts nowadays tell me that I can be a half-wit and still get it right. Maybe I am a half-wit because I believe the ads.' She smiled self effacingly. 'Preferably, the $1,000 should include a camera, some sort of underwater lighting or flash attachment, a light meter if you think I need one, and an underwater compass.'

'Well,' he answered with a conspiratorial smile, 'you're ahead of the game already, because my wife Barbara keeps telling me that I'm less than a half-wit, and I'm the one who has to explain this stuff to customers. So, let's see.' He lowered his gaze to inspect the computer monitor in front of him.

Tara was taken aback. Wife? He seemed barely the other side of twenty. She had no opportunity to explore the thought any further.

'As I see it,' he said, 'there are three choices which fit into the point-and-click category. All of them can be tweaked to get better photographs when you have learned the basics.'

The next few minutes were a blur of technical details.

'What's your recommendation?' Tara eventually asked.

His reply was a study in self-confidence—he had no doubt whatsoever about his conclusion.

'Sounds fine to me,' she responded. 'What about the other gear?'

'Give me a few seconds,' he said as his gaze dropped back to the computer monitor. He wrote the details on a scratch pad, which he turned to show her.

'Yes,' she answered, 'that'll be great. Thank you. I'm impressed you listened so carefully to my needs.'

'Well,' he smiled, so she didn't know whether he was joking, 'the good Lord gave us two ears and one mouth, and my wife keeps telling me that that's the proportion in which I should use them.'

Tara took the invoice from his outstretched hand. 'Barbara sounds like a very wise person. Forgive me for asking such a personal question, but how old is she?'

The assistant squared his shoulders and smiled at Tara. 'She turns twenty next Tuesday. She is expecting our second child around that time and, please God, it will be born on that same day … she will have a very special birthday present.'

'Second child? How old is your first child?'

'Our son Ari will be two in November.' He looked so proud, Tara thought he might bring out a wallet with family photos next.

Within five minutes, she found herself on the sidewalk with her new purchases safely packed in a B & H carry bag. Whew! Talk about sales efficiency.

She still had an hour to kill before her appointment with Dr Curlewis, so started walking in the general direction and looked out for a café. A Starbucks loomed at the next corner. She ordered a latté, found a comfortable seat and took out her Blackberry. It was the one thing that kept her in touch with her family wherever she was. She composed an email to her older brother in Hartford, and through him to her mother who occupied the granny flat at the back of his house. She told them of her vacation plans and that she'd be joining them for Thanksgiving in November. My God! Is it September already? Then, from the depths of her unconscious mind, she registered the sound of a voice at the next table.

'I can remember a time when we shared a party telephone line in our village in Turkey,' the dismembered voice was saying. 'We had maybe twenty or thirty such telephone lines in the entire village of around 500 people. Nowadays, anyone can sit with a personal wireless thingummy like yours, in just about any café in any city in the world and send instantaneous emails or make phone calls to people anywhere.'

She glanced up to see an unusually handsome man looking at her in a friendly manner. In his mid to late thirties, he had clear olive skin, wavy raven black hair and dark brown puppy dog eyes reminiscent of a young Omar Sharif. Tara felt a slight flutter in her stomach. She couldn't quite place the feeling. It wasn't sexual. There was something intangibly unusual about him, a quiet, non-threatening confidence—of a nature that was unfamiliar to her.

She smiled back at him. 'Where about in Turkey do you come from?' she asked.

'I was born in a little village between Afyon and Pamukkale,' he replied as he picked up his drink to join her at her table. The movement registered in her mind as seamless, and strangely non-threatening, as though she was watching an old Humphrey Bogart movie where the hero just assumes that the heroine is going to melt into his arms.

'You will probably not have heard of Afyon. It's the main opium producing region in Turkey, but you may well have heard of Pamukkale, which is world famous for its natural hot springs.'

'As a matter of fact I have heard of Pamukkale. I believe that's the place where there's a series of turquoise coloured, spring water pools down the side of a terraced hill. The water cascades from one to the next down the hillside.'

She could see he was impressed.

'My name is Mehmet.' He bowed his head slightly towards her. 'And yours?'

'I'm Tara,' she answered, 'and I'm also curious. Tell me more about this wonder of nature. Ever since I first heard about it I've wanted to go there. I've been to Ankara a couple of times, but always on flying visits and I've never had time to visit Pamukkale.'

'I was first introduced to Pamukkale when I was about seven years old.' He pronounced each syllable of the words with equal emphasis. 'My family and several other families from my village went there on a day's outing. I was a very impressionable child at the time, and I thought we had arrived at a fairyland. The pools, as you say, are bright turquoise—like topaz gemstones in the sunshine. It seemed like a fantasy land to my young eyes.'

Tara picked up her coffee cup to sip, but her attention was on Mehmet.

His puppy-dog eyes deepened even further as he recalled the occasion. 'In the blazing sunshine, the hillside seemed as white as newly fallen snow in winter, except that this was summer and very hot.' He paused for a moment to smile cautiously at his listener. 'All we children had brought our swimming outfits so that we could bathe in the pools. When you looked up at the edges of the pools, it looked as if crystalline spikes—like sugar or cotton wool—were hanging from the mouths of drooling giants. If it had been winter, I would have thought these spikes were frozen streams of water, but even a child could understand that such a thing would be impossible in the heat of summer. Behind them were brownish coloured walls of rock. I remember thinking they looked like the chocolate cakes with white icing that my mother used to make. That picnic, with my family and our friends, is amongst the most pleasurable memories of my life.'

'What causes those spikes?'

'The water from the hot springs is exceptionally high in calcium carbonate. As it pours down the hillside, the calcium is deposited. In time, these deposits harden. In fact, the name "Pamukkale" is a Turkish word that translates roughly to mean "cotton castle".' He paused again and this time he smiled broadly showing an even set of extraordinarily white teeth.

'And now, it is your turn to satisfy my curiosity. Turkey is a land that is far away from the USA, yet you mentioned that you have been to its capital, Ankara, on more than one occasion. Have you travelled much in your life?'

'I'm a commercial airline pilot … Boeing passenger jets.' Tara waved an outstretched hand into the distance. 'My job, has taken me to the far corners of the Earth. It's been some time since I last visited Ankara. It seems to becoming much more westernised.'

'You appear to be a very well informed lady,' Mehmet responded. Tara cringed inwardly just a little at his expression but put it down to language and cultural differences. 'There is still much tradition that the older people try to cling to,' he continued, 'but the younger ones want technology.'

'The country has such a rich heritage … biblical heritage,' Tara said.

'Yes—where Adam and Eve set foot after they were expelled from the Garden of Eden; where Abraham stayed for some years on his journey from Ur—which is today in southern Iraq—to Canaan. And 500 years ago, the tentacles of the Ottoman Empire stretched across much of south-eastern Europe, North Africa and the Middle East. When the Ottoman Empire finally came to an end following World War I … since those days the people have been living in poverty until relatively recently. Nowadays, we are still poor, but we are once again becoming a more industrious nation.'

'And now Turkey may become part of the EU?' Tara asked. 'I've always wondered about that—the fact that its only interface with Europe is via short borders with Greece and Bulgaria. It's always seemed to me that Turkey was more a Middle Eastern country than a European country. Why do you even want to become a member of the EU?'

'I am assuming that your profession has facilitated your good knowledge of geography?'

When Tara did not respond, he continued. 'Yes, it is true that there are those in the EU who are arguing that Turkey may grow to become the Muslim tail that wags the Christian dog,' he said. 'And that, by the end of the decade, our population of around eighty million will grow to become the largest in the EU. But this is really an emotional argument. The real reason is not difficult to understand.'

Tara heard a hint of emotion in his voice, and raised her eyebrows to look inquiringly at him.

'The mindset of the average Turkish citizen is now much more aligned with the West than the Middle East. They aspire to own better cars and furniture and clothing. My own situation is a good example of this. Although I now live in Haiti and earn my living as a metals broker, I have a degree in commerce from a Turkish university. I enjoy the fact that my work brings me often to the United States. In this globalised world, Turkey is really not that far removed from anywhere nowadays.'

Haiti! Tara felt the shutters in her mind come slamming down. This was the third time in two days that she had cause to focus on the subject of Muslims and Haiti and the West. Suddenly, she couldn't wait to get out of there. She rose to leave.

'You are going?' Mehmet asked.

'I have a doctor's appointment a few blocks away and I need to give myself time to get there. I see that you have hardly begun to drink your coffee. Please don't let me interrupt you.'

'Wait,' Mehmet protested. 'Can we not at least exchange phone numbers? I am often in the USA. Perhaps we could meet again?'

'I don't really see the point, Mehmet,' she said as politely as she could. 'You live in another country. My work takes me all over the world and I am hardly ever here anyway. But it was nice meeting you.'

With that, she picked up her things and walked out of the café as quickly as she could without appearing to be running.

CHAPTER 8

JET LAGGED AND punch drunk. That was how Patrick was feeling at 11.45 a.m. on Tuesday after landing in Santo Domingo less than twelve hours earlier. Including changeovers, he had been on the go for twenty-seven hours straight, catching flights that had taken him from Brisbane to Sydney to Los Angeles, and then to Atlanta, and finally on to Santo Domingo. After a few hours of fitful sleep he had walked into a high-powered presentation on 'Nickel and Oil in Tomorrow's World' in the boardroom of Eagle Mine's offices.

Ten of the mining company's most senior executives were seated around the large table. Some lounged in their chairs, others rested chins on balled fists or open palms as they concentrated on the projection screen in front of them. One rocked his chair precariously backwards and forwards, his knees wedged under the edge of the table. The tabletop was arrayed with drinks bottles and empty mint wrappers, and conspicuously virginal notepads.

'Titch' McCann, vice president of an organization that went by the name of Vancouver Consulting, or VC in short-speak, had just completed a presentation of numbers and graphs and was now summing up.

'So … in summary, worldwide demand for nickel exceeds supply and the shortfall seems likely to keep growing. As of last week, the available inventories in warehouses monitored by the London Metal Exchange represented substantially less than one half of one day's requirements. It's therefore self-evident that Eagle is facing a major expansion opportunity.'

He walked back to his seat and there was a smattering of applause and a sliding back of chairs as the meeting broke for lunch.

'Ladies and gentlemen,' McCann raised his hand above the chatter and continued in a slightly raised voice. 'Please ensure that we reconvene by two o'clock. We'll be focussing on the world's oil markets and I urge you not to go out and spend the nickel profits that you have not yet earned—the flipside of the nickel boom is that the world's oil industry is trending towards similar shortages. Let's not forget that the plant that generates the power for your electric smelters runs on diesel, and that any interruption in the flow of that diesel will likely cause major production problems. Let's also not forget that the nickel ferrocones produced by your smelters are delivered in diesel powered trucks from the mine in Bonao to the port in Haina and then transported by diesel powered ships to your markets.'

Patrick and Todd Allbright made their way out of the boardroom and into the street outside.

'The VP of VC is the ultimate good news–bad news guy,' quipped the man who controlled the mine's purse strings. 'Any plans for lunch?' he asked. 'I have a couple of things I want to talk to you about, not the least of which is a dinner party that Desirée is organizing for this coming Saturday night.'

'No plans,' Patrick answered, glancing up at the blackening sky. 'But I don't think we should stray too far. It looks to me like there's an unseasonal storm brewing. Why don't we just nip across the road for a sandwich?'

'Desirée is missing the social life she used to have back home in Boston,' Todd continued after the two men had bought lunch and found a table. 'I've been encouraging her to become more of a front-foot hostess, so she's throwing a formal dinner party on Saturday night for a few friends and business associates. Will you join us? And bring a date— sevenish for 7.30?'

'Thanks Todd. I'd love to come. But I'm not sure if I can scrape up a date at this stage. I haven't had much time for a social life these past few months I've been here. Can I let you know about that?'

'Of course.'

Patrick eyed the sandwich on his plate with suspicion. He picked it up and inspected its contents edge-on. He raised one corner of the top layer of bread, and his mouth turned down theatrically at the corners.

Todd laughed. 'The way you're looking at that reminds me of that movie with Walter Matthau and Jack Lemon. Did you ever see it?'

'Don't think so.'

'Yeah, well. Matthau holds up a plate and he asks his buddies around the poker table, "What kind of sandwich do you want? I got green ones and I got brown ones. The green ones are either very new cheese or very old meat".'

Patrick chuckled. He put the sandwich down, pushed the plate away and reached for a styrofoam cup of coffee. 'It's the jet lag, mate. Tell me something though, how does a guy like you—educated at Stanford and with a post-graduate degree from Harvard—come to land up in a country like this, particularly given that it seems Desirée would be more at home in Boston society? I hope you don't mind my asking.'

'Not at all. I suppose we rationalised it on the basis that we would be having a short-term adventure. We agreed that it would be for a maximum period of five years or until the kids came along, whichever came first. I'm sure we'll have some interesting stories to tell when we rejoin our circle of friends in Boston—including the one about my Australian associate who insisted on ordering sandwiches when everyone else around him was eating local food.'

Patrick cast his eyes around the room for a few seconds as if to verify Todd's observation before he responded. What he saw around him was a sparsely furnished room full of happily chatting Dominicans. 'Yeah. I hear you, but you and Desirée are delightful people who are certainly not airheads. There must be more to your decision than just interesting stories.' He took a sip of his coffee and grimaced.

'Most people would have been satisfied with that superficial answer,' Todd responded with a lopsided smile. 'I suppose that as a mining engineer, you're congenitally programmed to drill down deeper.'

Patrick acknowledged the crack with a tired sounding expulsion of air that might have been a laugh. 'Mate, let's leave my genitals out of this. Just think of me as a nosey Australian bastard who hasn't had a whole hell of a lot of sleep in the past couple of days. Come on. Fess up. What are you doing in the Dominican Republic?'

'There's no secret. My longer-term plans are to get into politics, and I didn't want to travel down the investment banking road like some of my friends who also want to end up in Congress. Sure, an investment banking career allows you to make contacts in high places, but you don't get to learn much about the real world at its coal face … where wealth and employment are generated.'

That perked Patrick up, and he gave Todd a look of encouragement. His response gave Todd's voice a more earnest tone. 'In these days of globalisation and the World Wide Web, most people seem to have forgotten that all wealth ultimately traces back to adding some form of value to Mother Earth's bounty. Collating and shuffling pieces of paper is where the wealth trail ends, not where it begins. It's one of life's ironies that the world's poorer nations tend to be at the beginning of the wealth trail. But if you follow the money, it eventually accumulates and concentrates within the world's richer and better organized nations … which tend to specialise in activities that are closer to the sources of the capital and closer to the markets. Eventually, the money is deposited into some bank account or other, and as often as not withdrawn for investment.'

'Those are admirable sentiments, sport, but I'm not sure that working as a finance executive in a mining company in the Dominican Republic is going to make you rich.'

Todd leaned back in his chair. He looked at his lunch companion across the table as if choosing his next words carefully.

'Please don't take this the wrong way Patrick, because I don't want to sound blasé about it. But my family is already rich, and so is Desirée's. And Desirée, she's not just a social butterfly. Sure, she had her coming-out party the same as everyone else in her circle of friends, but—like me   she also has a keenly developed social conscience. We see this stint as a fairly exciting way of getting to understand the Latin American and Creole mindset and, perhaps, of learning to speak Spanish—which is always handy these days.'

'Sounds to me like you have a flair for the art-of-the-possible,' Patrick said. 'Maybe I'll get to count a US congressman or even a senator in my own circle of friends one day. So what's on your mind, Todd? I'm sure Desirée's dinner party is not the only matter you wanted to talk about today.'

'You're right. While you've been away, I've been worrying about the prospects and possible consequences of mine flooding.'

'Why would you be worrying about that?' he responded, unconsciously glancing towards the window and the weather that loomed outside.

'Hurricane Katrina brought into sharp focus the general increase in extreme weather in the Atlantic basin. I've been keeping an eye on the forecasts, and it seems that in the coming years we can expect the number of named storms and hurricanes to run at around eighty percent above the previous fifty-year average. That's fairly concerning to me, and I think it demands risk management attention and, corporately, that's part of my responsibility.'

'I'm a mining engineer. My training's more in line with metallurgy than meteorology ...'

'If we have a flood and are unprepared for it, you're going to have to personally bear some of the consequences. It's my job to worry about financial consequences, but I'm thinking more about engineering consequences now. It seems self-evident that global warming is causing an escalation of a variety of technical risks, and we're going to have to learn to get to grips with them—now, rather than later.'

Todd's last statement seemed to hit a nerve with Patrick. He shifted his position so that he faced Todd squarely, his brow furrowed in a frown.

'Let me share something with you. I've come to realise that whatever we read on the front pages of the newspapers can usually be treated as history. Frankly, the real news usually doesn't make the newspapers until after it's too late to do anything about it. The real news is that there's no way that global warming has been *caused* by greenhouse gas emissions.'

'What are you talking about?' Todd looked at Patrick as though he had taken leave of his senses.

'These emissions are very probably exacerbating what other highly credible people have been arguing we would have been experiencing in any event. They're starting to become seriously concerned we might be missing the arrival of global cooling. Frankly, I'm not really arguing about whether there is global warming or global cooling. I'm focussing on the most likely cause of climate change. And I just don't accept the view that humans are the cause.'

'So give me a "for instance".'

'Well … two quick examples. The first is Melville Island, north of the Arctic Circle. It used to have an average temperature all year round of five degrees ever since they started keeping records in the 1950s. Recently, temperatures there have skyrocketed to around fifteen to twenty degrees. There's no way that carbon dioxide or any other greenhouse gas could have caused that to happen in such a localised area. It came as a total surprise to the CO_2–global warming camp. One conclusion you can draw from their shocked reaction is that their computer models are seriously flawed.'

'Okay. What's your second example?' Todd's expression was deadpan.

'Since 1992, there's been a dramatic weakening in the Gulf Stream that takes warm water in the Atlantic from the tropics to the Northern Hemisphere, and cold water from the Arctic region in the north—past the West Coast of Africa back down towards the Southern Ocean in the Antarctic. The Gulf Stream behaves like a sort of heat exchange pump; cold water is continuously replacing warm water, and vice versa.'

Patrick shifted forward in his seat. 'It takes over 3,500 times as much energy to heat a cubic metre of seawater by one degree as it takes to warm a cubic metre of air by the same amount. There's no way our warming atmosphere would have been able to transfer enough heat energy to warm our oceans so dramatically in such a short period of time. You can do the math yourself. Blind Freddy can see that there must have been other forces at work.'

'So you're not arguing that we haven't been experiencing global warming?'

'Of course not. Global warming is self-evident. What I'm focussing on is the most likely *cause* of that warming, which has far more likely been the increasing intensity of sunspot activity. These same credible people who are expecting global cooling are arguing that our sun has been unusually active of late, and that this active cycle will very soon climax before entering an unusually quiet period.'

'If it's that simple, how come everyone seems to have it so wrong?'

'We don't have enough time to discuss this further right now because we need to get back to young Titch, but you can now see why I'm focussing so intently on the subject of oil. Consumption could soar with global cooling.'

'Can we talk about this in more detail at a later stage? I'm still not convinced.'

'Of course. But be reassured, I hear you about the risk of flooding. Over the next few weeks I'll look into putting in place a fall-back plan to address what might happen if we have a flood.'

Patrick looked up towards the ominously pregnant skies as they walked out of the café, and did not at all like what he saw.

Half an hour later, lunch had long been forgotten, and the atmosphere in the boardroom was no longer either casual or relaxed. Titch McCann was causing a stir with the table of numbers that he was projecting onto the screen.

'Ladies and gentlemen,' he said, and rocked forward slightly on his feet. 'What you're looking at is an overview of the importance of oil in the world economy. Whilst I don't want to teach you guys how to suck eggs, it might be well to remember that the world economy is like a gyroscope—you know, one of those spinning wheels that stays upright on its axle precisely because it is spinning, and that is likely to fall over if the wheel stops spinning. Clearly, to stay upright, the economy needs to keep spinning around at a fairly fast pace.'

The room was quiet.

'Okay.' Titch looked around at his listeners. 'As you guys of all people know, wealth originates from the environment—from the raw resources extracted from the bowels of the earth or harvested from crops and forests, or pulled out of the sea. So ... iron ore is made into steel, the steel goes into motor cars, and the motor cars need roads, service stations, hire purchase finance, accident insurance and panel beaters. Ultimately, we owe our current prosperity to the fact that people such as your good selves are harvesting what Mother Nature has to offer.'

'I knew I was critically important to the future of the world economy,' one wag blurted out, cutting into their collective concentration. 'I just didn't know why.' There were titters of appreciation, but they soon died out.

Titch smiled in acknowledgment before continuing. 'Yes, but we should also not lose sight of the fact that none of this would occur if there was no artificial energy available. Since the 1700s, fossil fuels have provided the artificial energy that powered the industrial revolution.'

With that, he turned to face the image that was being projected onto the screen.

'The table of numbers can be summarised as follows: firstly, when oil was trading at $45 a barrel, the direct wholesale value of all the oil produced by all the world's oil producers accounted for roughly three percent of all the income generated on the planet. When we add up all the various incomes being generated by all the other oil dependent industries, we find that oil and its related industries accounted for roughly eleven percent of all the world's income in 2004.'

Titch looked around the table. Everyone's eyes were on him.

'Now, I want to introduce you to an economic concept, the multiplier effect. Does anyone here know what that is?'

'Yes,' Todd Allbright responded. 'If I spend, say, $100 on a shirt, then the person who sells me the shirt will probably spend most of that $100, and save only a small proportion of it. If he saves ten percent, then the next guy will receive $90 and if *that* guy saves ten percent, then the next guy after him will receive ninety percent of the $90, or $81, and so on, until all the money is finally spent. The total multiplier effect will be around nine times by the time the process ends, or around $900 because of the actions of everyone else down the line.'

'Exactly right,' said Titch. 'It's the multiplier effect that causes the economic gyroscope to spin and to stay upright.'

A few people nodded. No one around the table said anything, so he continued. 'For the record, the reality is that people don't typically save ten percent—more like 4.5 percent, and the less people save—and the more they spend, of course—the faster the gyroscope spins.'

At that point, a light went on for Patrick, as he remembered the discussion on bank lending and debt that he and Samantha had had two nights before.

'Holy mackerel,' he said aloud before he realised he was speaking his thoughts. Then, for the benefit of the people around the table who had turned to look at him, 'If oil and associated industries are accounting for eleven percent of the world's income, and the effect of the multiplier is that the original oil related income grows nine fold, then it must follow that oil and related industries are what ultimately drives the world economy.'

'There's a question of timing,' Titch said. 'It may not all happen within one year, but if we take Patrick's argument at face value, then here's something you won't hear or read about in the media. I want you to consider the impact on the total economic pie of an oil price rise from $45 to, say, $75 a barrel. In fact, the oil price has indeed risen to well over $75 a barrel, so it's not just a hypothetical question.'

He allowed a few seconds to pass before continuing.

'If, say, everything else remained equal and the world's total income remained constant, then oil's share of the world income—because of the price rise—would have risen from three percent to five percent. Trust me. I've crunched the numbers. Apply the multiplier effect and oil's total impact on the economic pie grows to forty-five percent.'

Titch rubbed a pencil between his palms, then spun it on the table in front of him. 'The key here is that if the economic gyroscope is going to keep spinning at the same rate and not fall over, then the whole world economy needs to keep growing at around its historical two to three percent per year in volume terms. But if volumes of sales of other things slow, then the world economy will be in danger of falling over.'

Patrick again remembered his discussions with Samantha. 'And what happens if the oil price is quoted in a currency other than US dollars, which is what Saddam Hussein tried to do?' He answered his own question. 'The US dollar will probably fall sharply relative to other currencies and the US economy would probably tank.'

'And the multiplier there,' broke in Todd, 'is that this will impact on the rest of the world that is exporting to the US.'

'My God,' a woman further down the table exclaimed. 'That would also partially explain why the Coalition of the Willing invaded Iraq. They needed to ensure that no one lost faith in the US dollar.'

'So.' Titch continued—rather too quickly Patrick thought. 'If we want to avoid a war of major dimensions, there appear to be three sensible answers from the perspective of the global economy. First, the oil producers may attempt to engineer a lower oil price by increasing output in the short term, but that's a very limited option. Second, the pain of price inflation will need to be shared around rather than confined to the USA. Thirdly, and most importantly, we will need to become less dependent on oil.'

Patrick turned to Todd and whispered, 'This is what I was hoping he would get to.'

Todd, for his part, was thinking that Titch had not made one single reference to global warming or CO_2 to justify the world's need to find a replacement for oil. And if Patrick was right about the sunspot activity, then what the hell was really driving the global warming soothsayers?

CHAPTER 9

TARA HAD CHECKED into her Santo Domingo hotel and freshened up, but hadn't bothered to unpack. The afternoon sky was becoming ominously overcast, she could always unpack later. The concierge had arranged a cab to take her to a store that specialised in blue amber. He had also handed her his business card, saying that if she mentioned his name, the manager would give her a discount. Five US dollars changed hands. Both were happy. Doubtless, he would also earn some sort of kickback commission from the store.

It looked like any jewellery store, except that it had been designed with an eye to lulling visitors into a state of relaxation. There were the usual display counters, but there was an unusual emphasis on seating and lighting. Several comfortable armchairs were dotted around the shop, implicitly inviting customers to take their time. Conventional fluorescent globes lit the store, as well as table lamps with incandescent light bulbs.

When the sales assistant heard that she was contemplating several purchases, the red carpet had been rolled out. Señor Fernandez, the manager, had magically appeared from the back office, the coffee had been poured and the smiles had broadened. In a holiday mood, with her brand new camera bag nestling at her feet, Tara was feeling somewhat frivolous as she sat talking to Señor Fernandez. There was a ghost of a smile on her lips. It didn't matter what country you're in, a salesman was still a salesman.

'No one knows for sure why it's blue,' Señor Fernandez was saying. Some believe that it has to do with volcanic ash or dust that embedded itself into the amber at the time it was formed, but I do not personally accept this explanation because Dominican amber is very clear and the ash would have made the amber opaque. Others believe the original honey-gold colour turned green and then eventually blue as it was exposed to extreme underground heat associated with volcanic activity. Again, I think this could not have been possible because it would have caused the amber to burn up and be destroyed in the process.'

Tara reached for an eye-catching piece that was lying on the counter. It was crystal clear and the colour of rich honey. Encapsulated within it was a perfectly preserved ancient leaf. The leaf must have been millions of years old, yet it looked as if it had just recently fallen off the tree. A tiny, equally well preserved insect was still sitting on the leaf's surface, doubtlessly pausing—at the time—to do what it was originally designed to do during its short life on earth. Talk about dramatic pauses.

'Perhaps I am mistaken,' Tara observed, 'but this doesn't look blue to me.'

'You are quite correct, señorita. That is not blue amber. There are three regions in the Dominican Republic where amber is to be found. The older and harder amber is mined around La Cordillera Septentrional in the north—that is where blue amber is mainly found. The nearest mines in La Cordillera are scattered around La Cumbre near Santiago about 180 kilometres from here. It is maybe a four-hour car journey away because of traffic.'

'Cordillera? That means range doesn't it, as in mountain range?'

'Si señorita. The name La Cumbre means "the peak". There are perhaps twelve separate mines high up in the mountains at about 1,500 feet. It is a very beautiful part of the island. The other two regions are close to Bayaguana and Sabana in the east. This piece was found near Bayaguana.'

Tara nodded, turning the piece over in her hand. It was an amazing example of nature as artist.

'All the amber in the Dominican Republic was formed between the Oligocene and Miocene eras,' he told her, 'between ten and thirty million years ago, but the amber in the eastern region is somewhat softer.' He handed her a magnifier to put to her eye. 'It also has fossil inclusions in it like you see in this particular piece.'

'How much is this piece?'

'It is a bargain at US$650, señorita.'

Tara smiled in reaction to the word. The game had begun. She handed him the concierge's card. 'Pedro at my hotel told me to tell you that he recommended I buy from you. If we can come to a satisfactory arrangement on this piece, I might be prepared to buy some others to give to members of my family when I visit them for Thanksgiving.'

'Señorita, I am not authorised to give discounts. It could cost me my job, and then how would my poor wife and my six children eat?'

'What if the piece was damaged?'

'The owner holds me personally responsible for damages.'

'Would you personally pay full price for this piece if it was damaged?'

'But this piece is not damaged, señorita.'

'Well, why don't we just pretend that it is? Then we can agree on how much I should pay in compensation to protect you from being fired, and then we can move forward. Why don't we start at $400 for this piece?'

Señor Fernandez wrung his hands in despair. 'It would be more than my pitiful life is worth, señorita.'

'How much would you have to charge to save your life, which I am sure is much more valuable than you modestly claim?'

Señor Fernadez looked down at his intertwined fingers. Then he looked up at the ceiling. He sighed theatrically and brought his gaze back to look into her sparkling sapphire eyes, which seemed to flicker with tiny, amber coloured streaks of flame. The clarity of his own brown-eyed gaze belied the hangdog look on his face.

'Would the señorita be prepared to settle for $500?'

Tara relented. 'Yes, and, as I promised, I would also like to see another piece please.'

With the first sale under his belt, Señor Fernandez became notice-ably more relaxed and warmer in his attitude. If he'd had a moustache, he would have twirled the ends, Tara thought, but stopped herself from smiling. He reached behind him to open a display case, and extracted another piece from it.

'I have read an explanation written by a professor of physics from the USA as to why the blue amber is blue, señorita. This explanation is the one that I feel is perhaps closest to the truth.'

'Oh?' Tara responded somewhat distractedly. Her attention was focussed on the countertop and an exquisitely carved turtle just two inches in length.

'Yes,' Señor Fernandez continued, holding between his forefinger and thumb the amber piece he had retrieved from the cabinet so that the closest source of available light—an incandescent lamp on the counter—was behind it. He gestured for Tara to look. 'What colours do you see?'

'It's beautiful,' she said. It had no inclusions, no foreign matter at all. It appeared to have been formed by swirls of resinous sap stirred together in nature's cauldron. 'It seems to have a variety of different oranges, browns and gold—like the colours of autumn leaves, only transparent. Wait! I thought I saw some blue as you moved your hand.'

'You did señorita.' He leaned closer towards her, holding the piece reverently in the palm of his hand in a manner so the light from the ceiling mounted globes fell directly onto its surface. The amber's surface seemed to fluoresce and to take on a range of blue hues.

'It's blue!' Tara said in delight. 'Goodness, it looks almost alive. The swirls move as the light hits it from different angles. Wait! They're not swirls. It's more like I'm looking at the ocean from thousands of feet above the surface and the darker orange colours are the coral beneath. It's quite magnificent.'

'*This* is Dominican blue amber, señorita,' the manager said with pride of ownership in his voice. It was as though he had a personal arrangement with its Creator Himself. 'It's a very fine piece, which is exceptionally well priced at $520.'

Tara knew intuitively that the price had suddenly risen from whatever its original level may have been, but even at $520 she was prepared to take it. Nevertheless, she shrugged her shoulders and gestured for him to put it to one side for the moment. She was warming to the game. Maybe he would offer her one of the hand-rolled Dominican cigars that she had spotted in a humidor on the display counter, but she doubted it.

This man was of the old Spanish school. Women were not supposed to smoke big fat phallic cigars.

'What was the professor's explanation?' she asked, harking back to his previous comment. She would stall the closing of the sale until she was good and ready.

'His studies concluded that blue amber contains minute aerosols of aromatic molecules of a substance called perylene, produced by a thermal polymerization process initiated by electromagnetic irradiation. They fluoresce under light to reflect the bluish colours that we see.'

Tara's eyes glazed over. 'Basically light bouncing off microscopic bubbles of transparent stuff,' she responded distractedly. But she wasn't really focussing on what he had just said, she was trying not to stare at the carved turtle that had so captivated her.

'Tell me about this piece,' she asked, off-handedly picking it up from the countertop. 'Is this a carving of a local turtle?'

'There are four main types of turtle living off the Dominican coast, señorita. This particular carving is of a hawksbill, which is prized for its shell.'

'It's exquisite. I've never seen anything quite like it,' Tara gushed in spite of herself. 'Look at this fault line in the amber in the turtle's beak area. Look how the sculptor used the fault to advantage so that it emphasises the feature.' Tara had quite forgotten that it was he who was supposed to be selling it to her.

'Maybe I can even find such a turtle to photograph whilst I am here,' she said —belatedly trying to convince Señor Fernandez that her interest was in the living animal.

This was a particularly exquisite piece, he told her. She knew he was not fooled by her ruse, and affable though he was, he had still stopped short of offering her a cigar.

'Is the señorita aware of the differences between Dominican amber and Baltic amber which is found near the Baltic Sea?' he asked.

'Not really, but I'm interested to hear. I want to learn all I can about Dominican blue amber.'

'Compared to Baltic amber, Dominican amber in general is much clearer. Also, Dominican blue amber gives off a unique fragrance when it is being worked on.'

'You mean like a perfume?'

'Si. It is released into the air as a result of the abrasion.'

Tara's mind started to drift as she continued to inspect the carved turtle.

'Amber is considered a gemstone,' Señor Fernandez was saying. 'It has been traded since earliest times because it was also believed to be possessed of magical and mystical properties.'

A few moments silence passed before she picked up the piece she had agreed to buy. 'There was a movie in the US called *Jurassic Park*,' she said, 'based on the idea that a mosquito had been preserved in Dominican amber and some scientists had retrieved dinosaur DNA from its stomach. Is it possible that such DNA could have been preserved in the amber for that long?'

'I'm afraid not, señorita. The last dinosaurs roamed the earth sixty-five million years ago. The oldest Dominican amber is only thirty million years old. The movie was purely the product of someone's over-active imagination.'

'Thirty million years is still older than my grandmother's cat.' Tara gazed speculatively at the amber for a few seconds, then lifted her head. 'But hang on a minute. How is it possible that this leaf could be so perfectly preserved after thirty million years? That's unreal.'

'In a sense it has been mummified—with no exposure to oxygen for all that time.'

'Could you show me that tray of amber pieces please?' she asked, pointing below the glass surface of the counter.

Señor Fernadez jumped up from his chair as if she had used an electrified cattle prod. He handed her the tray, which she placed on her lap.

A small and particularly striking piece of blue amber immediately caught her attention. It lent itself to being set in gold and worn as a ring, but Tara was superstitious about buying a ring for herself. She would prefer it to be given to her by the kind of strange man she and her flatmate had joked about. But, with her lifestyle, how would they ever find one another?

She caught herself muttering aloud, and to cover her embarrassment her hand moved to pick up another stone close by, which she felt her mother might appreciate. 'If we can come to an agreement on price, Señor Fernandez, I am prepared to buy a total of four pieces. This piece may be suitable for my mother to wear as a pendant. I think my sister-in-law would love to have the one with the inclusions in it that I have already bought. I would like to keep the turtle for myself, and also the first piece you showed me that reminds me of the ocean when I am flying above it. I think it could be incorporated into a very attractive necklace.'

'You have chosen well, señorita. Your mother and your sister-in-law will be very happy.'

'I hope so, but that still leaves me needing a gift for my brother Ken.'

And thus the business at hand devolved to haggling over price. After some serious discussion about values and inflation, and poverty and mouths to feed, and the usual tear jerking arguments, the final total was agreed upon. Señor Fernandez was even persuaded to throw in a box of twenty-five Tambor Dominicano Churchill cigars as a bonus, but only when Tara pushed him—for her brother, she told him. She knew of a company in New York that could make an embossed label with his name for the outside of the cedar box. The fact that Ken didn't smoke seemed irrelevant in the moment; he could offer them to his visitors.

'Señor Fernandez, would it be possible for you to arrange a visit to one of the mines in La Cumbra you were telling me about?' she asked. 'I am here on vacation, so I can make myself available at any time.'

'I will see what I can do, señorita. I will make a telephone call for you.' He directed his assistant to finalise the transaction and rose to make his way back to his office.

Presently, Señor Fernandez returned with the news. 'Good fortune, she smiles on you señorita. I have managed to make a very favourable arrangement for tomorrow.'

'You have? That's wonderful.'

'I have arranged for a young medical student by the name of Aurelio Duarte to collect you at your hotel at 6 a.m. tomorrow morning. He is on vacation too at present. He will take you to the La Toca mine, and bring you back to Santo Domingo between 6.00 and 6.30 p.m., in time for an early dinner. He is very reputable—I know his family—and he is a good driver. You should wear walking clothes and sneakers, señorita. It could take up to one hour to walk from the road to the mine.'

'How much will that cost me?'

Señor Fernadez looked across to his sales assistant, who nodded slightly—presumably confirming that Tara had paid. The assistant began to pack the now wrapped items into a glossy bag subtly embossed with the store name. 'Because you have been such a good customer of mine, Aurelio has agreed to act as your personal guide for a total of $250 including the use of his four-wheel drive vehicle, but you will need to pay for the gasoline and for his food and drink along the way.'

'That sounds reasonable,' Tara agreed. 'Thank you.'

Señor Fernadez personally saw her out to her cab, and opened the door for her. He glanced up at the sky and spoke rapidly in Spanish to the driver. 'I have instructed him to take the most direct route, señorita because I fear there is a violent storm approaching.'

CHAPTER 10

EXHAUSTED BY ALL the discussions on the economics of oil and the explorations for new and less damaging fuel sources, Patrick had left work early. The traffic had been flowing smoothly. He had passed the Juan Pablo Duarte Olympic Centre on his left travelling east towards the Rio Ozama. He headed towards the bridge—the Puente Ramon Matias Mella—that would take him to the other side of the river and then home and to bed.

Now driving by habit, he was daydreaming about how the stagecoach driver always sat on the *right* with the guy riding shotgun at his *left* elbow. Who the hell decided that the steering wheel would be on the *left* hand side of the car and that cars should drive on the right hand side of the road? It didn't make any sense at all. Most people are right handed. It takes much more effort to turn left if you're right handed. But if you travel on the right hand side of the road, then turning left turns out to be hard work for a right handed guy. What did the engineers in those days have for brains? Scrambled eggs?

Catching himself in this ridiculous train of thought he grinned inwardly. 'Gallagher,' he said out loud, 'your own brain is scrambled. Just make sure you get home in one piece. Then you can sleep all you want.'

The dismally grey afternoon had suddenly taken on a stygian sombreness. He switched on the Ford's headlights and then the windscreen wipers as rain suddenly pelted down. The traffic slowed. About five cars ahead someone must have stalled because he could see that the bridge in front of that car was empty.

What the hell?

Out of nowhere, and without making any sound at all, what seemed like a giant pterodactyl swooped down from behind, a few feet above the hood of his car, narrowly missing—by inches it seemed to Patrick—the roofs of the cars in front. It was hard to tell exactly what had happened because visibility was so poor. Raindrops were now hitting his windshield with the force of hail pellets. The noise on the roof was deafening. In the foreground, at about two o'clock he was able to make out the surface of the river, but only because it reflected the light of a terrifyingly large lightning bolt that leapt across the sky. There was a deafening crack, followed by an ear splitting roar of thunder that caused the Ford to shake on its suspension as the entire bridge seemed to reel.

Rivers of water gushed and splashed on the bridge's tarmac. The drainage system was clearly not designed to handle such a deluge. The cars ahead were soon up to their hubcaps in rushing, foaming, cascading water that seemed to come from nowhere.

The red tail-lights of the car in front moved forward. Instinctively, Patrick followed them, inching his way ahead onto the bridge itself. Just as suddenly, the tail-lights stopped moving. He braked hard, just managing to stop within an inch of impact. He was directly over the water. His windscreen was starting to fog up. The outside temperature must have dropped sharply. He looked around him. It was as if the fog and rain were slowly entombing him inside a metal and glass cocoon. He switched on the car's demister, turning the fan on high. Semi circles of shiny blackened glass began to spread upwards.

Minutes passed. The rain continued its steady onslaught, its noise abating from a cacophonic explosiveness to a low, continuous drumbeat. With visibility clearing slightly, Patrick craned his head forward, peering into the curtain of rain ahead, attempting to see what was going on in front.

Suddenly he saw a movement out of the corner of his eye, and before he knew what he was doing he had opened the door and stepped outside into the still pelting rain.

'*Mierde*! *Mierde*!' a young boy screamed at the top of his lungs. His arms flailed. The stamping of his feet as he ran caused great splashes of water to rain upwards.

Patrick recognised the boy's panic and lunged towards him, grabbing him firmly by the shoulders. 'Hey! Calm down. It'll be okay. I've got you. The worst is over.' He turned him bodily so that the boy was facing him.

At last the youngster seemed to focus on something other than his distress. He looked up into Patrick's face then threw his arms around his rescuer's waist.

'*Dio Mio*,' he sobbed uncontrollably.

'Well, at least you've stopped screaming now,' Patrick said, his voice soothing. He knew the boy wouldn't understand the words, but he seemed to take comfort from Patrick's voice. He moved his hand from the boy's shoulder, protectively stroking his head. The parental gesture seemed to have a calming effect.

The two of them stood there, exposed to the violence of the storm, the water on the bridge lapping at their ankles. Had there been an accident up ahead? Had the boy been involved ... or seen it happen? What the hell was happening?

Then he saw it. Through the curtain of still-cascading water, he saw the pterodactyl's silhouette. It was a twin-engine light plane that had crashed or made an emergency landing on the shallow lake of the bridge tarmac. It had fishtailed and was blocking all lanes on the bridge. Incredibly, unbelievably, it didn't seem to have hit any other vehicle or the bridge structure itself. At such close range, and with everything else that was happening, it was no wonder the boy was terrified.

The bridge led to a clover leaf interchange on the other side. It was bloody rush hour! Traffic would be piling up for miles around ... Damn! But he knew that would not be on the pilot's mind right now.

Still holding the boy protectively in his arms, Patrick turned to take in the salient details, the engineer in him assessing the options. With the traffic snarled up the way it was and, with the front cars so close to the plane that they were almost touching, there was no way the emergency services could reach the plane or move it anywhere. And the rain! He had never experienced rain like this before. Then, just as suddenly as it had started, the rain stopped.

He couldn't put the boy in his car. That was a no-go zone in this day—and particularly with their limited ability to communicate.

Emergency workers on foot were now making their way through the traffic. The *policía* wouldn't be far behind. He'd hand the kid over to them.

CHAPTER 11

ROOM SERVICE HAD packed sandwiches for their journey, and Tara had already eaten breakfast by the time her guide, Aurelio—the sometime medical student—had arrived at the arranged time. An impressive start, given the general Dominican attitude towards punctuality.

In their first half hour together, the conversation had been sparse, somewhat formal and stilted.

'Please stop calling me "señora" Aurelio. I'm not married. Please call me Tara.'

'Si Tara,' he replied, softly. His eyes shot sideways towards her, then away.

She tried to read between the lines of his response. The youngster's light brown skin still had the soft texture of youth. At around five feet six tall, he was at least two or three inches shorter than she. Was he shy, or was he just being respectful?

'Tell you what,' she said, 'its going to be a long journey unless we talk to one another. Why don't you tell me something about yourself and your home life?'

A further minute of silence passed. Just when she thought she would have to prod him again, he opened up. 'My family lives a humble life in Santo Domingo,' he began. 'I am attending the UASD.' (He pronounced it 'Uwaasd'.) 'That is the Universidad Autonoma de Santo Domingo—as a first year medical student—but it is my dream one day go to college in the United States of America. There are many Dominicans living in your country. We hear from them that it is a land of opportunity.'

It was like drawing teeth, but at least it was a beginning.

'But why would you wish to study in America? It is my under-standing that the University of Santo Domingo is one of the oldest in the New World. It must be a very good university.'

'In fact it is the oldest,' he said in a quiet voice, 'but an education in the United States is better because it is state-of-the-art. You have better funding than here. Some medical students at Uwaasd go to Mexico or Cuba to complete their studies; for me, I would prefer to go where I can get the very best education.'

'I suppose that an education in the US will also allow you to make many contacts amongst potentially influential people you would not otherwise meet?'

He nodded slightly, but said nothing.

Seeing that the point was certainly not lost on him, she continued her gentle probing. 'What does a young man like you do in his spare time?'

'Unfortunately, I have very little spare time. If I am not attending classes or studying, it is my responsibility to earn what I can to contribute towards my family's living expenses. When I can, I love to go to the stadium to watch baseball. In the Dominican Republic, we are all mad about baseball. It is our national sport.'

'Baseball? That's interesting.'

She was being polite, but Aurelio had no way of knowing this. He sat a little more upright and there was a new enthusiasm in his voice. 'Did you know, Tara, that the town of San Pedro de Macoris has produced more professional US baseball players than any other locality in the world?' He provided her with a mini avalanche of information. She heard the name 'Sammy Sosa' at least three times in an awed tone.

Tara listened politely. 'I did not know that,' she said when the oppor-tunity arose again for her to speak. 'It sounds very impressive.' In reality, she had only a passing interest in baseball and tried another subject.

'I am particularly interested in the life you live in this country and about the local culture. What can you tell me about that? How is the life here different from life in the US? '

'It is very difficult for me to answer that because except for what I have seen in Hollywood movies, and what I have heard from Dominicans who visit us from Nueva York, I do not know much about life in the United States.' The way he pronounced it, the name sounded like 'Nueba Yol'.

'What about your home life? Is the man in charge, like in the old days, or does the wife of the house have any say?'

He glanced at her, as if trying to gauge whether he should censor or tailor his response, and then shifted his attention back to the road ahead. 'It depends on how poor the family is. The very poor do not have strong family ties. Usually the man and woman just live together and they are not married. In such cases the woman will assume many responsibilities that would otherwise be the man's. Sometimes a mother will run the household and take decisions if the father is not living at home. Maybe he is living in America and sending money home every month, or maybe—if he works on one of the sugar farms in the north of the island—his family will only see him for a few months in the year. But that does not happen very often because most sugar workers are from Haiti.'

Tara had been watching him intently—trying to read his body language. She was pleased to see that his arms, which had previously been ramrod stiff as he held the steering wheel, were now more relaxed and bent at the elbows. The angle of his neck was also less rigid. He was unwinding. She glanced out of the window, and the ever vigilant professional pilot noted the traffic around them. It was increasing but running smoothly. They seemed to be making good time. Everything according to plan. Everything in place. Okay.

She leaned back in the seat and stretched her legs out in front of her. She thought of taking off her sneakers and socks, but discarded the idea. Too much like hard work to get them back on again.

'Amongst those you might call the middle class,' he continued, 'the family ties are stronger and there, the father is the decision maker. That is the case in my own family, where my mother defers to my father. But that is changing even in this type of family.'

'How so?'

'Women are becoming more educated in this country. They are going out into the work force and they are having fewer children as a result.

After a few moments, this time without her prompting, he broke the silence. 'Have you heard of *compadrasto*?'

'No. What is that?'

'It is the practice of appointing a godfather for a newly baptised child. Some people think of the word "*compadre*", when they hear this word, but the correct word is "*padrino*". A *padrino* is like a godfather. Usually he is—how you say—more powerful than the father of the child, or maybe a very special friend of the father. He is chosen when the child is baptised. The bonds between the family and the child and the *padrino* become stronger as a result. Sometimes a man's employer will be his son's *padrino*. It is a great honour.'

He took his eyes off the road and turned his head towards her. Seeing her nodding, he was encouraged to continue. 'General Rafael Trujillo, when he was still this country's dictator, would organize mass baptisms, so that he could be named *padrino* of all of the peasant children, but that was not so much a benefit to the children as to him. It was because he wanted the parents to become more loyal to him.'

'It sounds a bit like the old Japanese custom of moral indebtedness or, possibly, something like the Italian mafia. I suppose one would have to live in the community to fully understand what it really means. Do you have a *padrino*?'

'Si. My *padrino* is a distant cousin on my father's side. He is a rich man. He lives in *Nueba Yol*. I am hoping that one day he will arrange to sponsor me to obtain a student visa into the United States.'

Tara smiled to herself and looked out of the window to take in the passing scenery, which, disappointingly, she did not find particularly remarkable. It was not until they approached Santiago that Tara sat a little more upright in her seat. Before them loomed a huge building on their right, in the shape of a pyramid.

'What's that over there?'

'It is a hotel. And the one next door is a private hospital. And over there, in the distance in front of us is the Santiago Monument.'

'It seems very grand, but why is it pointing to the north, away from the highway? Surely it should have been built facing in the direction where most of the traffic will be approaching it?'

'I never thought about that. Maybe it's facing towards *Nueba Yol.*' He smiled at her to indicate that he was trying to be funny. Tara found herself easily slipping into her role of tourist.

'We are leaving the outskirts of Santiago,' Aurelio said, breaking the silence some minutes later. 'This road is known as the Carretera Turística— the tourist road.'

The terrain was becoming increasingly mountainous. 'The side of that mountain, it looks like it's been ripped away by a landslide,' Tara said. 'I noticed similar sights earlier on. What do you think causes that?'

Aurelio pulled the car up to the side of the road that was quickly becoming more and more like a levelled scar on the edge of the mountainside the further they drove. He got out to stand beside Tara who now gazed intently at a steep slope on the other side of a valley.

'You will see this more often as we get closer to La Cumbre. The sandstone is soft. Sometimes it is washed away by the storms. In this particular case I am not certain, but it might have been caused by Hurricane Katrina last year. The town of Tamboril is only a few kilometres from where we are now standing. It was completely flooded at that time.' He pointed into the distance. 'Can you see those parallel protrusions of sandstone—the veins of a different colour and texture between the sandstone?'

'Yes, I see them.'

'That is the geological formation in which amber is found. It is sandstone with occasional conglomerates that accumulated when this land was originally under water. That is where the miners will dig their tunnels.'

'They do it manually … with picks and shovels into the hillsides?'

'Si. It is not complicated. But sometimes it can be dangerous because the tunnels could subside. They can extend for long distances and sometimes the miners will use logs cut from large tree branches, or small tree trunks, to support the exposed sandstone faces on the sides and above to prevent collapse.'

Tara thought that she saw a movement in the dense undergrowth. She stepped quickly towards the four-wheel drive. They were being watched. She climbed back inside, but Aurelio took his time. After he closed the door he wound down his window and leaned his elbow on the ledge. Now he was in his own domain. Tara, by contrast, was feeling far less relaxed.

'I've noticed that we've also passed more than one row of these flimsy fruit stalls along the way,' she said. 'There must be dozens of them. Why so many?'

'It is because the Carretera Turística is travelled by large numbers of people who are on their way from Santiago to the coast. This road cuts through the mountain range on its way to either Puerto Plata or one of several beaches along the immediate coastline. You may have heard of Sosua? It is one of the better known destinations because of the scuba diving.'

'No. But I do scuba dive. At some point I would like to go diving amongst the wrecks off the island. Maybe you could help me with that on another day?'

'Of course, if you would like. I will be happy to help if I am able to.'

They drove on in silence until they came upon a few modest buildings. Aurelio slowed the car as they passed. Some were no more than huts, their walls and roofs barely able to protect the inhabitants from the elements, or so it seemed to Tara. One or two were reasonably sturdy. Of these one was a brightly coloured building that had been painted in primary red from its base halfway up its timber slatted walls, then with buttercup yellow to the point where the rusting corrugated steel roofing overhung slightly. The hut itself had been built on a foundation of rocks and what looked like dried mud, but was probably concrete—so that it abutted a twenty-foot steep fall to the forest floor behind it. Aurelio brought the car to a standstill.

From her vantage point Tara could see at least five red and yellow 'Maggi' logos emblazoned on its sides. The colour scheme was too coincidental.

My God. Even here, high in the Cordillera Septentrional, on a rutted apology for a road on a West Indies island washed by the Caribbean Sea, the tentacles of international commerce had reached out. Had she come all this way just to find yet more evidence that the entire world was becoming culturally homogenised?

'Would you like to stretch your legs?' Aurelio asked. 'There are some fruit vendors over there. Perhaps we can get something to eat.'

They wandered across to the nearest vendor's stall, where Tara's spirits lifted immediately. The fruit was displayed in a collection of mismatched old polystyrene boxes and polypropylene bread crates of various ages, but the display was magnificent. Individual bunches of plum-sized black grapes had been strung at intervals from the beams above, as had bunches of what looked like bananas.

'Are these Dominican bananas?'

'No,' Aurelio said. 'Those are what we call *plantanos*. They are similar to bananas, but I believe they are less sweet. When they are raw, they are best eaten after the skin has turned brown. Otherwise it is better to cook them. They form part of the staple diet of most Dominicans. They are usually sprinkled with salt, fried and eaten with rice and chicken or other meat.'

Apart from being noticeably more plump and appetising than the fruit she was used to, the varieties were much the same as could be bought back home; the main difference seemed to be one of emphasis. About a third of the space was taken up by the plantains—lined up like soldiers along the stall's perimeter. There were piles of sweet potatoes in greater abundance than would be on display in any US fresh produce store. Papayas and melons were shown off in the midst of all the other produce. And extraordinarily large pineapples had been strung together, hung from the stall's perpendicular support columns alongside dangling bottles of some type of homemade juice.

'This guy could decorate Bloomingdale's windows,' she said, more to herself than to Aurelio. 'He obviously has an eye for merchandising.'

'Please excuse, Tara. I would like to talk him about what we might see today,' said Aurelio and walked off to strike up a conversation with the vendor. The man may have been in his late twenties. He wore a sleeveless cotton vest and a pair of spotlessly clean, if old, blue denim jeans. His face seemed remarkably open and carefree.

It was at times like these that Tara wished she understood Spanish better. Suddenly, she found herself smiling again. Hanging from the vendor's leather belt was a bunch of maybe twenty keys, incongruously out of place in this little village where the huts would barely have had doors, let alone locks. They were a statement of his self-worth, a wonderful eccentricity.

'Aurelio,' she called out. 'Would you ask the vendor if I may take some photos of him and his stall please?'

She saw a short and animated conversation during which the vendor's nose seemed to twitch, until his face lit up with pleasure. He beckoned her over with a grin, then lined himself up alongside her with his produce displays in the background. He talked animatedly to her, but apart from an occasional 'señorita' she could only guess at his words by his happiness to oblige her request.

She hurriedly instructed Aurelio on how to point and click the camera, then rejoined the vendor who handed her a large bunch of grapes and motioned her to stand beside a bunch of plantains. He held a pineapple in one hand and an unusual green glass bottle of fruit juice in the other. He beamed at the camera.

Then, with much relayed instruction, Tara arranged for the vendor to take a photograph of her and Aurelio with the Maggi store in the far background. She draped her arm around Aurelio's shoulders. He screwed up the courage to hold her around her waist. It seemed to make his day—and probably the fruit vendor's too judging by the jocularity between them.

They bought a few bunches of grapes and two bottles of fruit juice and were on their way again. It was then Tara noticed that the red and yellow Maggi store was not the only colourful building. In fact, most of the wooden huts were painted in bright colours. One was even painted a combination of lilac and lime green. It seemed that Dominican peasants liked happy colours. Yes, things were definitely looking up.

CHAPTER 12

IT IS STILL early, Tara,' Aurelio said. 'There is a polishing factory nearby. Would you like to see how the amber is cut and polished?'

'Of course! Did you have to ask?!'

Within ten minutes she found herself in yet another world. The 'factory' turned out to be one of the little huts that lined the Carretera Turística.

'What a wonderful aroma,' Tara said as they entered through the front doorway.

Aurelio led her deeper into the hut, to a little workroom with a trestle table pushed up against a wall. On it were two or three small abrasive buffing wheels powered by electric motors. There, seated on an ordinary dining room chair at one of the polishing wheels was a man whose age Tara found difficult to guess. His milk chocolate skin and short black hair were covered in a white powder—as was everything else within a two-yard radius of where he sat.

'He looks like one of those oompah loompahs from *Willy Wonka*,' Tara said before she realised that Aurelio would have no idea what she was talking about.

Aurelio's nose wrinkled just like the fruit vendor's had.

'It's from a movie,' she said by way of explanation.

Like the fruit vendor, too, the polisher was wearing a sleeveless undervest and blue jeans, but his vest was more colourful, even under the snowstorm of white powder. At his right elbow, on the table's surface must have been thirty or so pieces of amber—some with a bluish hue. At the end of the table stood a shoebox piled high with yet more amber awaiting cleaning and polishing. The polisher looked up as they entered the room, smiled in friendly welcome.

'*Hola mi amigo,*' Aurelio said in greeting.

'*Hola.*' The polisher's greeting was friendly enough, but he had barely raised his head to look at them. Tara was not the first tourist he had ever encountered. He must have long ago learned that he would never get any work done if he stopped every time to chat.

'The aroma you noticed is the blue amber,' Aurelio was saying. 'The fine aerosols trapped inside the amber—they are what cause it to fluoresce in the light—also have aromatic properties.'

Tara lingered another couple of minutes, picking up a couple of pieces to inspect them more closely.

'It looks to me that this polishing is really just a means of cleaning up the amber sufficiently to enable him to see what colour it is, and whether it has any inclusions or faults. It seems that as soon as he is able to determine that, he goes onto the next piece.'

'You are very observant. It is not always the case in other factories, but this particular amber will be worked more carefully by someone else.'

She signalled to Aurelio that she would like to continue with her tour. In response to her polite *gracias*, the polisher looked up, smiled, nodded his head, and resumed his work.

'The walking trail that will lead us to the mine is very close to here,' Aurelio said as they re-emerged into the daylight. For the third time in the past hour, they climbed back into the four-wheel drive.

Very soon, Aurelio slowed to take a turn-off to the right. They hadn't travelled a hundred yards along the side road, when Tara began to feel a little anxious. She held tightly to the car's hand-hold to stop herself from being flung about.

'The quality of the road's surface is certainly deteriorating,' she said. 'And it looks even worse ahead. From those deep ruts it looks like the car tyres are prone to spinning when the sand is wet. Is it safe for us to continue further?'

'Yes. We are very close now, and the road is dry. There is no sign that there was any rain up here at all in the last few days.'

'Don't you find that strange?'

He shrugged, but offered no answer. 'From here we must continue on foot,' he said.

As Tara alighted from the vehicle, she found herself facing a ghostly white haze of wispy, low-lying clouds that hung as if suspended in time above the undulating hilltops. The peaks rose from the variegated emerald and olive valley below and stretched into the distance amid a virginal mixture of lush equatorial undergrowth. She drew a deep, involuntary breath.

'Wow!' There were no other words to describe the feeling of awe-inspired privilege that washed over her. The vista was about as far removed from Central Park as a New York city skyscraper was from the little pastel coloured huts lining the Carretera Turística.

Aurelio smiled. Intuitively, he seemed to understand that the most appropriate response to this magnificent sight was silence. It was a full two minutes before Tara gathered her thoughts.

'Let's get going,' she said.

They made their way carefully—gingerly climbing over dead logs, negotiating their way around rocky outcrops, and grabbing onto available plant life to steady themselves as they walked and stumbled their way towards the valley below. On either side of the track, a mixture of tall, fronded plants grew in an array of shapes and sizes beside stunted and gnarled old trees with deep green foliage. Tara thought of the trees like friendly bystanders, their leafy branches protectively shading Aurelio and her from much of the glaring sunshine above. They came across a trickling stream, which they followed for a while; Tara ever mindful and vigilant, watching for any sign of wildlife in the undergrowth. Except for the background humming of insects, the occasional noisy squawking of a flock of parrots flying past overhead and, once, the silent imprint of a shoe sole on the muddy banks of the stream, they seemed to be alone.

Then, in a clearing, they came across a group of young men standing seemingly relaxed and chatting. A few feet away, under a lean-to made of branches and palm fronds, one of them squatted while cooking something on a small paraffin or gas stove. Aurelio and Tara had arrived at the mine.

Again, there was a short conversation in Spanish. Again, there was a wrinkling of noses followed by broad smiles of understanding and agreement. There were also some side comments and laughter amongst the men. The word '*gringa*'—foreigner from America—came up a couple of times. Tara thought she also heard the words '*bonita*', and '*sexual*', but she couldn't be sure. She decided to keep a slight distance for the time being. They were in the middle of nowhere, miles from the nearest civilization.

Aurelio walked back towards her. 'They will be happy to show you around, but we cannot spend more that half an hour here if we are to return to Santo Domingo before dark.'

'Are you trying to protect me from these guys?' she asked with a smile. Aurelio looked embarrassed.

'What's he cooking?' she asked to change the subject. 'It smells great.'

'That is called *arroz con abichuelas*, a mixture of rice and beans. He is probably cooking some small pieces of beef with it, but it could be any meat.'

'Can one buy that in a restaurant in Santo Domingo?'

'Of course, but not exactly the same. This is a local dish for locals. To sell food like this to tourists would be like offering leftovers to your guests. It would not be right. In the restaurants it is much more carefully presented and is usually served with salads.'

The word 'dignity' popped into Tara's mind. Aurelio seemed to have it, and that was what she had seen on the faces of the fruit vendor and the amber polisher and, now, even the miners as she approached them. Other than their initial jocularity, they seemed to consider her as their guest and themselves as hosts who happily welcomed visitors into their world. The men were just being men.

As they approached the entrance to the mine, a happy looking miner wearing a backward facing baseball cap sat with a short-handled pick in one hand, a lump of soft rock in the other.

'*Hola*, señorita,' he said, grinning broadly.

She smiled back at him, lifted her hand in greeting, but continued to follow Aurelio to the mine entrance. It was like standing at the entrance to the burrow of a large animal.

Aurelio exchanged a few words with one of the miners. 'It is all right for us to go inside the tunnel. Would you like to?' he asked Tara.

'Very much so—yes please. I've come all this way. I want to finish what I started.' She saw that none of the miners wore a helmet or any other safety gear. They were just guys digging holes in the side of the mountain. Some wore shirts, some wore sleeveless undervests, and some were bare-chested. Obviously mining was warm work. She had the feeling that one or two of the better-built men had very recently become shirtless.

Gingerly, she stepped inside. The tunnel was dark beyond a couple yards, but she was able to make out a flickering light some distance away. As they approached, the bearer of the faint light looked up at her—she could see now that he held nothing more substantial than a candle. He beamed a welcome, his white teeth accentuated against his brown face and against the darkness of the tunnel. He moved the candle to set it down near the next section of rock he would attack with his pick.

Tara had to bend almost double to edge, crab-wise, beyond the miner. She thought that Aurelio, following close behind her, was probably having the view of his life. She felt self-conscious. Then, to hell with it—I'm never going to see these guys again. Her self-consciousness faded into insignificance in the next moment as she eyed the few wooden logs that had been wedged as flimsy supports between the two perpendicular walls of the tunnel. Thirty or so yards from the opening was another miner. Fate had led them to him just as he had 'struck gold'.

He pointed a rough, stubby finger at the rock face, holding up the candle for her to see. '*Tenga una mirada en esto.*'

A piece of amber was embedded in the surrounding rock. He handed her the candle to hold, and turned to pick up a small hammer and chisel. '*Agarro el vela aquí.*'

'He says to hold the candle here,' Aurelio translated. The miner took her by the wrist, guiding her so that the candle would shed light where he needed it. He expertly prised the amber loose then handed it to her for inspection. It looked like any other piece of amber she had seen that day, except that this one had pride of ownership. She was elated. She turned to Aurelio who was squatting behind her. 'Is it possible to buy this piece, Aurelio? It would mean a lot to take it home with me.'

The miner cocked his head to the side. '$30,' he said to Aurelio. She did not bargain with him—she was just as happy to pay as he was to receive. The rough piece that she had helped him prise out of the rock face would take pride of place on the coffee table next to her much more expensive turtle. She also had the photographs they had taken at both the fruit stall and the mine. It had been a wonderful day.

On their return journey along the Carretera Turística, revelling in the afterglow of their mission accomplished, Tara and Aurelio ate from a bunch of grapes that Aurelio had washed in the little stream they had crossed on their way back from the mine. They spat the pips out of the open windows, vying each other to spit the furthest.

'Hey!' Tara shouted over the sound of the wind that rushed in through the open windows. 'The grapes come out of the ground anyway, so if anyone asks, we're just planting a vineyard on the side of the mountain.' She felt like a naughty child, and laughed gleefully.

About an hour into the return journey she turned, more seriously this time, to Aurelio.

'What do you know of blue amber's mystical properties?'

'I do not understand what you mean by "mystical".'

'I have read that amber is believed by some to have healing powers. Can you tell me anything about that?'

'Am I not studying to be a doctor?' His laughter showed no trace of the shy Aurelio she had met earlier in the day. She waited expectantly.

'Did you know that the Greek word for amber is "elektron", and that the word "elektor" means "beaming sun"?'

'Err … no, I didn't know that.'

'The word "elektron" is the origin of the English word "electricity", and it is static electricity that is probably the reason why magical properties were attributed to amber. You would know that amber becomes strongly charged with static electricity when you rub it. We have known about this property of amber since around 600 BC and whilst I believe that this is probably the source of most of amber's mystical attributes, there may be more to it than just old wives tales.'

Tara perked up. 'Why would anyone keep such a random date in his head, for God's sake? Have you made a study of amber?'

'Not really, but I have learned quite a lot about it in the past year or two through my part-time job as a tour guide, and I have remembered because of my interest in medicine. For example, it was believed that the electrical charge that was built up was a negative charge, and that this negative charge would attract positive power and energy to the wearer of an amber amulet.'

'Surely they wouldn't have thought in those terms two-and-a-half thousand years ago?'

'Of course, you are right, but the belief of the power to attract positive forces was very real. For another example, it was also believed to aid intellect, and that might also have been a result of the static electricity. We know today—through electro-encephalography—that the human brain has very definite electrical energy patterns coursing through it. It is quite possible that we might one day discover a link that is based more on science than on superstition.'

'You are certainly building up a good circumstantial case, I'll give you that. Though I have to be honest, it sounds a bit like there may be more superstition and less reality here. But I am prepared to accept that where there's smoke there's fire and that there must be some basis of truth in at least some of the legends.'

Somewhat surprisingly, Aurelio's cerebral excursions had served another unexpected purpose; when Tara looked at her watch, she discovered that it was already five o'clock. They were approaching the outskirts of Santo Domingo, and on an impulse, she took a decision.

'Aurelio, as you know, I am here on vacation for the next couple of weeks. How would you like to be my guide when I need one?'

His response was eager. 'I would like that very much. Fortunately, my university is on vacation at present and I am available. What would you like me to do?'

'Right now I have two things in mind. I would really like to find out more about the physics of light and how it relates to blue amber. Any suggestions on how I might do that?'

'My brother is a post-graduate student in science—not in that area—but I'm sure he could explain anything you need to know. I can ask him tonight.'

'That's wonderful, and the other favour I have to ask is: do you have any experience with scuba diving? I'd like to explore the reefs around here, perhaps also do some underwater photography.'

'Unfortunately, this is not something in which I have experience. But I will ask some friends about locations and diving schools and I will try to make some recommendations when we meet again.'

'Good idea. How about we meet somewhere for lunch tomorrow?'

CHAPTER 13

TARA WAS SEATED at a table in a quiet corner of a restaurant around the corner from her hotel, absorbed in the story on the front page of *Dominican Today*, a local, English language newspaper. The waiter had brought it to her after taking her drink order. She had seen something of the lead story on the CDN TV channel that morning but hadn't been able to understand it fully, other than that a light plane had been forced to land on a city bridge during a freak thunderstorm that had come out of nowhere yesterday. It had caused serious disruption to the afternoon peak hour traffic—and it seemed the entire city was still talking about it.

The newspaper showed a head-and-shoulders photograph of a senior executive of the Eagle nickel mine.

Hero of the day was an Australian mining engineer, Mr Patrick Gallagher, who has been living in Santo Domingo for just over a year, the article read. *He was one of the hundreds of motorists caught in the traffic snarl. Being on the spot, he had offered to assist the emergency services with a load-bearing helicopter from Eagle's mine in Bonao to help clear the bridge.*

Tara skimmed the rest of the article: cables lowered from the helicopter had been anchored to the fuselage of the plane to airlift it to the local airport. After inspection and refuelling, the very lucky owner–pilot had flown it back to the USA from where he had come. There was speculation in the article that the plane's compass might have been giving false readings because of magnetic anomalies, or whether the agonic line adjustment mechanism had been properly set prior to the original take-off. Or perhaps, the plane's instruments may have been affected by the thunderstorm.

Tara frowned in concentration. No pilot worth his salt could possibly have overlooked such a basic checklist item as the agonic adjustment setting. Her thoughts were interrupted by two men holding a discussion at a nearby table. She recognised an Australian accent.

Tara caught the tail end of an explanation that seemed to be about how to get swing out of a baseball when pitching. 'It's a function of how the pitcher holds his fingers and the angle and timing of his wrist flick,' said an American voice.

'We call him a bowler, not a pitcher,' said the Australian voice. 'In Australia, a pitcher is a clay jug you keep water in.' He looked familiar.

Perhaps feeling Tara's gaze upon him, the man looked over to her. He carried on speaking to his associate as if nothing had happened but his eyes did not leave her face.

'On the other hand, the pitch is the twenty-two yards of impacted ground between the two wickets which has grass like a bowling green. Go figure, the bowler bowls the ball down the pitch.'

She was the first to drop her gaze, and her eyes went back to the newspaper in front of her. *Oh shit.* The same face stared back at her from the front page photograph. He probably thought she was staring at him for that reason!

'Iddy bloodiot!' she said to herself, then laughed. It was one of those spoonerisms that usually kicked in when she felt light-heartedness bubbling up. Now he would think she was demented.

'So tell me how your bowlers do it in cricket,' said the American voice.

'Your baseball is sewn together like a leather tennis ball,' she heard the Australian—this Patrick Gallagher—say to his associate. 'But a cricket ball has a raised seam at the joint of the two leather hemispheres that are sewn together to contain the inner core.' He continued to delve into the microscopic intricacies of how these design features could be used to manipulate the ball's flight path. Boring as bat shit. What is it that gets guys so worked up over this stuff?

Girl, you need to get a life. You're spending far too much time on your own when you expect eavesdropped conversations to entertain you.

In spite of herself, Tara turned her attention back to the newspaper article, which went on to explain why Mr Gallagher had felt compelled to help out. The Australian was sitting in his stationary car, stuck on the bridge in the storm, when he had seen a young boy of about nine or ten years old spooked by the thunderstorm and the crash. He had been in obvious distress. He was crying, trying to shelter by the stopped cars— running from one to another. Gallagher had left his car when he saw the boy heading in his direction. He had managed to pacify him somewhat, even though, as a relative newcomer to the Dominican Republic, he spoke only a little Spanish.

'Some people are more affected by electrical thunderstorms than others,' he had later told the *Dominican Today* reporter. 'Maybe it has something to do with the electrical wiring of the brain. Grasping him firmly by the shoulders seemed to calm him. Maybe he just needed to be held, because the tension seemed to suddenly drain out of him and he just hugged me. Or maybe it helped to ground him in an electrical sense. Who knows? It doesn't really matter. It worked. He simply needed some comfort.'

The story had continued for another couple of paragraphs. An interpreter had been found, and once the human mini-drama had been resolved, Mr Gallagher had been able to communicate his ideas to the authorities on how to clear the traffic blockage ...

Without looking in their direction, Tara sensed the American get up to leave, and that Gallagher had remained seated at his table. She lifted her gaze. Her eyes followed the American until he was almost at the restaurant's door. Suddenly she felt as if her heart had stopped beating. Just beyond the entrance, she saw a man whose face she had no trouble in recognising. It was the Turkish man who had come to her table at Starbucks in New York the day before yesterday.

What the ...?. Instinctively, she picked up her glass of wine and, before she had had time to think her actions through, had taken the three or four steps to Gallagher's table.

'Excuse me Mr Gallagher, I hope you don't think I'm crazy, but I need your help please. I'm a Delta Airlines pilot on vacation from the US and there's a guy about to enter the restaurant whose attentions I very much want to avoid. Please may I sit at your table for a few minutes, and if he comes over, pretend that we are on a date? If he sees me sitting with someone else he may not bother me.'

Gallagher blinked in surprise at the attractive—if flustered—woman who stood before him, glass of wine in hand. This couldn't be a pick-up? Classy … nice eyes. He decided to roll with it.

'The short answer is yes, of course. Please sit down.'

'I'm at a slight disadvantage here,' he said.

Tara hoped she hadn't chosen the worse of two options. He had a disarming smile though.

'I'm curious to know how you know my name … and if you and I are to be an item, it would also be fairly helpful if you told me yours.'

'My name's Tara Geoffrey,' she said quickly. 'Sorry, I was just reading about you in a news report, so I sort of felt I knew you—or at least something about you. Thank you. You're a lifesaver … well, yes—ha ha—twice in one week. This guy—the one at the door—scares me.' Then she did something even more unexpected. She leaned over and kissed him on the cheek in an affectionate sort of way, before seating herself with her back to the direction from which Mehmet would come.

Patrick hadn't seen that one coming.

'I promise to leave you in peace as soon as the coast is clear,' she said in a stage whisper.

Tara looked up at Patrick to see that he was looking past her, a big grin on his face.

'Hi Patrick,' said a voice behind her. 'I hope you haven't been waiting long?'

The accent sounded horribly familiar … *oh no.*

'Tara, may I introduce you to—' Patrick said, rising to his feet and stretching out his hand to greet the newcomer.

'Hey!' the newcomer interrupted, addressing himself to Tara. 'This is a pleasant surprise. We met in New York on Monday, remember?'

It was him … Mehmet … here to meet Patrick. Oh, this couldn't have been worse.

'Is he the reason you wouldn't give me your phone number?' Mehmet asked, pointing at Patrick, a resigned grin on his face.

A look of Mephistophelian glee crept into Gallagher's green eyes. 'Not at all,' he responded innocently to one or both of Mehmet's questions, in the process cutting off any reply she might have been framing. 'Tara and I were just about to order a pre-dinner cocktail. I assumed you wouldn't mind that I asked her to join us.'

'Of course not.'

'In any event, I'm pleased that you two have already met, but just remember to keep your distance mate. She's mine.' With that, Patrick wrapped his arm around her shoulders and turned his head to plant a proprietary kiss full on her lips.

The situation was now totally out of her control and it was Tara's turn to be taken by surprise. She felt herself grow hot from the neck up.

He brushed his mouth softly near Tara's ear. 'Relax,' he whispered, an infuriating smile on his face. 'Roll with it.'

Then he turned back to Mehmet. 'We've known each other for some time, but the distance between us keeps us apart for too long. Her airline pilot responsibilities keep her globe trotting, and my mining engineer's job has prevented me from putting down roots for any length of time, so we decided to spend some days together on the island during her vacation.'

Tara noted that he was offering just sufficient detail from his scant bank of knowledge to sound convincing. The guy was smooth.

'Tara was just about to explain this agonic adjustment mechanism to me. I assume you read about it as being the likely cause of the emergency landing on the bridge two days ago.'

Looking a bit confused, Mehmet smiled. 'Of course, I knew about the plane, but what's this about an agonic adjustment mechanism? I've never heard of it … I don't know what you're talking about.'

Tara saw an opportunity, and lunged for it. *If that was the way Patrick Gallagher was going to play this tennis match, she could play it just as well. Watch out buster, I'm returning serve.*

'Hey, where are your manners?' she demanded. 'Mehmet's just arrived. We haven't even ordered drinks yet and already you want to snuff out the glow of our happy reunion.'

The copper flecks in her sapphire eyes seemed to Patrick to flash like crackling flames.

'Forget about the agonic line,' she continued. 'We can get to the serious stuff later … maybe. Ask Mehmet what he wants to drink. I'll have my usual Barbary Coast,' she said, returning his opening serve kiss with a forehand cross-court sweep shot, as her mind went into overdrive. *Let's see how you handle that one.* She willed him to hear her thought, tried to smile sweetly at him, all the time suppressing the bubbles of laughter rising inside her.

Patrick's face was inscrutable. He turned to Mehmet. 'Did I say airline pilot?' he asked with a tinge of mockery in his voice as he lobbed the ball gently back over the net. 'My apologies, I meant airline pirate. What are you drinking, mate?'

'Unfortunately,' Mehmet responded, one eyebrow raised quizzically, 'you have forgotten, I cannot partake of alcoholic spirits? But I most certainly do not want to spoil the party spirit. What would I get if I ordered the same thing but without alcoholic beverage in it?'

Patrick's head cocked ever so slightly in Tara's direction, signalling *your ball.* But all he got from her was a matching raise of one delicate eyebrow. Her mouth was pursed, as if to stop herself from smiling too broadly.

Instead, she addressed herself to Mehmet, while still looking at Gallagher: 'You forgot to wrinkle your nose, Mehmet.'

Mehmet was taken aback by her *non sequitur.* 'Excuse me?'

She turned to face him with an angelic look on her face. 'In the last twenty-four hours I have discovered that the locals wrinkle their noses when they don't understand something. Everyone here seems to do it. You have to get with the program.'

Mehmet looked from one to the other, as if to ask *what is going on here?* Obligingly, he turned to Patrick and wrinkled his nose as he repeated the question. 'What would I get if I ordered the same thing but without alcoholic beverage in it?'

This time Tara decided to let Patrick off the hook. She leant forward, about to answer, when she heard Patrick's voice steal the ball from under her nose.

'Light cream … The gin, rum, scotch and crème de cacao all have alcohol in them.'

She swivelled to look at him.

'So, if you want to go straight to hell, Mehmet, this particular drink would be a great way to go about that. On the other hand, after one of these drinks you might find that your hidden Imam decides to reveal himself to you.'

It seemed to Tara that he had an altogether too beatific smile on his damned face.

'You make jokes about my religion, my friend,' Mehmet said, with what Tara thought was thinly-veiled mock sternness.

She blinked. *Oh shit! That's the last place we want to go.* She lunged again—this time in a desperate attempt to preserve the feeling of light-hearted banter. 'I've got a suggestion. Why don't you have a coconut milk drink mixed with pineapple juice and a dash of lime cordial?'

'I have never heard of such a drink,' Mehmet answered.

'Neither have I. But it will have all the flavours of the tropics. How about it?'

'I believe it's called a virgin piña colada,' Patrick chipped in. 'And what the heck, if you are going to insist on living so dangerously, then I will rise to the occasion. I will see your Barbary Coast and raise you a Bermuda Rose, given that we are on the edge of the Bermuda Triangle here. It's quite a smooth drink, actually—from gin, apricot brandy and grenadine.'

He looked around, expecting some argument or discussion. Getting none, he caught the eye of a hovering waiter and placed their order.

'Tell me,' Mehmet began, in an obvious attempt to bring the conversation down to manageable levels, 'how did you two lovebirds meet?'

With that particular question, the tennis match was quickly underway again. Patrick turned his body to face Tara. He leaned his elbow on the tabletop and rested a slightly forward-thrusting chin on a relaxed fist. Then, said—almost without appearing to move his mouth, which was twitching at the corners yet again, 'Why don't *you* tell him the story, my snookums?'

His green eyes seemed to engulf her.

She was silent for a few seconds, then remembered the discussion she had overheard about the cricket ball. She decided to go for broke. 'Well okay, but remember, my *smukoons*,' she said, as though she had done this sort of thing many times, '*you* suggested it.'

Just at that point, the drinks arrived, and Tara took a deep draft of hers before launching into an entirely imaginary story that she made up as the words came out of her mouth.

'I happened to be in Australia for a rostered flight a couple of years ago, when I decided to watch a game of rugby. I like to keep up with these matters just to hold my own at cocktail parties. It allows me to talk about sport without being treated like an imbecile by the Neanderthals. I've found that if I can talk about a sport that the guys in the US don't know much about, they will willingly let me have a beer or a glass of wine with them. It also allows me to have a lot more fun.'

Patrick listened with some interest to this woman who appeared to be in total command. He willed her to continue talking.

'Anyhow, there I am in Sydney, but the only male company is a flight steward and he doesn't really qualify, if you know what I mean. Fortunately, the guy was a real trooper. He agreed to go with me to a game of rugby that Saturday afternoon—provided I went dinner and dancing with him that evening. It was a fair exchange, I enjoy dancing.'

With the two men showing no signs of wanting to interrupt, Tara was in her element, enjoying the moment. She had found her stride.

'So I'm sitting there trying to fathom what's going on and I'm asking him questions that he has *no* idea how to answer. If I remember correctly, my *smukoons*,' she said, eyes glittering, 'I asked my flight steward friend to explain the essential difference between gridiron and rugby. While both games have similarly shaped balls, the guys in gridiron wear a lot of protective clothing. It seemed to me that rugby was just as dangerous a game as gridiron, but the rugby players were wearing virtually no protective clothing at all. I genuinely couldn't understand it. Unfortunately—or maybe fortunately, for me—neither could my friend.'

She turned to face Patrick, laying her hand affectionately on his arm. 'It happened that this particular Neanderthal was sitting immediately behind me in the stands.' She softened the words with a mock hug to show Mehmet that she and Patrick really did have a warm and loving relationship, then sealed it by kissing Patrick warmly on the cheek. 'He was there with a mate and he leant over, and said to me—she deepened her voice to parody Patrick's—"The essential difference between rugby and gridiron is that in rugby, the object is to play the ball, but in grid-iron, the object is to play the man. In rugby you need brains, but in gridiron you need brawn".'

She wrinkled her nose at Patrick. 'I guess that I must be more of an American patriot than I thought, because—for some reason, I did what I never do—I started to defend the game of gridiron and explained that a lot of thinking goes into developing game strategy. Well, to cut a long story short, I never went dancing with the flight steward that night.'

'Bravo!' said Mehmet, enthusiastically applauding. 'Tell me more. There must be more.'

In the meantime Patrick had found his interest turning into admira-tion. This was not just some girl with a pick-up line. He could feel the warm chemistry starting to stir. It was subtly out of the ordinary, in a way that he couldn't quite put his finger on.

The waiter came to take their order and when he had departed, Tara turned back to Mehmet.

'Okay, Mehmet. I kept up my end of the bargain. Now it's your turn. How do you and Patrick know each other? He has never mentioned your name to me before,' she said with an angelic smile.

'My story is not nearly as interesting as yours. Ah, well you know what Patrick does, and I am a commodity broker. I do a lot of business with Eagle and have gotten to know most of the senior executives personally.'

'That's it? Well, that turned out to be a bit of a *squamp dib*.'

The food arrived and the talk veered to revolve around food in general for a while, but it did not take Mehmet long to steer the conver-sation back to the 'loving couple' as he called them. Tara wondered whether he had seen through their ruse.

'Tara, I am curious to know how you managed to establish a relationship as close as yours so obviously is, when you live at opposite ends of the planet—particularly as you sounded so convincing when you put that forward as the reason why it would be pointless for us to swap telephone numbers.'

The two men had no way of knowing that Tara had had a lot of experience in the area of story invention. She had become quite the master of spontaneous fiction; it was her way of keeping people at arms length when she wanted to.

'Well, it all started when I was scheduled to go scuba diving in the Barrier Reef. This so-called gentleman had promised to join me and he was going to teach me about underwater photography which I was dying to learn, but he bailed and ever since I met him—and right up until this very second in time—we have never been scuba diving together. Patrick and I have shared an imaginary common interest in underwater sport for some time.' she said, with a meaning that was totally lost on Mehmet.

'But that doesn't explain anything.'

Patrick appeared to bristle at the innuendo that he might have churlishly dropped the scuba diving ball, and responded. 'Okay darling, now the gloves are off. You wanted to go scuba diving? Name the date. Right here and right now!' He was daring her, calling her bluff.

'This coming Friday,' she responded without blinking. It had been no bluff.

'Done!' said Patrick, sealing the arrangement. 'I'll take off work from around noon, and you can name the location. We'll meet at your hotel at 12.30. Okay?'

'Okay by me.'

Patrick wasn't quite sure who had cornered whom, but he had no time to dwell. Like a hare being chased by a greyhound, she was off again, racing to hide in the thicket of her imaginary story.

'Anyhow, getting back to your question, Mehmet, the next thing that happened was that Patrick looked me up in NYC. He was all apologetic, not knowing how I would react because we had never hooked up as promised, and he was like a golden retriever wagging his tail, all hopeful that we would go chasing sticks together.' At that point, she looked at Patrick with what seemed to him to be genuine affection—which surprised the hell out of him because he had already started to feel the same way about her.

'To be frank,' she continued, 'I was more than delighted to see him, so whatever awkwardness there might have been just vanished. We made arrangements to go to dinner and dancing as a foursome: Patrick and I, and my airline steward friend who went with me to the rugby match and his boyfriend … and the rest is history … never apart except by geography.'

Tara saw Mehmet's reaction when she mentioned the other 'couple'. He couldn't help himself. His nostrils flared as though at a bad smell, and although he tried to smile, his expression looked more like an animal baring its teeth. He was clearly uncomfortable at the thought, and was not particularly successful at hiding that fact. She felt the goose bumps rising on her arms—just as they had in New York two days before—but the moment passed as Patrick, also seeing the awkwardness, intervened.

'Let me remind you, that we have a dinner date on Saturday night. I told you, didn't I that Todd Allbright, our mine's GM of finance and his wife Desirée have invited a few people?'

'Including me,' Mehmet said rather quickly, obviously relieved that the conversation had moved on. 'And it is my hope that we can all enjoy a light-hearted evening such as this one: good food, good company, lots of laughter. Perhaps I can even research a joke or two.'

'Yes, Patrick. I do remember your telling me, but I don't really remember your asking me if I wanted to go.' Her expression was one of pure wickedness. 'The fact is that I won't know anyone except Mehmet at your stuffy old dinner party, and you did promise that you'd spend most of your spare time with me while I was here.' She paused.

Patrick could see she was enjoying this. He braced himself for what would surely come next. She didn't disappoint him.

'I think it's only fair, that in return you will take me on Sunday evening to La Guacara or maybe another disco to enjoy some genuine local merengue dancing. I'm not about to go on my own in a foreign country. In any event, I'm old fashioned. I don't *want* to go dancing on my own, especially since I've come all this way to be with you.' She turned to Mehmet. 'Does that sound fair to you?'

'Eminently.' He shrugged his shoulders apologetically at Patrick.

'Trapped by a vixen in his own lair,' was Patrick's response. 'You're more cunning than a fox. Did you know that?' The expression on his face belied the words. The way he was feeling right now, Patrick thought he might just be the luckiest guy alive.

At that, Mehmet stood up. 'It has been a wonderful evening, but I can see that you two lovebirds have a lot of catching up to do, so I will withdraw at this stage. Please allow me to pay for this evening. I will settle the bill on the way out.' He bowed slightly to Tara. 'It was delightful meeting up with you for a second time in three days. I'm looking forward to a very enjoyable evening on Saturday. Of course, I will expect you to be the life of the party—just as you were tonight.'

Tara and Patrick watched his departing back. The reason for their being together had evaporated. They looked at each other in silence until Mehmet had settled the bill and left the restaurant. Then, all the pent up laughter released itself.

'You are one wicked woman,' Patrick said. He was tempted to keep up the pretence and grab her hand. Instead he said, 'Want me to drive you somewhere where we can have a cup of coffee and maybe a snifter of Courvoisier Napoleon?'

'There's no point in leaving here. It's late, and I'm staying at the Conde de Penalba. It's only a couple of blocks away. Why don't we just stay here for coffee and a brandy?'

He received her subliminal 'not on a first date' message, but showed no sign of it. Strictly speaking, it was not even a first date, of course. 'Brandy! Have you any idea just how much of an insult you have thrown at our French friends?' he asked as he raised his hand to get the waiter's attention. After placing the order he proceeded to explain to Tara the difference between brandy and cognac; in particular about the Charente region in France. Tara knew he was really just trying to impress her—

well, that was an interesting sign—but if the truth be told, she was floatingly happy to be the impressee.

They had agreed to keep the dates they had made in Mehmet's presence, and were standing on the sidewalk saying their goodbyes when Tara reminded Patrick of Mehmet's obvious prejudice against gays. 'I think my instincts were right to turn to you for protection, my Neanderthal friend. Yes, the guy has a veneer of sophistication and bonhomie, but beneath that veneer run untold prejudices—probably including ones against unchaperoned women. I wonder what he's doing in Haiti?'

'Tell you what,' Patrick responded. 'I'll make you another deal. I'll make some enquiries into Mehmet's background between now and Friday provided you'll tell me what you know about the agonic line and how it relates to the Earth's magnetic field.'

'Sure. We can talk about that on Friday afternoon. If you want, between now and then I can ask some questions at the airport about the agonic adjustment on the plane. I assume that's also what's interesting you. As a pilot, I can tell you that it certainly raised questions in my mind.'

'Actually, my primary reason for accepting a job offer in this country was that I wanted to research the magnetic anomalies in this part of the world. I'm anticipating a period of global cooling and I'm interested in electromagnetic energy and its potential to replace oil. I've got a gut feeling you'll find there was nothing wrong with the plane.'

At that point, they kissed each other lightly on the cheek, hugged each other warmly, but fleetingly, and parted company. As he walked away, Patrick wanted to leap in the air and theatrically click his heels together. He resisted the temptation. Not bad Lothario, three dates in one week. Things were certainly looking up for young Gallagher. He wondered how Tara was feeling about it all.

CHAPTER 14

PATRICK WAS IN the office early the next day. He looked up from what he was doing to see Todd standing in the doorway, an early morning cup of coffee in his hand.

'Come on in, sport. Grab a pew. You missed a very interesting experience last night. The short version of a long story is that I had dinner with Mehmet and also a great looking American woman who came up to my table and introduced herself to me—out of the blue—just before Mehmet arrived.'

Todd seated himself comfortably in the visitor's chair. 'Okay. Now pull the other one,' he said, with a smile of studied tolerance.

'I kid you not. It was just after you left. I was sitting there minding my own business, when this drop-dead-gorgeous redhead with amazing pale blue eyes came up and asked if she could join me. She had been sitting two tables away, and recognised me from my photo in the news story she had been reading in yesterday's *Dominican Today*. She told me she had seen some guy coming into the restaurant that she wanted to avoid, and she reckoned I would at least be a safer bet. Problem was that the guy she was trying to avoid was Mehmet.'

'You expect me to fall for this garbage?'

'Well, you can take it or leave it, but I swear it's true. When Mehmet arrived at our table, he recognised her. I told him she was a long time girlfriend. Then, when he sat down to join us we had to invent our story as we went along. It was a weird experience. But, I'll tell you this much, the evening was a riot. I now have three dates with her.'

'Three dates? Amigo, one of us is losing his mind here, and it's not yours truly. A normal person would have made one date to suck-it-and-see. What if the first date is a wipe-out? How are you going to handle that?'

'I guess she sort of trapped me into going scuba diving with her tomorrow afternoon—which I was quite happy to do anyway because, as you know, I love it. It turned out that she's interested in underwater photography, so I reckon we can pass the time without the need for too much head strain. She was really fun to be with.'

'Okay, I'll grant you that sounds like it has reasonable possibilities. And you don't need to talk to someone too much underwater. But why not leave it there? You could have waited until afterwards to decide if you wanted to go out again.'

'Yeah, but that's your fault; I needed a date for Desirée's dinner party on Saturday night, and then I thought, what the hell? But now I'm in a bit of a bind, because Mehmet is also going to be there. I don't think it's such a bright idea to try to continue this charade. He's bound to catch on sooner or later. It's likely to land up an embarrassing situation.'

'Listen up Patrick. It may be a better idea just to tell him that it was all in good fun—before it all this starts to get out of hand. You'll have to work out a plausible reason as to why she approached you. Why did she, by the way?'

'As near as I could make out, Mehmet tried to pick her up at a coffee shop in New York a couple of days ago, and he sort of spooked her out. He was a bit too passionate about his Islamic beliefs. In NYC that subject's been a hot button since 9/11. Anyhow, because she had told me this I was paying attention, and I also saw it. Mehmet was super sensitive about everyday issues like gay rights and alcohol. He also got really defensive when I tried to make a joke about it.'

'Mmm, maybe we're all a bit over-sensitive these days?'

Patrick paused. Distractedly, he started rearranging the pens and pencils in the decorative glass container that stood on his desk. He placed all the pens with their points facing down, and all the pencils with their points up. He left the dagger shaped letter opener with its blade pointing upwards.

Todd leaned forward and turned it upside down. 'Safety first.'

'What do we know about this guy anyway?' Patrick asked. 'What's a died-in-the-wool Muslim doing in a political hot spot like Haiti? How long have we known him? Can we trust him?'

Todd took a sip of coffee, and gave his associate a speculative look. 'All I know for sure is that Mehmet originally hails from Turkey. He came recommended by a very credible mutual acquaintance, and we've been doing business with him for some years. More importantly, we've both benefited financially from the relationship. Why he lives in Haiti I have no idea.'

'Shouldn't we do some checking on him?'

'Who are we going to turn to? The authorities? Which authorities? Our company is Canadian. You're Australian. I'm a US citizen. He's a Turkish citizen living in Haiti. This is the Dominican Republic, and it's not too long ago that there was a politically destabilising scandal here. Let's face it man, this problem is one of those unintended consequences of globalisation of the world economy. At least in the old days we knew who was in charge.'

'I hear you. But we can't just sit around hoping that everything is on the up-and-up. Maybe I should have a quiet chat with him about life in general. I feel awkward about coming clean with him about Tara though. He probably won't see the funny side of it—particularly as we kept it up the whole time he was there.'

'I agree, but better now than later. And if you keep seeing this woman, it's bound to come out at some stage. Tara, huh? Unusual name. What's she doing in DR anyway—being as how she was in New York when she met Mehmet?'

'She's an airline pilot, and on her annual leave. My guess is she got the flight as a freebie. The only real date we have is that I'm taking her to a merengue disco on Sunday night. I can always let that one slide if she turns out to be a drag, but I've got a feeling about this one. She's different.'

Todd laughed 'Different? Now where have I heard that before?' He waved his hands in front of his face, as if fighting through a fog. 'Is that the dust that you're about to bite that I'm seeing around you?'

'Get out of here mate. I only just met her last night.'

'Actually, I'm not here just to pass the time of day. I wanted to explore why you think you're right about global cooling when the rest of the world is on about global warming.'

Patrick smiled. 'A sceptic, hah? Sure, why not? And not all the world ...'

With that, he opened a drawer in his desk, and pulled out a sheet of paper. He turned it to face Todd—so that it could be read clearly from the other side of the desk. It was a photocopy of a graph.

'The core question is,' Patrick began 'Are the temperature trends linear or cyclical? If they're linear—then the global warming guys are correct. But, if the trend is cyclical, then it's more likely that we may be experiencing the end of an old global warming period rather than the beginning of new one. Make sense?'

Todd shrugged non-commitally.

'Have a look at this chart. It reflects temperature changes going back 425,000 years. Their recent data comes from actual measurements—maybe over a hundred to 150 years or so; further back, they look at tree rings; and the oldest data they glean from ice core drillings. Now, tell me what you see.'

'The most obvious thing is that there seem to have been four periods of global cooling and five periods of global warming over that time. Am I right?'

'Yep. We're now at the peak of the fifth warming cycle.'

'Hmmm. That's interesting. Temperature changes in the very long term seem to vary only ten degrees from peak to trough. Not much change required to cause an Ice Age. I'll grant you that,' Todd said.

'Okay, so the historical facts suggest that global warming and global cooling are part of a mega-cyclical phenomenon, and we are about due for another Ice Age. Agree?'

'Well, yes, but 425,000 years is a bloody long time. And according to this chart, global cooling could occur at any time between now and within the next 20,000 years. C'mon, how does this help? Let's be practical.'

'It helps in one way. It tells us that we are closer to a peak than a trough at present, and that for global warming to manifest along the lines that the inter-governmental climate change scientists are apparently forecasting, we'd have to break a 425,000-year record.'

'Yes, but isn't that on the cards if industrialisation is a factor? All those millennia ago we weren't exactly burning fossil fuels to the extent we are now.'

'It depends on what is *causing* the climate to change, whether this is a natural phenomenon or man-made. And there is evidence to suggest that it is in fact a natural phenomenon.'

'You don't think man has the power to destroy nature?'

'Quite the opposite, but look at the facts.'

'Okay, so give me some.'

'For decades, scientists have been leaving pans of water out in the open and refilling them as the water evaporates,' Patrick said. 'In recent years the rate of evaporation in the pans has been falling. Doesn't that strike you as odd? With the environment getting hotter, you'd have expected the pan evaporation to be faster, not slower.'

'Well, if the atmosphere has become more humid because of global warming, that would account for reduced pan evaporation. It's not rocket science.'

'Oh really? If CO_2 has been warming our atmosphere, and this has been causing our ocean surfaces to evaporate, giving rise to higher levels of humidity, then why hasn't it *also* been evaporating the water in the pans? Why one and not the other? You have to be consistent.'

Todd absent-mindedly scratched his head, and looked expectantly at Patrick, waiting for him to continue.

'In any event, there's not enough energy in the warming atmosphere to cause either our oceans or the water in the pans to evaporate,' Patrick said.

'Okay. So, say I buy your argument. What do you believe has been the cause?'

'Well, you know when you eat an ice cream cone on a hot summer's day. As you walk, the ice cream melts and trickles down the cone onto your fingers. When you get out of the sun and stand in the shade and stop moving around, the rate of melting slows.'

'It's the heat of the direct sunlight and the movement of the air currents that accelerate the melting,' a female voice broke into the conversation.

Todd and Patrick looked up to see one of their colleagues leaning patiently against the doorway.

'Hi Rachel, we were just having a highly scientific discussion. Come and join us if you want.'

'Yeah, highly scientific: the rate of ice cream melting. Aah, happy memories,' Rachel said as she perched herself on the side of Patrick's desk. 'Speaking of which, there's a gathering in the boardroom—the pleasure of your company is cordially requested by Blackburn, a.k.a. "God".'

'What … happy hour, or something more serious?' asked Todd.

'Bit early in the day for happy hour, but there might be ice cream for you two boys to experiment with. See you in ten.'

'Come on Patrick, you've got ten minutes to solve the biggest question facing the world today,' Todd said.

'Well, I'm not trying to solve it, just explain it. I think I was trying to use the ice cream example to say that it's the sun's rays beating down on the surface of our oceans that have contributed to the warming of the oceans and that have also caused evaporation at their surfaces. This gives rise to a higher level of humidity. And, with water vapour also being a greenhouse gas—it and CO_2 have exacerbated what the sun's rays were already doing. There is definitely a greenhouse effect, but it hasn't been the *cause* of global warming.'

Todd said nothing. He turned his head to one side and looked out of the window. His eyes stared vacantly into the distance. He remained like that, immobile, thinking, for a while. Patrick seemed content to let him think it through.

'Raised levels of humidity would give rise to increased cloud cover. The clouds would have screened out the sun's rays.'

Patrick smiled in response. 'You've honed in on what may be the single most important clue in this mystery. But the fact is that there has been less cloud cover. An increasing proportion of the planet has been experiencing drought; and many scientists believe the reason for that is related to the increasing sunspot activity during the last seventy to eighty years or so. So here comes the multiplier fact again: since 1933, the general level of solar flare activity has been rising on a cyclical basis—which is one reason our oceans have been warming, and the warming oceans have in turn been releasing CO_2 into the environment. It's a cyclical phenomenon.'

'Four minutes left, and counting,' Todd reminded him.

'How about this then: the Centre for Sun–Climate Research, at the Danish Space Research Institute has discovered that clouds won't form in the absence of a certain type of cosmic irradiation. And when our sun becomes more active, the solar winds block these particular cosmic rays from reaching Earth's surface.'

'So you reckon we have been suffering from a triple whammy: hotter sun, higher humidity and fewer clouds? That's the cause of global warming?'

'It's not only me. Cosmological cycles are fairly easy to track. There's plenty of evidence that our weather patterns are ultimately driven by cosmological forces in general, and by our sun in particular. There are some experts out there who believe that the raised level of solar flaring will go through one last burst of unusually high activity—until around 2012. Then the sun is going to reach a particular position in the galaxy and start to go quiet.'

'So what does that mean?' Todd asked as the two men left Patrick's office to head for Blackburn's meeting.

Patrick walked a few paces in silence. 'Well, the first thing is that our humid atmosphere will start to form clouds because the cosmic rays will start to get through again; there'll be increased rain—and that by itself, is going to cool the earth's surface. With increased cloud cover, the sun's rays are going to be blocked from reaching us and that's going to cool the Earth's surface even further. With the ocean's heat pump no longer working properly, the cold water in both the Antarctic and the Arctic will get colder, and the ice caps will start to grow again. And those same experts believe we're going to land up in Ice Age conditions by the year 2050, because the 100,000-year cycle may be peaking, as we speak.'

Todd paused at the door of the boardroom. 'Buddy, if we're heading for global cooling, more energy will be consumed, and finding alternative energies to fossil fuels will need to become a top priority.'

'Yep, and this is no longer a heartbreaking story about the polar bears and penguins. This is for real,' Patrick said.

CHAPTER 15

TARA AWOKE FROM a deep sleep and stretched her slender body languorously, cat-like. After lying there for about a minute, just staring at the ceiling, she stretched again, propped herself into a sitting position with the bed pillows behind her and lifted her knees to her chin. With her arms hugging her legs around the shins, and her chin resting on her knees she found herself smiling broadly. In her mind's eye she saw his tanned face, piercing green eyes and quirky smile.

She swung herself out of the bed and padded barefoot through to the bathroom, shucked off her PJs, leaving them lying on the bathroom floor, and stepped into the shower. All of these actions were performed without much conscious thought. She hummed under her breath, her thoughts revisiting and reconstructing the serves and volleys of the previous evening's conversation. She could hear his laughter, see the raised eyebrow, how his chin jutted forward when he challenged her.

She remembered hugging this hunk of a man who, not two hours before, had been a total stranger … kissing him affectionately on the cheek. And he had seemed to like it too.

'Hmmm?' she mused, stopping short of examining an as-yet unformed thought. Better to let it just lie there and incubate.

She ran a comb through her hair and dabbed on just a promise of lipstick. She pulled on a sports shirt, left its top three buttons undone, and added a pair of slim jeans. The Tara Geoffrey body would not be hidden under its usual loose-fitting, figure-hiding clothes this day.

'Hey girl, snap out of it,' she muttered to the mirror. 'You've got things to do.'

First stop was Aurelio and lunch. They met in the Plaza Naco Food Court at Meli Melo. They had both ordered fresh fruit juices and Aurelio was tucking into *sanchocho*, a local dish—a thick stew with several different kinds of meat. Tara enjoyed the hearty approach he had to food. Perhaps it was because she was paying. That was okay too—he was a student, after all, with not much spare cash.

Aurelio had done his homework on her behalf. He flipped through his notes. 'If you are interested in underwater photography, I would suggest that you plan to visit an area where there are underwater wrecks. The fish are in great variety and numbers around wrecks.'

'Where are they, these wrecks?'

'Las Terrenas is on the Samana Peninsula that is due north from here, but it is a long drive by road. They have a coral garden, the *Dolphin* wreck, and there are several reefs and a deep canyon in the area,' he said, reading from his notes.

'Anything closer?'

'Si. The closest is La Caleta National Underwater Park—but you should know that Boca Chica is somewhat overdeveloped and it is very commercial. It has the reputation of being the Miami of the Dominican Republic.'

'Anything in the south?' She had ordered the *plato del dia*, local fish accompanied with rice and beans, a salad of cabbage, cucumber and green tomato, and was now enjoying a side order of *plantanos*.

'My recommendation would be the little fisherman's village of Bayahibe, near La Romana, where there is a Dive Centre called Scubafun. It is roughly a two-hour drive from here. There they have a coral reef too, with lobster, eagle rays, manatees, whales, shark, dolphins, turtles—depending on the time of the year. They are also able to offer a wreck dive to the *Saint George*.' He was starting to sound like a travelogue. 'There is also a tour of the nearby Casa de Campo, perhaps the finest resort in the Caribbean. It was designed by Oscar de la Renta, who was born in the Dominican Republic. Perhaps you could also take some photographs there.' Aurelio closed his notepad.

He was trying so hard. 'Thank you very much for doing such a thorough research job. You have given me an excess of riches to choose from. Maybe I can put that to Patrick to get his reaction.'

'Patrick? Who is Patrick?'

'Sorry. He is an Australian man I met yesterday. You heard about the aeroplane that landed on the bridge in the storm?'

'Si. Everyone was talking about it.'

'Patrick was the man who suggested the helicopter to lift the plane off the bridge … I met him in a restaurant.'

Aurelio nodded several times, looking impressed, if a little disappointed.

Then, by way of afterthought, Tara added, 'I don't know why, but I'm drawn to the area around Las Terrenas on the Samana peninsular. Perhaps I can convince Patrick to go with me next weekend, and you and he and I can take a short run up to Boca Chica tomorrow afternoon to get acclimatised.'

Aurelio didn't respond.

'Aurelio, this afternoon, instead of contacting the dive companies, I hoped you could run me out to the airport where they took that light plane for refuelling. I'd like to see if I can speak to the technical people there to see what went wrong.'

CHAPTER 16

MEHMET AND PATRICK sat in a café a short walk from Eagle Mine's offices. Although it was peak hour traffic outside, the café itself was almost empty. In contrast to Patrick's more formal work clothes, Mehmet was dressed in an open neck shirt and casual slacks. They had met at Patrick's request.

'We had a great time last night, but Tara's presence prevented us from talking about a business related issue that I wanted to explore with you,' Patrick began. He took a breath. He didn't know how Mehmet would react to what was coming next—nor how Tara would respond when he told her. It bothered him, but it was too dangerous to continue to live the lie.

'I'd like to set the record straight, because I think Tara and I might have dug a hole for ourselves. You should know that she and I only met last night for the first time. We were just having some fun and it continued a little longer than it should have—we were having fun making up all those stories. But—'

Mehmet broke into Patrick's confession with a delighted laugh.

Patrick was taken aback by his instant acceptance, and managed a sheepish smile.

'My friend, you and Tara were clearly on the same wavelength. It was also obvious you had good chemistry. I am curious, though—this never happens to me—please tell me how you do this!'

'It was just a coincidence. She was sitting a couple of tables away, reading a story about me in the newspaper at the time that Todd and I were talking together. I guess that when Todd left she thought she would have a go at striking up a conversation. You arrived soon after she had introduced herself to me. When she saw you, she raised the idea of this game, which I played along with just for fun. She must have heard Todd and me talking about sport before, so she just winged it.'

The explanation was delivered in a matter-of-fact manner. A white lie on this occasion was more constructive than the absolute truth.

Mehmet lifted his hand in salute. 'Well. It appears we were both on the receiving end of her sense of humour last night. She is undoubtedly an unusual lady. Good looking too, yes? I just wish she had been as friendly to me in New York on Monday as she was to you yesterday.'

Patrick laughed in response. 'Maybe it's because I was the hero "du jour" yesterday with my ugly mug plastered all over the papers.'

'Now, let us turn our attention to your other matter. I didn't realise you wanted to talk about business last night,' Mehmet said, changing the subject. 'I thought it was to be a social get together.'

'Actually it was both. You do a lot of business with us and we both benefit. The nickel price and the oil price have been very volatile in the past five years. As mine engineer I have to take a forward view on all matters which might impact my technical responsibilities.'

'So you want my opinion on where the prices of nickel and oil may be headed?'

Patrick hesitated before answering. His next sentence would need to be carefully considered in order to set the tone for the real agenda, and in a manner that did not cause Mehmet to become defensive.

Just then, their coffees arrived at the table. Mehmet had ordered a Turkish coffee, and he immediately took a tiny sip of the steaming liquid. Patrick, by contrast busied himself with his *café con leche*, adding two hefty spoonfuls of sugar, and then looked up at Mehmet.

'I wonder where the word "leche" comes from?' He had a wicked look on his face and pronounced it "let-che".

'Perhaps you should focus on the meaning of the word "con", which means "against".' Mehmet countered. 'Perhaps you are against lechery.'

Patrick's laugh was louder than usual.

'Getting back to your question, the answer is that I'm not really focussing on commodity prices. We have economists do that for us and it's not really my field anyway. I'm more interested in matters that it is unlikely they would be considering. For example, the Western preoccupation with lifestyle has caused an explosion of debt as people have borrowed to live beyond their means. And right now, I see several threats to consumer confidence that could destabilise the economy. One of these is coming from Islamic terrorist activity. If there was to be an increased level of terrorist activity right now, it seems to me that there is some potential we may experience oil supply interruptions. I was hoping you could give me a better insight into that subject—from a Muslim's perspective.'

Mehmet's eyes narrowed in discomfort. 'You are inviting me to talk to you about my views on politics and religion?'

Patrick leaned back in his chair with his palms turned upwards, as if to indicate that he did not represent a threat. He lifted his eyebrows in a gesture that indicated a hint of buffoonery. 'I'm Australian, mate. My forbears were convicts and we call a shovel a shovel. Nowadays we take our freedoms for granted and don't take politics as seriously as many other nations.'

'Forgive me, Patrick,' Mehmet answered. There was a note of caution in his voice. 'But I have learnt that one should never talk about politics and religion in social company. It is bound to end up in embarrassing disagreements. Everyone has a view that eventually turns out to be strongly held. Even, I suspect, you laid back Australians.'

'I can reassure you that you and I are unlikely to get into any arguments,' Patrick said, shaking his head. 'In my country, we don't like it when our own people get too full of themselves and become what we call "tall poppies". When our politicians grow to become tall poppies, we cut them down by voting them out.'

Mehmet did not look convinced.

'At the level of our ordinary citizens,' Patrick continued, 'we are more interested in sport and in living the quiet life. When I can, I scuba dive, take photographs, and read up on my other passion—electricity and its impact on our lives. Call it a hobby if you like.'

Mehmet looked mildly surprised. 'Electricity? As in power stations and copper cables? I mean you no disrespect, Patrick, but can anyone find such a subject interesting?'

'Probably not.' The response was delivered in a flat tone, as if intended to cut off further discussion on the matter. 'I am more interested in the bigger picture relating to electromagnetic energy in the environment, but that is a subject for another day. Today, I hope that you can feel sufficiently comfortable to share some of your views with me in our mutual interests.'

Patrick saw a strange expression wash over Mehmet's face. What had he said? Had he hit a nerve?

The moment passed, and Mehmet's gaze was once again focussed. 'Well, my friend,' he said, 'this certainly comes as a surprise to me. I also have an unusual hobby about which I am passionate. It involves the study of the history of human civilization. I am particularly interested in where mankind has come from, and where we may land up. Perhaps we can approach your question from that angle. That way it might be much easier for you to understand the mindset of the terrorists and the relative significance of what has become a subject of almost paranoid focus in the West.'

Patrick looked at Mehmet with eyes wide, a ghost of a smile playing on his lips. 'I will leave it to your judgement how you approach the subject, but it will be very helpful if I can get your views so, if you'll forgive the expression,' he said, with his eyes crinkling mischievously, 'why don't you just shoot?'

Mehmet lowered his chin towards his chest by about five centimetres. With one corner of his mouth twitching slightly, and his eyebrows raised in a manner reminiscent of Groucho Marx, he looked up at Patrick. He shook his head slightly from side to side and laughed softy. 'I fear that there is something seriously twisted in your Australian mind.'

He drew a deep breath. 'You know … materialism versus spirituality is like the clash of the tectonic plates. It's the epicentre of the modern day differences between core secular and core religious thought processes.'

Patrick nodded. 'And, nowadays, so much of the Western world has become secular. Someone was speaking to me just the other day about how ethics and morality are increasingly casualties in commerce and industry.'

'It is important to remember in all this, that both Judaism and Islam are Abrahamic religions, as is Christianity,' Mehmet continued as though Patrick hadn't spoken. 'Although there are differences between the cultures of the descendents of Abraham, all believe that man was created by God in the image of God. Muslims believe there is the one almighty God, Allah, who is infinitely superior to and transcendent from humankind. There is a heavy emphasis by us on the unity or singularity of God, but the primary reason for this is to ensure that God's second commandment in the laws he gave to Moses, is obeyed. Remember—"Thou shalt have no other gods before me". Our religion does not negate what went before it. Rather, it emphasises what was important. Indeed, our *Holy Qur'an* explicitly validates the historical importance of Moses as a prophet. It may even be of interest that, with the exception of the *Old Testament*'s reference to the Sabbath day, the Ten Commandments are also to be found in various verses in the *Holy Qur'an*, which we refer to as "Surahs". So, to all intents and purposes, in this specific area—namely, that there is one God, and that it is He who created the universe—there is unanimity of views in all three Abrahamic religions.'

Patrick nodded slightly. For the life of him, he couldn't see where this was headed yet.

'The fundamentalist Muslims believe that the Christians and Jews have by and large lost their way, that they have embraced materialism whilst continuing to pay only lip service to the core values of their religions—let alone the dogma. Indeed, from this perspective, the fundamentalists may well have a point. Forests have been denuded, the air and water have been contaminated and we are facing pollution of what was once a Garden of Eden. In good conscience, this should be addressed, but there is no sign that the West is predisposed to modify its behaviour in any serious way. Materialism always seem to come first.'

Patrick nodded. 'Yep. We gotta keep earning the money to keep paying the bills. It's a juggernaut treadmill.'

Mehmet paused, but he refrained from responding to Patrick's comment. 'Several highly advanced human civilizations in the Middle

East and Central Asia can be traced back by scientific means to just before 3000 BCE—more than 5,000 years ago. One of the most advanced of these was the Harappa civilization in the Indus Valley between India and Pakistan and might well have contained the seeds of the Hindu religion. Arguably, that may have also been where Abraham's ancestors originated. Separately from that, we have all heard of the technological wonders of ancient Egypt and the emergence of sophisticated farming techniques in the Fertile Crescent. We stand in awe of the knowledge of astronomy of those who built the pyramids and those who built Stonehenge in various stages over the course of the following thousand years.'

'Hmmm, I hadn't focussed on any ancient civilizations beyond the Egyptians. Now that I think about it, modern schools don't seem to teach kids much about ancient times.'

'Extraordinarily sophisticated ancient civilizations were not confined to what some anthropologists now refer to as Western Asia. For example, the Mayan temples, which were built around 1200 BCE, are reminiscent of the Egyptian pyramids and their priests were known as Blahm, pronounced by them as "Brahm". Like the Egyptians, the Mayans were certainly very sophisticated. Their calendar pinpoints the start of the current era of humanity to the *day*, in 3114 BCE. There is much that we can learn from these ancient civilizations.

'This is all very interesting Mehmet, but what does it have to do with us today?' Patrick rocked back in his chair, and swept his arm in a gesture which pointed to the few patrons sitting at the wooden tables in the café, to the service desk with its coffee machine, and to the phalanx of glasses on the wall mounted shelves behind it—their numbers multiplied by the mirror behind.

'In contrast to what I have just now been talking about, American civilization dates back to 1776, so it has existed for less than five percent of this total time line. There are some who deeply resent the arrogance of such a young nation as it flaunts its conviction—comparatively untested by time—that it knows what is good or bad for the rest of the world's nations. It is as if a five-year-old child is trying to dictate to his one hundred-year-old father what is right and what is wrong. By historical standards, the appropriate response of the father would be to discipline the obnoxious child.'

The two men were distracted by an uproar at a neighbouring table. As if on cue, a tantrum-throwing pre-schooler was being reprimanded by his exasperated mother. His tantrum turned to equally loud cries of misery.

Patrick cleared his throat and smiled. 'A fascinating perspective, but unfortunately, it has a serious error of logic.'

'Tell me.'

'The US was founded on Christian principles, so its origins *also* date back to before 3000 BCE. And the US is also home to a large proportion of the world's Jews—another ancient religion as you pointed out. So it begs the question as to what makes the Islamic terrorists think that they are the one hundred-year-old father who has the right to discipline the five-year-old Judeo–Christian child? Which group is the more arrogant? Is it the young USA which has only been around for five percent of the time line? Or is it the fanatical young Muslim terrorists, whose prophet was born 600 years after Jesus Christ was born, and more than 2,500 years after Abraham died?'

'I fear, Patrick, that you may have misunderstood me. I am trying to facilitate your understanding of the terrorists' orientation. These are people who measure the world against the yardstick of their own personal values, which are steeped in their own personal culture which, in turn, has not changed much over 1,400 odd years. They are incapable of seeing the world through American eyes because they look back into the tunnel of their own history for guidance. I hope it should be clear to you that I am able to see beyond their point of view.'

'Okay.'

'But let us switch our attention to the India–Pakistan border of today,' Mehmet continued. 'The Hindus believed that Brahma was the God of creation, and indeed that Brahman is creation. This represents a slight philosophical difference that appears to permeate Eastern religions. For the Eastern religions, regardless of dates, God does not reveal

Himself. The sacred scriptures of Eastern religions are not the word of God, but the studies and writings of men—philosophers, novelists, epic writers—who have concluded through a process of introspection and reason that God, the Creator, must exist.'

The mother at the adjoining table had given up trying to pacify her over-tired, distraught child and was leaving, making her way past Patrick and Mehmet. She smiled apologetically in their direction.

Patrick smiled sympathetically. Mehmet reached for an almond biscuit that had accompanied their coffee and missed the exchange.

'You may even find it of interest,' he continued single-mindedly, 'that the Brahma of the Hindus is believed by some to have been either the direct ancestor of, or *even* the very same Abraham who was the ancestor of today's roughly 3.5 billion Abrahamic descendants. It is curious, is it not, that the word "Brahma" is very similar to "Abraham". God Brahma is said to have had a consort who was also his sister, and her name was Saraisvati. As we of Abrahamic descent all know, the name of Abram's wife was Sarai before their names were changed to become Abraham and Sarah. Also, on more than one occasion in the *Bible*, Abraham referred to her as his sister. There have been various attempts to link the two—similar journeys between the two, or the same journeys, if they are one and the same. If we include the Hindus, the number with some directly traceable connection to Abraham becomes 4.5 billion, or nearly seventy percent of all humanity today.'

'Perhaps, rather than labour the points of disagreement, we should concentrate on what is common to that huge seventy percent,' Patrick suggested.

Mehmet was undaunted. 'To me personally, the differences between the various religions are cosmetic. I am even prepared to accept Charles Darwin's theories of evolution as being a subset of God's grand intelligent design. It is not difficult for me to embrace the idea that the universe that Allah created, and everything in it, is evolving according to His plan.'

'And yet you remain a devout Muslim. I find it fascinating that you are able to reconcile all of this in your mind. But I don't want to get side-tracked—what has this got to do with terrorism and the world economy in the twenty-first century?' Patrick asked.

'Your deceptively simple question cannot be addressed by a similarly simple answer, my friend.'

'Well, I'm happy to keep listening, but before you get to that, I wouldn't mind another one of those lecherous coffees. At the same time, can I order you another cup of that sludge you were drinking?'

'One day, my friend, I will prepare for you some genuine Turkish coffee. Unlike this coffee, which is prepared in under a minute, the genuine article needs to be heated slowly over charcoal embers for up to twenty minutes in a copper pot. It has to be watched carefully, and frequently taken off the fire to avoid burning, but the result is unsurpassed. Once you have acquired a taste for Mehmet Kuhl's homemade coffee, you will yearn for it, and you will never be happy with any substitute, lecherous or not.' Mehmet kissed his bunched fingertips to emphasise his point.

Patrick grinned. 'But if I never taste it in the first place, then I won't ever know what I'm missing and I can stay just as happy as I am right now. So I need think very carefully about that.' At that, he got up to go to the counter to place their order.

Mehmet sat by himself at the table, and did not move. It was as if he was already as comfortable as he expected to be.

Patrick returned. 'Sorry to waste your time, sport. Do you want to keep going?'

'Yes. We were going to talk about the spirituality that is common to all the world's religions.'

The waiter delivered their order and Patrick lifted the coffee to his lips, took a draught, expelled another sigh of contentment, and gesticulated for Mehmet to continue. 'Go for your life.'

'Do you understand the meaning of the word "dogma"?'

'Er ... a formalised set of religious rules dictated by the Church?'

'Yes, or by the Muslim Imams, or by the Jewish rabbinical courts, depending on which dogma we are talking about.'

'Of course.'

'Those who fervently believe in God ultimately *all* have one thing in common. Regardless of denomination or dogma, through prayer or meditation we all experience similar spiritual experiences which, we are convinced, transcend the physical or intellectual. Atheists argue that we are all genetically programmed to have these spiritual experiences, but listening to them is like listening to virgins talking about sex. From a religious perspective though, the spiritual experiences are similar, the perceived differences arise from the differences in the intellectual dogmas. One problem is that it is very difficult to separate dogma from reality. It is like trying to wrestle a cloud that keeps changing shape. The subject keeps moving. For example, are the attitudes of organized religion towards human sexuality a function of the will of God, or of dogma? If dogma, these attitudes may be causing more harm—at the level of the individual—than good.'

'I've always thought the test was whether a rule—the dogma—has to change over time as civilizations and lifestyles change,' Patrick said. 'Attitudes to sex change with almost every generation, so that's one that doesn't stand the test of time.'

Mehmet nodded slightly, but made no comment. 'The fact is that there are many commonalities and similarities between the various religions and it seems to me that the key to peace will probably lie in a focus on those similarities. The issue is whether those in charge of the religions will feel their positions of authority threatened if they do so. But if they were genuinely spiritual in their orientation they would have no need to feel threatened.'

'And vice versa,' Patrick said.

'In specific reference to your original question, there is too much egocentricity amongst the terrorists. It is therefore an open question whether those terrorists are capable of focussing on anything other than the *differences* between the religions. Ironically, they are as devoid of spirituality as those they accuse.'

'Whew! That's all pretty strong stuff,' Patrick said. 'But you mentioned that your own view is not the same as what you have just been explaining to me. So, where do you stand in all this?'

'Most importantly, I regard myself as a Sufi—a Muslim who seeks purity of the soul through inner enlightenment. I am not a violent man.

I personally believe we can and should all learn from one another. It is equally self-evident to me that the average person would prefer to live in comfort and good health rather than in poverty and sickness. Materialism has its benefits. Nevertheless, just as there are benefits flowing from the Western lifestyle, so too there are benefits to be derived from submitting one's soul to the will of Allah. The very word "Islam" means, literally, submission.'

Mehmet sipped quietly on his second coffee.

'It is submission of the ego that offers a pathway to inner peace that seems to be so lacking in the West, where your lifestyles have been built on a foundation of ego. The very fact that there has recently been an upsurge in so called New Age thinking in the West is evidence of a growing hunger for this inner spiritual peace. But when you dig deeply enough, New Age thinking is not new at all. It is merely a rehash of ancient Eastern philosophies mixed with the more spiritual elements of Abrahamic religions, with an emphasis on etheric energy and on the elevation of the human soul. Devout Muslims believe—and I myself do believe this—that the prophet Muhammad, peace be upon him, was God's last prophet on Earth. That is why I take the *Holy Qur'an* very seriously; at its heart, it contains a message of peace, not violence.'

Patrick swivelled away from the table to more comfortably cross his legs. 'It is one of the great ironies, isn't it, that religion has been at the core of so much of the world's battles for so many centuries.'

'My personal belief, as a devout Muslim and believer in Allah, is that there are misguided egotistical people in the world who extend across all religions and who twist the true words of God to suit their own ends. I believe these people are in the minority—at least amongst followers of the Islamic religion.'

As if reading Patrick's mind, he moved to address another specific question, which Patrick had not yet articulated. 'It has surely not escaped your notice that I have chosen to live in Haiti, a very unstable country. Perhaps you have been asking yourself why I have chosen to do this?'

Patrick ducked his head. 'To be honest, the thought had crossed my mind,' he said with a guilty smile.

'And, because I am a Muslim living in Haiti, you leapt to the conclusion that, therefore, I must be a terrorist mole?'

Patrick smiled again, but said nothing. The guy was spooky.

'There is an old saying that, "in the land of the blind, the one-eyed is king",' Mehmet said. 'There is so much instability in Haiti that there is no serious competition at the commercial level. I have found it quite easy to set myself up in business there. As a bonus, no one takes any notice of a religious Muslim in Haiti—where eighty percent of the population claims to be Catholic, but roughly half the population also practices voodoo. I have managed over the years to carve out a comfortable and relatively uncomplicated life for myself, where the biggest drawback is that it is lonely living under such circumstances. That is probably why I am spilling my guts to you here—to use an appalling Western expression.'

This last statement was made with a shrug of the shoulders, and a spreading out of both hands with palms facing upwards. Patrick felt some sympathy for his companion, but remained silent.

'My assumption is that one day I will enter an arranged marriage, as is the custom in more traditional Muslim families. You should therefore have no fear that I will try to win the gorgeous Tara away from you— even as we work together on Saturday night to drive her a little crazy, just for the fun of it.'

'You're an interesting and complicated guy,' Patrick said. 'For my part, I hope we can get to know each other better in the future. You might even find that you have an interest in the results of my own studies in the field of electromagnetic energy. But for the moment, I am single-mindedly wanting to get a handle on the terrorist question. So what's the bottom line? Do you think that terrorist activity is going to escalate or abate?'

'Their views are purely dogmatic, followed with deep conviction but without any deep understanding—evidenced by the fact that the concepts of spirituality and violence are mutually exclusive. Having said this, it also needs to be recognised that terrorism lies in the domain of that small minority of fanatical people who are rooted in history and who steadfastly refuse to adapt to modern day life. I believe that this is not necessarily the case with some Palestinians in Israel, but that is not relevant to this discussion. The most important factor, in my view, is that one would have to be deaf, dumb and blind to believe that the lives of six-and-a-half billion people here on Earth can ever revert to the simplistic lifestyle that prevailed in 687 CE, when the Al Aqsa Mosque was completed by Caliph Abd al-Malik on the site of the Temple Mount in Jerusalem. How much simpler must life in Palestine have been in 1517 CE, a mere twenty-five years after Columbus discovered this little island of Hispaniola and the continent of America? You will remember, of course, that 1517 CE was the year when Jerusalem came under the control of the Turkish Ottoman Empire.'

Mehmet paused to allow that last point to sink in, and Patrick recognised it for what it was: a cheeky dig at the child-like naïveté of the Americans in their world view.

'If terrorist activity is a reaction to the West's materialistic behaviour, their reaction will only get worse until the West begins to show a deeper respect for the Creator and His Creation, in particular, to one another and to our environment. As yet, there is no sign that the West is going to change its lifestyle aspirations. This raises the risk that the widening sphere of influence that the terrorists have amongst the have-nots may not be halted. Whether this terrorist activity will become so widespread that it will destabilise the planet's economy, I believe, will be a function of whether the leaders in the West are able to display sufficient wisdom. They need to stop prodding the hornet's nest and focus, instead, on repairing the damage that has been wrought on Mother Nature as a result of their preoccupation with materialistic matters.' Mehmet looked at his watch. 'For too long, the soul of humanity has been allowed to languish ... unlike me, I am afraid, for I cannot languish here with you much longer. I have an appointment I must keep.'

CHAPTER 17

THE PROLONGED RINGING of the phone next to her hotel bed finally woke Tara from her sleep. Aurelio had dropped her off at around six o'clock, and they were to meet again when he would collect her at 10.15 the following morning to meet with his brother at Uwaasd's Department of Physics.

The lights were still on. The TV was still murmuring in the background.

'Hello?'

'Hiii!' It was an unmistakably warm and friendly greeting.

'What time is it?'

'It's 9.20. Don't tell me I woke you?'

'Yep, but I'm pleased you did. I had a very full day today and I just passed out on the bed; simply couldn't follow the story I was watching on television.' She stretched deliciously. 'I need a bath.'

'I woke up this morning thinking about you,' Patrick said by way of an opening gambit.

'Mmmm,' she said, the hint of an invitation in her voice. 'Me too. What did you do earlier this evening?'

'I spent a couple of hours with Mehmet, as I promised I would. We spoke about his views on civilization in general, and terrorism in particular, and the bottom line is that I don't think you have anything to worry about. We might even become good friends, provided I can learn to understand what the hell he's talking about.'

Tara giggled. 'You poor man. But I also kept my end of the bargain. I went to check on that light plane. Do you want to know what I found out?'

'No.'

[126]   BEYOND NEANDERTHAL

'No?!'

'No, as in: why don't we talk about it tomorrow, when we meet? Perhaps we could go for walk on the beach and have a milkshake or something. There's a nice little café right on the beach at Boca Chica.'

'I thought we agreed to go scuba diving? Are you going to let me down *again*?' she asked, but her voice was teasing.

'Actually I have bigger things planned. That's why I don't want to feed you lunch. I want you starving by dinner time. Also, I'm thinking that if we go scuba diving tomorrow we'll be spending a lot of our time together under the water where we can't talk. And maybe I should get to know you better before I put my life in your hands ...'

'Poor Aurelio. After all his research.' Then, as an afterthought, 'And what do you mean you want me starving by dinner time?' He was being maddeningly vague.

'I'll tell you when we see each other. In the meantime, pack an overnight bag for tomorrow; smart casual for the evening and comfy clothes for Saturday. Also bring your bikini, preferably a small one. We won't be sleeping in Santo Domingo tomorrow night, but we'll be coming back Saturday arvo in time for the party.'

'And the diving? Are we going to give that a miss?'

'Tell you what. I'd be quite keen to do that next Saturday. I'm not trying to get out of it—you'll see. Was there any particular place you want to dive?'

'A choice of two places. We could go to Bayahibe near La Romana, or Las Terrenas on the Samana Peninsula, but that might take the whole weekend.'

'I like *that* idea. If I could get the use of the mine's turboprop, do you think you could fly us out there? Got your small plane licence with you?'

'Sure. No problem. I need to get some more miles up.'

'You serious?'

'No.'

Then she was struck by a thought. 'Patrick, would you mind terribly if I invited Aurelio, my guide, to join us? The youngster's been fantastic in the way he's shown me around, and I'm feeling a bit guilty about using and abusing him. He's been trying so hard to please me. He must have sat up half the night researching dive sites for me. And this would be quite a thrill for him.'

'Hey! Are you telling me I've got competition? Who is this guy?'

'C'mon! He's a nineteen-year-old first year medical student.'

'Well, I don't want some voyeuristic nineteen-year-old cramping our style. Maybe he should bring a girlfriend.'

'I'll ask him. I'm sure he'll love that.'

'What have you got planned for tomorrow morning?'

'I asked Aurelio to make an appointment for me to meet with his brother who is a physics post-grad. I've got this feeling that the blue amber may be blue because of electromagnetic anomalies in the region.'

'You have? What a strange coincidence! I'm sure I told you that I'm particularly interested in the electromagnetic anomalies in this part of the world. Did you know that the electromagnetic intensity of the planet has been waning?'

'Er, no, I didn't.'

'Yeah. Some people are arguing that we might be heading for pole flip-over and that the "colony collapse disorder" of the bees is an early warning signal—like the canary in the coal mine. They might just be getting lost because their homing devices are getting confused by magnetic anomalies. It all links in with this global cooling theory I've been reading about.. That's why I wanted you to educate me on the agonic line.'

'Well, we can do that tomorrow.'

There was a brief pause, where neither of them spoke.

'We don't have to go to Las Terrenas if you don't want to,' she said eventually. 'We could still go to Bayahibe. You can see manatees, sea cows. I understand that at Moreton Island in Australia you have a colony of dugongs which are closely related to the manatees.'

'Ho, ho. How the hell did you know that?' There was a new interest in his voice. 'Maybe you're not just a pretty face.'

'Some say I'm not *even* a pretty face—like my dad used to say. I've flown to Australia fairly often,' she continued. 'And Moreton Island is a magical place—I've snorkelled around the Tangalooma wrecks. And seen dugong there. There was also a fantastically friendly school of dolphins.'

'That's another coincidence. I've also been there. Admittedly it was a few years ago. But the fact is that I was at the Barrier Reef just couple of weeks ago. It's still fresh in my memory. Maybe we can leave Bayahibe for another day. My preference is go to Las Terrenas precisely because it's on the north coast of the island. If we go out to the reef, that'll put us in waters that are at the edge of the Bermuda Triangle. That's where the Bank–Barrier Reef is and I want to see how it compares with Australia's Barrier Reef. And I'll still get to spend the whole weekend up close and personal with you—that is, provided young Aurelio brings a girlfriend to keep *him* occupied.'

Oh damn. He already knew about the two barrier reefs. Aloud she said, 'If there are four of us, maybe we could all have fun together. You and I can still have the nights together.'

He heard that last unspoken promise and relented. 'Yeah, no worries. I'm sure we'll all have a great time. Listen, I can't keep the secret anymore. The fact is we're going to La Romana tomorrow evening and you wouldn't want to go there twice would you? You wouldn't want an overdose of Patrick Gallagher.'

'Try me,' she said, smiling into the phone. 'Hey, it's been fun talking to you and all, and we could carry on like this all night, but I want to have a bath and get a good night's sleep so that I can be chipper in the morning—as you Australians might say.'

'Chipper? Sure you've got the right continent? Anyway, I'll pick you up at your hotel at one o'clock—all chipper—and don't bother to pack pyjamas.'

All she heard after that was a click as he replaced his receiver.

There was a gentleness to her smile as she ran herself a hot bath. While it was filling up, she poured herself a drink. She was thinking about dance clubs and what she would wear on Saturday night to Desirée's party, but soon found her mind wandering.

What the hell's gotten into me? I'm behaving like a teenager.

CHAPTER 18

AURELIO'S BROTHER WAS taller, swarthy and un-athletic. They were not at all alike until they smiled, and it was the winning smile that greeted Tara as Aurelio introduced them.

'Tara, my brother Gerardo.'

Aurelio remained standing in the background as Gerardo gestured Tara to a seat, hurriedly removing a pile of journals and placing them on an already cluttered desk. Every surface was covered with work-in-progress, some gathering a fine layer of dust. Several well-worn jackets had accumulated on the back of the door as though their owner had forgotten to take them home. They looked distinctively old-fashioned—surely far too old for Gerardo.

He saw her look.

'Excuse me, this is not my office. My *professore* asked me to meet with him here in an hour and as I work here sometimes—using his books when he is not in—I thought it easier if we met here. I can give you half an hour, if that is enough for you.' It was not said with any trace of Aurelio's awkwardness.

Tara continued to look around the room but smiled at Gerardo in acknowledgement of his words, even though she had no idea how long it might take. She saw that the only sign of any attention to decorative detail was a small collection of framed, ancient maps that hung on the wall behind the professor's desk. Tara had never seen any maps that looked quite like these. She did notice, with some interest, that their protective glass sheets were uncharacteristically free of the dust or streak marks that she would have expected to see given the state of virtually everything else in this particular office.

Gerardo seemed impatient—or perhaps uncomfortable—with her

inspection of the professor's rooms, and after a short pause he asked without any further preliminaries, 'How can I help you?' His eyes were direct and businesslike.

'I don't know if Aurelio told you, I'm an airline pilot here on vacation in the Dominican Republic, and I find myself in need of a crash refresher course in one or two aspects of the subject of physics.'

'Please tell me what it is you wish me to explain.'

Tara sat quietly for a few seconds, trying to decide how best to broach the subject. 'One of the reasons I decided to vacation in the Dominican Republic is that I have become interested in blue amber. In particular, I am curious about two questions. The first is, why is it blue, and the second is, why is it unique to this small corner of the world?'

'Why do you think that I will know the answers to these two questions?'

'On Tuesday of this week I visited a retail store in Santo Domingo, where I bought some amber items. In chatting to the manager, he offered more than one explanation as to why it might be blue, the most sensible one, in my view, was in relation to aromatic aerosols. Frankly, the other explanations seemed to me to have been invented as an exercise in marketing. I was unable to take them seriously. Then, on Wednesday, Aurelio and I spent the day together. He took me to see a mine in the La Cumbre region. I noticed that in the room of a building where the amber was being cleaned and polished there was a distinctive aroma in the air—as if the abrasion process was releasing the aerosols into the air.'

Gerardo had an expression on his face that might have been interpreted as confusion. 'I find it strange that you should seek out the services of a physics scientist to address the question of why the blue amber may be blue. As any under-grad will be able to explain, it was Sir Isaac Newton, the father of modern day physics, who introduced the world to the concept that white light is really made up of a spectrum of seven different colours.' He turned to Aurelio. 'Even Aurelio will know what those seven colours are. Aurelio?'

Aurelio looked embarrassed—whether at the question or his brother's abruptness, Tara wasn't sure.

He answered his brother slowly. 'Red, orange, yellow, green, blue, indigo and violet.'

'It follows that blue amber is probably blue because the visible light it reflects is in the blue spectrum. You did not need me to tell you that.'

Hmmm, prickly fellow. 'It's not as simple as that. Firstly, it's only blue under certain circumstances, and it seems to fluoresce under those circumstances. In any event, the second question is the really important one as far as I am concerned, and that is, why is it only to be found in the Dominican Republic?'

'Do you have any theories in that regard?' Gerardo prompted. He seemed to be treating her like one of his tutorial students.

'As a matter of fact, I do. It occurs to me that light is really electro-magnetic radiation, and it also occurs to me that the Dominican Republic sits on the edge of the Bermuda Triangle, which is notorious for its electromagnetic anomalies. Although few physicists will agree with that word "anomalies", I am aware of several reports of unusual experiences within the Triangle which seem to have commonalities. I have been asking myself whether or not there could be a linkage here, but I don't know enough about the theory of electromagnetism. I would like you to give me a crash course in that, if you would please.'

Gerardo waited in silence, looking as though he expected more to be forthcoming and did not wish to interrupt the momentum of her thoughts.

Tara cleared her throat, and continued. 'There is another reason which only arose in the past day or so after Aurelio arranged this meeting. You may have heard on the news how, during that freak thun-derstorm on Tuesday night it was an Australian engineer who organized to clear the traffic gridlock that had banked up for miles around the Puente Ramon Matias Mella?'

'Yes, I am aware of that.' A look flashed across his face that Tara could not interpret.

'On Wednesday evening I met that gentleman. It happens that he is also particularly interested in naturally occurring electromagnetic energy—and especially as a possible replacement for oil. It transpires that he is also of the view that there may be a linkage between the Bermuda Triangle and blue amber. I told him I would explore this possibility in my discussions with you, but now I have a slightly wider brief in case you might throw some light on his area of interest.'

Another odd look crept into Gerardo's eyes; a look which Tara totally misread. She felt the heat rise in her face in embarrassment at the thought that Gerardo was focussing on her budding relationship with Patrick.

'An interesting subject,' said a deep voice behind her. She turned to follow Gerardo's gaze and the sound of the voice.

A man in his late sixties or early seventies stood in the doorway, a slightly bemused look on his face. His horn-rimmed bifocals gave him a distinctively old-fashioned academic look, a look somehow reinforced by his well-lived-in jacket—probably a cousin to the ones on the back of the door.

'*Professore*, I did not expect you for another three-quarters of an hour. Please, I am sorry, let me introduce you to Señorita Tara Geoffrey, and this is my brother, Aurelio. We were just meeting—'

'Señorita … and Aurelio—ah, the doctor-to-be.' said the professor.

'May I introduce you to Professor Rosenberg.' Gerardo managed to finish the introductions, his composure returning slightly.

Tara tried to come to his rescue. 'I hope you don't mind our taking over your office, but Gerardo was anxious not to miss his appointment with you.'

'Please … sit, sit. And tell me about this electromagnetism that interests you,' the professor said.

There was an aroma of pipe tobacco about him. His bushy grey eyebrows looked like a garden hedge gone wild.

'A mining engineer friend of mine believes that electromagnetic energy might someday replace oil,' Tara said.

'Coincidentally, I also have more than a passing interest in that possibility. Perhaps we might exchange views one day. My special interest is the history of science … the lessons of the past … but that does not pay the bills unfortunately.'

'I really don't know anything about electromagnetism myself … but, yes, I am sure my friend would very much like to meet you. I was about to ask Gerardo if he could explain to me—in simple language—the theory and the concepts surrounding electromagnetic energy.'

The professor held up one finger towards Gerardo, as if to halt his explanations. He sat quietly for a few seconds, and when he seemed to have resolved what was occupying his mind, he turned to Tara in a businesslike fashion.

'Well, Señorita Geoffrey, where would you like to start?'

'That's very generous of you … if you're sure it won't—'

'No, no … it will be a fair exchange—'

He left the remainder of his sentence hanging in the air. Tara studied him, wondering what he had left unsaid. She noticed that although he was clean-shaven, there were stray strands of white hair protruding under his chin where he probably had difficulty in seeing if he shaved without his glasses on.

'Thank you, and in that case you should probably proceed from the assumption that I have zero knowledge in the subject.'

'I doubt that that is the case, but that is probably a wise approach. That way there can be no misunderstandings. First, let us agree on our definitions. What do you understand by "energy"?'

Tara cast a sideways glance at Aurelio and Gerardo, who were quietly looking straight ahead. She was feeling mildly self-conscious in front of them, especially as Gerardo seemed to think she had been asking questions that were below a Physics 101 level. Steeling herself, she looked directly at the professor's bifocals instead of the hazel-brown eyes behind them. Like almost everything else in the room, the glass of his spectacles was also covered in dust. How in God's name could he see through them?

'If I want to pick up an object and move it from point A to point B, then it will require energy to do so. Without energy there would be no movement of anything. There would be no work.' Immediately she regretted the speed of her response. She looked at Gerardo tentatively, as if she was afraid of having made a serious mistake.

'So, in your definition, energy is what facilitates movement or work,' the professor responded. 'Yes, yes.' Then, by way of an afterthought, he said 'Of course, it will follow that this work will consume energy.'

Tara felt somehow relieved. She had overcome her first hurdle.

With what appeared to her to be the hint of a twinkle in his eye, the professor continued. 'I assume that you have heard the theory that energy cannot really be consumed or even destroyed, and that it can only be converted into something else? Thus when your energy is depleted, whilst you may be left with none of the energy in its original form, you will always be left with something else. By way of example, this something else might be heat—which is another form of energy. That is why when you engage in physical exertion you use up the store of calorific energy in your body fat, and you sometimes perspire because your body has generated heat energy in the process. In turn, that heat energy eventually dissipates in a process known as "entropy".'

Tara nodded to show that she was following him, but couldn't really see where this was leading.

'And now tell me what you understand by the word "electromagnetic"?' he asked.

She cleared her throat. 'It seems to me that the word is merely a combination of the two words "electricity" and "magnetism".'

'You are absolutely correct, señorita. A wave of electromagnetic energy is created when a group of electrons flows through a magnetic field.'

'Mmmm,' Tara said, non-committally.

'Perhaps we need to clarify that a little. Can you please explain to me your understanding of a magnetic field?'

Again, Tara cleared her throat nervously. This was not how she pictured it was going to be. 'I remember, when I was a child, playing with a bar magnet and iron filings. When you sprinkle iron filings on the surface of a piece of paper and hold the bar magnet horizontally under that paper some distance away, the iron filings arrange themselves into radiation lines. Those radiation lines represent the magnetic field of the magnet.'

'Now, finally, can you explain to me what you understand by electricity?'

'As I understand it, electricity is a flow of electrons as they move from the orbit of one atom to the orbit of another one that is very close by.'

The professor shifted himself in his seat. His right hand patted his jacket pocket, as if he was looking for something. He seemed to be distracted. Tara watched him quietly for a few seconds. It seemed to her that he must be a smoker. 'Professor?' she eventually said.

He looked startled. His eyes swivelled towards her. 'Hmmm?'

Suddenly he came back to the here and now. 'Yes? Oh! My apologies. I was thinking ... Can you tell me of any ways that one can deliberately cause these electrons to flow?'

She wondered what was pre-occupying him. 'One way would be to connect either end of a copper wire to a battery. This gives rise to an electrical circuit and the electrons flow out from the battery through one end of the wire and back into the battery through the other end of the wire.'

Gerardo chuckled, as if at some private joke.

'Close enough,' the professor responded, 'although that particular action would cause a short circuit. It would be safer to have something else like a light bulb connected to the opposite ends of the wires. Nevertheless, it appears to me that you have a basic understanding. I presume you also know that if you wind a piece of copper wire into the shape of a coil, and you pass a magnet quickly through the centre of that coil, that this is another way to cause the electrons to flow through the wire?'

'Frankly, I hadn't ever thought of that, but I'll take your word for it.'

'*Muy bueno*. But really, it is *you* who have explained this subject to *me* by answering my questions. So, you didn't really need me after all.'

She could see the laughter at last in his eyes behind the dusty spectacles. She wondered whether he was a bachelor or a widower. No woman would have allowed him out of the house looking so, so ... slept in. The thought that he might be a divorcee never entered her head.

Her father would have enjoyed the professor's subtle sense of humour.

'Unfortunately, we have not yet quite reached our destination. We now need to move onto the next principle so that I can begin to earn my keep.'

She wondered, too late, whether she should have offered to pay him for his time. No, surely … She looked at him expectantly.

'Please go ahead,' she said, pantomiming a mild curtsey from her seated position.

He rewarded her with a warm, paternal smile. 'I have told you that energy cannot be destroyed and that it can only convert from one form to another. I assume you know that it can also be converted to physical matter or mass under some circumstances, or vice versa. That is, mass can be converted to energy.'

'That was Einstein's theory wasn't it?'

'Yes it was, but there are a few of us who like to remember that it was a concept originally introduced by Sir Isaac Newton, although he chose to use the word "light" instead of energy. His view was that light would convert into matter and matter into light. In reality, Newton and Einstein were talking about light and energy interchangeably.'

Tara looked surprised.

'Now,' he continued, 'because your friend is interested in electromagnetic energy as a possible replacement for oil, I would like to take a much broader view than this. I would like you to think in universal terms.'

'Do you think I will understand what you are going to tell me?' Tara asked, apprehensively.

'Is there anything that you have explained to me so far that you have not understood?' he countered. He looked like a cat who had just finished a bowl of cream: comfortable, content, but not yet purring.

'I think I understand most of what I told you,' she answered with a smile.

'Well now, I assume you have heard of the Big Bang theory, which seeks to explain the origins of the universe?' he asked.

'Of course,' Tara responded. 'At the beginning of time there was a pinpoint of infinitely dense matter which exploded and converted instantaneously into energy.'

'If, of course, there was a beginning of time. Do you agree with that, Aurelio?'

Aurelio's head came up quickly. '*Como*? Pardon?'

'Do you agree with what the señorita has just said?'

'*Si professore, por favor perdóname.*' There was a hint of deference in his voice that Tara had not heard before.

'*Muy bien.*' The older man turned back to Tara. 'Do you understand, señorita, that the electromagnetic energy that was created as a result of the Big Bang was vibrating and trembling at various wavelengths and amplitudes?'

'Er, moving, yes.'

'This is a very important concept to grasp,' he said, 'Even today, maybe 15 billion years later, the universe is filled with either matter or trembling, pulsating electromagnetic energy. Many scientists believe this energy is dissipating. Some disagree and they point to some newly emerging evidence that supports their argument. We don't really know for an absolute certainty.'

She nodded just to acknowledge she had heard him. What he was saying was still basic stuff.

'What I would now like us to focus on is the spectrum of wavelengths of energy.'

He did not wait for her to say anything, but moved on.

'At the shorter end of the spectrum we have invisible high-energy waves like x-rays and gamma rays and invisible ultraviolet rays. Then, in the middle of the spectrum we have visible light waves ranging from violet through to red at the longer end of the mid range. Finally, at the long end of the spectrum we have invisible lower energy radio waves. This *entire* spectrum is known as the light spectrum—even though only the middle portion of it is visible to the naked eye.'

'Are there other forms of environmental energy which are not electromagnetic in origin?' she asked.

'An interesting question. I personally believe there may be other forms besides electromagnetic energy, such as etheric energy which has to do with the soul, but not everyone believes this and no one has yet been able to prove it. It is not a physical concept. Please let us not go down that road for the moment. It will merely be a distraction.'

Obediently, Tara remained silent.

'Now, the nature of light,' he continued. 'Sometimes it behaves like a wave, but sometimes it behaves just as if it were a particle. You know this?'

'Yes, but I don't understand it. Could you please explain it in simple terms?'

'In simple terms? Hmmm. Perhaps it will help you to understand if I explain the way a physicist's mind works,' he responded. 'When we are dealing with very tiny amounts of matter that are too small to be seen by any means known to man, then the physicist creates a name to explain what he cannot see. Armed with these imaginary inventions, the physicist will measure the outcomes of certain physical phenomena. If those outcomes match the expectation often enough, then he or she will start to believe that the mental invention is true.

'Like a photon,' broke in Gerardo. 'The physicists invented an imaginary particle called a photon, which they termed a light particle. But no-one has ever actually seen a photon, just as no one has ever seen a neutron. They just know that a neutron must be there, for example, because if it wasn't then there would be no other acceptable physical explanation for the behaviour of atoms.'

Tara looked from one man to the other. 'So you want me to accept the existence of a photon in my mind as being an imaginary particle?

'I would ask you to accept that something which defies all conventional logic does exist,' the professor said. 'A photon cannot be seen or touched. It has no mass, no electrical charge but it does have an indefinite lifetime. It is a tiny, sub-microscopic package of energy that behaves just like a particle would behave if it did have a mass.'

'Okay,' she answered. 'Now what?'

'We have been talking about colours. From a wave perspective, your eye detects a specific colour when light of a particular wavelength reflects off a material or a surface. Alternatively from a particle perspective and in very simple terms, an individual colour manifests when photons of a particular frequency or energy bounce back off the surface of that material or object,' the professor continued. 'That is the basic concept from the perspective of a physicist, señorita.' He paused.

'Do you remember how I explained that electromagnetic energy can convert to become heat energy?'

Tara nodded, but said nothing.

'The electromagnetic energy that is not reflected off a surface is absorbed. That energises and excites the atoms and molecules in and immediately below the surface and they bump against one another causing a sort of friction heat. That friction heat is radiated back as infra red heat energy.'

'Okay. I've got it. Thank you. But what about refraction? What happens when light is refracted?'

'When white light passes through a transparent or translucent prism, it splits into its components and you see all the colours of the visible spectrum. You see a sort of a rainbow. But when it bounces off an uneven surface it tends to scatter and you typically see the colour blue, which is at the higher energy, shorter wavelength end of the visible spectrum,'

'Aha. We're getting there.'

'An interesting example of a rough surface is the Earth's atmosphere,' he continued. 'Our atmosphere contains molecules of many different atomic structures, including nitrogen, oxygen, some ozone between the mesosphere and the stratosphere, water vapour and various pollutants. Incoming white light from the sun ricochets off the surfaces of these various molecules and this scatters the higher energy light waves, the ones we see as blue light. This is why the sky looks blue, and this is also why the blue changes in hue as the angle of the sun changes throughout the day.'

'Is that also why blue amber looks blue? Because the incoming light is scattered off the aerosols trapped below its surface? Is that why the blue seems to change in colour depending on the angle of the light?'

'You are absolutely correct, and that is also why the amber does not look blue when the light is behind it.'

Professor Rosenberg looked are Aurelio. 'Do you also understand?'

'Si,' he said nodding. It would be useful to him to be able to explain this scientifically to his tourists.

'Can we now turn our attention to why blue amber is only found in the Dominican Republic?' Tara asked.

The professor smiled. 'As they say in your country, "it's your dime".'

'Do you have any ideas?' she asked.

'Do I have any *clues*?' he countered. 'You need to bear in mind that the blue amber dates back to the Miocene era around 20 to 30 million years ago.'

'I have a clue,' Aurelio said suddenly. He looked like a young schoolboy who thought he was about to get a gold star. 'The clue is that Dominican amber is reputed to be much clearer than any other amber in the world,' he said. 'Surely that can tell us something?'

'A brilliant clue, Aurelio,' the professor responded.

Gerardo looked at his little brother with renewed interest.

Aurelio beamed.

Tara was confused. 'What's so brilliant about that?' she said, but not unkindly.

'For one thing,' the professor said, 'it introduces the idea that the atmosphere might have had a high concentration of ozone—thereby implying either electrical storm activity in the immediate vicinity or electromagnetic activity in the immediate environment.'

'How do you arrive at such a conclusion?' Tara asked.

'Do you know exactly what ozone is?'

'The stuff in the upper atmosphere that protects us from sunburn?'

'Yes, that is correct. But, more accurately, it is formed when ultra-violet light of a specific wavelength arriving from the sun excites the oxygen molecules—the O_2—in our upper atmosphere and causes them to split into two atoms of oxygen. Some of these single atoms temporarily join to become three atom molecules of ozone before reverting to oxygen molecules, but in the upper atmosphere it is being continually recreated by the suns rays and that is why there is always ozone present there.'

'Why temporary?'

'Because the additional atom of oxygen that has come along for the ride is not happy to be a so-called "third wheel on the bicycle" and ozone is therefore highly unstable. That third atom of oxygen is hungrily looking to join onto something else and so ozone is a virulent oxidising agent. It is a highly efficient killer of micro-organisms and destroyer of microscopic particulate matter, including pollen, for example.'

'Aah.' Tara responded 'So if there was a lot of ozone in the immediate vicinity, the atmosphere would be very clean because of the oxidising factor.'

'But lightning can also produce ozone,' Aurelio said.

'Yes, you can smell it in the air after a thunderstorm,' joined in Tara.

'What you are smelling is partly caused by the absence of particulates and partly as a result of ozone that has a unique odour.'

'Could it be the smell of ozone that has been encapsulated in aerosol form in the blue amber?' Tara asked excitedly.

'I don't know if the two aromas are identical, but I'm sure that could be tested somehow. Although ozone is very unstable, so its retention within the amber would be very unlikely.'

'Thank you professor … and Gerardo, too,' Tara said with feeling. 'You have given me exactly what I came here to find. I'm very grateful.'

'I would still advise caution, señorita. It would be wrong to treat this argument as anything other than a hypothesis. We have not actually proven anything. We are still speculating. Nevertheless, perhaps we should speculate a little more so that your engineer friend might also gain some benefit from this conversation,' he added cryptically. 'He is interested in the electromagnetic anomalies in this part of the world, is he not?'

'Absolutely,' Tara responded. 'But I can't see the connection.'

'You can't?' The professor turned to Aurelio 'And what about you, my first year medical student? Can you see the connection?'

'What caused the ozone?' Aurelio speculated.

'Precisely!' the professor exclaimed with enthusiasm. The question is either, what caused the highly localised thunderstorms that produced the ozone or, where did the highly localised electromagnetic radiation of the ultraviolet wavelength come from to produce the ozone?'

Aurelio looked like the cat that had swallowed the canary.

Tara was thunderstruck. From her perspective it didn't matter which answer was correct because, for the thunderstorms of this magnitude to have materialised in the first place—and be confined to the immediate area—there would have had to be anomalous electromagnetic activity here. That was probably what gave rise to the aerosols encapsulated within the amber in the first place. There *was* a linkage.

'Why do you think that my engineer friend would be interested to know this?' Tara asked. 'Does it have to do with his theory about electromagnetism as a replacement for oil?'

'Señorita,' the professor responded cryptically, with one eyebrow raised. 'I am going to respond to your question with a question of my own. This friend of your, this engineer, I am curious about something.'

'Yes?'

'He has told you he is interested in electromagnetic energy, and I have just explained to you how electromagnetic energy in the environment is linked to weather patterns … the electrical thunderstorms, the ultraviolet light rays of the sun, the ozone levels. My question is whether your friend expressed any views to you regarding the weather or the climate?'

Tara narrowed her eyelids and wrinkled her nose. She couldn't see any linkages that the professor seemed to be taking for granted. 'As a matter of fact, he made passing reference to his view that this period of global warming we are experiencing may soon give way to a period of global cooling.'

'Aha!' the professor exclaimed, rising from the chair behind his desk. 'Now you can do something for me, Señorita Geoffrey. I would like to meet your engineer friend personally, and then you will both have the answer to your question. But first I would like to tell you about these maps on my wall.'

CHAPTER 19

'ASALAAM ALEIKUM'—PEACE unto you.
'Wa-Aleikum Salaam'—and unto you, peace.
The two men greeting each other in Arabic stood on a street corner in one of the older sections of Port-au-Prince, capital of Haiti.

They turned to enter the little ethnic restaurant behind them and were greeted warmly by the owner.

'Masa'a AlKair, Mahmoud,' the two men greeted him in return. They had only ever exchanged pleasantries with him in all the years they had frequented his restaurant and knew him only by his first name.

The restaurant suited their purpose. It was too early in the evening for the dinner crowd and they would have at least an hour of private conversation before other patrons began to arrive.

Mahmoud led them across an unusually large Persian carpet, at the same time skirting several scatter rugs strategically placed to overlap the carpet's perimeter.

They walked past a makeshift service desk, really nothing more than a small table, in front of which had been placed a waist-high bookshelf. The older of the two men tilted his head as he passed, as though checking to see if any new books had been added since his last visit. The books would have been more at home in a scholarly library than a restaurant; there were titles in Arabic, in English and even one or two in French.

Mahmoud seated the two men at a low, square wooden table draped with a soft cotton cloth. The older man settled comfortably in his chair and looked around the room, re-familiarising himself with the deep reds, browns and desert sandscape of its Bedouin décor.

The other, Hussein Hashim, turned to the restaurateur. 'We are here to have a private meeting, Mahmoud … undisturbed.' His tone was perhaps a little too brusque. 'What specials do you have to offer us this evening?'

The restaurateur smiled, dipped his head slightly, and spread his palms upwards. 'We have flame grilled *shish tawook*—the chicken meat has been marinating overnight and the bird was freshly slaughtered by my own hands only yesterday. We also have a freshly made batch of *kebbe*, which the chef has spiced under my personal direction.

'Are they any good?' asked Hussein. The question was clearly super-fluous and delivered as if to put Mahmoud in his place.

'He who tastes, knows,' Mahmoud answered with a wry smile.

His double entendre should have been very meaningful to a man whose illustrious family name was revered by Sufis throughout the world—especially one also named to honour the grandson of the Prophet himself. It also indicated that Hussein's parents must have been particularly insightful and righteous people to name him thus. If Mahmoud was expecting a reaction to the allusion, he would have been disappointed for Hussein showed no recognition.

'Well, we will be upset if you bring us anything other than your best offering,' was all he said.

Unexpectedly, it was the older man, Mehmet Kuhl, who reacted. 'I see that you are a very learned man, Mahmoud. How did you come to understand the linkage between that particular expression and the Hashim family name?'

Both men turned to look at him with some surprise.

'But you are Turkish,' Mahmoud said. 'I must ask you how you, a Turk, know this Afghani meaning?'

'Aah! But you have avoided my question,' Mehmet protested, thereby himself neatly sidestepping Mahmoud's question. 'How did you come to understand this linkage?'

Unnoticed by the other two, a strange expression had crept into Hussein's black eyes. They were not to know this mental sparring somehow reminded him of his parents who, too, had enjoyed intel-lectual pursuits, but always meekly accepted their impoverished lot. They could not handle a son who demanded more, who was driven by the passionate belief that the Muslim faith was deserving of, and should henceforth command more respect throughout the world. He had fled their modest home when he was barely a teenager and joined a band of hard-eyed believers who could match his passion.

'Living in this godforsaken country,' Mahmoud said, 'populated largely by believers in voodoo, means there is little to stimulate my mind other than my books.' He bowed slightly towards the bookshelf. 'I have spent the past forty years educating myself in the history of our beloved Islam.'

Hussein, who had been watching from the sidelines with mounting irritation, took advantage of the pause. 'Enough of this. We have much to discuss. Mahmoud, please bring us a plate of your freshly baked flat bread, and some hommos and tabouli. Also, bring us one of each of the specials, with falafel and salads to accompany them, and also a jug of your homemade lemonade.'

'Certainly, Hussein,' Mahmoud said deferentially. 'Would you like the rose scented lemonade or the almond flavoured?'

'One of each please.' he answered and pointedly turned his attention to Mehmet.

'So, my brother,' he said. 'You are aware I have just flown in from Venezuela this morning and I am due to return to Afghanistan tomorrow morning. Time is short. What progress do you have to report regarding the pilot?'

Mehmet had been framing a humorous comment regarding the salesmanship of the restaurateur who had managed to sell two jugs of lemonade when only one was needed. He came down to earth with a thud.

'I feel awkward about this as you know. I am not used to these clandestine activities. But in the interests of helping you …' He fiddled absent-mindedly with the expanding wristband of his watch. 'As arranged, a taxi driver known to us was directed to wait outside the woman's apartment block.' On Monday of this week, after she hailed his cab, he took her to a camera shop on 34th Street. The driver alerted me and waited until I arrived. I followed her on foot to a coffee shop a few blocks away, where I attempted with little success, to make her acquaintance.'

'You have failed?'

'Only at first. It is not easy for women to talk to strange men these days … and with my background, it's not something that comes naturally to me, as you would know. But, fortuitously, I happened to meet her again only two evenings ago in a café in Santo Domingo. She was preparing to have dinner with a business acquaintance who I myself had arranged to dine with, and he unwittingly facilitated an introduction to her under circumstances where she was less defensive. I have also been invited to attend a dinner party hosted by his company's accountant this Saturday night, at which he and this woman will also be guests.'

Hussein was pleased. 'Clearly, Allah is working as our ally in this matter.'

Mehmet reflected on the arrogance of the statement, which sought to place Allah on the same level as the man uttering it. He refrained from commenting. Instead he said, 'I would like your reassurance again that you have no violence planned in regard to this task you have set me. As you know, I am a strong supporter of your objectives, which coincide with my own, but I have revulsion for your methods. My agreement to co-operate with you in this matter flows solely from the fact that you have assured me there is no violence planned.'

'My brother,' Hussein responded with a slightly supercilious tone creeping into his voice, 'you cannot eat eggs without breaking the shells. What you ask for is naïve in the extreme. Even your Ottoman Empire could not have been built without accompanying violence. However, in this case I can again reassure you that our objective is only to set up an information courier service. We need an American citizen to carry "commercially sensitive business mail" to help avoid the uncertainty of the Dominican mail system and the telephone and email networks that are vulnerable to eavesdropping and hacking. We need you to persuade her to carry letters on your behalf on both the outward and inward bound legs from the USA and the Dominican Republic. The letters will all be pre-stamped with the appropriate country's stamps. All she will have to do is drop the letters into a local post box from within the city of her destination.'

'Yes, you have told me all of this before, but nothing relating to the end which these messages will serve,' Mehmet said.

'Predominantly, the information will relate to routine intelligence gathering and dissemination, but you need not concern yourself with such questions.'

Mehmet reflected that only a fool would have accepted such a foolish answer, but what he knew of Miss Tara Geoffrey, he did not for one moment think she would agree to act as a courier. He did not pursue the matter further with Hussein and, instead, changed the subject.

'Perhaps we might now turn our minds to other matters?' It was his turn now to pursue his own purpose with Hussein.

'Of course. If that is your wish,' Hussein said leaning back comfortably in his seat.

'Whilst it is self-evident that the West is deliberately rattling its sabres at us, I have been trying to match the rhetoric of the Salafi jihadists with what I read in the *Holy Qur'an*. There is a particular Surah that is the source of some confusion in my mind.'

'Oh, and what is that?' Hussein tipped his chair back slightly and look around him at the waiters and the one or two other diners. Mehmet sensed that he did not ask the question with any discernable interest. It was as if the purpose of the meeting had been achieved and he was now merely passing the time as a matter of politeness before they went their separate ways.

Mehmet raised his hand to get Mahmoud's attention some distance away. 'I do not want to misquote the *Holy Qur'an*. I will ask Mahmoud if he has a copy amongst his books.'

'Go ahead.'

Mehmet raised his hand to get the restaurateur's attention. 'Mahmoud, I need a copy of the *Holy Qur'an*, if you have one here. There is a matter we wish to discuss; you are more than welcome to join us at our table to contribute to the richness of the discourse.' He looked inquiringly at Hussein who shrugged his shoulders.

Within seconds Mahmoud returned to the table and handed a copy of the *Holy Qur'an* to Mehmet. 'I would not like to interrupt your meal,' he said, 'but, with your permission, I might listen for a short time whilst your food is being prepared. In the meantime, I will arrange for the drinks, for which you are my guests.' He withdrew immediately but quickly returned to the table. He managed to seat himself just as Mehmet, having found what he was looking for, began to read.

'Surah 29.27 states: *We granted (Abraham) Isaac and Jacob, we assigned to his descendants prophethood and the scriptures, we endowed him with his due recompense in this life, and in the Hereafter he will surely be with the righteous.*'

A look of distaste washed over Hussein's face but he said nothing. By contrast, a look of amusement swept briefly over Mahmoud's face.

Mehmet continued. 'This information, passed to us by the Prophet Muhammad via our *Holy Qur'an* is very clear. Allah Himself was specifically acknowledging that Abraham's descendants would be included as beneficiaries of His goodwill. It also seems implicit to me from this Surah that Allah regarded Abraham's children, in the Hebrew lineage of Isaac and Jacob, as worthy of his special attention.'

'What are you saying?' Hussein shot the question at him almost accusingly.

'I am not saying anything at this point,' Mehmet said. 'I am merely reading to you what is written in our *Holy Qur'an*. But if you will indulge me further, I will present to you the difficulty with which I have been grappling.'

'Please to continue,' Mahmoud said.

Hussein brought his chair upright again and glanced at Mahmoud in irritation, as if to silence the disrespectful interruption.

Mehmet took no notice of the little exchange. His eyes were fixed on the book in front of him. 'Also implicit from this particular Surah, as well as many others that occur throughout the *Holy Qur'an*, is that the Book of the Jews contains historical information that we may regard as being accurate as to fact. The story of Noah is repeated. The story of Lot is repeated. And there are others.' He quickly flicked through the pages to find the correct Surah. 'Indeed Surah 29:46 is explicit on the place of the Jews in Allah's eyes: *And dispute ye not with the People of the Book, except with means better (than mere disputation), unless it be with those of them who inflict wrong (and injury): but say, We believe in the revelation which has come down to us and in that which came down to you; Our Allah and your Allah is one; and it is to Him we bow (in Islam).'*

Hussein ran the fingers of both hands through his hair, then held them in mid air by the side of his head. 'So, what are you getting at?'

'Before I come to the matter that is perplexing me,' Mehmet answered, 'I need to also refer to one more thing. There is a single sentence in the Book—or the *Old Testament* as the Jews and Christians refer to it—that has come to my attention. It is contained in the book of Genesis and it states, according to my memory, that Isaac and Ishmael buried their father, Abraham, in the cave of Machpelah. To me, this sentence conveys the fact that despite any differences they may or may not have had, Isaac and Ishmael were, ultimately, brothers in blood. If they did indeed have any differences then it is clear that they managed to rise above them when it became sufficiently important to do so.'

Hussein bristled. 'Are you defending the infidel Jews?' His hands now grasped the edge of the table, his elbows out from his body as though he was ready to suddenly stand. There was indignation and anger in his voice. 'Is that what this is all about? Does not the very Surah to which you have referred, explicitly state that we *should* "dispute by better means than disputation" the People of the Book who inflict wrong and injury. Does not this very Surah validate our jihad to fight for Allah's cause? It is you who have quoted this Surah, not I!'

Mehmet lowered his head below that of Hussein and extended his arms slightly, his hands pointing up towards the ceiling in a placatory manner. In a voice that was softer by a few decibels than that of his dinner companion, he answered, 'But this Surah does not equate "war" or "extermination" with "better means".' He paused while he turned the pages before him. 'Indeed Surah 2:143 explicitly extols the followers of Islam: *And thus have we willed you to be a community of the middle way, so that (with your lives) you might bear witness to the truth before all mankind, and that the Apostle might bear witness to it before you.* Clearly, Allah's intention is for the followers of Islam to set an example that is the middle way and *not* at the extreme.'

Hussein seemed to have decided that this conversation had gone far enough. He pushed his chair back from the table as if to end the discussion. 'You are forgetting that Allah also exhorts all true believers to eliminate the infidels,' he retorted with an air of superiority and triumph in his voice.

But Mehmet was not to be intimidated. 'The particular sentiment you have just expressed is what brings me to the very Surah that has been causing me some considerable perplexity,' he said, taking trouble not to make eye contact. Again he turned the pages until he found the Surah that he had been looking for, then went on quickly before Hussein had a chance to derail his train of thought. 'And this is what Surah 9:5 says: *But when the forbidden months are past, then fight and slay the pagans wherever ye find them, and seize them, beleaguer them, and lie in wait for them in every stratagem (of war); but if they repent, and establish regular prayers and practise regular charity, then open the way for them: for Allah is Oft-forgiving, Most Merciful.'*

A mixed look of triumph and relief crept into Hussein's eyes, as he lunged to make his point. 'Do you not see that it is this very Surah which justifies what we are doing?' he asked, his voice straining. 'We are specifically exhorted to seek out and fight and slay the pagans using every stratagem, until they repent.'

'My brother,' Mehmet responded, his demeanour calm. 'I fear that I have not communicated to you precisely what it is that has been the cause of my perplexity. By definition, the word "pagan" or "infidel" is used to describe an unbeliever in Allah or an idolater or those—such as who live in this country—who practise voodoo. How can the Jews or even the Christians for that matter—if they also embrace the Book to which our *Holy Qur'an* refers—how can these people be classified as unbelievers or idolaters?' Mehmet's eyebrows were raised questioningly at Hussein as he spoke. 'Further, the fact that they are our blood brothers and will remain so for eternity, or at least until the day of Judgement, is validated by the fact that both Isaac and Ishmael were present to bury their father, who is the father of us all—Jews, Christians and Muslims alike.'

Mahmoud looked as though he would burst, but it behove him to say nothing. Instead, he looked from one to the other and back again, as though following a tennis match.

Mehmet continued, his body still lacking the tenseness of his companions. 'How can we Muslims justify the murder of people who our own *Holy Qur'an* tells us are believers in Allah when what we are being exhorted to do by the *Holy Qur'an* is to set a good example of how Allah intended man to conduct his affairs? We are instructed to take matters into our own hands and lead by example. We need to show them the way forward, not blow them into oblivion.'

'And what if they will not follow our example?' Hussein said at last, his voice laced with both anger and sarcasm. 'What if they are deaf and blind to the message that we are trying to communicate? What then?'

Mehmet turned to Surah 2:113 and read, his head bowed, his finger on the page, '*Like unto their word is what those say who know not; but Allah will judge between them in their quarrel on the Day of Judgment.* The wording is clear, Hussein. It is not for *us* to judge. It is for *Allah* to judge. We submit to Him. He does not need anyone's assistance.'

Hussein played his last card. 'And what if they attack us? What if they declare war on us?'

Mehmet cleared his throat, his finger still resting on the page before him. 'Here I will quote three subsections of Surah 2. First, *Fight in the cause of Allah those who fight you, but do not transgress limits; for Allah loveth not transgressors.* Then, *And slay them wherever ye catch them, and turn them out from where they have turned you out; for tumult and oppression are worse than slaughter; but fight them not at the Sacred Mosque, unless they (first) fight you there; but if they fight you, slay them. Such is the reward of those who suppress faith.* And the third, *But if they cease, Allah is Oft-forgiving, Most Merciful.*'

'So we are all in agreement then. If they declare war on us we can fight them to the death.' There was triumph at last in Hussein's voice.

'Absolutely. I have no argument whatsoever with that logic.'

'So what is your concern, my brother?' Hussein shot back. 'We are clearly at war.'

'My concern is that the word "jihad", which we so freely use, is a word that implies aggressive behaviour and not defensive behaviour. We all know that jihad means to strive for a better life, but the accent is on *strive*—which implies forward movement and that one's weight is on the front foot. When you are defending something your weight is on your back foot. And the word "catch" in Surah 2:191 does not imply "chase". In this war, it is becoming difficult to distinguish the aggressor from the defendant. Nowhere in our *Holy Qur'an* can I find any justification for waging war on another man's land, if that man is not a pagan. That is why I am against the use of violence within the borders of the USA, or any other God-fearing country that is not already governed by an Islamic theocracy. To do so would be to transgress the limits, and Allah loveth not transgressors.'

Mahmoud looked from one man to the other, as if preparing himself to say something but also pondering on the wisdom of taking sides between his customers. Just at this point, the first course of food arrived and Mahmoud was forced, reluctantly, to excuse himself. He disappeared in a jangle of glass beads as he parted the heavy strands that shielded the entranceway to his kitchen a few feet away.

Hussein's fist was tightly curled on the table before him. He leant forward towards Mehmet, then back again into the burgundy upholstery of his chair, his forefinger now polishing the line of brass upholstery studs embedded in the gold braiding of the armrest. He was clearly agitated. Mixed emotions were written on his face: anger that the fundamental tenets of his organization were being brought into question; frustration, too. Mehmet was not the enemy, he had an important role to play but, because he was not a formal part of the organization, he, Hussein, could not merely give Mehmet instructions. He had to cajole and convince him into assisting; he could not afford to destabilise the relationship.

Unexpectedly, his discussion with Mehmet had resurrected painful memories. He had heard the arguments before … in his parents' home. He had been too immature to have the words to argue effectively with them or indeed to understand at any depth—he could see that now. He had not thought he would one day long to discuss those same issues with them … and that he would cherish the feeling of safety in revealing himself to them. He leant his arms on the table and unconsciously formed a circle with the fingers of both hands. He stared into its centre, still feeling the same inadequacy here with Mehmet; unable to negate the argument that had relied for its impact on direct quotation from the *Holy Qur'an.*

He took a breath and gestured towards the food. 'Please help yourself first, and then I will also partake.' He looked intently at the tablecloth for a long minute, his fingers now curling and uncurling slowly on the soft fabric.

'I am not a learned man such as yourself, so I cannot express an informed opinion regarding the issues you have raised, but it seems to me that there is one subject that has not yet been explored, and that subject is Palestine.'

Mehmet looked up, pleasant surprise written on his face. He took a moment to respond. 'My brother, that question lies at the heart of why I have chosen to help you in your endeavours. To me, the answer to the Palestine question is very complex. In my mind, it does not automatically fall in favour of *either* side in the dispute.'

'You are not saying you believe the Israelis are entitled to the land the British and the United Nations just summarily took for them without thought given to the then existing Palestinian inhabitants?'

'*Opposite things work together even though nominally opposed.* They are not my words but those of the great Sufi poet, Jalal al-Din Rumi,' Mehmet said, smoothing the tablecloth in front of him with the palm of his hand. 'After some years of contemplating their wisdom I finally concluded that the conflict between Muslim, Jew and Christian was part of Allah's Divine plan.'

'That is one of the strangest observations I have ever heard. Do you have evidence to support such a conclusion?'

'Shall we invite Mahmoud to rejoin us?'

'Why?'

'I see from his books that he hungers for the stimulation of knowledge. And I think he is a very learned individual.'

'Who are you, really, Mehmet?'

'Patience, my friend. I am no-one special, merely a man with an interesting history.'

CHAPTER 20

THE COLLECTION OF three framed maps on the wall behind Professor Rosenberg's desk formed a triangle, with one map at the top and two below.

'Professor,' Tara said, as he rose from his chair to lift the top map off its hook, 'in my country we are much less formal, and now that I know we are going to spend more time together, I would be more comfortable if you would call me Tara.'

'It will be my pleasure, Tara. Then you should do likewise. My first name is Yehuda.'

He walked back to the front of his desk where she and Aurelio were still sitting. He held the map with what seemed to Tara to be excessive gentleness and care. He turned it to face them, so they could see its detail.

'You and your engineer friend are both taking the trouble to satisfy your curiosity about the electromagnetic energy anomalies in this region, and it seems to me that you are travelling down a road of enquiry which will inevitably intersect with mine. You should know there is something very special about this particular university.'

'Oh? What is that?'

'Originally it was a seminary operated by Catholic monks of the Dominican Order in the fifteenth century. Then, in 1538, the institution was reorganized as a university by a papal bull, although the university was then called Universidad Santo Tomás de Aquino.'

Tara frowned, puzzled. Yehuda saw her look.

'I am trying to reinforce the idea in your mind that the Uwaasd of today was originally established not long after Christopher Columbus discovered America. What is particularly important about all this information is the dates. The important fact is that this university was established almost in parallel with the time that Columbus explored this region and, because of its history, it became the repository for some of his documents and memorabilia.'

A glimmer of understanding started to emerge in Tara's mind.

'The maps?'

He nodded. 'One particular map—from which we might deduce that the Ancients, long before Columbus's time, had access to very sophisticated technologies. These maps are just copies of course, the originals are in humidity-controlled, secure rooms. They are maps of the world as it was then believed to have been—at the time of Columbus.'

Tara leaned back in her chair. This had the makings of something unexpectedly interesting. Yehuda's face suddenly looked quite vibrant. He was obviously passionately interested in whatever information he was about to impart. Well, she was on vacation and had all the time in the world. She was not scheduled to meet Patrick until much later. Tara glanced sideways just to check on Aurelio. His concentration was focussed on the professor.

Yehuda pointed with his free hand to the circular map he was holding. 'This was drawn in approximately 1490 AD and it was argued by some that Columbus himself, or perhaps his brother Bartolommeo drew it. But most researchers now prefer to believe that Columbus commissioned it in Portugal. That is not important. What is important, is that it is generally thought that this is one of four or five maps or charts Columbus had at his disposal and which facilitated his discovery of the New World.'[1]

Tara looked more closely. At its centre was the continent of Africa with Europe above it.

'There's no landmass at all to the west of Africa, and yet there is a huge landmass to its east. And the cartographer has drawn what seems to be China in the north-east and, possibly, India directly to the east. And the ocean he has marked as "Oceanus Oriental"—Eastern Ocean.'

'Yes, but, to me,' Yehuda said, 'the most interesting thing about this map is that it sheds some light on why Columbus referred to this group of Caribbean Islands as the West Indies. He thought he had sailed around the world, and that he had found the East coast of India.'

'Why would he not have called them the *East* Indies in that case?'

'The thinking about geography in those days was not as precise as ours is today. The answer may be as simple as the fact he was travelling in a westerly direction away from his point of departure. For example, when we talk of wind direction, a westerly wind blows from the *west*, as opposed to *towards* the west. It is also clear, from the way this map was drawn, that the cartographers of those days had only a hazy under-standing of the concept of latitude. We should be careful not to apply our current terminology to a situation where the minds of those days may have thought differently.'

'Didn't the majority of the world believe the earth was flat in those days?'

Yehuda smiled in mild amusement when he heard this, as if he had just heard a student make some off-the-wall observation.

'My dear, as is implied by the circular border of this map, people knew by then that the earth was a sphere. Kings were normally portrayed, on coins and elsewhere, holding a stick and a ball. The stick was the sceptre of imperial authority, and the ball was the *orbis terrarum*, a symbol of the sphere of the earth.'

Yehuda walked back to the wall to replace the first map on its hook. It hung a little lopsidedly, with the world tilting easterly. Tara's fingers twitched to straighten it but she remained seated.

He pointed to the framed map at the bottom left of the triangle. 'This second map was drawn in 1507 by a German cartographer, Martin Waldseemuller. As you can see, it shows North and South America as two very large island continents, both having a mountainous west coast, and beyond them an ocean stretching some thousands of miles west to the coast of China. And here, it also shows the large island of Japan.'

'Why is this one of interest?'

'It is clearly much more accurate than the first map,' Yehuda answered. 'It was drawn following the return of Amerigo Vespucci from his own explorations in 1502. Vespucci claimed that he had sailed down the South American coast to a point which would have brought him to within a few hundred miles of Cape Horn—virtually to the mouth of the Magellan Strait through which Magellan was to eventually sail into the Pacific in 1520.'

Tara remained silent, curious to see the point the professor was trying to make. Again, she glanced across at Aurelio. His face was blank, but he appeared to be interested.

'When I came across this Waldseemuller map some thirty years ago,' Yehuda continued, 'it reminded me that even after its publication, Columbus still adamantly believed that the east coast of South America was actually part of the eastern coastline of India.'

'I wonder why? Surely it would have taken nothing away from his discoveries?'

'That was my conundrum too,' he said. 'And twenty years ago it expanded into something of a mystery of some significant dimension. It was then that I discovered the original of this third map that I have hanging here on my wall, and to which I wish to draw your specific attention.'

'*You* discovered the original?' she asked. 'What ... this map?'

'The original.' He looked at her over the top of his glasses, one eyebrow raised slightly at her. 'In respect of your second question, let me draw your attention to what this map contains.' He lifted the third map off its hook, the wire behind it making a dull twang as it was lifted from the wall. He presented it to Tara so she could take it in her own hands to inspect it close up.

'You see here, it shows the western coast of North Africa, the eastern coast of what Columbus adamantly believed to be the east coast of Asia. And here, the northern coast of Antarctica in the south.'

Tara had only known him for less than an hour, but already she understood that Yehuda had a flair for the dramatic. His mouth twitched at the corners, and this time both garden-hedge eyebrows lifted above the rims of his bifocals. He looked like a little boy on the verge of doing something mischievous.

'This particular map was drawn on the skin of a gazelle and signed by an admiral of the Turkish Navy, Piri Ibn Haji Memmed, also known as Piri Re'is. It was found in 1929 in the Imperial Palace in Constantinople. It was dated 919 AH, in the Islamic calendar, which corresponds to 1513 CE. So—'

'Excuse me, but didn't you just say you discovered the original? And also, if it was dated 1513 it could not possibly have been available to Columbus.'

A hint of a smile played around the corners of Yehuda's mouth as though Tara had walked into his mischievous trap.

'Isn't it more probable that the guy who drew this map—Piri Re'is—was able to draw it by applying information that was made available to him after Columbus and Vespucci returned from their respective voyages?' she asked.

Yehuda pulled off his bifocals, looked at Tara with a short-sighted squint before inspecting the glasses closely, then seemed surprised to discover that they were covered in dust. He leaned across to pull open a drawer in his desk and took a facial tissue from its box. He breathed on the glass, then busied himself in smearing the moistened dust from one end of his spectacles to the other.

Tara looked on at this somewhat endearing pantomime. He seemed so dishevelled, so vulnerable. Not for the first time she wondered what a physics professor was doing delving into historic maps? There was bound to be an interesting story behind that one.

'My dear, your logic would be impeccable if it were not for two facts. First, what I discovered was—as I said—the *original* of this map or, more explicitly, I discovered that this map was based on an earlier map virtually identical in its detail. It is reasonable to conclude that the Piri Re'is map was a copy of that original. It was signed by one Albertinus de Virga, a Portuguese cartographer, in the mid 1400s—just before his death.'

That got her attention. '*Before* Columbus discovered the New World! How could that have been possible?' His eyesight might be veiled with the dust of his spectacles, but there was nothing wrong with his mind. He was smoothly and effortlessly laying out the trail of his story for her and Aurelio to scamper along.

'I believe that the original was one of the four or five maps that were actually used by Columbus,' he said. 'Twenty years ago it was in the possession of a family friend—the son of a very rich sugar farmer here on the island. Our friend claimed that his father had purchased the map in a secret transaction from Uwaasd in the 1940s, when it was in financial difficulties at the time of World War II. The transaction was kept secret for obvious reasons. The university was extremely reluctant to part with an item of such value, but found itself forced to do so as a means of ensuring its survival. Clearly, a large sum of money must have changed hands.'

Tara tried to unravel the implications of what he had just told them.

'This brings me to the second point of interest,' Yehuda said, 'which is that the northern coastline of Antarctica is perfectly detailed.' He paused for effect. 'And in a manner which charts the land that is *under* the ice. And it's surprisingly accurate. One implication might be that this map was based on information that must have been known thousands of years ago. In modern times, we have been able to determine what the landmass under the ice looks like, but only by means of sophisticated technology, which became available in the middle of the twentieth century.'

'Why do you say *thousands* of years?' This time it was Aurelio, breaking his protracted silence.

'Because for the entire period of modern man's history on this planet—dating back to 9500 BCE—the Antarctic has been covered by ice. The fact is that the land under the ice was accurately drawn by both De Virga and Piri Re'is 300 to 350 years before modern man was able to determine this information to be true and correct. Either the information predates the most recent polar shift of our planet, or it predates the Ice Age before the current Interglacial Holocene Warming period. Without the sophisticated technology that we have today, these maps could not have been drawn based on the physical state of our planet during the past 11,500 years.'

Yehuda seemed content to allow them to absorb the information. He said nothing.

Tara fixed him with a penetrating stare but remained silent for some moments.

'Why are you telling us this?' she said at last. 'Frankly, I'm having difficulty coming to grips with the fact that not much more than an hour ago we were total strangers and you kindly agreed to give of your valuable time to talk to us about electromagnetic energy. You have generously shared this amazing information with us—but I have no idea whether this is just a most interesting sidetrack, or whether the two subjects are even related?'

He looked at Tara with a look that reminded her of her father. 'My purpose is merely to pre-empt where we are heading. With your permission, I wish to make five points.'

'I'm sorry … please go ahead.'

Yehuda extended his left hand forward in the form of a fist with the back of his hand pointing towards the floor. 'One,' he said, extending the thumb of his left fist. 'There *is* another way this third map might have been drawn. If we were able to map the Antarctic under the ice by making use of sophisticated technology, then that possibility should not be discarded from the perspective of historians. Let's say, for the sake of keeping an open mind, that earlier civilizations might have had access to similar technology.'

'Two.' He extended his left index finger. 'There is evidence in the form of the pyramids of Egypt, and the sophisticated construction methods used in the city of Machu Picchu in Peru, for example—as well as from various other sources—that early civilizations had access to astonishingly sophisticated technologies. One conclusion may be that whoever built them must have been less reliant than we are today on "Neanderthal fire" as a source of energy. For example, even to this day, our fossil fuel energy-dependent technologies do not have the power to lift some of the foundation stone blocks of the Great Pyramid of Giza.' He paused to let his words sink in.

'Three. As a physicist and as a historian, I am personally convinced that the reason for this lesser reliance on fossil fuels was that the Ancients had already developed, or had access to, more sophisticated and more compact energy technologies.' Again he paused, '… which enabled them to overcome the forces of gravity.'

Tara opened her mouth to say something, but no words came out.

With a slight nod of his head, Yehuda acknowledged the dilemma he had placed his listeners in. 'Yes, I understand it may be a great leap of faith to think that the ancient civilizations had access to technology which we can only dream about in science fiction today. But explain this, for example: the Hebrew *Old Testament* contains references to at least one such gravity defying technology that existed in the days of Egypt.'

He looked at each of their faces, paced the length of his desk in front of them, as though in a classroom, then continued. 'For another example, the Rigveda—an ancient Indian religious script written in Sanskrit—has several passages that refer to a flying vehicle. The Rigveda predates the *Old Testament*. It was written between 1700 BCE and 1100 BCE.'

Yehuda picked up a pencil from his desk and held it at eye level as though to help him make his point. 'For yet another example, the Surya Siddhanta, which is an Indian book on astronomy, also makes reference to ancient Sanskrit texts that talk of sophisticated energy technologies. It specifically pinpoints the commencement of the current epoch in human history as February 18 in 3102 BCE, which happens to coincide roughly with early references to the birth of the Egyptian civilization.'

And didn't the Mayan calendar start roughly around that time too? Tara did not voice her thoughts, not wanting to interrupt his train of thought—and being a little unsure of her ground on this subject.

'And finally, the Catholic Church lists some 200 saints who were alleged to have performed anti-gravitational feats. All-in-all, there is corroborating evidence from various sources that suggest some of the Ancients may have been more technologically advanced than we are today.

'Now, point number four. After nearly twenty years of research, I am virtually certain—as opposed to your engineer friend, who now only suspects this—that one of the energy sources on which these earlier and more sophisticated civilizations relied, was the electromagnetic energy that is ubiquitously pulsating throughout the entire 14 to 15 billion-year-old universe of God's Creation.' Yehuda sat on the edge of his desk and faced Tara.

'And … that brings us to point number five. As I have already mentioned, I would like to meet with your engineer friend, please. He comes from a different discipline so it could be useful to compare notes. That way I might understand better what he has in his mind, and also the avenues that he is investigating.'

Tara stole a sideways glance at Aurelio and Gerardo before responding to Yehuda's astounding theory. Aurelio's back was ramrod stiff, his fists clenched in his lap. He seemed to be hardly breathing. Gerardo lounged against the wall. His look seemed to say he'd heard all this before.

She leaned forward to place her hand gently on Aurelio's arm—an instinctive motherly act of reassurance. Aurelio jumped at the touch. He drew a sharp, short breath. She smiled reassuringly at him and turned to Yehuda.

'Patrick and I will be out of town this evening, but we'll be returning from La Romana tomorrow morning. I could arrange for Aurelio to pick you up tomorrow at around noon, if you are free of course. Perhaps the four of us can have lunch together at my hotel?' She looked over at Aurelio and back to the professor. 'From what I have heard here today, and from what little I have understood, it seems to me that Patrick will consider himself lucky that Aurelio— and Gerardo—brought us together. I hope you don't mind my wanting to include Aurelio in these arrangements? After all, if it hadn't been for them, we wouldn't have met. Gerardo, you are welcome of course, but I take it this isn't new to you?'

Gerardo had stopped leaning against the wall at the mention of his name, and looked happy enough at being given a way to excuse himself from further meetings. He inclined his head non-committally towards Tara.

'Why should I mind?' Yehuda's tone was old-worldly and civil. 'Yes, I will make myself available at that time. I look forward to meeting up with you and Patrick tomorrow, and I will be happy if Aurelio can act as my chauffer. Thank you for offering. Shall we say 12.30?'

'Yes. I have just one final question that I can't leave unanswered until we meet again.'

Yehuda raised his eyebrows questioningly at her.

'I don't understand … I'm curious why you are so convinced that the energy technologies of the Ancients were based on their under-standing of electromagnetism?'

'Certainly, it boils down to the fact that all electromagnetic energy travels at the speed of light.' He paused once more. 'It may interest you to know that our modern day understanding of the exact speed of light was first calculated by one Leon Foucault, in 1862 CE. It may further interest you to know that all three—the *Old Testament*, The *New Testament* and The *Holy Qur'an*[ii]—contain references to a mathematical formula that allows for a quantification of the speed of light. I have applied this formula myself and I found it to be astonishingly accurate. This suggests to us that these tomes are not just full off apocryphal stories, myths and dogma, and that the gravity defying technologies that were referred to within the texts of the *Old Testament*, the *Rigveda* and the *Surya Siddhanta* were not just figments of someone's overactive imagination. They were real.'

CHAPTER 21

TARA WAS IMPATIENT to tell Patrick of Yehuda's revelations. And yet she was also hesitant. A long scientific–historic discussion would set a different tone to the day that she was hoping for. She would have to pick her moment.

She put off the inevitable on their drive to Boca Chica—it should not be the first thing they talked about. Then, they'd spent a glorious hour or so wandering aimlessly around Boca Chica, exploring the palm lined beach, their hands and shoulders occasionally touching and bumping in their closeness. They had stopped to watch a couple of sun-grizzled old men playing dominos on a makeshift table under an equally ancient beach umbrella, Patrick's arm around her shoulder. She had snuggled up to him and then forgotten to watch the outcome of the game.

They walked under an avenue of coconut palms, the afternoon breeze gently stroking the rustling fronds above them. Tara felt a wave of contentment wash over her. She was alone in an idyllic location with a man to whom she felt unusually attracted.

'It's so quiet and peaceful here,' she said, looking at the rows of thatched umbrellas with their empty seats. 'I was expecting a madhouse. Aurelio told me that Boca Chica is like Miami.'

'It's Friday. Everyone's at work or at school. But if you had only told me you were attracted to insane asylums ...'

'Then what? You would have taken me home?'

He laughed, and squeezed her hand in a veiled promise.

They continued walking, all the while exploring the newness of their relationship and the mindless nonsense of a shared sense of humour.

'I can see us, in fifty years time,' Patrick said, 'sitting on that bench over there, contentedly gazing out to sea, fondly reminiscing about our first date.'

'Lend me your dentures, dear,' she said, in a quavering little-old-lady voice, 'I need them to peel this orange.'

'You use your own dentures you old bat,' he countered in a grizzled octogenarian quaver. 'The last time I lent you mine, you broke them trying to tighten that nut on your wheelchair.'

'Well dear, if the nut in question hadn't been sitting on my wheelchair in the first place, then I wouldn't have had that problem. Would I?'

They wandered around, happy smiles on their faces, and at the end of the promenade, Tara pointed. 'Look. Paddle boats for hire. Why don't we go out onto the bay? We'll have it all to ourselves.'

'Sure. One of those twin hulled two seaters.'

The slap, slap, slap of the revolving paddle had a mesmerising effect as they slowly drifted like a half-submerged log in a lazily flowing river. They fell quiet and at the end of their hour they returned to the boathouse, pleasantly relaxed but also exercised.

It might have been fifteen minutes later, back on land, that they found themselves standing beside a little fountain at the entrance to the old thatch-roof building that housed the Neptunos Restaurant. Unbeknown to Tara and Patrick, it was one of Boca Chica's most famous restaurants. Jets of water sprayed upwards from submerged spigots in the fountain, then cascaded over the feet of the graceful Italianate statue at its centre. The equatorial vegetation on the other side of the pathway, and the palm trees dotted around in the background, stood in sharp contrast.

Patrick took two coins from his pocket, and flipped one in the air towards her. She caught it with both hands. 'Howzat!' he said. 'Let's make a wish.'

With feigned little-girl obedience, Tara closed her eyes and tossed the coin over her shoulder but, unlike the little girl, her thoughts were decidedly grown up. When she opened her eyes again, she turned to face Patrick. 'I wished that we could go inside,' she said with a demure smile, but the fire behind her eyes showed the faintest crackle of humour.

He grinned. '*Now* you're in trouble! You're not supposed to tell. But don't worry. I shall be your personal genie. Your wish is my command. After you, my fair damsel.'

A waiter led them to one of the rough wooden tables on the pier overlooking the bay. Water lapped lazily at the wooden pylons beneath them.

For a few moments a silence descended between them as they took in their idyllic surrounds. Tara had still not told Patrick about her meeting with the professor. It was as if she was savouring the information she had unearthed. For his part, Patrick was playing her at her own game, as if he had no interest in that subject. It had become a game of unspoken words. They were communicating without communicating.

'So,' Patrick said at last, 'why don't you tell me everything I ever wanted to know about the agonic line but was too shy to ask.'

'Must we?' she pleaded. 'We've had such a gloriously relaxing afternoon.'

'Yeah,' he answered in a casually fatalistic tone of voice. 'Let's get it out the way. Then we can enjoy the rest of our time together.'

She sighed in mock resignation.

'Well, okay then. It's not all that complicated. I presume as a mining engineer you know that the Earth is composed of a solid core at its centre, and that between the core and the Earth's surface is a sea of molten lava, and that floating on that sea of lava is the Earth's crust which is made up of the tectonic plates that shift slightly from time to time?'

'Yes, I think I heard that vaguely in Mine Engineering 101—in case we ever dug that deep. And that the solid core is even hotter than the lava, and that the reason it's not molten is that it's under enormous pressure.'

She nodded. 'So of course, you also know how the Earth's rotation on its axis causes the molten lava to move relative to the core?'

'Yes, teacher. And even that it's the movement of the molten lava relative to the Earth's core that gives rise to the magnetic field that surrounds the Earth.'

Well, I just spent this morning listening to a professor of physics explaining how the movement of electricity through an electrical conductor gives rise to a magnetic field. Presumably, the molten lava—which I understand is mainly iron—carries some sort of electrical charge which travels through it as it moves relative to the Earth's core, which is also mainly iron.'

'There's a slightly more involved scientific explanation,' Patrick said, 'but you've got the drift.'

'Okay, thanks muchly. Who's supposed to be telling who here?' Tara squinted her eyes dangerously at him.'

'Whom.'

'Okay—whom's supposed to be telling who here? I'm on a roll here buster, just let's keep this rolling, shall we?

Patrick nodded contritely, a smile twitching at one corner of his mouth.

'A complication arises because the Earth is tilted slightly at an angle, and so the *magnetic* North and South Poles of the planet and the *geographic* North and South Poles are not in exactly the same places.'

The beers Patrick had ordered arrived at that point—a Presidente Light for her and a Presidente for him. The waiter placed the opened bottles and chilled glasses before them. When he didn't pour their drinks for them, Tara made a point about pouring hers without creating a foaming head. Patrick, on seeing this, made a show of pouring his beer so that it foamed and spilled over the rim of his glass onto the wooden tabletop.

He lifted his glass. 'S'looking at you kid.'

'May you turn out to be a very strange man,' she said with a whimsical smile as she lifted her glass to touch his.

He raised his eyebrows in query as he drank, but she offered no explanation.

'When you think about what I just told you,' she continued, 'you'll remember that the longitudinal lines on any map of the globe all radiate from the extreme geographic north to the extreme geographic south; from the very top of the globe to the very bottom—or vice versa if you want to be a pedantic Australian.'

He smiled in acknowledgement. 'So?'

'So, if you were trying to navigate using a compass which points *magnetic* north, and you were trying to reach a particular spot on the map that is designated by the intersection of geographic longitudinal and latitudinal lines—say, for example, eighteen degrees north of the zero latitude line at the equator, and seventy degrees west of the zero longitudinal line which runs through Greenwich, you would probably get yourself lost given that a compass does not point due north … *except* if you were flying from, say, Miami. Those are very roughly the co-ordinates of where we are sitting right now, by the way.'

'I'm impressed that you can just reel those co-ordinates off the top of your head. What's so special about Miami?'

'It so happens that the magnetic line running through Miami points *both* due north and magnetic north. It's one of the few places on the face of the globe that this occurs, and those places are all located on a magnetic line called the agonic line.'

'Aha!'

'Strictly speaking, there are actually two agonic lines, which are sometimes called zero declination lines: one emanating from the magnetic North Pole and one from the magnetic South Pole. They are not really straight lines, but I don't want to get over complicated. Let's just say they are two lines of a pattern that forms an electromagnetic grid around the surface of the globe. There are also a couple of magnetic lines which have zero declination along part of their length, but that's not relevant here.'

'Okay, my exquisitely beautiful and also brilliant pilotess, you've got my attention. I would assume that the agonic line that runs through Miami also passes close to the Bermuda Triangle?'

'No, you increasingly strange mining engineer from the land of Oz, your assumption would be wrong. As you know, Miami lies at one tip of the Bermuda Triangle. Another tip is at the island of Puerto Rico, which is almost due east—to the right of Santo Domingo. The third point of the triangle is at the island of Bermuda itself, which is north and slightly west of Puerto Rico. The agonic line we're talking about travels from the magnetic North Pole, through the great lakes and then Miami, and then continues south of Miami across eastern Cuba, and then down into South America. It bypasses the Bermuda Triangle completely.'

'Whadda ya mean calling me "strange"? You've used that word twice now. You mean strange as in fruitcake, or strange as in unusually mysterious, brilliant and debonair?'

'It's a family joke. But you're closer with your second question. Now, do you want me to finish or not?'

'Go for your life,' he said with a mock flourish of his hand while trying to bow chivalrously from the waist to acknowledge her throwaway compliment.

'I don't know if you're aware of it, but there are maps available which show these magnetic grid lines I've been talking about. In fact, some of the magnetic lines actually do run through the Bermuda Triangle to the right of the agonic line, but there is nothing particularly unusual about those lines.'

'So, does this prior knowledge about declination imply that a pilot who is navigating by means of a compass would have a fairly simple adjustment calculation to make?'

'Nowadays, we are a lot more sophisticated than that. First of all, most planes are fitted with electronic GPS monitors, which enable the pilots to rely on orbiting satellites to determine the precise position of their planes. Also, most planes are fitted with computers that automatically adjust for declination.'

'I see. So, given what you've just told me, it seems that the Bermuda Triangle should be a relatively easy area to navigate in spite of all the lost ships and planes.'

'Yes, and that's precisely why I was so surprised that the pilot of that light plane got lost.'

'Can we talk about that for a minute?' He put his hand, cold from the beer glass, on top of hers and drew a line on the back of her hand with his finger. 'What if the magnetic lines shift, which I believe they do? How will the computerised equipment adjust?'

Tara kept her eyes downcast, focussed on the watery imprint of his finger. *Concentrate girl.*

'The computerised database on the plane needs to be updated once a month as a matter of routine maintenance. And, yes, you are quite correct—the magnetic grid lines do shift around slightly from time to time. But if the maintenance procedures are regularly followed, then all the pilot needs to do is enter his airport of departure into the on-board computer, so that it can automatically make the appropriate adjustments. In the case of this particular light aircraft that went off course, I had a chat with the maintenance crew at the airport yesterday. The database had been routinely updated, and the pilot had routinely entered his point of departure.'

'Was there anything at all that was out of the ordinary?'

'Yes.'

'Don't be infuriating woman, just when we're getting to the good bit!' Patrick said when Tara, grinning, went no further.

She relented. 'The automatic adjustment mechanism had been switched off. The only conclusion I can draw from that, is that it must have been giving the pilot readings that were conflicting with his other equipment and causing him some confusion.'

'You don't think that the reason that the pilot got lost had anything to do with the shifting agonic line?'

'Well, it so happened that this plane wasn't fitted with GPS, so he was probably relying routinely on his magnetic compass and gyroscopic compass as well as the computer adjustments.'

Patrick took another long draft from his beer and wiped the froth off his top lip. He looked out across the bay, but his gaze was not focussed.

'You missed a spot,' she said, leaning over to wipe it off with her finger. It was an unconsciously proprietary gesture. She toyed with her own glass and took another diminutive sip of beer. She watched the rippling of his jaw muscles, and found herself distracted by this small oddity. This was a man who clenched his teeth when deep in thought. She wondered if he did that in his sleep too.

'Tell me more about how he would have used the compasses,' he eventually asked.

She forced herself to concentrate again.

'In most light aircraft, the magnetic compass is mounted above the instrument panel to avoid magnetic interference from the other instruments. Within the instrument panel, the aircraft is also fitted with a gyroscope, which acts as a sort of a compass but uses a different principle. The gyroscope needs to be manually aligned with the compass from time to time because it often goes out of alignment if the plane is, for some reason, not flying level. It follows that it's the magnetic compass, and not the gyroscope, that is the ultimate source of reference if there's no GPS system, and if the computer database has not been updated or is switched off—from what the ground crew told me—my guess is that the pilot was probably not even making manual adjustments for the agonic line, and that he was just winging it, if you will excuse the expression.'

'That doesn't make any sense at all. Why would he disconnect it?'

'According to the ground engineer, the pilot noticed that the magnetic compass and the gyroscopic compass were continually moving out of alignment, and that the computer adjustments were causing the plane to travel along a compass course that was significantly different from what the map was showing he should have been travelling.'

'So he thought that the computer system was malfunctioning?'

'Yes, but in reality, it wasn't a *computer* malfunction at all. The *compass* was giving false readings. That's why there was this mismatch between the two compasses, and that's why he got lost.'

'How the hell could the compass have been giving him false readings … a variation in the magnetic field?'

'That's what I thought of too, at first, but that explanation doesn't make sense in light of the fact that the magnetic grid lines are known to change slowly and smoothly over time.'

'So the most logical conclusion is that Bermuda Triangle struck again?' It was more of a statement than a question.

'I hate to say so, because I've never personally experienced anything like that before. But, given that he was apparently flying on a course that was taking him roughly from Miami to Puerto Rico, I can't offer you any other reasonable explanation.'

CHAPTER 22

HUSSEIN WAS DELIBERATING Mehmet's startling remark that the conflict between Muslim, Jew and Christian was part of Allah's Divine plan, and the more he thought about it, the more odd it seemed. His thoughts were interrupted by Mahmoud, who delivered the main course to their table. The restaurant was still almost empty except for some patrons sitting at two other tables out of earshot. A waiter hovered in the background, with nothing yet to occupy him.

'My friend,' Hussein said, 'it appears that you have impressed my brother Mehmet here. I have asked him to explain a rather strange statement he has made and to provide me with some greater detail of his personal history. He has requested that we invite you to join us while he does so. Please, if you would care to—'

Mahmoud hid his surprise at Hussein's change in attitude. With some confusion he sat down, then called to the waiter that he would not be available to deal with patrons until further notice. 'Please eat, my friends,' he said. 'Do not mind me. I will eat later, as is my usual habit.'

Mehmet started to speak almost immediately, as if to defuse any tension that might have been building in Hussein's mind. 'I have quoted the great Sufi poet Rumi who said that, *opposite things work together even though nominally opposed*,' he said before continuing to recap the end of his conversation with Hussein. 'It is a commonly accepted fact that most humans rise to apply themselves to challenges—even to oppositions—and grow as a result. Our friend Hussein has asked if I have any evidence to support a conclusion I have come to, and I was about to present this to him.'

'That is the second time tonight that you have displayed evidence of an understanding of the Sufis,' Mahmoud observed.

'Yes, but the first reference was made by you yourself, when you displayed an understanding that the name Hashim has been associated with Sufism for hundreds of years. That is one reason why I asked Hussein if he would allow you to join us. There is another, but that will wait until later.'

'I sincerely thank you for your generosity of spirit,' Mahmoud answered. He extended his hands outwards in a gesture intended to convey that he did not wish to interrupt the proceedings any further.

'Certainly,' Mehmet replied to his unspoken request. 'Some time ago, I took it upon myself to generate a timeline of key historical events relating to the land that was originally called Canaan, dating back to 1410 BCE. It is debatable as to which date should be the start date of occupation of that land because between then and 1052 BCE the twelve tribes of Israel were not united, and the nation of Israel was not ruled by anyone.'

Mahmoud looked curious, but said nothing. Finally, it was Hussein who spoke. 'Why would you want to do this research?'

'It was because there has been so much argument raging about who is entitled to claim Israel or Palestine as their rightful home,' Mehmet responded with humour, 'that I decided to calculate the number of years that Jerusalem was specifically under the control of either Jews, Christians or Muslims—since the Jews first lived there as a nation.

'And what did you conclude?' Mahmoud asked.

Mehmet smiled enigmatically. 'If you take 1052 BCE as the starting date—the year that Saul was crowned first King of Israel—then the numbers are Jews, 983 years; Christians, 392 years; Muslims, 1,176 years, with roughly 400 of those years under the Ottoman Empire of Turkey. However, if you take 1410 BCE as the starting date—the year Joshua conquered Jericho and led the Children of Israel in the land of Canaan—then the numbers are Jews, 1,341 years; Christians, 392 years; Muslims, 1,176 years.'

Mahmoud closed his eyes as he concentrated on the numbers. 'But those numbers are inconclusive,' he said after a pause. 'Under the first scenario, the Muslims are the leaders by themselves, but the Christians and Jews together can claim longevity. Under the second scenario, the Jews are the leaders, but the Muslims and the Christians together can claim longevity.'

'Precisely,' Mehmet answered. 'And the position is further confused by the fact that Palestine was controlled by the Turks, and not the Arabs, for around 400 years during the occupations by the Muslims. And we Turks were not even present, but were controlling from afar. We never actually lived there. Also, just to confuse matters even further, the name Palestine is derived from the word philistine, and the Philistines were Aegean in origin. They had migrated to the country by way of the Island of Crete. The original Palestinians were neither of Arabic nor, probably, of Turkish extraction.'

Hussein leant forward and looked from one man to the other. 'So what you are saying is that, on the basis of longevity, no one can legitimately and irrefutably claim the land as theirs?'

'On the basis of longevity that is precisely what I am saying,' Mehmet answered, with a smile in his voice and a flash of mischief in his dark eyes. 'And that is how I came to the conclusion that Allah has been playing with his children and taunting us—pitting us against each other through the millennia—so that we may grow as a species to mature adulthood, which we are now rapidly approaching.'

'I find myself needing to ask you the question again,' said Hussein. 'Who are you really, my brother?' His perplexed expression seemed to indicate that he wasn't sure if he was dealing with a fool, a madman, a spy or, something else that he was too afraid to articulate.

'I am sorry to inform you that I am really just an ordinary human being,' Mehmet answered. 'There is nothing special about me other than my upbringing. In truth I am nobody. I am, like Adam before me, merely like the dust of the Earth.'

'Perhaps you will allow us to be the judges of that,' said Mahmoud, taking the role of hospitable host. 'I, too, am curious to know more about the man sitting at the table with us this evening.'

Mehmet nodded his head from side to side in acknowledgement. He had taken a mouthful of the *kebbe* on his plate, and was in the process of piling some tabouli salad and hommos onto his fork. Hussein followed his lead. It was not until Mehmet had taken a sip of lemonade that he spoke.

'Mahmoud, you are to be complimented on preparing a fine meal for us this evening, which I am afraid you may now have to spoil by reheating it for me later on if I am to tell you my story. But let us begin.' He pushed his plate away slightly.

'When I was a young boy of ten years and living in Turkey, my parents, who were, and still are, very religious and practising Muslims, were approached by an elder in the community. I had come to his attention; I don't know how this happened but he recommended that I be selected to join the monastery at Sarmoun, in northern Afghanistan. I was to be educated under the ultimate guidance of Baba Amyn.'

Both men sucked in a breath through half-closed teeth, their eyes focussed on Mehmet. This monastery was legendary as an educational centre for Sufi students.

'Are you, yourself a Sufi?' Mahmoud asked.

'No, I am afraid not,' Mehmet answered. 'It takes upwards of sixteen years of study and practise to become a Sufi, and then only at the ultimate discretion of your teacher. The nature of my recruitment was different. I attended that monastery as if I were attending a school. I was then discharged at age seventeen to go to university in Turkey where I gained a conventional, secular commercial degree. The curriculum of my education at the monastery was a mixture of languages, grammar, science, history, mathematics, geography, Islamic religion and Sufi philosophy and practice. In short, I was an experiment, a sort of a guinea pig.'

'What was the purpose of this?' asked Hussein, who was now leaning forward in his chair. He had forgotten his food.

'If you understand anything about the Sufis, which you must, given your name,' answered Mehmet, 'you will understand there are some matters I am not at liberty to speak about with full frankness. Suffice it to say that I am not a fully fledged Sufi, and that I am still regarded by the Sufis as an initiate. There are, however, some basic principles, which it was decided I should attempt to apply in my day-to-day secular life. I live an ordinary life in the secular world, unsupervised by anyone at the monastery.'

'Are you at liberty to talk about *any* of these principles,' Mahmoud asked.

The tremor in his voice made it clear Mehmet had struck a chord.

'Yes, I will be prepared to discuss four specific principles, but no more. It would be best if you refrained from asking me questions relating to any other matters. That way I will not be put into a position where I have to choose between offending you by avoiding any answer, or by lying to you. If you will forgive me for one or two minutes, perhaps both Hussein and I may take another mouthful or two of this delicious food and this will allow me to order my thoughts.'

Mahmoud sat like a stone statue, barely breathing. It was as if he was afraid that any sudden movement on his part would disturb the *jinni* who had made this dream appear in his mind, and the table would disappear in a puff of smoke.

Hussein's movements, on the other hand, were those of a man eating by habit. There was no expression on his face. His gaze was fixed on some point inwards in his mind. He chewed steadily.

At length, Mehmet cleared his throat, and prepared to continue. 'Probably the most important principle that I need to communicate today, is that at the foundation level of the Sufi way of life stands the basic principle that there should be a total absence of ego. In the world of Sufism, ego is the most significant barrier between humanity and God. Unfortunately, this presents us with a conundrum in our day-to-day lives. Whilst in the spiritual world one cannot progress without total annihilation of the ego, in the secular world, one cannot survive— psychologists believe—unless the ego is allowed free reign in competitive situations. And, Hussein, to partially answer your question, it was to test this hypothesis of the psychologists that it was decided to use me as an experimental guinea pig. My ego was to be annihilated, and I was to be let loose into the secular world with nothing but my education to see if I would be able to survive without its re-emergence.'

Mahmoud looked stunned. 'But what if the experiment had failed and it turned out that the psychologists were correct? You would have been destroyed as a human being.'

Mehmet considered this. 'That appears to have been a risk that my parents were prepared to take. They are deeply religious people who had total faith in the judgement of the elder concerned.'

'You appear to have survived intact.' Hussein observed. 'So either your ego has re-emerged, or you have learned some other principles that have allowed you to cope in the world in which we live.' He appeared to have undergone a metamorphosis of understanding following his introspection. He had finally come to understand that what he had witnessed in his own parents was now explainable as an absence of ego. He had broken the Sufi line in his family when he had run away from home.

No one spoke. Eventually, Mahmoud broke the silence. 'Please to continue.'

'The next foundation principle is that a closed mind cannot grow. In order to keep open the possibility of personal spiritual growth, one needs to dispense with dogma.'

'What does that mean?' asked Hussein.

'Imagine, if you will,' Mehmet said, 'a picket line, such as was involved in demonstrations in Europe not too long ago, with committed Muslims holding placards and banners with messages like, "Slay those who insult Islam"; "Europe will pay"; "Islam will dominate the World". In the context of the need to demolish ego and dispense with dogma, how does one interpret the sentiments reflected in these messages? What do you think, Mahmoud?'

Mahmoud was somewhat taken aback at being singled out. He shifted from one haunch to the other on his chair. 'Certainly, those slogans are a reflection of the thoughts of people whose egos have been dented and they are feeling angry.'

'I agree, but what about the question of dogma? Do these slogans sound dogmatic to you?'

'What are you getting at?' Hussein asked.

'Well, you know what dogma is: a body of doctrines that an organized religion imposes on its followers—based on blind faith and not necessarily needing any real understanding. I have earlier read quotes to you from the *Holy Qur'an*, none of which would support the ideas articulated on such placards and banners. This implies that the people who held these banners and placards were driven by dogma. Their minds are closed. It is as if their souls have become like bonsai trees. Their shape is perfect, but their growth has become stunted.'

Hussein nodded, conceding somewhat grudgingly. 'Yes, I suppose I can see that. But how else can these people let go of their frustration?'

'Frustration from what? Spiritual growth does not rely on other people's behaviour. A man's spiritual journey is intensely private. One does not need the co-operation of others to attain oneness with Allah. Neither can the behaviour of others inhibit you on your personal spiritual journey. What does it matter whether another man thinks of you as a king or a knave? It is only a matter that will affect your ego. Frustration can only be in relation to the material world, in which ego supposedly plays a large part.'

'If I remember correctly, the poet Rumi to whom you referred previously also made a similar observation,' Mahmoud ventured hesitantly.

'You are right, my friend,' Mehmet said. 'In fact, he said, *we have taken the essence of the Qur'an, and thrown the carcass to the donkeys*, which, at face value is heretical and insulting to the Prophet Muhammad—peace be upon him—who brought us its contents. And yet this man Rumi retains respect of Muslims world-wide. Why? Because he was talking sense. What he was referring to when he mentioned the carcass was the *dogma* of the religion, not the religion itself. People cannot benefit from dogma which they do not, or cannot, or will not understand. The people who held these placards and banners are not true Muslims as Allah intended us to be. They, like those Christians and Jews whom we criticise, have also strayed from the path of righteousness.'

Mahmoud had listened with a furrowed brow, wanting to say more but also taking care to avoid being seen as disrespectful. 'Are you saying that these dissenters had no right to voice their opinions, and no right to stand up against their oppressors?'

'It is not I who am saying anything. I am merely quoting to you what the *Holy Qur'an* says. There can be no room for interpretation. We Muslims should be leading by example. We should be pursuing pagans who do not believe in the one Allah, not Christians and Jews who clearly do. We should be avoiding excessive behaviour. And, finally, we should be defending with our lives attacks against our own homelands, which might very well require us to catch and slay the invading enemy. That is what all of the Surahs, which I quoted today, in fact say in combination. No more and no less. The *Holy Qur'an* does not exhort us to attempt to dominate, as was inferred in one of those banners. Dominate who? The very word "Islam" means to *submit*—which is the exact opposite of dominate. We submit to Allah and we aspire to dominate no one because we should have no egos to satisfy. What Allah wills is clearly stated for anyone to study and understand in our *Holy Qur'an*.'

Hussein's body language had become neutral, unreadable. 'Let us assume for the moment that you are correct in these last observations, you have only articulated two of the four principles to which you originally alluded. I, for one, would like to see the whole picture before I form a view.'

At this, Mehmet smiled. 'An admirable approach my brother, so let me now continue. If I have managed to annihilate my ego, and I have also disposed of my dogmatic approach either by deep study of the true meaning of the words of the *Holy Qur'an*, or by choosing to gloss over the detail and rather live my life by Islam's core principles, how can I work in a practical manner to protect myself from the dangers in the competitive environment in which I am expected to live on a day-to-day basis? This question brings us to the third principle which I would like to put forward, which is that *he who would change the outer world should begin by changing his world within*.'

Hussein chewed at the inside of his lower lip. 'You will need to explain further before I understand fully what you are driving at.'

'The point I am trying to make here,' Mehmet said, 'is based on a historical context. In the early days of Islam, murder, assassination, death and war were what drove the spread of Islam. We were not then a peace loving people. We were explicitly following Allah's instructions to *fight and slay the pagans wherever ye find them, and seize them, beleaguer them, and lie in wait for them in every stratagem (of war).*

'And why is this of significance?' asked Hussein. He scratched at his beard thoughtfully. 'After all, that is who we were then, and it was very successful. We brought culture, medicine and mathematics to the world beyond our borders. We were feared and revered. At the very least, we were respected.'

'Ah yes, but those who have no ego have no need to be feared, revered or respected. Furthermore, except for countries like those in which we are now, the Western world is largely rid of pagans.'

Hussein interjected. 'You are saying that perhaps the time has come where we need to change our inner selves in order to redirect our attention away from the concept of spreading Islam?'

Mehmet was slow to reply as he considered the question and marshalled his thoughts. 'That appears to me to be a loaded question. What I am saying—no, what the *Holy Qur'an* is saying—is that, *amongst believers*, we should lead by example. That is where we should now be directing our energies. In my own experience, if you smile at a stranger, he tends to return the smile. We should not be waiting for the other man to smile in our direction. It is we who should be changing our world from within if we want the world without to change.'

Hussein did not look like a man convinced. 'That sounds to me to be altruistic and very impractical. What if whilst we are smiling and spreading charity, and throwing rose petals in the path of our duplicitous enemy he is stabbing us in the back and plundering us?'

'Under such circumstances, the *Holy Qur'an* is clear. We should defend ourselves and catch and slay the enemy, provided we do not overstep the boundaries.'

'If I am correct in understanding you,' Mahmoud said, 'the fourth principle, which you have not yet articulated, should complete the explanation.'

'It will take far more than four principles to complete the picture, my friend, but I applaud you on your clarity of thought.'

Hussein remained silent, but his body language was not combative. Mehmet took this as an optimistic sign that they might not, after all, have been dealing with the closed mind of a fanatic.

'The fourth principle that I am able to share with you this evening is *far* more difficult to communicate. It has to do with projection of a form of energy, and it is not generally discussed outside the Halka, which is, as you know, the learning ring of Sufi students chosen by their teacher.'

'You are about to share an undisclosed secret?' Mahmoud interrupted.

Mehmet looked at him in some surprise. 'No, my brother, what I am about to tell you has been known about since the time of the Prophet Jesus, but it is not particularly well understood. Some people believe it is aligned with the Sufi power of the projection of will, but it is more subtle than that.'

His companions, he noted, both sat forward in their seats, waiting for his next words. The time had come to stretch their minds.

'It needs to be recognised that the human body is really an electrical system with electrons moving from cell to cell, through various meridians that course through it, and also surround the body at its surface. You will best be able to understand this if you think in terms of an ECG machine or an EEG machine that measures heart waves or brain waves via the minute electrical signals that emanate from the body.'

Mahmoud nodded slowly. There was a clatter of plates in the background and the increasing hum of patrons, but he seemed oblivious to the buzz of business around him.

'And whilst all human bodies have measurable electricity coursing through them, the intensity of this electrical energy will vary, depending on two factors: first, the intensity of energy which naturally flows through their bodies—some of which, incidentally, may be channelled or scavenged from the environment; and second, the relative amount of resistance within their bodies to that electrical flow.'

Hussein's swarthy features were furrowed in the manner of a child trying to understand something that was beyond him because he lacked the inner tools to process the information. He said nothing. His look of almost childlike confusion would have been endearing to Mehmet under other circumstances.

'I cannot yet see what your purpose is. Why does it matter if the human body is an electrical system that can interface with environmental energy?' Mahmoud asked, his hands raised at his sides, palms upward.

'You will understand why it matters if you can accept, as the Sufis do, that there is *more than one* type of energy in the environment. The one that we all know about may be described as physical energy—also known as electromagnetic energy. Another type of energy may be described as soul energy, otherwise known as the energy of the ether, or etheric energy.'

'What is this soul energy ... or etheric energy?' Hussein asked.

Mahmoud leant forward, as if to answer. Mehmet's eyes flashed at him for a brief moment. Mahmoud understood their message and remained silent.

'It is an energy that has the power to overcome physical energy,' Mehmet said to both men. 'Logic dictates that etheric energy must be the supreme power behind the will of Allah. The Prophet Jesus also preached etheric energy. He chose to describe it as Love, with a capital "L". Although its existence cannot be scientifically validated, logic dictates that it must exist.

'The reason that the scientists will never be able to prove that Allah does not exist is that they have no understanding of this etheric energy. They have no way of validating it or invalidating it, so they merely assume that it does not exist. But their alternative is logically ridiculous. They continue to talk about the Big Bang, which they themselves should—and some do— reject as impossible in terms of their own laws of physics. The Big Bang could only have occurred as a result of some external force, and that force could not possibly have been electromagnetic or physical energy ... by their reasoning, of course.'

Mehmet smiled broadly, as if he had told some sort of joke. He looked hugely amused.

'And what has this to do with us ordinary mortals?' Mahmoud asked.

Mehmet paused before answering. He looked across to see Hussein's reaction, but received no clues. Hussein was sitting passively. It would be better just to press forward.

'The Sufis believe that the human organism—just as it can be characterised as an *electrical* energy system with its own internal electrical flows and its ability to interface with the physical energy in the environment—can *also* be characterised as an etheric energy system with its own internal powers of love, and its own ability to tap into the Soul of Allah.'

Mehmet could see the window of Mahmoud's mind opening wide to embrace the idea. Hussein's raisin eyes remained opaque. If responses were anything to go by, then Mahmoud was clearly way ahead of Hussein.

'One could argue that personal love is etheric energy of a particular wavelength and, for example, when two people fall in love, they are merely on the same etheric wavelength. Of course, there is also a varying intensity of chemistry, which gives rise to lust—but chemistry wanes and love still remains. It may even grow over time as the wavelengths synchronise in the absence of ego. That is why arranged marriages work, provided both parties are committed to the union.

'The Sufis have learnt a technique for opening their hearts to allow the energy of will to flow from the sender to the receiver. But, in opening their hearts, they are actually harnessing the power of Love that the Prophet Jesus, too, was able to harness and which gained him so many followers. In simple terms, the Prophet Jesus was channelling the Love of Allah and projecting it through to his followers. That he was uniquely able to do this with such forceful impact implied that he must have had a unique relationship with Allah, and it is therefore not surprising that he came to be known as the Son of God. Similarly, Sufi masters are able to project a positive attitude of amplified intensity such that the people with whom they interact absorb this energy and are comforted. The recipients feel no external threat emanating from the sender—indeed they feel exactly the opposite—they feel an intensified stream of goodwill and Love. Thereby, they feel energised and willingly become collaborators rather than adversaries. And this brings me to my second reason for inviting you to join us at the table here this evening, Mahmoud.'

Mahmoud looked taken aback. He had forgotten that Mehmet had wanted him there for a reason 'Oh? And what is that?'

'I have informed you that I am still regarded as an initiate, and I have also informed you that I am nothing other than an ordinary man. Is that correct?'

'Yes,' Mahmoud responded.

'I would like to pose a question to you, and I ask that you be fully open and free of fear from consequences from either myself or Hussein when you answer.' He looked towards Hussein for his confirmation, and received it with a slight dip of Hussein's head.

'I shall try my best,' Mahmoud answered.

'Please describe to us, the changes in behaviour that you have observed in Hussein since we walked through your door this evening.'

Mahmoud's mouth opened, but no words came out. He looked from one man to the other. He closed his mouth, swallowed, then spoke in a voice that was just audible. 'Forgive me Mehmet, but you ask too much of me.' He looked furtively in Hussein's direction.

Unexpectedly, Hussein raised the palm of his hand towards Mahmoud. 'By all means, please feel free to be as honest as it is possible to be. I will bear you no grudges because I myself am intensely curious to hear your answer.'

Mahmoud lowered his eyes as he considered for a few moments before responding in a slightly tremulous voice. 'With the deepest respect and honour, Hussein, I was painfully aware that when you first walked in through the door you spoke to me as if I was a servant. You were dismissive of me. Then, not thirty minutes ago, when you invited me to sit at this table to join you, you actually referred to me as "my friend". I was pleasurably aware of that shift in your attitude.'

Hussein's lips were pressed together in a thin line. He nodded slowly. 'I am inclined to agree with your observation. I apologise to you for my earlier discourtesy.'

'And that,' said Mehmet, 'is how I have been able to function in the secular world on a day-to-day basis. I have learned from my Sufi master the rudimentary method of projecting energetic Love. It is an art that anyone on earth can learn, because it requires virtually no talent at all—merely a change of attitude. One merely needs to adapt one's thinking to project positive, caring and loving thoughts.'

There was a protracted silence as the other two men took in his words, absorbing the enormity of what had been told to them. Their eyes were on Mehmet, while he, seemingly unaware of their gaze, started once again to eat his food which, by now, had become cold.

Hussein was the one who at last broke the silence. 'Forgive my bluntness, but with an outlook such as yours, why did you even consider participating in the arrangements we were discussing earlier … the reason that we met here today?'

Mehmet raised his head to look at Hussein. He slowly chewed a mouthful of food, then swallowed. 'I am afraid that I will need to ask you, Mahmoud, to give us a few moments of privacy, so that I might answer that question with frankness.'

The request brought Mahmoud back to his own reality. He noticed with some surprise that the restaurant was almost full and that his attentions were needed elsewhere. He turned first to Hussein and then to Mehmet. 'I wish to thank you for allowing me the privilege to participate in this evening's discussion.' He bowed slightly to both men, then faced Mehmet. 'I am indebted to you.' He took a step back before adding, 'I am disappointed to see that your food has now become cold. Please, I cannot accept any payment from either of you for your dinner this evening. And I hope we will meet again at some point in the near future.' He took another step back before turning his back to walk away.

Mehmet turned his body to face Hussein. 'You are a man who is fairly senior in his organization, are you not?'

Hussein merely nodded.

'Then here is my answer to your question. By my accepting your request to assist your organization, it put me into a position where I was able to have this particular conversation, and it has, demonstrably, had a constructive outcome. The channels of communication between us are now wide open, and there is a matter that needs to be communicated by you with some conviction at the most senior level within your organization.'

There was a barely perceptible stiffening in Hussein's posture. 'What is it that you wish me to communicate?' His voice was guarded.

Mehmet paused to structure his thinking before responding. At length, he said: 'Some months ago I was contacted by my Sufi master from Afghanistan. He instructed me to contact your organization, and you in particular. He informed me that the conflict in Palestine has escalated to a point where outside intervention is now required.'

'But it was I who contacted you.'

'Let me put it this way,' Mehmet said. 'You contacted me because I arranged for my presence and activities here to be brought to your attention.'

'How could you possibly have arranged that? My very existence is not known to more than a handful of people outside my own organization.' Hussein's fingers drummed on the tablecloth, his eyes sharply focussed on Mehmet.

'The answer to that question is complex. In any event, it is not relevant to what I have to say. We have limited time for what I have to communicate to you now, and, with your permission, I would prefer to focus on that.'

Hussein was torn, but indicated with an upward palm for Mehmet to continue.

'What I am about to communicate to you goes beyond the four principles that I revealed when Mahmoud was at the table. The only reason I am sharing this information, is that you need it as context in your communications with your superiors. In your heart, you are a still a Hashimite. You will therefore understand that what I am about to tell you is the absolute truth.'

'I can make you no promises, but I will listen to what you have to say.'

'Thank you.' Then, with no further preamble, Mehmet began. 'The famous scientist, Albert Einstein, brought to the world's attention that there is a phenomenon now known as the space–time continuum. From the perspective of man on earth, time moves in one direction only, namely forwards. We look backwards into history, and we look forwards into the future. From the perspective of Allah, however, the past, the present and the future co-exist. Time is therefore an illusion. Einstein's work validated this fact.'

He paused for a few seconds to allow Hussein to respond or ask questions. Receiving none, he continued. 'Nearly a thousand years ago, the Sufi masters—and your own ancestors were amongst them—had developed an ability to cognitively gather information from anywhere on the space–time continuum. Just as the biblical prophets had done, and just as our own prophet, Muhammad had done—peace be upon him. Specifically, they developed the ability in broad terms to "see" the past and also the future, and what my master sees in the future is the reason he has asked me to make contact.'

'What does he see?'

'He sees that mankind has reached a fork in the road in our journey towards adulthood. If we choose to go down one road, the disagreements and the violence will escalate to the point that the entire world will be drawn into the conflict. Under such circumstances, mankind will experience escalating conflagration and, ultimately, destruction. However, if we choose to go down the other road, mankind faces enlightenment beyond description. We will emerge into an era characterised by a millennium of peace. By analogy, the caterpillar will emerge as a butterfly.'

'And how can I do anything about this?'

'My master in Afghanistan would like to meet with your leader, who is currently in hiding in Pakistan. My master has asked that I request you to facilitate such a meeting to be held in private at the monastery.'

CHAPTER 23

IT TOOK TARA and Patrick a leisurely two hour car journey during the late afternoon on Friday to drive from Boca Chica to the Sunscape Casa del Mar in La Romana. Tara had filled Patrick in on her meeting with Yehuda and felt his focus suddenly sharpen when she mentioned the ancient maps.

'He wants to meet with both of us, so I took the liberty of arranging to have lunch with him—and with Aurelio—at the Zona Colonial tomorrow.'

'Good idea. And I get to meet the wonderful Aurelio at last.'

'Speaking of whom,' Tara said, as they were now driving through San Pedro de Macoris. 'Did you know that this town has spawned most of the famous Dominican baseball players in the US?'

'Really? That's interesting … which ones?'

Tara pulled a face. She had almost immediately forgotten most of the baseball related detail after Aurelio had told her, and now struggled to recall just one or two names. They rang no bells for Patrick, and the conversation ambled into their childhood sports and activities.

'I was more into ponies than ball sports,' Tara said. 'I had a pony my father named "Donkey". The name stuck, poor old thing. We used to ride all through the countryside in Massachusetts—we had a hobby farm there. Most of all, I loved the fall, with its blazing pastiche of reds and oranges, browns and gold. It was as if the leaves were preparing, gloriously, to meet their maker. It gave me such a sense of inner peace to be quietly at one with it all. Ultimately, that's probably why I took up flying. I get that same feeling when I'm at the controls of an aeroplane high above the Earth. I feel almost as if I was born to it.'

'I had the same with kayaking around the Ku-ring-gai Chase waterways at home,' Patrick reminisced. 'I could launch my kayak at any one of half a dozen places within fifteen minutes of our home. I'd sit there quietly, all on my own, in my kayak in the middle of the river, and all I could hear was the chatter and chirping of the birds, and the lap of the water against the hull. There were forests of powder-yellow acacia trees dotted between the eucalypts up and down the sides of the hills that rose up from the riverbanks. That's when I began to play around with nature photography. And that experience *also* led me to conclude that if I were to become a mining engineer, I could spend a lot of my time communing with nature.'

They drove in comfortable silence for a while until they reached La Romana.

'The hotel is more a family style resort,' Patrick said. 'We had a weekend executive offsite seminar here not too long ago. So the manager knows me, and has given us the penthouse suite they normally reserved for visiting celebrities ... which I of course told him you were.' There was laughter behind his eyes as he looked over at her.

'I shall do my best to behave disgracefully in the best celebrity tradition—so I don't let you down,' Tara said.

The look on her face led Patrick to believe she was somehow not talking about public displays of behaviour.

As the bellboy ushered them from the elevator and into their suite, Tara felt the tingle of excitement, anticipation and—unexpectedly—shyness at being in a hotel room with Patrick for the first time. She looked around her, wishing for the bellboy to disappear. Everything looked pristine—from the elegant cane furniture, to the collection of framed tropical gardens painted in oils. Freshly cut flowers stood on a small dining table beside a large crystal fruit bowl filled with an abundance of tropical fruits as well as strawberries, cherries and peaches flown in from who knows where. But no champagne chilling in an ice bucket?

When at last they were alone—with Tara feeling even more deliciously like an inexperienced schoolgirl—Patrick walked to the open sliding door onto the patio beyond. She followed, and there was the champagne with two chilled flutes. He busied himself for a few moments opening the bottle. The cork flew off towards the palm trees and the

Caribbean beyond. He handed her a glass and looked silently at her for a few more seconds before raising his own to toast her.

There was nothing of the jocular Patrick in his voice now. 'To the most beautiful woman I have ever laid eyes on, and to the something magical that's happening here.'

'To a time to remember,' Tara managed, a little overwhelmed by his words.

They sipped their champagne, each feeling the proximity of the other's body, and yet not touching. The waves whispered their way to shore and a slight rustling of the palm fronds announced the arrival of the evening breeze.

It was with a feeling of mounting anticipation that they left the privacy of their suite to walk to an Italian restaurant that Patrick had booked for dinner. Its front lawn reached to the silver sands of the beach, and diners sat sheltered from the weather by a thatched overhanging roof. The table to which Patrick and Tara were led had an exquisite, uninterrupted view of the beach and the ocean.

As the maître d' seated them, he addressed himself to Patrick. 'May I recommend the chef's special of the day, an entrée of lobster spaghettini? The lobster meat has been cooked in fresh tomato basil cream sauce served with asiago cheese.' Patrick looked at Tara inquiringly. She nodded.

'For two, thank you,' Patrick answered. The maître d' bustled around, unfolding white linen napkins with a flourish onto their laps and calling a waiter over to take the balance of their order.

Patrick put a hand on his sleeve before he could leave them. 'Also, the señorita and I would like to go for a walk on the beach after dinner. Could you please ask the chef to make us a flask of coffee with cream, when we have finished our dinner?'

'Of course sir, and a perfect evening for it. I hope that you and the señorita will enjoy a memorable occasion.'

Tara had been studying Patrick's features while he talked to the maître d'. His mop of unkempt dark blond hair framed a happy, uncomplicated face and a slightly receding hairline. His eyebrows were arched in a manner that was altogether too sexy. She wanted to laugh out loud in delight, and realised it was not the first time this had happened to her in his company. Her stomach tightened ever so slightly in anticipation of what lay ahead.

The restaurant, the meal and the evening combined into a memorable, 'proper' first date as Patrick called it, and when the waiter brought their thermos of coffee in a basket with fine china cups and four gold-wrapped chocolates, they made their way to the sand and into the moonlit darkness. Halfway along the beach they stopped to sit under a coconut palm, facing the ocean. Patrick propped his back against the trunk, patting his legs to invite Tara to sit with her back leaning against his chest. Her head rested comfortably on his collarbone, his mouth was at the level of her ear. The sound of his breathing was erotically audible to her whenever he kissed her lightly on her exposed neck or around the soft curve of her ears. He seemed to be in no particular hurry. When she could stand it no longer, she turned her body to face his.

He kissed her sensuously, exploring all her senses, and just when she thought she would burst with desire he broke away from her. He turned her gently to lie on the sand. She cushioned her head on her folded arms as he stroked the small of her back with his thumbs. Now and again his hands found the rounded mound of her buttocks. Then his fingers trailed the backs of her legs down to the soles of her feet. He stroked her insteps, her toes. Tara felt herself floating.

There had been no conversation for some time. They both lay on the sand now, gazing silently upwards at the night sky decorated with myriad twinkling pinpricks of light. Patrick was running his fingers gently through her hair, stroking her scalp lightly with his fingers when he broke the silence.

'The sky in the Northern Hemisphere looks very different from the one above Australia. From there the Southern Cross is always somewhere to be seen.'

She had been too spaced-out to respond with anything other than what sounded like 'hmmm,' breathed dreamily from the back of her throat.

She looked up at him. *Was he never going to suggest they head back to the hotel?*

'I really would like to go back now, please,' she whispered at last. He smiled in response, moving—with some difficulty, she noticed—to stand up.

They headed back the way they had come until Patrick stopped, a sheepish smile on his face. He put the basket down, opened the thermos and quickly poured the forgotten coffee onto the sand beside a palm tree.

'Some day, someone will be mystified by the coffee-flavoured coconut milk from this tree,' he said. They giggled conspiratorially.

'Do you want to shower the sand off?' Patrick asked as they entered their hotel suite.

'Good idea, it seems to be everywhere,' Tara answered, walking into the bathroom even as she started to disrobe.

When he heard the sound of the running water, Patrick turned to his luggage and took out an oil burner with a tea candle that he placed next to the hotel's CD player. Beside them he set down a small bottle of essential oils: yohimbe, sandalwood, woodruff, rose oil, jasmine, neroli oil. He selected a peach and a couple of strawberries from the fruit bowl, poured two snifters of Courvoisier that he found in the mini bar, and took the drinks and the plate of fruit out onto the balcony.

When Tara emerged from the bathroom minutes later she heard the barely audible strains of a Mozart string symphony emanating from the CD player. There was an aroma in the air that seemed to be a mixture of flowers, spices and something slightly more pungent, which she couldn't quite place. The bedside lamp furthest from the open sliding door sent its feeble light into what was an otherwise darkened apartment and patio beyond. She saw Patrick's outline as he sat on one of the outside chairs, and called out softly to him, 'Hello stranger.'

He had discarded his clothes and donned one of the hotel's towelling robes. He was on the point of lifting the balloon glass of cognac to his lips when he turned to face her. He rose and took a couple of steps towards her back into the apartment. 'You look magnificent,' he whispered, as he moved to embrace her. He covered her mouth with his, as her arms snaked under his gown to pull his body roughly, closer to hers. She felt his building erection under his shorts as, skin to skin, their torsos made contact down the lengths of their bodies.

'Darling, you're going to have to allow me to take the lead here if you don't want me to lose control,' he whispered. 'I need to stay off the fast track for a little while.' He kissed her again, with much more passion this time, before pulling himself away altogether. 'Why don't you put on your gown to keep warm, and sip the cognac very slowly while I take a cold shower? You might want to nibble on some peach and strawberry in between sips—the mixture of tastes is sensational. I'll be back in few minutes.'

'Hurry back,' she breathed.

When he came out of the bathroom it was Tara's turn to stare in admiration. Patrick did not have the body of an Adonis, but his wide shoulders and narrow hips formed a visual "V" that she found highly attractive. This time it was Tara who walked back inside the room towards him. Unselfconsciously, she let the gown slip from her shoulders as she embraced him. She found herself having to stand slightly on tiptoe to compensate for his height advantage. Her hand moved towards his inner thigh.

With that, he leaned over, picked her up and laid her down on the bed.

Time ticked by in slow motion. One corner of the un-drawn curtain in front of the open patio door twitched slightly, as a gentle breeze blew in from the sea.

Patrick sensed her skin texture was changing. The previous porcelain smoothness had been replaced by a slight roughness—indicating a damming up of electrical energy that would have nowhere to go until it was eventually released by orgasm. He kept the pressure mounting within her.

CHAPTER 24

TARA AND PATRICK woke soon after dawn the following morning, luxuriating in their feelings of newfound intimacy. It was not until around 8.30 that they emerged onto their patio. It was a bright, cloudless day. Two hungry gulls circled in the sky above the glittering sea where the fringe reef began. Occasionally one dived into the water, once re-emerging with a small fish wriggling it is mouth.

The sight of the gulls fishing for their breakfast reminded them that they were both, by now, ravenously hungry. Patrick phoned for room service to send up a gargantuan, calorie replenishing breakfast which they ate at the table on the patio.

They were both wrapped in their own cocoons of thought. Their feelings of inner contentment negated the need for any conversation beyond a few monosyllabic sounds like, 'aah!' and 'huh?'; and inconsequentials like, 'look at that sailboat over there', and: 'uh huh', and 'would you like some more juice?', 'mmm.'

Eventually, they had checked out of the hotel to drive back to Tara's hotel in the Zona Colonial. Neither paid any attention to the scenery, both basking in an afterglow which neither wanted to disturb. The miles and the minutes disappeared, and at a little past noon they walked into the hotel lobby to find the professor and Aurelio already waiting for them. Neither she nor Patrick particularly felt like eating but, out of politeness, Tara decided that it would be important to show some deference to Yehuda. After all, she *had* invited him to lunch.

About fifteen minutes into the lunchtime pleasantries, Tara looked across the table at Aurelio and noted the same saucer-eyed expression that she had seen on him the previous morning. From her perspective, all Patrick and Yehuda had been doing was exchanging basic, getting-to-know-one-another information. Patrick had been giving Yehuda a potted version of the history of the Federal Reserve System. Yehuda had been telling some anecdote about a secret society called the Skull and Bones, or something to that effect. It turned out that Yehuda was an only child, and that he had arrived in the Dominican Republic with his parents as refugees from Austria in the early 1940s. Although he had been brought up and educated on the island, he had earned his degrees at Harvard and M.I.T.

Tara kicked Aurelio lightly under the table and winked at him, smiling at the same time as if to say, 'Hey, don't worry about it. It's only two guys establishing their turf.' He smiled back sheepishly. At least Tara was paying him some attention.

'I understand from Tara that you are interested in the possibility that electromagnetic energy might one day replace oil,' Yehuda was saying. 'I am curious to know how your interest came about.'

Patrick raised his eyebrows and shrugged. 'There's nothing particularly startling about how I got the idea. A couple of years ago, I read a book called *The Shadow of Solomon*, by Sir Laurence Gardner.'

'I have not heard of this book,' Yehuda responded.

'The story you just told me about that secret Harvard alumni society was quite a coincidence. Gardner's book was about Freemasonry, and how the Freemasons might have had access to information that was known to King Solomon in biblical times. But I was less interested in the Freemasonry angle than in Gardner's speculation as to what that information might have been.'

'I myself am a student of the *Old Testament*,' Yehuda commented. 'King Solomon was certainly famous for his wisdom, and he was also a man of considerable influence and power, but I have not heard of any especially influential information to which he might have had access. Can you be more specific?'

'Well, I don't want you to think I'm crazy or anything like that, but something in that book captured my imagination.'

It seemed to Tara that Patrick was hedging. Was he nervous of sounding like a fool, or was he just reluctant to part with his information?

'Why don't you let me be the judge of that?' Yehuda suggested. 'I assume that Tara has told you that I also have an interest in electromagnetic energy. That is why I requested our meeting in the first place. Its very purpose is to allow us to compare notes.'

Patrick drew a breath. 'Well, okay, but I think it's important for you to understand that my only exposure to religion was when I was a kid, and my parents had to force me to attend Sunday school. I remember how, at one of those Sunday school classes, the teacher read us the story about how the children of Israel, who had escaped from Egypt under the leadership of Moses, had wandered through the desert for forty years, and how they had survived by augmenting their diet with manna that fell from the heavens.'

'Yes. I know that story well. According to the *Old Testament* it was a gift from God, who was protecting them in their wanderings.'

'Ah, excuse please,' said the waiter as he reached between the two men to place their food on the table.

Patrick glanced across the table at Tara and then Aurelio to discover that they too were showing more interest in his story than in the arrival of the food. *Full house.*

'The story made an impression on me too,' Patrick said. 'I don't want to insult you, Yehuda, but the reason it made an impression is that I thought it was nonsense. I remember thinking how gullible anyone who believed that story had to be to believe it.'

Yehuda did not react. Whilst he himself had developed a fairly sophisticated understanding of the *Torah*, he could see how, in a vacuum, such a story might sound ridiculous to a non-believer ... perhaps like a fairy tale. 'But if you thought that, why were you interested in what Gardner had to say in his book?'

'Towards the end of the book, Gardner told of a white powdery substance he had come across in *today's* world that is edible.' Patrick held his bread in the air to make his next point. 'Apparently it tastes like bread. But it also has some other properties that caught my attention, one of which is that this white powder can store an electrical charge. It is apparently superconductive.'

Yehuda's posture echoed that of Patrick's. 'And Gardner thought it may have been the manna referred to in the *Bible*?'

'That's the impression I got. He also seemed to be implying that if this was so, there might have also been a linkage between that powder and the Ark of the Covenant which the children of Israel carried around with them in the desert, and which was, of course, eventually housed in the Temple that Solomon built. The view expressed was that the Ark of the Covenant may have been a giant electrical capacitor that scavenged electromagnetic energy from the environment and stored it as an electrical charge in the manna that was housed inside it.'

A peculiar expression had crept over Yehuda's face. 'Interesting,' he said, noncommittally. He moved the food around on his plate but did not yet eat. 'Did Gardner speculate how the children of Israel might have come into possession of such a sophisticated energy technology?'

'Not really.'

'Do you have any views of your own, Patrick?' Yehuda probed.

'Again, not really, but I do have an, as yet, unformed view that maybe the ancient Egyptians had access to other very sophisticated technologies, because some of the pyramid stones—those that were not cast in situ—must have been extremely difficult to cut with such precision. For example, I read recently that the inside of the huge granite box in the King's Chamber of the Great Pyramid was finished off to an accuracy that modern manufacturers reserve for precision surface plates. It would have been impossible to get that degree of accuracy by hand.'[iii]

'Where would they have acquired such technologies?' Yehuda asked. It seemed an innocent question. 'There is no evidence to suggest that they evolved any technologies—other than circumstantial evidence.'

'Tara has also told me about the maps in your office and about how you think that civilization may have predated the current Holocene interglacial. I suspect that you are trying to prod me in that direction. Am I right?'

'Science is about evidence, not speculation, Patrick. I am keeping an open mind on what you are telling me, because I assume that Gardner did unearth some evidence regarding this white powder you speak of.'

'I tell you what, I'll make a trade with you,' Patrick countered. 'Energy is not my field, it's yours. But I do have some palaeontology related information that you might find of some interest regarding the history of civilization. As a mining engineer this is a subject that crops up from time to time because, when we dig deep beneath the Earth's surface in our mining activities, we sometimes uncover more than just nickel or tin or silver, or whatever it is we happen to be mining. My deal is this. I'll share my palaeo-anthropological information with you if you can tell me something about how the Ark of the Covenant might physically have scavenged electromagnetic energy from the environment.'

Yehuda smiled. 'A poker player I see. I'll see your electromagnetic technology and raise you a palaeo-anthropological discovery. Is that it?'

Patrick just looked at him. He really didn't know where to go from here. The professor seemed to be laughing at him.

What Yehuda said next therefore came as a surprise. 'I agree. Why don't we meet next Sunday evening at my home, and between now and then I will research the subject that is of interest to you? In the meantime, what palaeontology information do you have?'

Patrick looked at Tara and then at Aurelio and then back to Tara. She was smiling encouragingly. 'Go for it. It's a generous offer on the part of a busy professor of physics.'

Patrick said nothing for a minute or two. He played with his food for a bit, but he wasn't really hungry. He noticed that of all of them, Aurelio was most intent on his food and had almost finished the enormous meal he had ordered. Patrick looked into the distance before speaking.

'Do you know what a clovis point is?'

'If I'm not mistaken, it's an ancient spear point that was chipped out of stone by prehistoric man. It connected to a short wooden shaft that fitted into a heavier and longer wooden handle so that it became a reloadable throwing spear.

'I'm impressed. But do you know when these clovis points were made?'

'I'm no expert on the subject, and on top of that my memory is hazy, but I seem to remember that the hunters in question lived around the end of the last Ice Age—so that would be around 11,000 years ago.'

'Spot on, Yehuda. Now here's an interesting twist. It might be of interest to you to hear that in the 1950s, a Canadian anthropologist at a dig called Sheguiandah on Manitoulin Island in Lake Huron between Canada and Michigan found several clovis points at that site.[iv] Four geologists inspected the site to determine how old it was, and three of the four thought that the site was from the interglacial period *before* this one.'

Yehuda stared at him, his brow furrowed. 'That's impossible. There must have been an error of some sort. The last interglacial was the Eemian interglacial, and that peaked about 125,000 years ago.'

Patrick was unfazed. 'I invite you to consider your initial reaction. You used the word "impossible". Presumably, that's what the fourth geologist thought, and that's why they issued a joint statement—signed by all four of them—that the site was a minimum of 30,000 years of age. There was apparently a temporary period of warming within the Wisconsin glaciation period that followed, and that occurred roughly 75,000 years ago, and that's what the most outspoken of the geologists settled on. The 30,000 number was a meaningless compromise.'

'But that's still impossible. That would mean that the Americas were inhabited 19,000 to 64,000 years before our history books say they were. It would mean that the anthropological text books would all have to be rewritten.'

'I absolutely, agree with you. And guess what happened to the anthropologist, when he continued to insist that the conclusions drawn from that dig were conclusive?'

'Well, as an academic myself, I would imagine that his reputation was placed on the line.'

'Exactly right. In fact, he lost his job at the National Museum of Canada, and was unable to find another job for a prolonged period. His boss, the director of the museum was fired because he had refused to fire him. Several articles that the anthropologist submitted for publication were refused, and it was reported that the artefacts that he had found "vanished into storage bins" at the museum.' Patrick raised his fingers to draw the quotation marks in the air.

'Have you considered the possibility that he was wrong in his conclusions, and that, therefore, he should have been fired?' Yehuda asked with a tolerant smile.

'I guess it's possible, but the story doesn't end there. In 1954—before he started to publish—the site was visited by a party of geologists from the Michigan Basin Geological Society. None of these geologists expressed any dissension to the geological conclusion that the excavation was from a formation known as an "ice-laid till"—referring to the Wisconsin glacial till. The objections only started to manifest after the anthropologist began to argue that the clovis points he had uncovered must have been from the same era as the glacial till.'

'So what did the geologists say when he began to argue this way?'

Patrick smiled. 'Modern day lecturers on the subject accept everything about Sheguiandah, but they explain to their students that the deposits date from a period of post-glacial mudflow, rather than Wisconsin glacial till. The post- glacial mudflow would have occurred around the commencement of the current Holocene Interglacial—around 11,000 to 15,000 years ago. And the package is now tied up with neat pink ribbon, so to speak.'

'Do they submit any evidence to justify this conclusion?'

'To my knowledge, not one skerrick of proof has ever been offered to validate the post-glacial mudflow hypothesis.'

'So what conclusion do you draw?'

Patrick did not answer. Instead, he lifted the glass of cola that he had ordered with his meal, and drained it. The four were seated in a manner where he and Tara were sitting on one side of the table, and Yehuda and Aurelio were on the other. He turned his head to look directly at Tara, only to find that her face mirrored Yehuda's expression of anticipation. Aurelio looked out of his depth. Why was Tara was so insistent on including him?

'Earth to Patrick,' Tara prompted. 'Have we lost contact?'

He moved his knee over to rest against her thigh—he couldn't resist it—after all she had asked for contact. He suppressed a smile, then turned back to face Yehuda, to find that he was looking at Tara and smiling at her fondly. At least it was a paternal smile.

He cleared his throat. 'One needs to understand that the reason the anthropological establishment community is so adamant, flows from DNA markers, amongst other things.'

Aurelio said nothing, but Patrick could see he was certainly paying attention now that his meal was finished. It was then that he remembered Aurelio was a medical student. Maybe he wasn't as far out of his depth as he seemed.

'Biologists have identified a DNA marker that traces back to a Bushman tribe in the Kalahari desert of Namibia—the SAR Bushman. Precisely the same DNA marker is also present in the Chukchi tribe living today at the edge of the Bering Strait that divides Siberia in Russia from Alaska.'

'Why is that relevant?' Aurelio asked at last.

'Because there is evidence to support the conclusion that about 11,000 years ago the ancestors of present day Chuckchis crossed dry land that is now covered by the waters of the Bering Straight, and migrated to North America via Alaska. Exactly the same DNA marker has been found in tribes of the North American Indians and, in fact, this same DNA marker is present in much of present day mankind. Against a backdrop of this "hard" DNA evidence, the anthropological establishment is unable to embrace the idea that there may have been other, modern human inhabitants of the Americas prior to 11,000 years ago—or anywhere else, other than Africa, for that matter—prior to 50,000 years ago.'

'At face value it appears to me that these two thought paradigms may indeed be irreconcilable,' Yehuda said. 'The dates attributable to the clovis points must therefore be erroneous.'

'Alternatively, the two thought paradigms could *both* be correct,' Patrick countered. 'Our current thinking on DNA markers is still relatively new and the conventional wisdom is that 99.9 percent of the more than 6 billion humans alive today are similar when it comes to genetic content and identity. However ... there was a recent journal article which pointed out that, until now, analysis of the genome has focussed overwhelmingly on comparing flaws, or polymorphisms, in single "letters" in the chemical code for making and sustaining human life. It now appears this approach may have been flawed and that there is a wider variation amongst humans than was previously believed to be the case.'[v]

'But it would not necessarily negate the Out of Africa conclusion,' Yehuda countered. 'It might just prove that there have been mutations along the way.'

'Or it might be that the marker in the Bushmen may have been inherited from humans who had populated the earth during earlier times. Human DNA strands are sufficiently long to accommodate more than one marker. It's quite possible that there may have been interbreeding with different strains of humans along the way.'

'So what's your conclusion regarding the dating of the clovis points from that island in Lake Huron?' Tara asked.

'I'm inclined to believe that those clovis points were far older than conventional wisdom would allow, and that throws some significant doubt on the straight line evolutionary theory that Darwin was proposing.'

'In practical terms, have you found any other evidence that would suggest that the Sheguiandah dig was not an isolated case?' Yehuda asked.

'Actually, yes, I've come across a plethora of examples that do not fit neatly within the context of a linear evolution of humankind.'

'Can you give us more examples?' Yehuda asked.

'Well, for one, there was an extraordinary report early last century in the *New York Sunday American*, of a fossilized human footprint found in a rock surface in Nevada by a mining engineer by the name of Reid.[vi] That was what made me pay particular attention because I too have seen some strange things in my time.'

'A footprint doesn't sound too strange though,' Tara ventured.

'Well, firstly, the print was not of a bare foot, but of the sole of a manmade shoe.'

'How did Reid validate that it was the sole of a shoe, and not something that just coincidentally looked like the sole of a shoe?'

'I can see that you did not become a professor by being sloppy in your methodologies.' Patrick said, a wry smile on his face. 'After showing the fossilized imprint to a geologist at Colombia University in New York and three professors at the Museum of Natural History, these four men unanimously concluded that it was, quote "the most remarkable natural imitation of an artificial object that they had ever seen", unquote.'

'You mean, nature imitating man-made?' Tara asked. 'That's a new twist.'

'Well, I think Reid probably was of the same mind because he had microphotographs taken of the imprint and had them blown up to twenty times in size.' Patrick paused with the hint of a mischievous smile.

'What did they show?' the three asked in chorus.

'They showed—in the minutest detail—the twist and warp of the thread that had been used to sew the sole of the shoe to its body. It was definitely man-made.'

'And the estimated age of the rock?' Yehuda asked.

'Now that's the second fact which I found so strange. Two separate geologists have validated that the rock came from the Triassic period, which dates back between 213 and 248 million years.'

Tara looked shocked. 'Whoa. Are you trying to tell us that a fully evolved man—wearing the equivalent of modern day shoes—walked the Earth 250 million years ago?'

'Absolutely not. No, the purpose of these two examples is to illustrate the principle that one cannot rely on the precision typically associated with palaeo-anthropological dating techniques.'

'O … kay, so why's that important?' Tara asked.

Patrick leant forward, the sides of his hands rigidly poised on the edge of the table. He looked as though he was about to go in for a kill. 'Because if the dating techniques are so rubbery in their results, the argument that man evolved in a stepped fashion from apes to humans is probably facile. This does not mean that Darwin's entire theory of evolution is flawed. That would be like throwing the baby out with the bathwater. It merely demonstrates that to draw a trend-line of evolution, which does not allow for parallel developments, is too simplistic and childlike in its logic.'

'What's the alternative?' Tara asked.

'It's conceivable that sophisticated humans have been present on this planet for far longer than the anthropologists are allowing for in their compartmentalised logic,' he responded. Out of the corner of his eye he detected a slight movement of Yehuda's head as the professor nodded in agreement.

He turned to address Yehuda directly. 'Apes and missing links notwithstanding, it seems highly probable—based on the large body of evidence that does *not* fit comfortably within the neat and tidy evolution model—that the population of thinking man might have waxed and waned over the aeons, as the Earth was subjected to a series of environmental catastrophes. Alternatively, thinking man might have evolved differently in different parts of the world, and today's population might be made up of more than one strain of humanity—but all of whom finally came together at a convergence point.'

'Getting back to your shoe sole example,' Yehuda interrupted. 'I am reminded of an interesting coincidence in timing.'

'Coincidence?'

'Not very long ago, I read a news report describing an observation by a geologist associated with the Ohio State University,' Yehuda answered. 'Apparently, recently available satellite data suggests that a crater impact that had been discovered in Antarctica dates back 250 million years. The 300-mile wide crater lies more than a mile beneath a sheet of ice in the Wilkes Land region of the east Antarctic ice sheet, and this geologist—von Frese is his name—he observed that this was sufficiently large to represent the probable cause of extinction of ninety percent of the species on Earth at that time, paving the way for dinosaurs to rise to prominence.'

'You have to admit that these and other examples like them certainly lead to the conclusion that one at least needs to keep an open mind regarding the origins of man.'

Tara felt the need to add her two cents' worth. 'Maybe all this evidence also points to a possible explanation regarding the source of information on the map that Yehuda told me about the other day?'

Her observation caused a lull in the conversation, which Yehuda was the first to break. 'In the context of that map, another of von Frese's observations is highly relevant. He believes the crater's size and location are such that the impact could have been the catalyst to the break-up of the Gondwana supercontinent.'

'I haven't seen the map; why is that relevant?' Patrick wanted to know.

'Because, at the time of the impact, the point of impact would have been free of ice, and since that impact, the continents have been slowly drifting further away from the Antarctic. Both the Piri Rei's map and my friend's map show the landmass below the Antarctic ice as it is today. As far as we can tell, the first Ice Age began 40 million years ago, and the land under the Antarctic must have been buried under ice for at least that long.'

'Alternatively,' Patrick chimed in, 'the map on your wall was able to be drawn because the technology to facilitate it was available thousands of years before it was reinvented by modern man after World War II?'

'Well, gentlemen,' Tara said by way of what she intended would be a wrap-up. 'After listening to what both of you have had to say over the past few days I, for one, am prepared to accept the physical evidence that humankind of today is not the first, nor the only group of intelligent inhabitants of our fair planet. I may even be receptive to an argument about extra terrestrials, and the introduction of a new genetic strain around 5,200 years ago.' The smile on her face implied that she was only being half serious. 'Either Adam lived much earlier than we thought, or he was the first of a brand new human community that suddenly emerged back in the dawn of modern civilization.'

Yehuda, turned to Patrick. 'Do you agree?'

'Unless one believes in extra terrestrial visitors, which I'm not inclined to do because there's no immediately apparent reason that they would have come and then just gone away again, it's hard to argue other-wise,' Patrick responded. 'I guess that's the only logical conclusion I can come to. I'm more inclined to accept that waxing and waning has occurred as a result of natural catastrophes from time to time.'

'Well now.' Yehuda said, in what seemed to Tara to be a conscious effort to embrace the dramatic. 'I think that the time has come for me to pass on some other information to you, so that we might pool our intellectual resources.'

'Shall we order coffees first?' Tara asked as the waiter hovered. Orders were taken and then the professor leant forward, almost conspiratorially. Tara thought there was a hint of mischief in his brown eyes.

'Do you remember that thunderstorm of a few days ago?'

'Do I ever! I could hardly forget it given that I was right in the deep end of it.'

The professor looked like a man who had a point to make, and nothing was going to stop him from making it. 'Would you be surprised to hear that the thunderstorm was a direct consequence of an experiment in physics that I had my students conduct?'

Tara's head swivelled to face Yehuda.

Aurelio, who had only spoken one sentence during the entire lunchtime, sat stiffly upright.

Patrick's head jolted back slightly and he arched his eyebrows. 'Are you telling me that you manufactured that thunderstorm?' he asked.

'Yes, that is what I am telling you. Gerardo—your brother—was part of it,' he said, turning to Aurelio.

The three listeners remained silent. It seemed an outrageous claim. And yet, in the short time they had known him, it seemed out of character for him to joke or exaggerate. Eventually, it was the professor who broke the silence.

Patrick, one reason I wanted to meet with you today is that Tara told me about your view that we might be facing the possibility of a global cooling period. Is this correct?'

'Yes. But the thunderstorm experiment?'

Yehuda smiled infuriatingly, but did not elaborate further. 'Although I would still like to meet next Sunday evening, as we discussed earlier, I would also appreciate an hour or so of your and Tara's time on, say, this coming Wednesday in my office at Uwaasd. There is some important related information that I have there which I would like to share with you. Would six o'clock be convenient for you?'

CHAPTER 25

PATRICK TURNED HIS car into Todd Allbright's driveway. The house was located in a quiet, tree-lined street a couple of blocks away from the US embassy and maybe a kilometre away from the National Palace. On the drive over he'd told Tara a little of Todd's background. She could see he hadn't been exaggerating—this was prime real estate. It must have cost in the multiple millions of dollars.

Desirée greeted them at an imposing oak front door. She looked elegant and understated, even in a couturier designed silk dress. Tara felt self-conscious in her own simple cotton print dress and flat-heeled shoes. Patrick had neglected to inform her that this was to be anything other than a casual dinner amongst corporate peers. Okay, this was something she'd learnt about him today. That and what he'd chosen to wear himself: a plain white shirt, brown slacks and tan coloured casual shoes. Only his leather Gucci belt was at all sartorially noteworthy, and had probably cost more than the rest of his clothes put together. *Ah men; got to love their social graces.*

Desirée shook Patrick's hand first, then turned to hug Tara. There was just the faintest hint of what might have been Clive Christian No. 1.

'Welcome, Tara and thank you so much for agreeing to join us at such short notice,' she said with what sounded like genuine warmth.

Something Tara's father had once said echoed in her mind—that the definition of a lady is a woman who can make any man seem like a gentleman, and any woman feel like an ally. She felt her embarrassment quickly recede. Regardless of Desirée's own stylish attire and the simple silver and pearl jewellery, she impressed Tara as someone who did not need to judge others by what they wore.

Their hostess led them into a high ceiling lounge room where several other guests were gathered, and began to make the introductions.

'Aha, so you were the man with Patrick at the restaurant,' Tara said on being introduced to Todd.

'Welcome, Tara. We feel honoured that you accepted Patrick's invitation to join him at a dinner party full of strangers.' Desirée's husband was equally charming and gracious.

She took his outstretched hand. 'You and Desirée have already made me feel as if I belong here, Todd. Thank you.'

Mehmet was there too. Tara had noticed him talking to a school-marmish young woman when they entered the room and now Todd led her towards him. 'I believe you know Mehmet,' he said, 'and may I introduce you to Juanita.'

Mehmet and Juanita's body language did not suggest two people who knew each other well and Tara surmised that Juanita had been invited to even the gender balance.

'Juanita works at the National Library across the road from the US embassy,' Todd offered as if telepathically responding to her thought. 'Juanita and Desirée met there when Desirée was reading up on the history of Hispaniola.'

'*Soy muy feliz encontrarle*. I am very happy to meet you, Tara and Patrick.'

There were two other couples present: Eugenia Alvarez, who Desirée had met through Juanita; Professor Carlos Alvarez, a professor of history; Peter Haddon III and Dawn Haddon. Peter was introduced as a fourth generation expatriate American, and a sugar farmer.

Peter rose from his chair and shook their hands, whilst Dawn remained seated, accepting first Tara's proffered hand and then Patrick's.

'The Haddon family has retained its American ties,' Desirée explained, 'but they've become so much part of this country that some people now describe you as a Dominican sugar baron, don't they Peter?'

'Not to my face,' he responded, with a faint smile. In those few moments his manner exuded wealth and power, with an edge of hardness about him—a killer instinct close to the surface. By contrast, Dawn looked to Tara much like someone who lacked the courage to express herself. The monochromatic hue of her clothes and lack of jewellery let her blend into the background of the room and the flow of conversation. She hadn't yet uttered a word.

Tara turned her attention back to Desirée and Peter, then heard Patrick's voice behind her.

'So Baroness, what do you think of life on this idyllic island?'

What? How did he know about that? She swivelled on her heel to face him, only to discover that he was talking to Dawn, not her. She relaxed, and quietly observed him. With unerring instinct, he had honed in on Dawn as the one person in the room who needed attention.

'Something wrong?'

'Err, no. I'm fine. Thank you, Desirée.' She had to pull herself together. After all, she and Patrick were supposed to be a long standing item. Could she carry it off? Her thoughts trailed away and she found herself thinking of the comic strip *Peanuts* with the Red Baron flying ace, and how she had come to be referred to as 'baroness' by the immediate members of her family. *There's no way Patrick could have known about that. Just relax girl! Go with the flow.*

Tara's reverie was interrupted by Todd, who appeared by her side with a sharply triangular, long-stemmed cocktail glass.

'Dominican Rum and sour cream, with a hint of maple syrup. I call it my ambrosia.'

Tara enjoyed the relaxing effect of the cocktail. She tuned in and out of the conversations that flowed around her. She caught the words 'Napoleon' and 'Haiti' and 'uprising'. Professor Alvarez was telling Mehmet about how the Haitian slaves were emancipated … She looked at Patrick again; he seemed unconscious of the wealth around him—or at least not intimidated by it. Tara had to admit to herself, that she was just a little over-awed. Peter III's diamond studded solid gold Rolex could not have cost anything less than $50,000.

'The idea for the lighthouse as a monument to Columbus was originally conceived in 1878,' she heard Juanita saying. 'But it took until 1923 before it was formally resolved to build it.'

'That's forty-five years from thought to deed,' Patrick observed.

'One needs to understand, Patrick,' Peter III said, 'that in our part of the world, the wheels of politics turn slowly.'

'It was built in the shape of a huge cross and it is longer and wider than a football field. Two beams of light are projected forty-four miles up to form a gigantic cross in the sky. On a clear night the light can be seen as far away as Puerto Rico.'

'Puerto Rico! How far away is that from the Dominican Republic?' Patrick asked.

'It's around 250 miles from Santo Domingo to San Juan in Puerto Rico,' Tara broke into the conversation.

'Tara's a pilot with Delta Airlines,' Patrick said with a smile in her direction that seemed to exclude everyone else in the room.

'Nowadays, people pay to fly to this country in your comfortable aeroplanes,' Juanita continued. 'But in the old days, they travelled mostly as unwilling passengers—as slaves in the holds of ships. It's because of these varied backgrounds that there still lingers today a superstitious view of life amongst many of the illiterate population and even amongst some of those who are literate. For example, did you know that, according to Dominican folklore, many still believe the name Columbus to be cursed—the *fucu de Colon*, the curse of Columbus?'

There were polite murmurs.

'Yes, really,' Juanita continued to her captive audience. 'These people believe the very name of Columbus is jinxed; and that if his name should be uttered aloud, the jinx can only be warded off by shouting "Zafa"— as if the devil could be chased back into his box. For this reason he is referred to as the "Great Admiral" or the "Discoverer", and many believe that Columbus Day itself will bring bad luck.'

'I must say I found it very interesting,' Desirée said, 'that when the Dominicans first flirted with democracy, they tended to elect either weak or corrupt leaders. But it seems that, since 1996, the country has been moving more steadily towards genuine democracy.'

'A fragile one, as is so often the case,' Todd said, 'with the conservative Christian Socialists formed by Balageur aligning with the leftist PRD in the 2006 elections.'

'Men using any means available to them to grab personal power. Testosterone politics,' Desirée said with a teasing tone to her voice.

Tara smiled at Desirée's mischief and noted that while Eugenia also smiled, Dawn seemed somewhat discomforted. Intuitively, Tara glanced at Patrick to discover that he was also looking in Dawn's direction. She had been right. Patrick did have a protective instinct about him. The feelings of warmth towards him were the same she had experienced when she'd read about the way he had empathised with the young boy on the bridge during the storm.

One of the servants stood discreetly in the doorway and signalled to Desirée. 'Ladies and gentlemen, dinner is ready to be served,' she announced. 'Shall we make our way through to the dining room?'

The dinner table in the adjacent room was picture perfect it seemed to Tara—as if set to be photographed by *Architectural Digest*. The fine bone china had a cobalt white glaze edged with silver leaf. The heavy silver cutlery looked like a family heirloom.

The guests seated themselves according to place cards, and as the first course was served, it was Patrick who opened the conversation.

'Your reference to Napoleon reminded me of the story of Mr Smith,' he said, addressing himself to Carlos. 'Mr Smith was visiting a psychiatrist,' he began. 'He was dressed exactly as Napoleon would have dressed—a three-cornered hat and the same type of waistcoat that you see in Napoleon's portraits, with his hand tucked into one of the openings between the buttons.' Patrick undid a button and inserted his own hand into his own shirt front.

' "How can I help you?" asks the psychiatrist.

"You can't help me," the man answers grandly. "I'm Napoleon. I don't need any help. I'm a powerful man. I have a powerful army. I am rich. I have whatever I need." '

Patrick paused, looked at the listening faces, then continued.

' "Then why are you here?" asks the psychiatrist.

"It's my wife," answers Napoleon. "She thinks she's Mrs Smith. Do you think you'll be able to help her?" '

There was a ripple of laughter around the table.

The attention around the tabled turned to the food and as the conversation waned, Tara turned to Desirée but spoke loudly enough to address the rest of the table. 'Speaking of Mr and Mrs Smith, Desirée, it occurs to me that you and Todd have very interesting initials. I imagine if I had been the master of ceremonies at your wedding reception, I would have been tempted to say, "Ladies and Gentlemen I have pleasure in introducing Mr Todd Albright and Mrs Desirée Albright: TA DA!" '

It took a moment for the joke to be understood, and surprisingly it was Dawn who laughed the loudest. Todd looked at Tara appreciatively. Mehmet clapped his hands softly. 'Tara,' he said, in a tone of voice that was clearly intended to be teasing 'I see that your mind is embracing wedding related thoughts. Am I to infer from this that you and Patrick are starting to make plans?'

The silence was deafening. Tara felt the flush rise up her neck. She couldn't look at Patrick—the look would be misinterpreted by everyone present.

'Mehmet, do you know something that the rest of us should be told about?' Desirée asked.

Mehmet's face was a study in innocence. 'Until three days ago, I never knew that Patrick had a girlfriend. The three of us had dinner together on Wednesday evening, and that was when I discovered the two lovebirds have been evolving a long distance relationship for a couple of years now. It appears that Tara has been Patrick's well kept secret, but I am pleased to tell you all that it seemed obvious to me they are very well suited to one another. Now I hear Tara talking about what she might have said at your wedding. Naturally, I am curious.'

Tara's eyes darted to Patrick. He was looking intently at Mehmet. All other eyes were on Tara.

Patrick was torn between his inclination to run with the impromptu charade and wanting to protect Tara. The practical reality of teasing Tara wasn't half as much fun as the theory of it. He took the middle ground. 'Come on, Mehmet, that's an unfair question. Tara and I have had no serious discussion on the subject. On the other hand, though,' he continued, turning to face Tara, 'you were going to flag the idea to your family about my meeting them. Any possible dates on the horizon? Have you run it past them yet?'

Okay, he was giving her a way out. She reached down into her handbag and pulled out her Blackberry. 'Fortunately, Mehmet himself is my witness. I think I still have the email that I sent from the Starbucks café on Monday where he and I met.' She scrolled through her emails, head down and in the process managed to avoid everyone's gaze.

'Here it is,' she said triumphantly, handing the Blackberry to Mehmet. 'I'll be happy for you to read it out to everyone.'

'*Hi Ken,*' Mehmet read aloud. '*Just a quick note to confirm our Thanksgiving dinner arrangements. Off to Dominican Republic on my three week vacation this afternoon. Love to mom. Tell her I'll be thinking of her and I'll be bringing her a surprise from DR when we get together. Love Baroness.*'

Mehmet looked at Tara with an odd expression in his eyes. 'This is the message you were composing when we met at Starbucks?'

'Baroness?' This, from Patrick, who seemed to have forgotten the charade they were supposed to be playing.

Before she could answer either question, Todd interrupted. 'You first met Mehmet on Monday?' he asked, a wide-open smile on his face. He seemed to be bursting with curiosity. Did he really not know, or was he rescuing her?

Tara's eyes were on fire. She was back in control. 'Yes I met-Mehmet-on-Monday,' she said, slowly emphasising the alliteration 'And she-sells-sea-shells-on-the-seashore.'

She saw the stunned look on Patrick's face. 'What's the metter with you?' she asked, with an expression of child-like innocence.

For the first time in his life Patrick was unable to think of anything to say. He and Mehmet had agreed they would work together to pull her chain—she was the one who was supposed to be scrambling here. Not only had she wriggled out of it, but she had come up with this impossible email. Spooky.

The seconds passed. He was not going to be left high and dry. He turned to Dawn. 'Wheht deh yeh mehk ehf ehll thehs?' he asked, continuing to play on the vowels from Mehmet's name as Tara had seemed to do.

Dawn looked at him like a frightened rabbit caught in crosshairs. Then, from somewhere in her girlhood came, 'Eh hehv neh ehdehya,' She giggled at herself. The look on her face said she really had no idea where her answer had come from.

Peter looked at his wife in amazement. How long had it been since he had heard her crack a joke like that? Ten years? Twenty years? He reached over and playfully took her hand. 'Dehn't yeh thehnk theht weh shehld ehsk Tehreh?'

A rush of hibernating confidence seemed to flood back to Dawn as a smile lit up her face. 'Ehbsehlehtleh,' she said, turning to face Tara. 'Explehn plehs!'

All eyes were once again on Tara, including Patrick's.

They waited for her to say something.

Tara's mind raced through the possibilities. Eventually, she sighed, and a single word escaped her lips. 'Busted!' She turned to Mehmet. 'I have a confession. Patrick and I only met a few minutes before you walked into the restaurant on Wednesday. We took an impromptu decision to kid around. We thought it might be fun.'

'I know,' Mehmet answered, smiling angelically. 'Patrick told me the next day,'

'You knew!' she turned accusingly to Patrick. 'You told him, and … and didn't tell me?' She turned back to Mehmet. 'And *you* threw me this marriage hand grenade, knowing that we had only just met?'

'What?' Mehmet responded. 'Did you think you had cornered the market on fun? You forget you are dealing with a commodity trader. No one can corner the market in anything anymore.'

There was laughter around the table.

'Do I still get to meet your family on Thanksgiving?' Patrick asked with a hint of boyish naughtiness, and then before she could answer, 'How the hell did you happen to have that email in your Blackberry? That was spooky.'

Tara cleared her throat. 'Remind me to drown you when we go scuba diving.' Then she smiled. 'The email was just a coincidence. My brother wanted me to confirm our Thanksgiving dinner—to which I hereby invite you by the way—and that's what the email was about. I was expecting to buy some blue amber while I was here. I wanted to give one piece to each member of my family, but I wanted it to be a surprise, so I didn't tell him what I was planning.'

Their host took the lead and called from the other end of the table, 'Bravo Tara.'

'The course of true love never did run smooth,' Eugenia said. 'Patrick, I hope you will have the good sense to accept Tara's gracious offer—notwithstanding the ungentlemanly behaviour that you and Mehmet have just now displayed.'

'*Moi*?' he answered with a pained expression on his face, the palm of his right hand flattened against his chest. 'Hey, I'm the innocent one here. This one started it all,' he said, gesturing at Tara. 'And Mehmet is also innocent. All he did was to return the serve she gave him on Wednesday night.' Patrick gazed at Tara with affection. 'But I'll tell you what. I *am* prepared to admit to anyone who will listen, that in three days flat you have managed to capture my heart.' Then he took her hand, lifted it to his lips and kissed her fingers. 'Thank you. I would love to meet your family on Thanksgiving.' His words were clear enough for all to hear.

The women smiled, and there was a touch of nostalgia and even envy on some of their faces. Dawn blinked her eyes, then launched into a laughing conversation with Desirée. Peter emptied his wineglass and looked in happy amazement at his wife.

Mehmet and Juanita, seated next to one another, became engrossed in an animated conversation. Eugenia joined in the conversations to her right and across the table, while the academic in Carlos quietly observed the cultural differences around the room.

CHAPTER 26

IN A DRABLY furnished room, on the day after Todd and Desirée's dinner party, two men sat comfortably in each other's company. Along the full length of the two longer walls were floor-to-ceiling bookshelves stacked end to end with volumes, some packed two deep. Between their two chairs stood a wooden coffee table that despite its age still showed hints of its origins at the hands of a master craftsman. The older of the two men relaxed in a rocker-recliner smoking a briar pipe. His head rested against the olive coloured leather which, by no stretch of anyone's imagination, could be said to coordinate with any other item in the room. From time to time the professor's thoughts became so engrossed that he forgot to draw on his pipe. The tobacco stopped smouldering. When he eventually became conscious of this fact, the ritual of packing, lighting, drawing and puffing would begin all over again.

A cloud of distinctively aromatic tobacco hung between the men. Even as a devout non-smoker, the younger man found the aroma pleasant. He sat meditatively, feet flat on the floor, hands lying loosely in his lap, palms facing upwards. From long experience, he knew that after his companion's deep contemplation, the forthcoming conversation would be thought provoking. For his part, he was content to focus on a single imaginary and repetitive sound that allowed his mind to drift formlessly.

His thoughts quietened as the wavelengths of electromagnetic energy within his brain began to harmonise. Gradually, they evinced a languid elongation from their normal, relaxed alpha frequency. His heartbeat slowed. His blood pressure fell. His breathing became shallow—the theta waves kicked in. His mind edged ever closer towards the universal consciousness until, eventually, his fully harmonised brainwaves reached the delta frequency. It was the closest he could approach to a state of enlightenment. Except for the faint glimmer of pineal activity that tethered him tenuously to Earthly consciousness, his mind had merged with the greater whole—a single drop of water in the ocean of space and time.

The professor broke into Mehmet's meditation. 'Have you ever contemplated the process of annealing steel?'

Slowly, the electrical flows within Mehmet's brain reactivated, as his consciousness resumed normal earthbound functionality. It took about fifteen seconds. He opened his eyes, smiled, stretched.

'Not really.'

He showed no curiosity, made no move to continue the conversation. From their regular monthly meetings, he understood that the professor's rationale would not be immediately revealed and that this was his way of embarking on a journey of communication which, eventually, would land up with the annealing of steel being applied as some form of esoteric analogy.

The older man looked at his friend and smiled. 'One day I would like you to teach me how you do that—your meditation,' he said. 'I imagine that it was in a similar manner that Muhammad and all the prophets before him communicated with God's angels.'

'I am afraid that you would be wrong, Yehuda. You forget that I am merely an initiate, a baby who is still learning to crawl. All I am able to do is *merge* my consciousness—a trivial accomplishment relative to the manner in which the Sufis are able to *expand* their consciousness, and to how the Prophet Muhammad—peace be upon him—was able to expand his own consciousness even further to receive information that ordinary mortals could not.'

Yehuda sighed. 'Yes, I suppose so.'

Mehmet had been down this path before. He said nothing, waiting politely for Yehuda to finally reveal what he had been contemplating.

As if in response to his unstated cue, Yehuda continued. 'History tells us that the Prophet Muhammad's visions were associated with his epilepsy. Of course, we will never know, but it would be interesting to discover whether his fits were the results of the enormous energy that surged into him as he tapped into the universal consciousness, or whether the electrical surges within his own brain caused these fits and facilitated his visions.'

'It probably doesn't matter,' Mehmet responded. 'The result was that he was able to give mankind the *Holy Qur'an*, and to deliver the message that we should humble ourselves before Allah, submit ourselves to His will. That is all that matters.'

'I agree with you. We should concentrate our attentions on that which matters. The descendants of Abraham certainly do have a tendency to want to throw out the baby with the bathwater.' Yehuda chuckled as if at some imagined vision. 'It's as if we are like baboons beating our chests to establish our supremacy. "My religion is stronger than yours", and thereby dismiss the value of what we have to offer one another.' He beat his chest with a closed fist. 'Why is it so difficult to understand that we are all a hundred percent correct? It's just that we are looking at different surfaces of the same Rubik's Cube. The Jews see blue, the Christians see white and the Muslim's—if you will excuse my weak attempt at humour—can only see red.' He chuckled again.

'Apart from your gloriously mixed metaphors, if you are going to use that logic, then the Christians will win the argument, because white embodies all the colours of the rainbow. It is lucky that you and I both understand this is not a contest.' He smiled congenially.

They lapsed into silence for a while until Mehmet looked at the professor with the expression of a naughty child. 'You dragged me away from the edge of heaven to contemplate the process of annealing steel.'

Yehuda pointed the stem of his pipe in Mehmet's general direction. 'What I have in mind has to do with human characteristics. Let us first talk about halal food.'

Mehmet knew better than to ask what halal food had to do with annealing steel—or with human characteristics, for that matter. He waited.

'You know, of course, why devout Muslims eat only halal food,' Yehuda said.

'Of course. The word halal means "permitted". Of the plants, we are permitted to eat anything that is not intoxicating or hazardous. Of the animals, we may eat only the flesh of those that have been slaughtered with a sharp knife in a humane and painless fashion. We are prohibited from eating the flesh of a list of animals that are haram—"forbidden"—pigs, monkeys, dogs and many other beings, and we are also forbidden to eat or drink blood.'

'I did not ask you what halal food was,' Yehuda remonstrated with a smile that reminded Mehmet of his own teacher's smile at the monastery many years previously. 'I asked you if you know *why* you eat only Halal.'

Mehmet shrugged. 'It is part of Islamic Law that we should strive to eat only food that is clean, hygienic and safe for human consumption.'

'An interesting answer. Do you know where this law comes from?'

'My memory is somewhat hazy as to the exact Surah in the *Holy Qur'an*, but I believe there are at least three that specifically tell us we may only eat that which is Halal.'

'Do these Surahs contain the list of permitted and forbidden foods to which you referred?'

'No, the information on the actual foods comes from the Hadith—the narration of how the Prophet Muhammad lived his life.'

'Would it surprise you to discover that the Jewish *Torah,* the *Old Testament* is the original source of this list? Specifically, the foods which you call haram are listed in the book of Leviticus, which was part of the *Torah* given to the Jews, by God Himself through the Prophet Moses—roughly two thousand years before the Prophet Muhammad was born?'

Mehmet's expression reflected confusion as he waited for his friend to continue.

'Please allow me some leeway,' Yehuda continued. 'For the moment, I would like to focus on something else you said—that blood, in particular, is expressly forbidden.'

'What is the significance of this in your mind?'

Yehuda got up out of his chair and looked around the austere room then walked towards the trestle table behind his chair on which stood an urn that every now again rumbled with the roil of simmering water. He reached for a cup among an odd assortment of various teas, a can of instant coffee, sugar and a thermally insulated jug of cold milk. He paused, put the cup down again, then walked across the room to the bookshelf on his left. He tilted his head back to read the spines through the lower half of his glasses. 'Ah, yes.' He reached for a book and leafed through it. 'I am going to read to you from the *Old Testament*, Leviticus, Chapter 17, from verse 10 onwards. *If any man of the house of Israel or of the strangers that sojourn among them eats any blood, I will set my face against that person who eats blood, and will cut him off from among his people. For the life of the flesh is in the blood …*' He moved his glasses down his nose with his index finger and looked over the top as he skirted a threadbare sofa bed and carried the book back towards Mehmet. 'There are more verses that reinforce what I have just read to you, but the message is already crystal clear and unambiguous. Both the Jews and the strangers who live among us are expressly forbidden by Allah Himself to eat blood.'

Mehmet sat quietly, struck by Yehuda's apparent willingness to use the words Allah and God interchangeably.

Yehuda looked over the top of his glasses at Mehmet. 'Have you heard of a television program, *The Horseman without a Horse*? It is a series that was aired recently in both Syria and Egypt, around the time of the Muslim holy period of Ramadan.'

'You know that I do not waste my time watching television. What is your interest in this TV series?'

'There is one episode where two Jewish men are depicted as having kidnapped a young Christian child. There is a scene in that episode which shows the Jewish men slaughtering the child by cutting his throat with a knife to draw his blood—ostensibly to use it as an ingredient in the baking of unleavened bread for the Jewish Passover dinner—the same remembrance dinner, of course, that the Prophet Jesus attended two thousand years ago, just before He was crucified, and which the world has come to know as the Last Supper.'

Mehmet drew his eyebrows together quizzically but said nothing.

'What can one reasonably conclude about the levels of ignorance, stupidity and arrogance of the person who produced such a television program,' Yehuda asked, 'given that not only are Jews expressly forbidden to eat the blood of any living or dead creature, but that Muslims themselves recognise blood as haram, and derive their *own* understanding of this from the Jewish *Torah*? What motivated such a program?' He brought the open sections of the *Old Testament* together with a dull *thwack*, then answered himself, 'One can only conclude that the TV producer's brain had become so twisted and addled with acerbic hatred that he was incapable of rational thought.'

'Are you sure of your facts?' Mehmet asked. He scratched his brow with one finger.

'As sure as I am that you are sitting in that chair! I have watched this particular scene with my own eyes on more than one occasion. Furthermore,' he jabbed the coffee table between them with an index finger, 'the program itself was screened at peak family viewing time during the Ramadan period when the *hajj* takes place.'

'You know what the *hajj* is!' Even as he said it, Mehmet knew nothing should surprise him about Yehuda's knowledge. 'Of course.'

'Yes I do.'

'If you understand the reason for the *hajj* pilgrimage, then you should also understand the rationale for the timing of the screening of that TV show,' Mehmet said in a low voice. 'Regardless of whether or not the show is sensible in itself, the timing of its screening is understandable.'

'Why is that?'

'One of the events commemorated in the *hajj*,' Mehmet answered, 'has to do with the ritual of the stoning of the three *jamarat* at Mina. Every pilgrim must throw pebbles to strike each *jamrah*—each of the three walls. A total of forty-nine pebbles from each pilgrim must strike the walls. The first wall must be struck twenty-one times over three days. The other two must be struck fourteen times each over the last two of the same three days.'

'Yes, that I know, but what is the significance?' Yehuda asked.

'It goes to the heart of the dispute between the Muslims and the Jews. Your *Torah* seems to infer that God's covenant with Abraham was in respect of Isaac—his son with Sarah.' Mehmet tapped the ends of the fingers of his hands together, his eyes lowered in thought. 'Although our *Holy Qur'an* does not specifically state which was the son, Islamic tradition holds that the covenant was in respect of Ishmael—Abraham's son with Hagar, born many years before Isaac.'

'Yes, yes, I also understand this as the core point of contention,' Yehuda responded. 'And the Muslims believe that Isaac stole his older half-brother Ishmael's birthright. The Jews believe that because Hagar was not Abraham's lawful wife, Isaac, the son of his lawful wife Sarah was his rightful heir.'

'Well, in terms of Islamic belief, our tradition also holds that the Devil appeared at each *jamrah*. At the first, he tried to influence Abraham through temptation not to sacrifice Ishmael according to Allah's command. At the second he tried to influence Hagar through temptation to get her to prevent Abraham from sacrificing Ishmael. At the third he tried to influence Ishmael not to allow himself to be sacrificed. Of course, Abraham's commitment did not waiver, but Ishmael's life was nevertheless saved through Allah's mercy.'

'Do you personally believe this?' asked Yehuda.

'It is not important what I believe. What is important is that you understand the significance of the stoning. And there is yet another aspect to this stoning,' Mehmet continued, 'which is that it is also symbolic of the trampling of Satan who might be in one or more of three places. He might be one's internal despot, as represented by one's hopes and wishes which need to be kept under control. Or he might be hidden from view altogether in the persona of a *jinni* named Iblis, or he might be hidden amongst the enemies of religion and humanity which, as a matter of fact if not logic, they believe may include infidel Jews and Christians. In the process of this stoning, the *hajji* works himself into a frenzy of hatred of Satan and of the enemies of Islam. The process has the effect of reaffirming his faith.'

Yehuda stood and absent-mindedly re-tucked a stray end of his shirt into his trousers. 'So, an implication is that once a year at Ramadan, millions of Muslims all over the world reaffirm their traditional view that Isaac stole Ishmael's birthright, and many hundreds of thousands of *hajjis* work themselves into a frenzy of hatred as they stone the imaginary Devil, whom they have convinced themselves over roughly 1,400 years may be hidden amongst the Jews—the descendants of Isaac's son Jacob. This is the core: the flame of hatred that is fanned every year, over and over and over again as part of a religious ritual that has been perpetuated to this very day.' He paced the floor.

'It is probably more subliminal than that, but that is essentially the issue, which is more than likely why Ramadan was the time chosen to screen that particular TV series to which you referred.'

'Hmmm,' was Yehuda's only response. He paced to the end of the room, turned and paced back again. With two fingers he tugged at the collar of his shirt, a ritual Mehmet had often observed when the professor lapsed into thought.

After a few moments Mehmet, too, stood and in doing so, blocked the path of Yehuda's pacing. 'You know, the evidence throughout the ages has a central theme surrounding the behaviour of the followers of Islam.'

Yehuda looked at the younger man in front of him, his eyes filled with an expression that might have been interpreted as sadness. 'In my experience, once a problem is understood it can be solved. The difficulty lies in cutting through the prejudice, the dogma, the closed-mindedness that often obscures the issue. So I am interested in whatever you have to say.' He sat back down and the olive leather seat expelled a sigh under his weight.

Mehmet remained standing. 'The common thread is frustration. For over 1,400 years, the followers of Islam have been struggling to deliver a simple message to the world—that all of humanity must submit to the superior power of Allah if we wish to enjoy a life hereafter. Too few have paid attention. The harder Muslims strive to deliver this simple message, the more disrespectfully we are treated. By way of one example of this disrespect, one only needs to examine how the British behaved as they manipulated the Middle Eastern countries to finally bring down the Ottoman Empire. Their actions were interwoven with a deal to profit the Anglo-American alliance, to gain iron-fisted control to distribute Middle Eastern oil. It was okay to let these countries bring the oil out of the ground, but it was a case of "our oil companies will put in the production equipment and our oil companies will distribute worldwide".' Mehmet sat down again. 'There are many other examples of this nature that I could give you.'

'Perhaps the problem is more related to the method of delivering the message, than to the truth of the message or its value,' Yehuda suggested. 'And for that, too, there are examples on both sides. Throughout the ages, the Muslims have relied more on force than on reason. For example, when your Prophet Muhammad was originally expelled from Mecca, he relocated to Medina, a town occupied largely by the Jews. When he attempted to convert the Jews of Medina they ignored him. His response was to amass an army, conquer the town and murder most of them. Calif Omar drove out the Jews of Khaibar, but there he relied more on deception and duplicity when he violated the treaty of Muhammad.'

Mehmet nodded slightly; his response was not at all defensive. 'It cannot be denied that Islam was heavily reliant on the sword in those days. The Prophet Muhammad—peace be upon him—is famous for his view that war is deception. His Quraysh model of lulling one's enemies into a sense of false security, preparatory to turning on them and conquering them, is still admired by those who believe that the end justifies the means. For example, Yasir Arafat tried to use that very strategy in his dealings with the Israelis. But you must remember that Muhammad was motivated by his belief that he was acting under the instructions of Allah to deliver His message.'

Yehuda's knees jiggled, as if of their own accord. He moved to the edge of his seat, his elbows resting on his quietened knees. 'I am not questioning the message itself. Indeed, the evidence is now before us. The world is in a mess because humanity has effectively raped and pillaged our Mother Earth. We have denuded our seas and forests. We have polluted the water we drink and the air we breathe. Tens, if not hundreds of millions now live in the stench of squalor, suffering from malnutrition if not starvation. Human immune systems have become compromised as a result of this environmental degradation. HIV/AIDS is but one consequence. Even the body temperature of Mother Earth herself is rising as she battles against her fever. We have tried to conquer and dominate nature, notwithstanding the Prophet Muhammad's message to the contrary.'

'Are you not playing with words here, professor?' Mehmet asked his voice rising a little, as if on the brink of being offended. 'You appear to be substituting the word nature for the word Allah.'

'Mehmet, my son, nature is all around us and within us. Arguably, all of creation—the entire universe and everything within it and beyond— is encompassed in the word nature. Therefore, what is all of creation if not the manifestation of the Creator? They are one and the same, just as you know that the Jewish and Christian God is one and the same as Allah. From your own earlier meditation you must understand that we are all part of the greater whole that is God. It seems to me that the real message that Muhammad received during his visions was that all of humanity should be humble and submit itself to the power and laws of nature.'

The word 'son' had not been lost on Mehmet, just as 'professor' had not been lost on the man who had up until that point been addressed by Mehmet as Yehuda. He needed time to order his thoughts.

The minutes ticked by. Neither man rose from his seated position, neither said anything. Yehuda's eyes were again closed as he leant his head against the back of his chair. Mehmet seemed to have entered a meditative or at least a contemplative state.

When eventually, Yehuda heard a muffled sound from his companion, he looked up to see tears wet on Mehmet's cheeks.

'Forgive me,' Mehmet said in a voice that would have been inaudible at the end of the room. 'I was almost angered by your words, which—it turns out—were the catalyst to a revelation that I have just now experienced.'

Yehuda smiled. 'Tell me about this revelation,' he said, his own voice gentle.

Mehmet drew a breath through his teeth, paused, then brought his steepled fingers together. 'I had a vision that the Imam Mahdi is about to reveal himself. He is the Hidden Imam of the Shiites whose return will be a precursor to the arrival of the Jewish Messiah or the equivalent in Christianity—Christ's second coming.'

'I'm genuinely pleased that we have made this breakthrough,' Yehuda said. It was as if he had been expecting this outcome.

Yehuda waited a few seconds, more by way of a courtesy to allow the younger man time to savour his epiphany. Then, with the hint of a smile he continued. 'Of course, you understand that this arrival would have to be accompanied by a wave of Love that would wash over the world, and that this would seem impossible given the current clash of civilizations which the world is now experiencing".

'It would certainly be a miracle.'

'Mmm. Perhaps now we can talk about the annealing of steel?'

CHAPTER 27

THE TWO DANCERS, their torsos rhythmically united, swayed their hips from side to side to the music. For no longer than a few seconds, the long lengths of their bodies were suggestively joined. Then, the male smoothly disengaged to take his partner's hand. Their connected arms snaked over and around one another's heads and necks. And still their hips swayed to the incessant merengue beat—the repetitive, hypnotic beat. Their dance was a celebration of joyous sensuality, stirred for 300 years on the sugar plantations of the Dominican Republic in a cauldron of African, Hispanic and French cultures.

To Tara, it was as if the animal skin drums of the African savannah had been magically transported to this discotheque in Santo Domingo. She found herself imagining the movements and sounds of the tribal dancers of the African continent—from whose bosom the Dominican sugar plantation slaves had been torn—their feet stamping rhythmically into the twilight dusk. She could dreamily see an orange sun sinking behind the silhouetted thorn trees and the song leader's haunting, high pitched tenor call interweaving with the lower octave bass of the tribal chorus—like the shuttle on a loom repeating the same soulful call-and-response, call-and-response. The hips of the two dancers swayed, back and forth, back and forth.

The female dancer thrust her back against her partner's chest. Suddenly Africa gave way to Spain as she arched, then stroked the back of his head, her facial expression reflecting the concentrated, scowling suggestiveness of a Spanish dancer. His right arm wrapped around her shoulders, moved downwards, brushing lightly over her breasts.

Then he twirled her, French minuet style, the palm of his free right hand lightly, suggestively, stroking her entire torso as she rotated—from her left armpit to her right hip and then back again.

Tara felt herself seduced by the pulsating sounds and movements as she peered through the smoky haze. She was mesmerized by the dancers' movements—like hot lava rising, swirling, twirling, ebbing and falling—tantalizing and fleeting.

Patrick watched the couple with the fascination of someone watching a snake charmer. He leaned over and shouted into Tara's ear. 'You don't seriously expect me to do that, do you?'

'Of course!' she shouted back. 'Do you think I dragged you here to watch?'

'How the hell am I going to learn those moves?' he asked with his mouth closer to her ear than it needed to be. Lingeringly, he rested his chin on her shoulder.

'Just shift your weight from one foot to the other in time to the music!' Tara said as she got up from the table. 'Watch what the couple next to you is doing!' She grabbed his hand in a gorilla grip and pulled him onto the crowded dance floor.

At first both Tara and Patrick moved clumsily, but Tara's swaying soon merged with the rhythm of the music. Her eyes were focussed inwards, feeling the music rather than listening to it. Her arms were raised above her head like those of an enraptured singer in a spiritualist choir.

Patrick was engulfed by the sensuality of her hip movements. He felt extremely self-conscious. In his imagination all eyes in the room were trained on them. With Tara lost in a world of her own, he was forced to face the fact that his choice was to shape up or ship out. There would be no hiding behind jokes or banter. Tentatively at first, then with increasing confidence, he mastered the swaying movement. It was easy, really. As Tara had suggested, all he had to do was shift his weight from one foot to the other allowing his hip joints to swivel—first sideways as his feet moved and then slightly upwards as he settled his body weight on each alternating leg.

He tapped her on the shoulder and she beamed a smile at him, her eyes drawn to the movements of his body before her. She grabbed his hands in hers, and rotated slowly, sensually, like an Arabian Nights belly dancer, so that she gradually turned from him. In the process, she had to lift her arm so that his hand hovered above her head.

Casting aside all his Anglo-American inhibitions Patrick threw himself into the dancing with a gusto he never knew he had in him. What the hell, why fight it? The key, as Tara had demonstrated, was to feel the music, not listen to it. He let it wash over him. Soon, he was comfortable in his mastery. *You want dance? I'll give you dance.*

He grinned. It wasn't necessary to copy the couple next to them. Except for the need to maintain the rhythm, there were no rules. As long as he maintained the metronomic swaying rhythm of his feet and hips, he could give his hands and arms the freedom to move to the music in any way he liked. His upper torso would automatically follow in whatever direction he pointed it. Look and learn, he thought with more than a little male arrogance as he launched them into a series of hand, arm and body movements that came out of nowhere.

Tara was twirled, twisted, stroked, swivelled and even lifted off the ground and swung around in his arms. When she recovered from her initial shock, her reaction was to exaggerate her own movements. Her facial expression took on a look of wicked sensuality as she challenged him to ever greater heights. She arched her body backwards. It was instinctive and she knew, now, that was how the sensual merengue movements must have evolved. Their gyrations became even less inhibited.

They were oblivious to the fact that they were two gringos in a Caribbean environment; oblivious, also, to the fact that they had become the centre of attraction.

Eventually, it was Tara who succumbed to exhaustion. She stopped in her tracks. With her legs as straight as two stilts, she let her upper torso fall forward—the limp rag doll bowing to her marionette partner. Patrick came down to earth. He gathered her in his arms. They leant against one other to avoid falling, then became aware of the crowd as it roared its approval, clapping and cheering. Tara and Patrick made their way to the nearest available table where they collapsed, trying to catch their breath.

There was a contraption bolted to the edge of the table which looked like a juke box. Patrick punched a button which would order him a rum and Coke. 'What'll you have?'

'Same as you.'

This floored him. Should he press the same button twice? Was there another button that registered the number of drinks? His mind was too exhausted to think about solving a simple problem.

He stopped trying. 'Let's get out of here,' he said. 'It's too hard to work this out and I'm too tired. Let's go back to your hotel for a quiet drink. I've got to get up early to go to work tomorrow.'

CHAPTER 28

YEHUDA LEANED BACK in his chair and crossed his legs comfortably, careful to keep the soles of his shoes in a direction away from his guest. 'As a religious Muslim, Mehmet, how do you picture Allah in your mind?'

'A very strange question. What do you mean?'

'What is the image in your mind when you think of the Creator, the supreme architect of intelligent design? Does He have a form? Is He a grey bearded gentleman sitting with a ledger on a mountain top on some planet or star watching your every move, documenting your sins and your good deeds? Can He read your thoughts? Is *He* really a *She*?'

'I never really thought in terms of an image,' Mehmet answered. 'Truthfully … I'm still having some trouble in understanding what you are getting at.'

'Muslims talk about submitting to the will of Allah. Does that imply that you are being monitored in your behaviour to determine whether you are or are not submitting? Is He monitoring the behaviour of all six and a half billion people living on this planet on a daily basis, 24/7?'

'You have a very strange turn of mind. I imagine Allah as a supreme, all powerful, all knowing being without shape or form. He is timeless, indestructible, immortal. He pervades every corner of the infinite Universe.'

'Why would He have a gender?'

'I think the word is merely a convenience. I imagine He embodies both female and male characteristics in orientation and attitude. Sometimes He is strong, sometimes nurturing.'

'The Christians say that "God is Love". What do you think they mean?'

'I imagine they are talking about His attitude or predisposition towards humanity. His intentions are benevolent. He loves us as a parent would love His children—unreservedly.'

'Could it be that what the Christians are really talking about is a Universal Soul that permeates the ether of all existence—a sort of positive energetic force, as opposed to a negative energetic force, which some might use as an image to describe the Devil?'

Mehmet nodded slowly several times. 'Yes, I agree with that. As a Sufi initiate, I have some personal experience in the projection of positive energetic force, and when the receiver is bathed in that energy, the result is a feeling of wellbeing. I have even read of scientific experiments which show the impact of positive thoughts on the molecular structure of water ice crystals.'[vii] He paused and let his head lean against the back of his chair. 'Yes, I could accept that the Love that permeates the Universe is a positive etheric energy force into which anyone who opens his or her heart may tap at will—to use a modern phrase.'

'And what of the physical matter that permeates the Universe? You are aware, no doubt that the physicists argue that at the beginning of time, around 14 to 15 billion years ago, all matter in the universe was compacted into a single point of infinite density which exploded in what we now describe as the Big Bang?'

'Of course, of course. What about it?' Mehmet asked.

'Could that physical matter be an element of God or Allah?'

'We have earlier agreed that the physical universe and everything in it is a manifestation or embodiment of Allah. You will also remember my reaction. I am hardly going to argue with you now on that particular point.'

'So we can agree on that?'

'Yes.'

'What about the concept of a universal consciousness, a universal awareness?'

'You refer to the mind of God, I assume?'

'I do.'

'Clearly, for Allah to have a will or an intention, He must have a Mind, though not a physical one, of course—so, yes, I would agree with that also.'

'So, in summary, God or Allah has a universal consciousness, a physical embodiment that pervades all tangible matter, and a universal etheric soul that is charged with energetic Love? In short: a Mind, a Body and a Soul?'

'I see where you are headed with this,' Mehmet said, with a smile. '*God created man in His own image*, from the book of Genesis.'

'Precisely, but I would like you to think one step further than the individual. Think in terms of human society which is half male and half female—in particular, the descendants of Abraham.'

'You will have to explain.'

'There are three strains of the descendants of Abraham, are there not? Each had a prophet who delivered a message. Moses delivered a complex cerebral message; Jesus delivered a spiritual message that emphasised Love; and Muhammad delivered a message that we need to submit to the supreme power of Allah, which the followers of Muhammad have been attempting to physically enforce since the days of Quraysh. It is for that precise reason that the history of Islam is replete with conquests and an emphasis on the importance of *jihad.*'

Mehmet's smiled. 'We may not be very far apart, you and I, my friend. You are telling me you believe humanity has been created in Allah's image at both the individual level and at the level of the collective according to the same principle as—let us say—the individual bee and the beehive to which the bee belongs? You believe that, like the beehive, the collective humanity has a discrete identity? You believe that, like the beehive, each discrete element has its purpose?'

Yehuda laughed. 'As my students would put it, "you are cooking with gas".' He leant forward and pressed the palms of his hands together. 'For the human race to survive the challenges which confront it, and to evolve to a higher level, we need to coalesce into a single group and leverage off each other's strengths.'

Mehmet nodded slowly.

'If any one element attempts to ignore any other element,' Yehuda continued, 'or to stifle or dominate or annihilate that element, we will delay the arrival of your Imam Mahdi … and of the Jewish Messiah …

and of the second coming of the Christ. Essential to peaceful coexistence is the recognition by each group that the others all have something unique to offer. Even the followers of Buddha or L. Ron Hubbard—to name but two examples—have something unique to offer. These various uniquenesses need to be embraced, not scorned, rejected or modified or proselytised.'

'Like a healthy beehive. All working together in harmony, each performing its unique function.' Mehmet closed his eyes in thought.

Yehuda sat tapping his hands together quietly while the younger man considered the implications. Then, with an impish smile on his face, he continued. 'Which brings me back to the point I raised at the beginning of this evening. I would now like to address the subject of annealing steel.'

'Ah, the full circle!' Mehmet's black eyes shone in satisfied pleasure.

'The father of physics, Sir Isaac Newton himself was convinced—as am I—that the *Old Testament* is more than just a book of apocryphal stories. I believe it contains codified information that was deliberately placed there, waiting to be decoded when the time was right. It is my intention to reveal one example of one such decoded message next Sunday evening. I have invited a young couple to attend: she is an American pilot here on vacation; he is a mining engineer—'

'For Eagle Mines, the company you originally introduced me to,' Mehmet broke in, a smile spreading across his face. Patrick Gallagher. And Tara … Geoffrey.'

'Well, well, well. I might have realized, knowing you.' Yehuda bounced the palms of his hands up and down on his knees. 'My purpose on Sunday is to report on a particular technology that Patrick believes was specifically referred to in the *Old Testament*. And of course, you are also invited to join us.'

'Thank you. I will be particularly interested to attend.' Mehmet chuckled, as if at some further internal amusement. 'But I'm not sure I follow your intent here. What has this all to do with annealing?'

'The process of annealing—of tempering steel—involves exposing it to extreme heat, and then working it by beating it, applying pressure and abrasion, and then slowly allowing it to cool again.' Yehuda patted his pockets in search of his pipe that lay on the low table next to him. 'Do you agree?'

'Err … yes.' Mehmet said, then pointed to the table.

'Aah, thank you. I should give it up … perhaps, one day.'

'I hear gum is a good substitute.'

Yehuda put the pipe in his mouth, searched for his tobacco, then waved the unlit pipe in the air to make his next point. 'The key to ensuring that humanity would be able to eventually crack any code which might be embodied in the *Torah*, or the *Book* as you call it, would be to ensure that not one single letter of that code book ever changed throughout the millennia, would it not? Does that not make sense?'

'Well, without thinking about it at length … yes, I suppose.'

'The *Old Testament* explicitly states that God Himself appointed the Jews as the custodians of that codebook. So … what would be the best way, the key, to ensuring that the Jews remained sharp, on their toes, mentally honed, resilient and fiercely dedicated to protecting the integrity of every letter of the *Torah*?'

Mehmet smiled. He decided to allow Yehuda the pleasure of articulating the answer himself.

'Would it not be by the application of heat, impact, pressure and abrasion?' Yehuda asked. 'Like annealing steel, by heating it in a flame. And then by beating it on an anvil—as when manufacturing a sword of the finest calibre. And then, by allowing periods of peace for the heat to slowly dissipate before commencing the process all over again.'

'You are telling me that you believe it was part of Allah's plan to ensure that the Jews were persecuted throughout the millennia,' Mehmet said, 'To keep them annealed and razor sharp?'

'It seems that way to me,' Yehuda offered.

Mehmet smiled a knowing smile. Not a word escaped his lips. He was remembering his discussion a few days earlier with Hussein and Mahmoud. The principle was precisely what he had been proposing to them at that time. Yehuda was merely filling in the details.

Yehuda withdrew the still unlit pipe from his mouth. He pointed its stem in Mehmet's direction, his eyes widened, his eyebrows raised. 'If I am correct in this—if it was the will of Allah that the Jews would protect the integrity of the *Torah* until the Messianic era was upon us—then it will follow that no one will ever be successful in wiping out the Jews. It will be like an irresistible force applied to an immovable object. Throughout the millennia, all that this heat and pressure and abrasion of anti-semitism has been able to achieve, is to anneal the Jewish sword—which becomes ever stronger, ever sharper.'

'The bee and the beehive,' was all that Mehmet said.

After a few seconds, Yehuda continued, but his tone held a finality as though he now wanted to round off the evening's conversation. 'I believe the time has come for that sword, and for the swords of the Muslims and Christians, to be beaten into ploughshares. I believe we are standing at the threshold of the Messianic era that all three Abrahamic religions have been anticipating.'

This time the silence lasted for a full five minutes. Both men sat quietly, their heads resting against the backs of their chairs, their arms relaxed in mirror images of each other.

Mehmet cleared his throat. 'I think you might have overlooked something.'

'Oh?'

'The descendants of Abraham only account for roughly fifty percent of humanity. What about the other fifty percent?'

Yehuda smiled. His facial expression softened, his eyes crinkling a little at the corners. 'The followers of the Hindu religion also believe in a Supreme Creator.' He held a finger up in the air. 'Together that would account for over two-thirds of humanity. Bearing that in mind, what you are really talking about is the other thirty-three percent of humanity, which is made up of those of the Mongoloid and Negroid races.'

Mehmet stared at the bookshelf in front of him, then murmured, as much to himself as to Yehuda. 'The traditionally recognised Abrahamic religions—or descendants, if you will—Jews, Muslims and Christians ... Caucasoid, Mongoloid and Negroid ... Father, Son and Holy Spirit ...

Mind, Body and Soul. God created man in His own image ... the Universal Trinity ... the Hebrew triangle—the triangles that make up the Star of David permeate all of creation. One points up, the other down. As above, so below.' He lapsed into silence, his lips silently repeating his thoughts over and again.

Quietly, Yehuda reached across to his side table. From it he retrieved a page scattered with illustrations. He handed it to Mehmet.

'The Hindus also think in terms of God as a trinity. They think of Brahma, Shiva and Vishnu,' he said. 'And, like the Jews, they have also incorporated the triangle into one of their emblems. As you will see from these emblems, the truth has been there for all to see, patiently waiting for recognition and understanding.' He paused, to dramatise the impact of his next statement. 'I believe that the time has arrived when the secrets which have been patiently hiding behind the codes will be increasingly revealed.'

CHAPTER 29

T ARA AND PATRICK arrived separately at Uwaasd, and had made their way across the campus to reach Yehuda's rooms a few minutes before six o'clock. Other than late night, lingering and susurrated telephone conversations from the comfort of solitary beds in their respective domiciles, they hadn't managed to catch up even once during the past three days. Patrick had worked twelve-hour days to get on top of his workload following his holiday in Australia, and to justify—at least to himself—taking off a long weekend so soon after his return to work. They had arranged to depart for Las Terrenas early on Friday—in two days' time. He had confirmed the availability of the mine's King Air aeroplane. She had confirmed that Aurelio would be joining them—with a girlfriend to accompany him. All systems were 'go'. For Tara, the time had passed slowly. She had occupied it mainly with sightseeing under Aurelio's guidance.

They met outside Yehuda's rooms. There was no time for personal conversation. There hadn't even been time for more than a fleeting greeting: a 'snug hug and a blissful kiss' as Tara thought of it with a tinkle of internal merriment. Was it only she, or was everyone designed to think icing-sugar thoughts when they found themselves on the warm threshold of love?

'I want to thank you young people for humouring an ageing professor, and for meeting me here this afternoon. Unfortunately, I am unable to provide you with any refreshments here, but these rooms give me the benefit of handy access to my research files and other papers. Perhaps we can try to make this a relatively short discussion.'

Patrick looked around the office to get his bearings and saw exactly what Tara had seen on her first visit. How could anyone concentrate in this box-like environment? Either Yehuda had an incredible ability to focus on the job at hand, or he lived in his head and it didn't really matter where he parked his ageing buns.

'After you told us that you and your students had caused that thunderstorm last Tuesday, wild horses couldn't stop us from joining you.' There was a tone of schoolboyish glee in Patrick's voice.

'I hope you will forgive me, Patrick, but that is not the main reason for today's meeting. I have other serious matters I wish to discuss.'

'You're sounding very formal and very mysterious,' Tara interjected. 'Of course, we'll be happy to discuss whatever you wish.'

Yehuda nodded. Absentmindedly, he fumbled in his pockets for his pipe. It wasn't there. He patted another pocket and looked around the room before giving up the search. 'I must, I must buy gum,' he said.

Tara and Patrick's eyes glanced sideways towards each other, their heads unmoving, their expressions politely blank.

'Patrick,' Yehuda began 'when Tara first mentioned your interest in electromagnetic energy I was only mildly intrigued. There are many people in the world who have such an interest, and most of those I have met appear to me to be romantics. It was primarily because she told me you were *also* concerned about the possibility of a coming era of global cooling that I asked her to arrange our meeting. There are not many people who hold that view. Like you, I happen to be one of them, although I suspect that global temperatures might continue to rise during the summers until around 2012.'

'I appreciate that you did. I found our conversation the other day very stimulating, particularly from the palaeontology perspective,' Patrick responded. You and I seem to share more than one common interest.'

'Yes.' Yehuda's answer was perfunctory, distracted. 'To be honest, the opportunity you raised regarding the Ark of the Covenant also came to me as an unusually pleasant surprise.'

Tara sensed a tension in the professor that hadn't been there last time they met. His words were delivered in a manner that was patently building up to something else—as if he was an athlete running on the spot. She looked at Patrick. He sensed her look and raised an eyebrow slightly at her. Neither said anything. The room was silent as Yehuda sat gathering his thoughts.

In the prolonged silence, Tara soon found her mind wandering. Today was Wednesday, a little over a week since she had arrived. Why *had* she felt so powerfully drawn to spend her vacation here? She vividly remembered her own intransigence when her flatmate had queried the sanity of her proposed visit to Santo Domingo. Since her arrival she'd experienced a tectonic shift in the boundaries of her life. A little smile crept its way around her mouth. In that short time Patrick had acknowledged, to a room full of people, that she had captured his heart, and Yehuda claimed to be able to manufacture thunderstorms … and was about to share some deep inner thoughts about who knew what?

Yehuda's words broke into her reverie. 'If you seriously believe that we might be heading for global cooling, then it seems to me you will probably also be focussing on matters unrelated to the subject of carbon dioxide emissions. It will not have escaped your attention that the primary cause of climate change is more likely to be related to recent discoveries in the field of astrophysics—which might also go some way towards augmenting our understanding of glaciation cycles.'

Astrophysics? That caught Tara by surprise. She was doubly surprised to see the serious expression on Patrick's face as he nodded silently.

'Excuse me?' she asked, looking quickly from one man to the other.

Yehuda turned to face Tara. 'Forgive me for being brief today, but for the purpose of this discussion, I would ask you please to just accept that the cause of the cyclical climate heating and cooling of the Earth's surface ultimately appears more likely to be a function of the waxing and waning of the amount of energy arriving from our sun. In turn, this is influenced by three factors. First, the distance of the earth from the sun, which varies because the earth's orbit is elliptical as opposed to round. Second, the angle of inclination of the earth relative to the sun as our planet wobbles on its axis in a 26,000 year cycle—the precession cycle it's called. And thirdly, it has recently been discovered that it is *also* influenced by sunspot activity that waxes and wanes as our sun proceeds along its own cyclical pathway through our Milky Way.' He smiled his professor smile at her over the top of his glasses before continuing. 'Whilst there is no question that carbon dioxide emissions have added to the problem of global warming it is equally certain, at least to those who subscribe to the astrophysicists arguments, that the rising CO_2 level in our atmosphere has not been the ultimate *cause* of global warming.'

Tara raised both eyebrows in polite acquiescence.

'There are also those who would argue,' Yehuda continued, 'that the positions of the heavenly bodies, relative to each other and to Earth, should be taken more seriously for metaphysical reasons. I hasten to add that the scientist in me cannot take the arguments too seriously at his stage.'

'Are you talking about the astrological horoscopes we read in our daily newspapers?' Tara asked. This was an unexpectedly unscientific side to the professor.

Yehuda looked directly at her, his hazel eyes unblinking. 'No, my dear. Horoscopes do seem to me to be of some value, but purely from an entertainment perspective.'

His words were straight forward enough but Tara sensed a glimmer of humour behind the direct gaze.

As if reading her mind, Yehuda continued. 'There can be no doubt that the Ancients had a remarkably clear understanding of the subject of astronomy because there is hard scientific evidence to support this conclusion.'

Tara couldn't let this go by without exploring it further. 'Can you give us an example, please?'

'Certainly.' Yehuda swivelled in his seat and his chair creaked in a grinding, oil-thirsty manner. 'Do you recall that, at our meeting last Saturday, Patrick made reference to the sophisticated technologies to which the Egyptians must have had access?'

Both Tara and Patrick nodded.

'I have a copy of an article here, somewhere ... which was published in the *New Scientist Magazine* in November 2000 ...' He stood up, leaned forward and rummaged in the debris of journals, theses and papers that lay there. Within seconds he found what he was looking for. She expected him to look at them triumphantly, but he seemed to take his discovery as a matter of course. She smiled secretly. *How in God's name could he keep track of everything on his desk?*

Yehuda sat down again to another squeaked sigh of his chair. 'This article reported on the findings of Kate Spence, a British Egyptologist who used astronomical records to pinpoint the date of the construction of the Great Pyramid of Giza at between 2485 BCE and 2475 BCE. Her methodology was subjected to arms-length validation by an astronomer of some credibility. The dates are therefore believable.'

'How could the dates have been pinpointed with such accuracy?' Tara asked.

'It had been discovered previously that the Egyptian tombs are aligned north–south with an accuracy of 0.05 degrees. Now that's amazingly accurate when you think that the North Star was not aligned directly over the North Pole in those days as a result of the precession wobble in Earth's rotation on its axis.'

'And the precise position of any particular star relative to Earth will only repeat itself once every 26,000 years?' Patrick asked.

'Yes. The Egyptians couldn't possibly have used the North Star for the purpose of arriving at such accurate north–south alignment of the Great Pyramid. But Kate Spence was able to work out an alternative method by which this degree of accuracy might have been possible in those days.'

'How?' Tara asked. She couldn't help the question springing out.

'She discovered that when two particular stars—Mizar which is located in the Big Dipper, and Kochab in the Little Dipper—were aligned vertically, one directly above the other, an imaginary straight line drawn through both of them would mark the position of true north for the pyramid builders. That alignment occurred during the time of the pyramid's construction.'

'Spence must have used extraordinarily sophisticated computer technology to replicate the position of the heavens in those days.' Tara wrinkled her nose in some exasperation. 'Come on, Yehuda, the Ancients wouldn't have had access to that. The telescope wasn't even invented.

You're telling us that she just assumed that the ancient Egyptians were able to align these remote stars *with the naked eye*?' Her eyebrows collided quizzically. 'And even if they could, how would they have known that the alignment of the two stars would have pointed due north? And even if they had compasses in those days, they would have had to adjust for agonic line declination.'

Patrick laughed. 'Don't confuse us with practical facts, Tara.'

Unexpectedly, Yehuda came to her rescue. 'Tara happens to have asked a particularly incisive question.' He leaned forward yet again over the rubble of his desk and, within seconds, had pulled out yet another piece of dog-eared paper from close to the top of the pile. *Abracadabra.*

'This is a photocopy of a news item that reported on a device known as the Antikythera Mechanism, which had been discovered in an ancient Roman shipwreck over a hundred years ago. It has taken modern humans until now to put together the eighty-two pieces of this shattered mechanism. When it was finally reconstructed, the researchers were able to determine that the device was a complex and uncannily accurate astronomical computer that could predict the positions of the sun and planets, show the location of the moon and even forecast eclipses. It was something of a coup to discover such an ancient piece of scientific equipment.'

'Could it have been used by the Ancient Egyptians?' Tara asked.

'I'm afraid not. The Antikythera Mechanism is believed to be only 2,100 years old, and the Great Pyramid of Giza was built 4,500 years ago.'

Tara glanced sideways at him. 'I'm guessing you are trying to draw a long bow here—that it's reasonable to assume that the Egyptians had access to things like telescopes even though they were only *re*discovered relatively recently.'

'Aha,' Yehuda responded nodding his head several times. 'I agree that would be a very reasonable hypothesis, but it gets even more mysterious than that.'

Now it was Patrick's turn to voice his incredulity. 'Yehuda, you've already stretched the elastic band of credibility to snapping point,' he said in good humour.

Yehuda looked unconcerned. 'Studies have been done which, adjusting for precession, suggest that the shafts emanating from the King's and Queen's chambers in the Great Pyramid aligned precisely to particular stars of great symbolism. Specifically, the southern shaft from the King's chamber would have pointed to the brightest of the three stars making up Orion's belt. The northern shaft was aimed at the star Kochab.' He looked over at his guests, obviously enjoying his moments of revelation. 'According to Egyptian mythology, Orion's belt was symbolically identified with Osiris, their high God of resurrection and rebirth. On the other hand, Kochab was a star associated by the Ancients with the immortality of the soul. These concepts are either laced with superstition, or they are very sophisticated ... depending on your perspective of life.'

Tara stirred in her chair. 'Now, I have to say that does capture my imagination. Here we are, 5,000 years later, and the Flat Earth atheists are still arguing that there is no such thing as etheric soul.' She shook her head from side to side. 'Anything they can't see past the horizon with their own eyes doesn't exist.'

Yehuda looked at her with renewed interest, then smiled and chuckled softly in agreement. 'It has only been very recently discovered that some of the massive blocks from which the pyramids were constructed, were not quarried at all. As Patrick mentioned the other day, they were more likely compact-cast in situ, on top of the quarried foundation stones, using a material that was so sophisticated that, apart from the man made nanospheres of material it contains, it is virtually impossible to tell it from naturally occurring stone. The material is far superior to our modern-day concrete.'

'So what's the point you're trying to make?' Patrick asked.

Yehuda didn't answer immediately. He scratched his chin, then swivelled in his chair to face the maps on his wall. His fist supported his chin, while his other arm was folded across his body. Finally, he cleared his throat and swivelled back to face his guests.

'Imagine, if you will, the architectural design complexities associated with aligning those pyramid shafts with such precision.' He spoke slowly, each word clearly articulated. 'And then try to imagine the level of sophistication … the knowledge of specialised materials, materials handling, astronomy and mathematics that would have been required to allow for the incredibly precise construction of those shafts—quite apart from the construction and alignment of the pyramid itself.'

Yehuda paused, and began to drum the fingers of his right hand on the arm of his chair. His gaze was focussed on some faraway point above the heads of his visitors.

'Don't get me wrong, Yehuda, I'm enjoying this information, but it's a long way from global cooling and I'm still looking for the ulti-mate point you're trying to make,' Patrick said. 'Why are you telling us this?'

'What I am attempting to do here is establish the bullet-proof cred-ibility of the Ancients' technological sophistication in general, and of their knowledge of astronomy in particular. At the same time, I am trying to plant the idea in your minds that they had a predisposition to think in metaphysical terms—the language of the *Old Testament*, in which those references to the Ark of the Covenant and gold were recorded. For example, you may or may not be aware that the story of the resurrection of Osiris from the dead predated the *New Testament* account of the resur-rection of Jesus Christ by some 3,200 years.'

Patrick jerked his head back. He had never heard *that* before.

'I am also attempting to get both of you to focus on the egocentric manner in which modern humanity appears to view the Ancients,' Yehuda continued. 'On the one hand, because we have come to worship at the altar of science, we are agog at the unbelievable physical precision of their achievements, some of which we are only now learning to repli-cate ourselves—let alone explain how they achieved these things. On the other hand, because science cannot adequately explain their preoccupa-tion with the immortality of the soul, we seem to have no trouble at all in writing off as "primitive" their metaphysical views in general. But let us apply some common sense here. How could they have been so far ahead of us in one area, and so far behind us in another? Such an argu-ment reflects a ludicrous disconnect in logic.'

'Okay,' Patrick ventured, 'let's say, for the sake of argument, that we accept this last statement of yours without reservation, and let's agree that we will keep our minds receptively open to the subject of metaphysics. You must still have a deeper purpose here, if I'm not mistaken?'

'You are correct but, before I jump to that, I want to beg your indulgence for just a little longer. I want to also draw your attention to the superior knowledge of astronomy of another advanced race, the Mayans, the seeds of which can be traced to the Olmecs as far back as 2600 BCE. They lived in what is today Central America, the other side of the world from Egypt. You have heard of the Mayan calendar, yes?'

Patrick wasn't sure whether it was more important to answer that question or focus on the coincidence of timing when the Great Pyramid was built, and the Mayans. He also suddenly became conscious of the fact that, a week earlier, he and Mehmet had also been talking about the Mayans. Intellectual circles in Santo Domingo were probably as incestuous as anywhere else; he wondered if they knew each other. The question popped out of his mouth before he knew he was asking it. 'Yehuda, do you by any chance know a guy by the name of Mehmet Kuhl?'

Tara looked sharply at him. *What had brought that on?*

'I most certainly do,' Yehuda answered, smiling broadly. 'He is an old friend of mine. In fact, I was the one who introduced him to Eagle Mines. Why do you ask?'

'*You* did! Is this a small town or is this the universal six degrees of separation? By further coincidence, Tara met him in New York. And it was only last Wednesday—exactly a week ago—that he was telling me about his research into ancient civilizations. He specifically mentioned the Mayans, and for some reason I remember he made a tongue-in-cheek reference to the fact that the word "priest" in the language of the Mayans sounds like a variation of the name Abraham.'

'He told you that? Hah. Well, we meet regularly on a social basis and we often discuss our mutual interest in ancient civilizations. He has never mentioned that particular linkage to me before. Perhaps I should ask him about it.'

It was at that point that Tara felt a chill run down her spine. Yehuda and Mehmet knew each other too! How many coincidences would it take for a coincidence to be something other than a coincidence? What was this, some divine plan? Or something sinister? With a heroic effort, she pushed these thoughts aside, forced her mind back to the subject at hand, and turned to face Yehuda.

'I would ask you to be patient for just a little while longer,' Yehuda said to her, perhaps in response to the look on her face. 'All of this has to do with Patrick's concerns regarding global cooling and what we might do to prepare for that, but I have been forced to talk to you about more wide ranging matters to give you context.'

A feeling of fatalistic powerlessness washed over Tara. She leant back in her seat and let herself be carried by the tide of events to take her where it may.

'Their calendar was believed to have been devised around 300 years earlier,' Yehuda continued, addressing himself to Patrick, 'but only came into general use from about 355 BCE. That's when the first evidence emerged of their preoccupation with a concept called "the long count".'

'Some 650 years after the start date of the Hebrew calendar,' Patrick said, pleased with himself for remembering the figure.

'Well, I'm impressed that you should remember that relationship, but there is an argument that *both* the Mayan calendar and the Hebrew calendar triangulate back to 3113 BCE. There is an argument that there was a human error in interpreting some information recorded in the *Torah*.'

Tara and Patrick's looks of surprise echoed each other.

'Without getting too technical, the start date of modern civilization is calculated from that information source. The years prior to Noah's death were added up based on Noah's age and the age of all the patri- archs in the generations which preceded him. That is how the year 3761 BCE was derived as the year in which God is said to have created Adam.'

'So?' Patrick asked.

'It has recently come to light that the biblical estimate of Noah's age and Methuselah's age, for example, may have been based on an incor- rect numbering system—one that only came into being after Noah died. If the numbering system that was in use when Noah was supposed to have died was applied, then his adjusted age and the ages of all the people who preceded him would allow for an adjusted birth date for Adam of 3113 BCE.'[viii]

'It seems to be a highly esoteric subject.'

'It gets less esoteric, Patrick, when you start to focus on the so-called start date of the Mayan calendar of August 11 in 3114 BCE, and the start date of the current Hindu epoch of February 18, 3102 BCE,'

'But how does it affect us today?'

Yehuda held up a finger and smiled. 'I am far more interested in the *end* date of the Mayan calendar, which is expected to be December 21, 2012 AD in your terminology. If three separate and apparently unrelated calendar models are triangulating back to the same *start* date, then I am inclined to take the Mayan calendar's *end* date more seriously.'

'End date?' Tara asked. 'The Mayan calendar is forecasting the end of the world?'

'Nothing so dramatic, my dear.'

Both Tara and Patrick looked at Yehuda expectantly.

'Computer models based on up-to-date knowledge of our galaxy are forecasting that at precisely noon on that day in 2012 our sun will be located at the epicentre of our Milky Way; the elliptic of our sun will intersect with the galactic equator. It is an event which recurs only once in 26,000 years.'

Tara was the first to get the connection. 'Aha, so at one minute past midnight on December 22, 2012, the next long count cycle will commence—and the next 26,000 year cycle?'

Yehuda nodded and scratched his temple energetically. 'Remembering Patrick's earlier comments regarding the Egyptians, I would ask you also to consider this,' he said, a touch of dramatic tension creeping into his voice. 'Supposedly without any telescopes to aid their viewing of the stars; supposedly without any equipment to plot the precise movement of the stars; and supposedly without any computerised maps at their disposal to forecast how the galaxy was going to appear in the future, the Mayans were able to pinpoint this event with absolute precision.'

Patrick and Tara were falling into natural step with Yehuda's long pauses, and a couple of minutes passed before Patrick broke the silence. 'It sort of puts into perspective the relative importance of the preoccupation by some people with the accumulation of personal power,' he said, a wry smile on his lips.

'What made you think of that?' Tara asked.

'Nothing earth shattering, really. I was just thinking about the clash of civilizations, about the need to accumulate land and wealth … people's dreams of becoming billionaires. What Yehuda has just shared with us is pretty humbling, don't you think?'

'Allow me to say that Christ himself tried to guide us on the importance of humility some 2,000 years ago, but we seem to have had some difficulties with either our eyesight, or our hearing, or our memories.' Yehuda absent-mindedly massaged his right knee, stretched it in front of him then rose out of his chair. He paced around the room, stopped at a bookshelf and balanced himself with one hand on the shelf as he swung his right knee backwards and forwards several times.

'Having said this,' he continued as though there had been no pause, 'I would now like to turn our attention to the primary purpose of this meeting.'

'Global cooling?' Tara asked with a smile.

'Certainly. If our sun is going to be at the epicentre of the Milky Way in 2012, then one consequence may be that the earth's surface may then begin to cool for the foreseeable future. I am mindful of the 100,000-year glaciation cycle which was originally identified back in the 1920s. And also the potential for sunspot activity to quieten down from 2012 onwards. I hope you didn't think that I asked you here today just to "shoot the breeze" if I may use that term.' Yehuda looked at his watch. 'My goodness,' he exclaimed. 'It is now seven o'clock. I seem to have seriously underestimated the time required.'

'Well if we are about to reach the main item on the menu, why don't we head off and grab a bite to eat and continue our discussions over dinner?' Patrick suggested.

'Food! Great idea,' Tara agreed.

Yehuda nodded, then rummaged around to find some other papers on his desk, folded them lengthwise and pushed their bulk into the inside pocket of his professorial looking jacket.

CHAPTER 30

WITHIN HALF AN hour, they were all seated al fresco in La Quintana restaurant in the Plaza De Espana.

'Patrick and I would like you to be our guest tonight,' Tara said as the waiter handed around menus.

Yehuda inclined his head to one side, squinting his eyes slightly, a comically hesitant look on his face. Tara recognised that, however open-minded he was on so many other matters, he was still of that older generation of Latin males who found it difficult to accept a woman paying for him. She came to his rescue.

'There is a price to pay, of course, and that is you must choose the food on our behalf. My Spanglish isn't good enough.'

Patrick had no such language inhibitions and ordered aperitifs for Tara and himself, and a Presidente Light for the *professore*, as he had now taken to referring to Yehuda. There was the hint of a devilish smile on his face and even in the short time they had known each other, Tara recognised it as the signal that he was about to launch into a story or—even more probably—an irreverent joke. She knew that one day, his cheeky sense of humour would get him into deep, deep trouble; she just hoped today would not be that day.

'Let me tell you about these two Jewish guys who had grown up together in Connecticut,' Patrick began, modifying the identity of the heroes for Yehuda's benefit, and the location of the story for Tara's sake.

Tara stole a glance at Yehuda, cringing inwardly at Patrick's political incorrectness. No, she couldn't even pass it off as that. It was just plain lack of social sensitivity … social manners. To her surprise, Yehuda was grinning at Patrick and with each new irreverent turn in the story his grin widened. Patrick might be many delicious things, but a gentleman with social graces this mining engineer would never be. It was time for her to take temporary leave of them, on the excuse of freshening up before the food arrived. She couldn't resist a playful, if hard bump on Patrick's shoulder as she stepped past his chair.

Just at that moment Patrick had rocked back, his centre of gravity directly above the two back legs of his chair. He threw his arms forward to try to rebalance, grabbed at the edge of the table … missed, and caught a fistful of tablecloth instead. Blissfully unaware of the chaos she had helped create, Tara was already through the door when gravity claimed Patrick. As his arms went skyward after missing their grab for the table, the fistful of tablecloth went with him. He kicked his legs forward in a last desperate action. They caught under the tabletop but, instead of saving him, the table, the white linen cloth, crockery, glassware and cutlery came crashing down with him.

Almost as quickly as disaster had befallen, Patrick was surrounded by waiters, the restaurant manager and adjoining diners. He was helped to his feet, brushed off, and the table replaced on its legs. Everything else was swooped up in the tablecloth with an efficiency that suggested this was a regular occurrence. Patrick offered profuse apologies, which the manager accepted fairly good-naturedly.

After the initial shock, Yehuda had giggled behind his hand, more like a schoolboy than a professor.

'Well, they were most pleasant about that … I guess it means an enormous tip at the end,' Patrick whispered to Yehuda, grimacing in his embarrassment.

By the time Tara returned, two waiters had, between them, more or less made all the necessary repairs and brought fresh drinks. Tara, and a third waiter bearing the food, arrived simultaneously. She noted the silence that had descended between Patrick and Yehuda, and assumed the worst.

'Yehuda, I want to apologise if you felt that Patrick and I were behaving in an undignified manner,' she said. 'Patrick,' she continued, turning to face him 'you should be ashamed of yourself!'

To her surprise, Yehuda seemed not in the slightest put out. He stifled a giggle and seemed unable to speak. Then Patrick chipped in.

'Talk about the pot calling the kettle black. All *I* did was tell a joke. *You* damn near caused the destruction of the restaurant.'

What on earth was he talking about now?

Patrick looked from Tara to Yehuda, then the two men looked at Tara. They seemed to be enjoying something she was not part of.

When Yehuda could not contain his laughter, Patrick told her what her actions had led to. 'We're probably going to get a bill for at least $100 for broken crockery.' His voice was still tinged with laughter, and there was certainly no remorse.

Tara looked at him in open-mouthed horror.

'Tara,' Yehuda said, 'I beg you to please not take this too seriously. We will all three of us share the check. I will gladly pay my share. I have not had this much fun in years. It is good to let one's hair down now and then, and there has been no real harm done.'

A happier silence descended as Tara found herself unable to maintain the momentum of her adult role amongst these two overgrown school-boys, one of whom was old enough to be the other's father.

It wasn't until they were nearing the end of their meal that the mood returned to a somewhat more serious discussions. Yehuda pulled out a piece of paper from his jacket pocket. He passed it across the table to Patrick.

'I would ask the two of you to indulge me for just a little while longer please,' he said. 'I want to draw your attention to the primary reason for wanting to meet with you.'

They both nodded, although Patrick's eyes remained on the paper Yehuda had given him.

'I have observed a pattern emerging over the past few years, which has been causing me some concern,' Yehuda began. 'It relates to the "distributed electricity" model that is now routinely relied on world-wide, and in particular in the Northern Hemisphere.'

'By distributed electricity, I assume you mean producing electricity at a central power station and delivering it via conventional powerlines to users?' Patrick enquired.

'Yes, exactly.'

'Well, that sounds pretty standard—pretty universal. Why is that a concern?' Tara asked.

Yehuda looked her in the eyes before responding. She was learning to read the signs. He was about to make a point that was important to him.

'I personally monitored the internet on a daily basis over the winter of 2006–7,' he said. 'I was specifically looking for electricity blackouts across North America arising from the unusually cold weather. You know, snowstorms, blizzards, that kind of thing.'

'What did you find?'

'Four million people went without electricity for short periods during the three month period I was checking.'

'Why would you even think of doing that?'

'The scientist in me likes facts. And because that winter was unusually severe, I wanted to get a hands-on feel for the possible impact of global cooling. The currently fashionable explanation on climate change is that carbon dioxide emissions are causing global warming. The other is that variations in the intensity of the sun's irradiation are causing climate change. Even if we cannot agree on which scenario is the more likely, can we agree that this is the status quo?'

Patrick nodded.

'That's what I get from the media,' Tara said.

'Good.' Yehuda rubbed his hands together, as if already experiencing the cold. 'Now we can examine one other anomaly that has come to my attention. The rate of growth of world energy production has been slowing down in the past three years—oil, coal, natural gas, nuclear fission and solar power all added together. In the past two years it has grown at an even slower rate than the rate of growth of world population. The implication of this is that energy production has been falling on a per capita, or per person basis.'

He paused. They looked at him expectantly. He patted his jacket pockets as he did so often when searching for his pipe, but this time he retrieved a pen, turned over his piece of paper, smoothing it out on the table before him.

'You will have noticed that the oil price has been rising strongly.' He doodled an oilrig and a nuclear power symbol. 'This is because the oil industry is facing supply challenges, ones that are likely to manifest more broadly in the next few years. We have passed "peak oil".'

'Which means that the world is now depleting its oil reserves,' Patrick added, perhaps for Tara's benefit.

'Which are expected to be effectively used up within the next forty to fifty years,' Yehuda continued. He added a few lines that rapidly became a car driving downhill, complete with an over-active exhaust.

'Is that what has been worrying you?' Patrick asked.

'In the context of the imminent arrival of global cooling—yes. It's important to remember electricity is primarily generated by coal fired plants. It seems to me, that because of our preoccupation with carbon dioxide emissions, the rate at which new coal-fired power generating plants are being built has been slowing down ... and has not been keeping pace with growing demand.'

'What about nuclear fission power stations?' Tara asked. 'Isn't that *du jour* with some of the world leaders at the moment?'

'Nuclear ... there are still so many unknowns, so many questions without answers, so many problems without solutions, perhaps also so many issues we have not yet foreseen. I'm afraid that nuclear as the answer is not as simple as they suggest.'

'Then there must be supply stresses building within the electricity distribution grids.'

'Uhuh ... and bearing in mind that over ninety percent of all trans-portation within the US is dependent on oil, what do you think will happen to coal deliveries to existing power generating plants, if the US starts to experience oil shortages?'

'Why wouldn't they increase oil output?' Tara asked, ignoring his question.

'Aah, but it's not just a matter of pumping the oil,' Yehuda answered. 'The oil that comes out of the ground needs to be refined, and refineries are very expensive to build. It is a *Catch 22*, as you say. Most existing refineries are operating at close to capacity; very few new ones are coming on stream in the West. And the US has passed the point where it can satisfy any further growth in demand for refined oil products. But the building of new oil refineries cannot be justified in any quantity if the supply of oil is limited.'

'Brown-outs,' Patrick said, answering Yehuda's earlier question.

'And overlay that statement with the possibility of global cooling. What do you think will happen?'

'A surge in demand during winter. Blackouts.'

'And finally, what do you think will happen to the overhead power lines if global cooling gives rise to significantly increased snow precipitation?'

'Ice on the wires, and more blackouts from power interruptions. Maybe even dysfunctionality of the grids.'

'The way you put it, Tara observed after several moments, 'if global *warming* continues we will at best experience rolling brown-outs … unless we install, say, solar power plants. If global *cooling* manifests, solar power will be far less effective anyway. We will experience debilitating blackouts.'

'Maybe even a collapse of the system. It's virtually inevitable,' Patrick added in a low voice.

Yehuda put both his hands under his chin and faced Tara. 'As an American citizen, I'm sure you will be aware of an electrical overload incident that occurred in the summer of 2003 which gave rise to a cascading power blackout across the Northern USA and in Ontario. Fifty million people were without electricity for some hours as a result.'

'I was outside the country at the time, but I heard all about it on my return.'

'What's the timing of all this?' Patrick asked.

Yehuda turned over the paper he had earlier passed to Patrick. 'Let's have a look at that chart.'

ENERGY PER CAPITA: 1930–2030[ix]

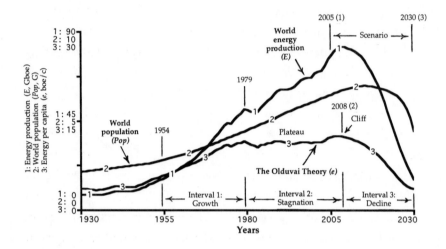

THE OLDUVAI THEORY DISAGGREGATED: 1930 TO 2030. THE MILESTONES ALONG CURVE 3 DEPICT AND DELIMIT THE OT'S THREE INTERVALS. NOTES: (1) DATA FOR 2005 ARE: E = 78.5, POP = 6.5 AND e = 12.2. (2) THE SCENARIO VALUES FOR 2008 ARE: E = 82.8, POP = 6.7 AND e = 12.4. (3) THE VALUES FOR 2030 ARE: E = 15.1, POP = 4.4 AND e = 3.4. DATA SOURCES: [1] FOR ENERGY—ROMER (1985) AND BP (2006). [2] FOR POPULATION—UN (2006).

'What *is* this?' Tara asked.

'A pictorial representation of an argument called the Olduvai Theory—an argument based on observable historical trends within the areas of world energy production and world population density.'

'An argument? What do mean?' Tara asked.

'If you look at the graph line marked #1,' Yehuda said, pointing with his pen, 'you will see that world energy production grew strongly for about fifty years, beginning in around 1955—a decade after World War II had ended—and ending in 2005.'

'The steepest curve,' Patrick observed. Tara nodded.

'If you now look at the line marked #2, you will see that it represents the growth of human population of the planet. According to the notes that accompany it, the graph shows world population at 6.5 billion people in 2005, peaking in 2008 at 6.7 billion souls. Thereafter population is forecast to decline.'

'And the graph line marked #3,' Tara said. 'It's flatter than the other two—particularly since 1980.' She turned her head sideways. 'Energy per capita,' she read.

'That's a *ratio* of #1 and #2. It is a graph of actual historical energy per capita dating back to 1930 and, going forward, it is a graph of forecast energy production per capita.'

'It's now falling.' Tara said.

'That's what I was trying to communicate earlier. And it turns down strongly in 2008 because the Olduvai Theory forecasts energy production to *fall* in absolute terms even though population continues to grow right up to 2012. After 2012, the theory forecasts that human population on Earth will begin to decrease in absolute terms. And that population numbers will begin to collapse, eventually reaching around 4.4 billion in 2030.'

'2012.' Patrick leant forward. 'That coincides with the Mayan calendar date.'

'Very good,' Yehuda replied.

'I wouldn't have put it quite in that way,' Tara observed, the humour in her remark softened by the look she gave Patrick.

'But how can those two be related?' Patrick asked. 'At face value, the two models have nothing to do with one another.'

'The only logical way that these two models can both point to the same date, is if we think of the Earth as a biological system in its own right. Our earth itself and all biological life in it and on it would have to pulse to a rhythm which is governed by cosmological forces.'

'Aha. That's why you spent so much time earlier this evening talking about the Egyptians and their attitude to metaphysics. You believe they must have understood this. The Mayans too,' Tara said. 'And that would seem to imply it's happened before. The map on your wall … earlier civilizations. It all fits.'

Patrick nodded. 'Okay. On the assumption that global warming is being caused by sunspot activity, and given that sunspot activity is expected to peak in 2012, I can now see why you are linking the Mayan calendar date with the Olduvai Theory date. Though the cause of both might be something else, something outside our biological system.'

'Yes, but what's the Olduvai model's underlying rationale for the expected fall in per capita energy production?' Tara asked.

'I'm afraid that if we go into the detail of the Olduvai Theory we might be here all night. Suffice it to say that one primary driver is population shifts and the other is a forecast decrease in total energy production.'

'How sadly ironic if we slowed down on construction of power plants when we should have been speeding up,' Tara said, folding her arms tightly in front of her. 'So where does all this leave us? Up the proverbial creek without a paddle?'

'Strangely, we are not really being proactive—even though up to ninety percent of humanity is at threat,' Yehuda responded. 'We are blithely relying on private enterprise to solve these life threatening problems. It's as if the collective psyche of the human race has gone into neutral as far as our survival is concerned.'

'Like the deer blinded by the headlights of the oncoming car,' Tara said.

'But I have a plan.'

'Aha. Would you care to share?' Patrick asked.

'Of course,' Yehuda said. 'Why else would I have asked you to meet with me this evening—which I now notice has turned late—with a minute to midnight rapidly approaching?' He smiled.

'Time flies ... as you were saying,' Patrick said with a forced smile of his own. He had not missed the professor's meaning. 'Let's hear your plan.'

'The National Centre for Atmospheric Research in the US, which forecasts the incidence of sunspot activity, projects a peaking of sunspot activity, also in 2012. Because this date coincides with the Mayan calendar forecast, and because they—and the Olduvai Theory—all triangulate to

2012, I am prepared to accept at face value that 2012 may turn out to be a watershed year. If humanity has not begun with urgency to broadly embrace an alternative energy or energies to both fossil fuels and nuclear fission by 2012, then the Olduvai Theory's prediction may turn out to have been prescient. As matter of pragmatism, we should not get too hung up on our disagreements as to causes. We need to *do* something!'

'But what?' Tara asked.

'We can do what Patrick had concluded we should be doing before I met him,' Yehuda answered. 'Find a mainstream alternative to fossil fuels, and the place to look—again as Patrick has intuitively under-stood—is in the environmental energy arena.'

'But my views are merely conceptual,' Patrick protested.

'But *mine* aren't!' Yehuda paused with dramatic effect. 'I have been testing just such an energy alternative for over twenty years. It is ready to be launched in test sites.'

'Your weather control energy?' Tara asked.

A look, which Tara could not interpret, washed over Yehuda's face. He appeared to be collecting his thoughts, as if what he had to say was inordinately important. 'Patrick and Tara,' he demurred, 'I want you to forget that I ever mentioned its ability to impact weather. Yes, guided by the research into cloud formation by the Dane, Henrik Svensmark, we were able to replicate his laboratory experiments in the sky above Santo Domingo using the energy technology I have been testing.' He pushed his chair back, as if to stand up, then appeared to remember he was in a restaurant. 'There is no way that we can really control cosmological forces. So it is my guess that if ever there was other intelligent life on this planet, one reason they didn't survive may be that they arrogantly believed they could control the environment. As our Muslim friends have been telling us for over 1,400 years, the key to humanity's survival this time around will lie in *submission*. We need to submit to the superior power of these cosmological forces. We need to submit to the inevitability that global cooling will eventually manifest. We have 425,000 years of accumulated data that tells us it will, versus a few decades of accumulated data that argues it won't.'

'It's a bit like the story of the one hundred mile race between the marathon runner and a horse,' Patrick concurred. 'It doesn't matter if the horse walks the first mile or how fit or how fast that marathon runner may be, the horse will win the race. It's inevitable.'

The three faces around the table reflected varying emotions.

Yehuda nodded slowly. 'To bet the farm—or the world—on the marathon runner would be madness. Our most sensible way forward will flow from acknowledging that the forces of nature are more powerful than humanity can ever hope to overcome or even influence.'

'Okay, we hear you,' Tara said, by way of acknowledgement. 'I, for one, am prepared to accept your philosophical argument, but what about the practical side? What, specifically can we do?'

'The timing of the arrival of global cooling is not particularly relevant if we acknowledge that we need to act with urgency. Frankly, what I have in mind will even render it irrelevant whether we will be experiencing global cooling or global warming. In my view we should move with a sense of urgency to harness the power of nature to ensure our survival.'

'As they say, planning is all about being where the puck is going to be,' Patrick interjected. He lifted an unused spoon from the table and swiped it theatrically above the table. 'But I'm afraid that merely adopting the appropriate attitude falls far short of a practical plan.'

Yehuda nodded. 'Agree, agree.'

'Okay,' Patrick ventured. 'So, let's get our feet back on the ground. How, *precisely*, is this energy technology of yours going to avoid blackouts and brownouts—whichever?'

'We won't even try to avoid that outcome,' Yehuda said. 'Instead, we are going to adapt our behaviour. If the politicians foolishly remain wedded to the distributed energy model currently in place, it appears they will seek to power it with nuclear fission, a technology that was fundamentally inappropriate to begin with.'

Tara and Patrick said nothing, waiting for Yehuda to explain his idea.

'I want you to think of the history of computing,' he said. 'How did that evolve?'

'You mean from huge mainframes to desktops and laptops?' Patrick could almost feel his brain synapses crackling from the surge of mental electricity as he put two and two together in a sudden jolt of understanding. 'Holy sh ... mackerel!' he exclaimed. 'You want to generate energy at the point of consumption ... turn the power generation model on its head—just like PCs took computing power away from the remote mainframe and onto the desk. You want to finesse the blackouts ... to, to change the model from distributed energy to on-site energy production ... dodge the consequences rather than have to fight them.'

'In a word—yes.' Yehuda pumped his fist excitedly on the table and Tara lunged for his glass as it was jolted into the air.

'And if the new technology is based on electromagnetic energy, that will automatically give rise to a cleaning up of the environment as a bonus side-effect,' Patrick said, the excitement in his own voice rising. 'And the argument over greenhouse gases and global warming becomes irrelevant.'

'Can your energy technology achieve all these things?' Tara asked.

'I believe so.'

'Can you give us details?' Patrick asked.

'Again, yes, but not at this stage. Right now, all I want you to focus on is that this technology will allow a private householder or a factory, or an office block, or a hotel, or a suburb within a city to generate electricity for on-site consumption at a peppercorn operating cost, and that it may even have the capacity to revolutionise transport.'

'When can you tell us?' Tara asked.

'I want to give you more than just details,' Yehuda answered. 'I want to ask you and Patrick to use your network of contacts to guide me in how this technology might be commercialised across the world ... but we must not get ahead of ourselves. Don't forget that we will be meeting on Sunday night to discuss the results of my research into the Ark of the Covenant flowing from Patrick's questions. I would like Mehmet to join us. You will discover that he and I have already been working together— which is why much of what I have told you this evening about the Ancients is already known to him.'

CHAPTER 31

'I CAN'T BELIEVE that I am going to the Samana Peninsular with the most beautiful woman in the world and that she's the one flying the plane,' Patrick said, looking sideways at Tara in the pilot seat of the King Air. 'And I barely know her.' There was an exaggeratedly fatalistic tone in his voice.

'There's still time to change your mind.'

'Naah. I wouldn't be dead for quids.'

She looked at him quizzically.

'It's an Australian expression,' he said. 'It means I'm deliriously happy.'

'Hmmm. Delirious sounds about right.'

The Santo Domingo air traffic control tower crackled through their earphones and Tara put a finger to her lips to silence further conversation for the time being. She pushed all else out of her mind as she busied herself with the pre-flight checklist and, minutes later, they were airborne.

Aurelio and his friend, Beatrix Cruz, were seated a couple of rows behind Tara and Patrick. Safely stashed with its own seat belt was Aurelio's guitar, an inclusion that had surprised Tara; he'd made no mention of his interest in music during their trip to the amber mine the previous week. When he'd introduced Beatrix to them just a few minutes before boarding the plane, Tara's initial assessment was of a young woman, reed thin, an attractive aura of nascent sensuality about her, but with way too much makeup. Tara's eyes had tracked down the girl's figure: a white tank top that was a size too small, blue jeans that could have been painted onto her slender figure. She was probably around seventeen or eighteen and rapidly growing out of her clothes, but by the look of Patrick's enthusiastic welcome, he didn't share her reservations.

Tara had taken the time to study Beatrix further. She seemed ill at ease. It was probably her first time in a small aeroplane and Patrick was trying hard to charm her, allay any fears. Perhaps her first impression was a tad harsh. Beneath the make-up and costume jewellery she could admire the youngster's high Creole cheekbones. Her mid-length shiny black hair had been pulled back to expose a wide and attractive fore-head. Her brown doe eyes were large and clear, and despite the surface trappings, they radiated innocence—even a suggestion of mystery. Some big sisterly guidance … and she could be very attractive.

A few minutes after takeoff, Tara flicked on the automatic pilot switch, and her mind drifted back to Beatrix. There was something compellingly unusual about her. She would have to ensure the young-sters enjoyed the weekend. Perhaps some sort of a party on the beach this evening?

It seemed they had barely taken off before Tara was banking the plane for the approach to the short landing strip. She was pleasantly surprised to discover that the grass runway she was expecting had been recently tarred. A positive omen. Remarkably, the flight had taken only around thirty minutes. According to Aurelio, the same trip by car would have taken over four hours given the traffic and the mountainous terrain landwards of Las Terrenas, their ultimate destination this morning.

'Lady and gentlemen,' Tara announced in her best airline captain's voice, as the wheels smoothly stroked the tarmac. 'Welcome to civilised paradise. It's 8.30 a.m. local time. The day is young, the air is fresh and clean, and we have the whole weekend ahead of us. It's great to be alive!'

Patrick leant across from the co-pilot's seat to kiss her affectionately on the cheek. 'That was such a buzz—putting my life in your hands— you can fly me anytime,' he said with a cheeky grin. He turned to face Aurelio and Beatrix, each seated at a window on opposite sides of the aisle. 'Okay troupers let's get this show on the road.'

Aurelio favoured him with a sheepish grin, while Beatrix's mouth barely twitched at the corners. Patrick was conscious that she had diffi-culty in making eye contact with him. This must be a new and intimidating experience for both of them and they were not yet sure how to behave. A gossamer thought insinuated its way into his mind and began to take shape. They should have a lobster barbie on the beach that night. Aurelio could bring his guitar ...

He glanced back in Tara's direction, but decided that this was not the time to voice the thought. She was otherwise occupied with shutting down the plane. His mind conjured up a salacious vision of her erotically swaying hips during the merengue dancing the other evening. He smiled. She would more than likely jump at the opportunity of dancing on the sand.

'Wait till you see where we're staying, guys,' he said to Aurelio and Beatrix.

'You know I would have been happy to have booked it for you,' Aurelio said. 'Where are we staying?'

'Aah, I have my networks and contacts too, you know. But it's a surprise.' Patrick rubbed his hands together in impish evilness. 'All I will say right now is that it is normally rented out by the week, but I managed to strike a deal because it was not yet the high season. All I will say is, Playa Coson, on Punta Bonita.' Then for Tara's benefit, 'Punta Bonita is a spit of land jutting out into the Atlantic Ocean slightly to the west of Las Terrenas. Playa Coson is a seven kilometre stretch of wild and untouched beach at the end of a private access pathway.'

They collected the rented Jeep from the hire car desk, and Patrick bounced the keys happily in the palm of his hand. 'Punta Bonita is only a 150-metre walk from where we'll be staying. On the other side is Playa Bonita, a surf beach. And from there, you can see over to the islands of Las Ballenas.'

'Sounds like just this side of heaven,' Tara said.

'Guys, we gotta do whatever it takes to make this weekend a lifetime experience,' Patrick shouted twenty minutes later as the Jeep bounced along the six kilometres of winding gravel road that would take them to Las Terrenas. 'We all need to relax and make ourselves at home.'

A little while later, he stopped the Jeep outside Jessie Rentals, a bike rental shop on Calle Carmen in the fishing village of Las Terrenas. Patrick turned to face Aurelio in the back seat 'Hey mate, d'you know how to drive a motorbike?' His tone was teasing—motorbikes were a primary mode of transport in Santo Domingo and the village was full of the four-wheeled variety.

Aurelio nodded happily. 'Si señor.'

'Cut the señor crap, Aurelio. I'm Patrick, she's Tara, and you and Beatrix are our guests for the weekend. We're here to have a great time— all of us together.'

'Si señor.' The voice was deadpan, but Aurelio's chin had dropped fractionally towards his chest and he looked up at Patrick with a hint of mischievousness. Patrick understood that his leg was being gently pulled.

He turned to face Tara. 'Aurelio and I are going inside to meet with the owner, whose name believe it or not, happens to be Patrick. He's arranged for someone to show us how to drive one of those quads over there.' He pointed to a row of four-wheel Yamaha motorbikes. 'Why don't you and Beatrix go for a walk to check out the lie of the land around here and we'll meet in, say, half an hour?'

'But we've already got wheels,' Tara protested. 'What do we need more for? We're only here for three days.'

'Yeah, but we can drive along the beach, and it'll give Aurelio and Beatrix some independence if they want it.'

Tara shrugged. It sounded like a boy thing. But even so, she couldn't see why she and Beatrix needed to be excluded from the driving lesson. She saw no purpose in arguing the point if this was to be a pleasant holiday. 'Fair enough. See you back here in thirty.'

The two women meandered down a gravel lane dotted with outdoor cafés, absorbing the ambience of the village. Tara was not surprised to see the same coconut palms from La Romana resort beach here too. And she was enthralled to see that the roofs of many of the huts along the side streets were covered in palm fronds, and that some of their walls were painted in the same attractive pastel colours of the huts along the Carretera Turística.

As soon as Tara began to focus on the charm of the little village, her enthusiasm bubbled over to Beatrix and the ice between them was broken. Beatrix took pride in showing Tara aspects of her culture, even though she, too, was a visitor to the village. It took less than five minutes for the two women to begin chatting as if they had known one another for years.

'How did you and Aurelio meet?'

'We have known each other all our lives. Aurelio he ees my cozen.'

'A close relative?'

'No.' She pronounced the word as 'nor', with a silent letter 'r', in a way that Tara found endearing. 'Our family ees a big one. He ees a distant cozen. I think Aurelio, he invited me because to show off.' The smile was demure, conspiratorial.

'You like him, don't you?'

Beatrix did not reply. Tara thought she saw a slight hunch of the shoulders and a barely perceptible nod. The girl stared at the ground as they walked, her head slightly forward.

'Aurelio never told me he could play the guitar. Does he play well?'

'*Muy, muy bueno.*' There was something in the enthusiastic way Beatrix delivered the message, and both women laughed. They understood each other.

Beyond the cafés was a blue painted entrance façade to what might once have been an old church building. Through the entrance were shops. It was not quite as big as a mall, more like a gallery. Tara cast her eye over the stone mosaic floor and the clear lacquered wooden poles that graced the external covered walkways. A timber slatted ceiling covered with palm fronds was designed to shelter the shoppers in wet or hot weather. The shopping gallery was both practical and comfortably inviting.

A fruit vendor, selling pineapples, coconuts and sugarcane from the platform of a rickety old open truck, made Tara smile with a sense of familiarity. This particular vendor was not wearing a colourful singlet, but a check shirt that must have been through a hundred washes.

The village seemed to have a feeling of carefree tranquillity and comforting friendliness. It had something distinctive. Character? Charm? Tara couldn't quite put her finger on it.

They continued their wanderings. The main road through Las Terrenas was tarred, but this did not detract from the sense that they had arrived at a sleepy country town. Everything seemed to move so slowly. Tara took in the scene which encompassed a dozen or so motor cycles parked at the edge of the roadside under the shade of a huge old tree, and two parked F100 style trucks with their windows left wide open. Further down the road, on the opposite side, she saw a couple of quads. In a moment of wry amusement she realised that this was city central. There were around twenty parked vehicles and maybe six or eight pedestrians in sight. But they weren't really going anywhere; they seemed to be lolling around in pairs, just chatting to one another. Smiling, she found herself wondering what they did to relax.

As they stood there taking in the scene, two young kids wobbled by on a pushbike. Tara couldn't help notice how remarkably clean they were for kids riding along a dusty road, and their chocolate-toned skin gave them a healthy outdoors look. One, probably about eight or nine, was seated on the crossbar, awkwardly battling to keep the bike upright as he steered it. The other, maybe a couple of years older sat on the saddle as he did the pedalling. He smiled at them through missing teeth as they passed by, and he waved cheekily to her, a perfect stranger. Or maybe he had been waving to Beatrix? A Toyota truck rolled soporifically past at about fifteen miles per hour, its driver looking for all the world like his mind might just as easily have been on fishing as driving.

Tara and Beatrix turned down a side road.

'What's that building?' Tara pointed to a double storey building that stood out amongst its neighbours.

'It ees, how you say? ... an agent for property?'

'You mean a real estate agency?'

'Si.'

It was a hive of silence and inactivity. Other than a few pictures in its windows—the details of which they couldn't make out from this distance—it looked to Tara more like an art gallery.

'You seem very much at home here Beatrix.'

'Si. I know this places well. Long ago it was jorst a little fishing village, but now many people from all over the world they come here to their holiday villas. Mainly they are from France, because the French were the first to come in the seventies. Then later, people from other countries in Europe, they also came here. Most of the restaurants in the village today they are owned by people from Europe.'

Tara looked at Beatrix with mounting interest. There was a bright young woman beneath the plastered makeup.

'In the fisherman's village near where Patrick parked the Jeep, there is the Indiana Café. That one is owned by Franky. He is a Frenchman. The Mosquito Bar is owned by Alex. I think maybe Alex, he is Spanish. And the Café Atlantico, it is run by a man who comes from the Principality of Andorra, between France and Spain,' she said. 'His name is Sergio.'

'Wow, you do know this village well. But how do you know all these people?'

'Aurelio and me, we have a cousin who works here as a *camarera*—a maid I think you say—in one of the vacation villas.' There followed a long genealogical explanation of the exact relationship of the cousin to both her and Aurelio. Tara was lost after the first sentence.

Then, in front of them was the fruit vendor in the check shirt again. He had either moved his truck or they had come full circle. Tara looked at her watch. 'Oh my God! It's ten o'clock already. We've been gone an hour. Patrick and Aurelio will be wondering where we are. Do you think you could find us the quickest way back?'

Beatrix laughed. '*Ciertamente.*' She reached out to grasp Tara's hand. We should walk this way.'

They walked hand-in-hand in silence for a while, concentrating on their hurried steps. Eventually, Tara broke the silence. 'Patrick says there is a beach within walking distance of where we are staying. Perhaps we could make a fire this evening ... barbecue some lobsters. Maybe we could persuade Aurelio to play that guitar he has brought along. What do you think?'

'I would like that very much. And you should not worry too much about Aurelio. You can be sure that you will have no *problema* with him. 'She paused and then giggled knowingly. '*Ciertamente*, he will play.'

This time their laughter was more like schoolgirlish giggles.

Patrick saw the two women laughing as they turned the corner near the bike hire shop. 'Where the heck have you been?' he asked, a worried frown creasing his forehead. 'I thought you must have had gotten lost, until Aurelio told me that Beatrix knows the village. Did you stop for a cup of coffee?'

'I'm so sorry,' Tara said, he voice full of contrition. 'We just got carried away—it's such a delightful village.' Before Patrick could respond, she dislodged her hand from Beatrix's and reached up to put her arms around his neck. 'I'm *so* pleased we came.'

What could he say to that? He felt a surge of warmth from Tara's body against his. He was mildly embarrassed by this open show of affection in front of Aurelio and Beatrix. 'We went for a five minute quad ride while you were gone,' he said rather quickly and a bit too woodenly. 'And we found a dive centre at the Hotel Palapa on Punta Popy. I spoke to the guys there and they agreed to make a special trip this afternoon, just for us.'

'Do they have a specific destination in mind? How long will it take?' She asked the questions in a business-like tone, picking up on his awkwardness. She was not one to hide her feelings if the occasion didn't demand it—it had been a long drought—and she was enjoying not being 'Captain Tara Geoffrey'. It wasn't often that she could wear her emotions on her sleeve.

'They took us onto the Playa Popy, a beach very close to their shop,' he answered. 'From there we could see Las Ballenas, a couple of nearby islands—so named because they look like they could be whales swimming out in the ocean. It's only about a fifteen minute boat ride to the fringe reef around the islands and apparently there's plenty to see.'

'Do you think we'll see any turtles? I especially wanted to photograph a hawksbill turtle so I can hang it on my wall at home.'

'I imagine it's possible, but I wouldn't want to hang around too long there, because after that we're going to another dive site. There's also an underwater canyon nearby—maybe a five minute boat ride from the Las Ballenas dive site. Apparently it's also a magical experience. All in all we should be home by six o'clock.'

'Fine by me. How about you?' she asked Beatrix.

Beatrix hesitated.

'Aurelio and I had a chat while you guys were out getting lost,' Patrick interjected. 'They are not really into diving, so he and Beatrix won't be coming with us. And Beatrix has a cousin who lives in Las Terrenas. They want to look her up.'

Tara was amused to hear that *Beatrix* had a cousin living in Las Terrenas. Men and their egos. Obviously, Aurelio had seen fit not to inform Patrick that Beatrix was also his cousin.

'But there's also another reason,' Patrick said, trying to sound mysterious.

'Oh? What's that?'

'Aurelio and I decided that we're going to have a party on the beach tonight. He's going to make all the arrangements. Apparently he knows a few people in Las Terrenas. In fact, he seems quite at home here. It turns out he even knew the manager at Jessie Rentals, a girl by the name of Soya. She seemed quite taken with him.'

Tara looked at him askance. 'What kind of a party?' Was he a mind reader?

Patrick looked at the odd, but unreadable expression on Tara's face. 'We were thinking of a two stage process. The four of us could have a lobster barbie—'

'A what?'

'A lobster barbie. Oh, sorry. You Americans call it a barbecue … with crayfish.'

Tara just looked at him. She said nothing.

He mistook her silence for disapproval. Perhaps his reaction to her hug had been too cool and he had pissed her off. He waited. Still nothing.

'*i pardon*, Patrick,' Beatrix interjected, 'Tara and me, we were talking about that jost before. She was telling me the same thing.'

'You're kidding me.'

'No.' This time the 'nor' sounded more dramatic than endearing to Tara.

'When did you get that idea?' he asked Tara.

'Oooh, when we were about ten minutes into the flight.'

'I got the same idea around the time we landed.'

'Lobster barbecue and all?'

He nodded, grinning.

'And the second stage?' she asked.

'Aurelio offered to play his guitar for us ... some dance music—you know, merengue and maybe also some bachata music.' The words tumbled out of his mouth in a rush. 'I thought you and I would give him some cash to go and buy the lobsters and some grog. He thinks he can rustle up a few people to join the party at around nine ... to give some local flavour to the music and the dancing. He knows someone here who plays the bongo drums or something. We can dance the night away.'

Tara looked at Beatrix, and Beatrix looked at Tara. Both laughed and put their arms around each other's shoulders.

'*Now* what have I said?'

Tara turned to Aurelio, gave him a sisterly hug around his shoulders, and planted a kiss on his cheek. 'Thank you! I think it's a wonderful idea. I'm so looking forward to dancing tonight—especially the bachata ... I think!' Turning to Patrick she did a little wiggle of her hips that showed what she meant. Then, for the second time in ten minutes, she threw her arms around his neck, leaned her body onto his and kissed him fully on the mouth. With gleeful laughter in her voice, she said, 'You guys have honed in on exactly what I was hoping to do. We're going to have a fantastic weekend!'

'We should get going to the villa,' Patrick said. 'I've got the directions here so—Aurelio and Beatrix—you can follow us on the quad.'

Patrick still hadn't told them where they were staying and it wasn't until the mansion came into sight at the very end of Bonita Road that he proclaimed, 'Voila! Villa Sofia!'

Tara did a double take. She recognised this house ... or, at the very least there was something faintly familiar about it ... about the architecture. It had an unobtrusively low-pitched roof and, from what she could see, seamless transitions between indoor and outdoor living. 'Have you ever heard of a guy by the name of Frank Lloyd Wright?'

'Was he related to those two guys who pioneered aviation?'

She laughed. 'Good guess, but no prize. No, Frank Lloyd Wright was the greatest American architect of all time. I visited his home in Chicago a couple of years ago. It's a museum now. The man was a genius; generations ahead of his time. He specialised in the principle of organic architecture, which allowed his buildings to blend in harmoniously with their environments. He'd have melted the hearts of the modern day greenies.'

'Why are you raising this now?'

'There's something about this Villa Sofia that reminds me of the house that Lloyd Wright designed for a Mrs Clinton Walker in California. I remembered her name because it was the same as President Clinton, and the name Walker stuck because Hillary must have come close to walking because of his womanising.'

'You've got a strange turn of mind, linking this house with Clinton and his philandering. Why are you raising this now, oh light of my life and fire of my loins?'

'Fire of your loins, huh? Later tonight, we'll need to investigate that in a little more depth,' she said, and then continued to expound her original thought. 'This is no ordinary holiday home. It's magnificent! How did you find it?'

'Only a *little* more depth? Ouch!' He rubbed his arm where she had playfully thumped him. 'I found it on the web. I sent the letting agent an email and the owner himself responded. Apparently he lives in France. He and his family use it as a holiday home. They let it out when they're not using it. Great guy. Very helpful.'

'Big for a holiday home. Look at the size of the gardens. Do you often conduct two simultaneous conversations?'

'It's my split personality, dear pot-calling-kettle-black.'

They got out of the Jeep at the front gate. Aurelio and Beatrix drove up behind them, but remained seated on the quad, its engine running. They were in deep conversation.

Tara opened the gate. She walked through it into the garden and stopped to gaze at the pristine pool and the surrounding emerald lawn dotted with coconut palms. The low-pitched roof at the front of the house extended well beyond the outer wall to provide shade over an inviting patio. A solid timber dining table and six sleekly modern chairs sat at its centre.

Through the window Tara caught a glimpse of white tiled floors, stark white walls and ceilings, and dark contrasting brown timber beams. There was a splash of blue and red colour from a painting hanging above a modernistic settee.

'This place is amazing,' she said, just as the door was opened by a plump maid. The roundness of her face made it difficult to guess her age, but she was probably around forty.

She beamed at them. 'Welcome señor and señora to Villa Sofia. My name ees Josefina.' The woman's eyes radiated warmth and welcome, and her figure suggested she was prone to over-sampling whatever cooking she might do for the owners or visitors.

Josefina moved forward to help carry their luggage from the vehicle outside, then stopped dead in her tracks. Several emotions seemed to flash across her face: confusion, consternation, concern and impending conniption. She stood as though planted in the pathway, her gaze on Aurelio and Beatrix. They, in turn, were not looking at the house or the maid, but arguing sotto voce with one another with an excessive use of truncated, jerky hand and arm movements.

'Is something wrong?' Patrick asked.

'Hhrmmph. I weel go and ask, señor.'

She brushed past them, determinedly making her way towards the garden gate. Patrick decided to follow. Tara trailed behind him.

'*Hola* Beatrix,' Josefina said. A torrent of Spanish followed, then an equally excited reply. Then Josefina turned to Aurelio. Her confusion seemed to mount but there was also a rising trace of anger building her voice. 'Aurelio!' she exclaimed '¿*Que tu haces aqui?*' What are you doing here?

Tara's gaze flicked from Josefina to Aurelio. Finally, it settled on Beatrix who, she saw, had tears rolling down her cheeks. *What the…?* 'Is Josefina the cousin you were telling me about?'

'Si Tara. I cannot stay in a house where Josefina is the *camarera* and I am a guest. It ees not right.' Her voice was close to a wail.

'You are a guest?' Josefina demanded. She turned to Aurelio. 'And you!' It was more of an accusation than a question.

'Si.' The single word croaked with the misery and anguish of someone who knows beyond a shadow of doubt that he has committed a heinous crime against all of humanity, but does not know what to do about it.

'*She* is your cousin?' Patrick asked Beatrix, pointing to Josefina. Then, not waiting for an answer, he turned to Josefina. 'How do you know Aurelio?'

'He is also my cozen, señor and I would like your permission to keel heem!' Even in her current state, her respect for class barriers overpowered her inclination to take matters into her own hands in front of the paying guests.

Patrick put two and two together. He turned his back to them, raised his eyebrows and winked at Tara. 'Busted times two,' he said in a whisper meant only for her ears.

Tara gave him a discreet nod. The executive pilot in her was about to assume command of the situation but Patrick beat her to it. He wrapped an arm around Josefina's shoulders, like a coach on the rugby field with an injured player. 'Come with me,' he said authoritatively and began to march her up the garden path towards the house and through the front door. He looked back over his shoulder at Tara. 'I'll be the home captain. You captain the visiting team.'

She nodded to him and turned back to Aurelio and Beatrix. 'Let's all go and sit down on the patio,' she said in a tone that would brook no argument. Beatrix was still tearful. Aurelio looked as though he would have been happier hiding under a rock with the other reptiles.

'Even I had no idea where we were would be staying. Patrick made the arrangements and he wanted it to be a surprise. So it's no one's fault: not you, Beatrix, or Aurelio … or Josefina's.' Beatrix nodded in dumb acknowledgement. Aurelio looked relieved to have the blame shifted from him.

'Do you recognise that you are really upset for Josefina because *she* has been put into a position of embarrassment?'

Beatrix nodded assent.

'Okay. So it is Patrick's and my responsibility to worry about Josefina, and we will not let you down on this. Josefina will not be embarrassed. Okay?'

They both nodded like scolded children.

'Now here's the thing.' She turned to Beatrix. 'We've all agreed that we are going to have a party tonight and I cannot allow my houseguest to come to my party looking so unhappy. So tonight I want you to look extra specially beautiful, Beatrix, for me and for Patrick and for Aurelio—especially for Aurelio. I want him to be very proud of you when you help him to make the party a happy occasion. I want him to be able to tell everyone in Santo Domingo that you were the most beautiful woman there, and there is no reason why you can't be. So I want Josefina to ensure that you dress appropriately for my party. She will know how all the other guests in this house dress.'

Beatrix looked alarmed. 'But all my clothes look like these,' she said. 'I cannot dress any differently.'

'You can if I send you out shopping with Josefina. I will give *her* the money, and I will give *her* instructions on how I want your makeup to look, and your hair and your clothes. You will go together to the beauty parlour and the clothing shop, and *she* will choose what a guest in this house should wear to a beach party. You would be doing me a favour to let me do this for our party … and of course, you may keep the clothes afterwards.'

Beatrix opened her mouth to say something; closed it again, looked at Aurelio, then at Tara. The confusion of emotions on her face was easy to read: surprise, happiness, indebtedness. Tara knew the whole exercise wouldn't cost more than a couple of hundred bucks. It would be cheap at the price and it would make five people a lot happier.

'Aurelio will be making all the preparations for tonight while you are out shopping. Patrick and I will be out diving. And the only thing I want Josefina to do this evening is make a Dominican Creole sauce for the lobster, and maybe some plantain pancakes and salads for the five of us, so there is nothing else for Josefina to do this afternoon.'

'*Five* of us?'

'Of course. We want Josefina to join us at the beach party. Patrick and I will probably want to have an early night after our scuba diving this afternoon, and then Josefina can be *your* guest.'

Beatrix beamed. Her face was split at mouth level from ear to ear. '*Muchas gracias*,' she said, tears once more brimming her eyes. You have made me *muy felize*, Tara, very happy, and I think that Josefina will feel *muy importante* when she chooses my new clothes for me.'

That left one loose end. Tara turned to Aurelio. 'There is no need to waste money on new clothes for a man who already looks like he belongs in these surroundings, but I would like to give you $300 to cover whatever arrangements you need to make for the party please.'

Aurelio looked shocked. '$300 is a lot of money. What can cost that much?'

'Patrick has paid from his own pocket to rent this house and I want to contribute my share, so I will pay for the party.'

'But $300?'

Beatrix grinned conspiratorially. She knew what was coming.

'Aurelio, this will not be a party for just five people. We would like you to invite some of your local friends who love to dance and play music. Patrick and I would like to learn the bachata, and we hope you will play your guitar. You may have to pay other musicians.'

Aurelio's face lit up. This was more than he had been expecting. Tara could almost see his thoughts broadening to encompass who else he might invite.

'We will have dinner just for the five of us at seven o'clock, and then the guests can start to arrive at the beach around nine … maybe twenty or thirty people. So, from the $300 you will buy the lobsters and anything else you and Beatrix and Josefina would like for dinner, and you can buy beer and soft drinks, and also charcoal for the barbecue. This will be my party but you and Beatrix will be the host and hostess. If there is any money left over, I don't want to know about it. It will be your money. I will be happy.' She handed him a bundle of notes.

'The only thing I ask,' she added, 'is that you should make sure that Patrick and I will have the opportunity to dance the bachata, and we may need someone to teach us. Maybe you and Beatrix can teach us?'

Now it was Aurelio's turn to beam.

At that point there were sounds of raucous laughter from inside. Tara rose, and walked in the direction of the noise. Her shoes tapped on the dark wooden floor as she walked towards the rear of the building. It made her feel elegant just being in this stylishly understated house. The predominant colour was ivory but with surprising touches of dramatic colour. There were glimpses of the main garden as well as intimate outdoor alcoves from several of the rooms that she passed.

The laughter came from a large airy kitchen where Josefina and Patrick were huddled together sharing a joke—no doubt one of Patrick's irreverent classics. He had a wicked look in his eye. Tara nodded in amusement at him. She wasn't sure she wanted to know, but her curiosity got the better of her. 'And?'

'Later, maybe ... mmm, I was just comparing the ancestral similarities between Dominican slaves and the Australian penile colony.'

Tara couldn't even begin to imagine what Patrick had been telling Josefina, but it had to be something seriously raunchy. Judging by the hysterical laughter, it had seemed to do the trick. 'Okay your side?' she asked.

'Yep. Yours?'

'Dandy. Now, maybe we can organize the bedroom arrangements and unpack. Separate bedrooms for the B and A, please!' She paused. She looked at him, waiting for his reaction and got a knowing grin. 'You know, you're the kind of guy my mother told me never to play with. You're a baaaad influence,' she said in return.

'I know, my mother felt the same ... it was a lonely childhood.' He sighed melodramatically.

He jauntily kissed the back of her neck as he walked passed her. He threw his bunch of car keys in the air like a cricket ball and sang tunelessly, flat, and at the top of his voice as he walked back to the car. *'When you're smiling, when you're smiling, the whole world smiles with you ...'*

CHAPTER 32

PATRICK AND TARA were changing into their swimwear before their dive trip. They had chosen an upstairs bedroom with a balcony and a view of the ocean through the trees. Aurelio and Beatrix had been given separate rooms on the mezzanine level—a queen-sized bed for her, two single beds for him.

'I have a slight suspicion Aurelio might not be happy with the sleeping arrangements when he sees the new Beatrix in the flesh tonight,' Tara said to Patrick.

'You are a scheming woman, from whom no mere male is safe.' He was wearing his Aussie brand Speedos. Tara leant against the wardrobe and watched appreciatively while he searched for a towel. 'Let's not wear wetsuits for the dive. The water around the island is as warm as you'll get, and we're doing a relatively short dive this afternoon.'

He laughed self-consciously at her gaze. 'They call them "budgie smugglers" in Oz,' he said, strutting towards her. 'And you … you wanton woman, look obscenely attractive in that bikini. It's even more seductive than your being stark raving naked. Did you know that?'

She dodged nimbly out of his way. 'Eat your heart out, buster. I'm off limits 'til after the party tonight. No toucha da merchandise.'

'Yeah, whatever, but I'm not going to sit still while you parade yourself around like that in front of Aurelio. Please put on a shirt. The guy's got the hots for you and you're going to drive him up the wall looking like that. Hell, you're driving *me* up the wall and we haven't even left the room yet.'

She rewarded him with a breath of tinkling laughter and a flash of fiery eyes, then obligingly reached for a long sleeve cotton shirt. She fastened two buttons only, and tied the ends of the shirt together above her midriff.

He let out a low whistled breath. 'I'm not sure if that's better or worse. How have you managed to stay single up to now?'

'You mean all these years?'

'I'm not walking into that trap, thank you very much. Are we going downstairs to swim or talk?'

'Actually, I need the expert photographer to give me some pointers. I've bought this brand new underwater camera and strobe light, which I haven't used yet.'

'Sure. Let's go down to the pool and I'll take you through it ... after all we've got an hour with absolutely nothing else to do.' He raised his eyebrows questioningly at her. She flicked him lightly with a towel and ran out of the room before he could seek revenge.

Josefina had whipped up a shrimp and avocado salad with a light Dijon sauce. She brought it to the poolside table, beautifully arranged on a platter, together with a bowl of locally grown fruit laid out in slices. A tempting jug of whipped cream sat alongside. Tara was so impressed she aimed her camera at them before Patrick could disturb the display.

The aroma of fresh coffee and newly baked pastries drifted from the kitchen. When Josefina eventually brought them out, the taste of both surpassed anything they had had before. But when Patrick asked for another helping, Josefina clucked like a mother hen and haughtily refused. It was a charade; they were feeling one another's boundaries, and Patrick and Tara were happy to just roll with it.

'I'll steal a handful for the boat ride,' he whispered to Tara, sounding like a naughty child.

'Josefina, is there a beauty parlour nearby?'

'Si señora', there ees one in the Bahia Las Ballenas Hotel, which ees not too far from here.'

'It's for Beatrix. I want her to look beautiful tonight and hope you can supervise her new look—clothes too. Do you need me to make the appointment?'

'No señora. I am known to one of the girls who works there and I will make an appointment for later. But forst I will make sure that Beatrix washes that *mock* off her face, and that she ees dressed in her new clothes with none of that *jonk* jewellery. Then they will be happy to treat her like they would treat any guest at Villa Sofia.' Josefina's emphasis showed Tara that she had an ally.

'That will make me happy, thank you,' Tara said, delighted that Josefina understood her aim. Somehow, the word 'señora' didn't have the same effect on her as it had had only a week or two ago. In fact, truth be told, she quite liked the sound of it.

'And me,' Josefina replied. 'You are a very kind lady, Señora Tara.'

Patrick and Tara headed for the dive centre where it transpired that their dive master was not a regular dive instructor. Putting the pieces together, Patrick concluded that his cold-call earlier that morning had caught them flat-footed. They had wanted his business, so they had accepted his booking, even though they didn't really have the capacity to deliver at the time. The boat was obviously a fishing vessel, but it looked sturdy, and the deep growl of the inboard motor as it sprang instantly to life was reassuring.

It had taken Patrick all of two minutes to form the view that 'Just-call-me- Charlie' was a prick or, as Tara might have put it, a smart-Alec. Likeable, perhaps, but a smart-Alec nevertheless.

Just-call-me-Charlie was visiting from Washington Heights, and was staying in Las Terrenas with family. He was a third cousin twice removed on his stepfather's second wife's side, to one of the guys in the dive school—or some such equally unfathomable relationship. He knew both the local waters and the local diving, having grown up in the area before migrating to the States. As it turned out, Just-call-me-Charlie offered value for money.

'Amigo,' he said, 'if you slip me an extra twenty-five bucks I'll take you to a dive site near Las Ballenas where the school doesn't normally take casual visitors. It's a cool place. The locals don't like to take dumb-fuck tourists there who might damage it.'

Patrick and Tara had looked at one another. Patrick shrugged. What the heck? If it turned out that Just-call-me-Charlie was a bullshit artist then he just wouldn't pay. Tara shrugged in response. She would leave to him to decide. 'No worries mate,' Patrick said, 'I'll pay you the cash when we get back to shore. Go for your life.'

The guy openly ogled Tara's body, took Patrick's answer for a 'yes', then turned his back to concentrate on the task at hand. When they arrived at the dive site he made sure he helped Tara adjust her weight belt and hoisted the tank onto her back. He straightened her buoyancy jacket and tested her air valves.

Patrick watched him closely and quickly followed Tara into the water. He felt a bit disoriented and found himself adjusting first his facemask and then various elements of his breathing apparatus after his back-flip entry. Tara tapped him on his shoulder, pointing with her other hand. He turned to face an almost overwhelmingly beautiful panorama—so beautiful that it caused him to catch his breath. It was a fairyland.

Off to their left was a forest of elkhorn coral. To their right he saw what looked like a field of feather dusters waving back and forth in the currents and eddies. There was a lone speckled grouper hovering above and just out of reach of the swaying plumes. Each feather duster had what appeared to be a flexible beige-coloured tube that looked as fragile as papier-mâché. Each tube was like a scabbard for long orange coloured plumes tipped with white at their ends. The creatures must be alive because the feather dusters kept extending then retracting into their tubed housings.

Tara brought her camera up, aiming it in the direction of a shoal of silver coloured fish—about thirty or forty of them—darting for cover amongst the elkhorn. The fish had disproportionately large black eyes, and with the light of her strobe reflecting off their bodies, their sides shone like silver mirrors. The shoal seemed to arrive at a collective conclusion that the intruders did not pose a threat and, as one, they wheeled to make another inquisitive pass—yet still remained within easy reach of the protection offered by the elkhorn. They were cautious, but their curiosity had gotten the better of them.

How could anyone not be impressed by such a sight? Whoa! Where the hell was Tara going? Patrick saw that she had drifted forwards and away from him. He followed the sight of her fins kicking smoothly ahead of him. Something had caught her attention. That something turned out to be a few metres ahead. He strengthened his own kicks to propel himself across an open expanse of sand to catch up with her.

Before her was a piece of modern sculpture, something that would have been at home in the Guggenheim in New York or the Museum of Contemporary Art in Sydney. She began photographing it from various angles. It was about ten feet tall and five feet across. The entire piece was composed of varying forms of either coral or sponge. Some of it soft and wavy, other parts appeared brittle, still others, delicately fragile.

Tara half closed her eyes to get an outline of what she was looking at and, with a bit of imagination, she could just make out a man's head. There were sea fans or sea plumes of a brownish beige colour on top, which could have been an artist's impression of surrealistic hair. They stood out in sharp relief against the blue background of the water that fluoresced as the sun above tried valiantly to penetrate the gloom.

Out of the corner of her eye she registered a flicker of movement behind the natural sculpture, and propelled herself gently forward to investigate. Perhaps it was just a speckled tubular plant waving in the current, poking out from the greenery in the base behind the coral sculpture. On closer inspection, she saw it was a moray eel, which she knew was typically a nocturnal animal. It came as a pleasant surprise to find herself the focus of attention of its gold-rimmed black eye and she lifted her camera to photograph it, her strobe light aimed directly at it.

The sudden movement and the bright light caused the creature of the night to panic. It shot out of its lair, and its two metre long body slithered, lightning-like, across the expanse of open sand which lay between the back of the coral tower and what looked like a very large multi-fingered succulent plant. The plant's translucent pale green fingers waved to and fro in the current. Each finger culminated in a bright lilac coloured tip the shape reminiscent of the head of a safety match.

Within seconds, the expanse of sand across which the eel had fled was a bed of mayhem. The eel's vibration had disturbed a camouflaged stingray causing it to erupt violently in a cloud of sand, its murderous looking barb waving behind it. In turn, its sudden and violent movement alarmed a large shoal of French grunts that had been hovering inno-cently above the succulent plant. The hundred or so yellow–gold grunts with their pale metallic blue stripes had been peacefully minding their own business. Now, the shoal darted upwards and away in unison but, somehow, the action must have caused a downdraft. One of the stragglers touched the bed of match heads waving below. Immediately its movements became jerky and uncontrolled.

On instinct, Tara propelled herself forward. Maybe she could free it from its entrapment. She was half a metre from the plant when, out of the midnight blue silence behind her—without warning—her ankle was caught in a vice-like grip. The pain seared up her leg. In the shock, she dropped her camera and strobe light, and in the same motion whirled around to fend off her attacker.

Patrick!

His right hand was clenched around her ankle, and with an extended finger was pointing at the succulent plant. Only when he saw he had her attention did he release her ankle. Then we wagged his forefinger urgently at her, in the way a father does to a child he catches doing something wrong—all the while continuing to point at the plant with his other hand. She understood that he had wanted to prevent her from touching that plant. Somewhat shaken, she carefully retrieved the camera and strobe light where they had fallen, inches from the plant, and made her way back to Patrick's side. He hugged her as best he could with masks and mouthpieces and fins between them, then gestured with his right hand that they should make their way back to the surface. It had been a close call and she had no inclination to resist.

'Thanks for that,' Tara said when they surfaced, her voice still emotional from what may have been a near-death experience.

Patrick smiled in silent understanding. 'What you nearly touched wasn't a plant. It was a giant carnivorous anemone. The fish must have been paralysed when it accidentally touched the stinging tentacles. You probably wouldn't have died, but you would have likely experienced a lot of pain had you touched it. How are you feeling?'

'I'm okay. Just give me a minute or two alone and I'll be fine.'

'Sure.'

They rested on the boat for a few minutes while Patrick confirmed with Just-call-me-Charlie that they would now like him to take them to the canyon. He didn't ask Tara whether she still wanted to go, and she understood that when you fall off a horse, the most sensible thing to do is to get back on again. As a rider in her childhood she had had more than one spill when her pony had shied, or stopped suddenly at a jump. There was no need for further discussion.

He came back after talking to Charlie and pointedly handed Tara her shirt. The independent woman in her—her ego—was irritated that he should presume to prescribe how she should comport herself. They were on a diving excursion, for God's sake—why was he acting so possessively towards her—and, earlier, in relation to Aurelio, too. The rational part of her mind was confused, the emotional part of her was strangely pleased, He didn't strike her as a prude, and neither did he strike her as particularly modest himself. If anything, he was an unusually gregarious guy, and certainly had no sexual hang-ups. Was Patrick starting to think of her as 'his'? She wasn't sure how she felt about entering into such a protective, Neanderthal relationship. She resolved to leave it for later discussion.

Tara busied herself, first with her shirt, then with an inspection of the compass on her left wrist. She tried to fathom the direction in which the canyon lay relative to the dive site, and relative to Las Ballenas, which they were just now passing on their left. To their right lay the Atlantic Ocean, probably due north. Yes, due north, as the compass was now confirming. The boat was travelling west, into the four o'clock afternoon sun.

'You should go deep down into the canyon, maybe forty or fifty metres,' Just-call-me-Charlie told Patrick when he idled the boat over their dive site. 'That way, when you look back up towards the surface, you can see whatever's swimming in the canyon.'

'Thanks, we'll do that,' Patrick said as he defogged his mask. He launched himself backwards into the water, followed by Tara a few seconds later. They began their descent, swimming down, down and further down, into the increasing gloom. It was an eerie feeling. They were making their way into a stygian cavern, where there appeared to be no sign of life—an illusion, as they both discovered when Tara switched on her strobe light.

They were conscious of the stealthy movement of half-formed shapes. Tara peered into the gloom to see if they were fish or crustaceans or even eels—maybe even a shark. They could make out an imposing canyon wall festooned with waving seaweed and a tapestry of other plant life. It was as if they had swum into a sunken, light-deprived medieval castle. She felt mildly threatened by this environment, but consciously clamped the feeling under control. She was determined to just get a-hold of herself. *Get back on the horse,* Tara. It was okay.

Patrick gestured at her to look up towards the daylight. If she could have opened her mouth in awe, she would have done so. There, between them and the light that penetrated the surface, about twenty metres above them swam a fish ball—like a swirling storm cloud she'd often viewed from the cockpit of her Boeing—hundreds of thousands of little fish taking shelter in the canyon. She couldn't make out the species, only that they were small.

The two human intruders hovered, awestruck, staring up at the writhing tornado of living, darting organisms. In the foreground, between the divers and this wonder of nature, about twelve metres up, were vague shapes of other fish swimming up and down from one wall of the canyon to the other: angel fish of different sizes and hues, a couple of butterfly fish and a lone spade fish.

Patrick couldn't see their colours in any detail, even though several of them swam only a few feet above him. Tara's strobe light was pointing in a different direction. He turned to see what her light was focussed on. What he discovered made him smile inwardly with pleasure. There, directly in front of Tara—not two metres away—was not one, but four turtles. Highly unusual. From what he knew, most turtles either travelled alone or in pairs. Hawksbills! He felt a burst of happiness for Tara that he'd been able to help make this experience possible for her.

They almost appeared to be posing for her camera. They seemed fearless—quite happy for her to approach them.

Then, in front of them, one of the turtles left the group and swam directly for the canyon wall. Tara's strobe light followed its progress—right up to the point where it collided head first into the wall.

What the ... ?

Tara turned her light back to the other three. One was swimming in circles. The other two were bumping into each other—as if arguing about which direction they should be travelling.

Patrick experienced a flash of intuitive understanding as his brain made the connection. He tapped Tara on her shoulder and pointed to her wrist compass.

She shone the light so that they could both see its dial.

Its needle was spinning erratically!

CHAPTER 33

YEHUDA AND MEHMET sat in their usual chairs in the study of the older man's home. It was Friday evening. The empty containers of their vegetarian take-away dinners added to the clutter on the tabletop. Yehuda looked distracted.

'You should know that I have invited Patrick and Tara to join forces with us,' he said at last.

Mehmet considered the statement for a few seconds. The professor was not one to make impulsive decisions. The young couple—Patrick in particular—must have made a deep impression on him. Nevertheless, he did feel the need to respond—if only for the sake of good manners.

'I am concerned about you, my friend. Ever since you met with Patrick, your demeanour has changed. Why is that?'

'Even though he is an amateur in the field of energy, he has already opened my eyes to two subjects on which you and I had not been focussing before I met him.'

'And they are?'

'I think I told you that he drew my attention to the possibility of a sophisticated, energy related technology that may have been incorporated into the biblical Ark of the Covenant. As you know, I want to address that particular subject on Sunday night.

'I will just have to contain my curiosity until then. And the second subject?'

'He explained the manner in which the world of politics is symbiotically intertwined with the worlds of banking and finance.'

'But we already knew that,' Mehmet protested. 'That is elementary nowadays.'

'Yes, but he demonstrated an unusual understanding of that subject. For example, he explained the mechanics of how central banking works, how they use the commercial banks to create money out of thin air … and how the politicians now actively encourage this because it gives them virtually unlimited access to money.'

'And the implications of this information?'

'The making of large sums of money for one's personal account seems to have become something of an exclusive country club game in the modern world,' Yehuda answered.

Mehmet shifted his position in the wing chair in which he was sitting, before looking up at his companion, his eyes screwed up in concentration. 'A country club? I don't understand.'

'To play in the game, one needs to understand the rules of the game.' Yehuda seemed even more distracted. 'I have been applying my mind to more practical matters of late. Most recently, how we might go about commercialising the new power generation technology. Frankly, I have no idea where to even begin. I don't know how to qualify for club membership. That's one reason I was attracted to the idea of Patrick joining forces with us. He seems to understand the money world and have connections with people who are senior members—"the big end of town" I've heard it called.'

'Ahh.' Mehmet's face lit up with a wicked smile, and he chuckled. 'My friend's mind has been coming out of the ether to focus on more mundane and earthly matters. *Now* I understand the look of pain on his face this evening. Welcome to the real world Yehuda.' His words were tinged with laughter. It wasn't often he was able to have fun at his friend's expense.

Yehuda did not rise to the bait. 'As a physicist who is unversed in such matters, it seems to me that anyone may become a member of the money country club. Provided you play by the rules, and provided that what you have to offer is seen by others to be potentially profitable, then you may participate in their game.'

'Yes,' Mehmet replied, 'it is called free enterprise. Everyone is free to participate, even you. So, what exactly is concerning you?'

'The energy technology is new. It will still need to be refined. It has and will have high costs of production to begin with. If a business was to be established to manufacture it, it will probably not deliver the required return on investment for some time. I don't even know what that return should be, but I imagine that it will be too high to achieve. I doubt, therefore, whether the country club will be interested in welcoming us into the ranks of its members.'

'So you can't see how it can possibly be broadly embraced across the world in a short space of time—within the next five to ten years?' Mehmet leaned back in his seat and scratched his chin. His gaze became preoccupied as his thoughts focussed inwards.

'To gear up for that kind of market penetration will require extraordinary financial resources. Where do we get this if the financial system is geared to expect a competitive return on investment? As a physicist I don't have the necessary understanding of business matters to thread my way through and around the obstacles.'

Mehmet did not answer immediately. Instead, he stood up and walked the couple of steps needed to get to the bookshelf, where something had caught his eye. He straightened one of the books that protruded so far forward from its companions on either side that it was only a matter of time before it fell to the floor. But his mind was elsewhere, his brow furrowed in thought. 'Let me ponder on it for a while. This problem is closer to my own field of training. I operate in the commercial world, perhaps I can think of a way forward.' He took a few more seconds to make his way back to the chair and seat himself again, his gaze still unfocussed. 'How much will one of these energy machines have to sell for at the current cost of production?'

'I have no idea. The original prototype must have cost around $100,000. Bear in mind we have been evolving it for twenty years.'

Mehmet looked shocked. 'That is far too high a price for the average person to afford. Certainly too high to sell the hundreds of millions of units that will be necessary if the technology is to replace the distributed electricity model across the face of the planet.'

'Those who can, do. Those who can't teach,' Yehuda quoted, his voice tinged with self-deprecating irony. 'I don't know how to do it.'

Mehmet steepled the fingers of his hands, his elbows resting on the arms of his chair. Yehuda fussed with his pipe. He sucked deeply, then coughed. The tobacco glowed in pinpoints but did not catch. He scraped out the pipe's bowl, and repeated the procedure. He sighed. He couldn't even light a pipe today. Then he noisily knocked its rim on the side of the ashtray. Still knocking his pipe, he looked across at Mehmet. The ashtray overturned, tipping its contents onto the floor.

Mehmet raised his eyebrows, sighing in mild frustration.

'I cannot think for all the movement and noise. Perhaps it will help you if I first explained exactly how the world of finance looks upon the question of return on investment. Then, while you are thinking about that, I can do some quiet thinking of my own.'

'Please.'

'Do you know what a treasury bond is?'

'Of course. It is a piece of paper that is evidence the holder has lent money to the government.'

'Would you agree that a loan to the government is, to all intents and purposes, risk free ... you are virtually guaranteed to get your money back?'

'Yes. That makes sense to me.'

'So you would imagine that the price of that risk-free money that you have lent to the government—the interest rate that the government will pay you for having lent them your money—would probably represent some sort of benchmark or reference point, would it not?'

'I imagine it would.'

'In fact it does. The interest or yield on a long term treasury bond is the benchmark against which all other long term investments are measured for the purposes of comparing risk and return.'

'How?' Yehuda automatically picked up his pipe, then put it down again. Mehmet smiled at his friend's action. Were the clouds of smoke, which normally billowed up when he was deep in thought, a metaphorical screen behind which Yehuda was able to hide?

'Does it sound fair that if an investment has a higher risk than a government bond, then it will need to generate a higher return to compensate for that higher risk?'

'Yes, yes.'

'Good,' Mehmet responded. 'One category of risk is investing on the stock market, and the second is in the type of venture you are contemplating, which would be referred to as a "start-up" or a "greenfield" venture. Very roughly, if you look back into history, you will find that investors regard the stock market as having three times the risk of a long term government bond, and a start-up as having three times the risk of the stock market.'

Generously, Yehuda avoided pointing out to Mehmet that, mathematically, three times zero risk was still zero risk. This was not the time for semantics. 'Are you telling me that my venture needs to generate a return of nine times the interest paid by the United States Government on its ten-year bonds?'

'I am.'

'And the current interest payable on its ten-year bond?'

'Around four percent, per year.'

'Dear God,' Yehuda responded. 'That means that the stock market should be yielding around twelve percent per year and my venture should offer a return to investors of over thirty-six percent per year?'

'Including capital gains, correct. And, yes, your energy technology will need to generate this return to its investors if you raise the capital to commercialise it. But it will become even more difficult to finance if interest rates on government bonds rise, because investors will require a higher return from you. For every half percent rise in the government bond rate, your technology will need to offer an additional 4.5 percent per year return to investors.'

'But that is an impossible target. What about the value to society? Does that not count for anything?' Yehuda leant forward in his chair.

'The simple answer to that question is "no". Investors are interested in return on investment, nothing else. The country club's rules of the money game do not allow for philanthropy.'

Again the two men lapsed into silence. 'I am going outside to think … and to let you think,' Yehuda said after less than half a minute. 'What you have just told me is deeply disturbing. I cannot see any way around this problem.'

When, at last, Mehmet went out in search of his friend. He found him pacing up and down, muttering to himself. Yehuda was not used to being faced with problems he could not apply method and logic to. If anything, he was looking even more distressed—grumpier than when he had fled the room.

Mehmet placed his arm around his friend's shoulder in a gesture of empathy and pacification. 'I think I may have a way forward. You need to calm down, my friend. Let's go inside for a cup of coffee. I will explain what I have come up with. It is quite a straightforward approach.'

That had been an hour earlier. The two men were again seated in their usual chairs, but any air of calm had once again deserted Yehuda.

'I need details,' he demanded. 'Your summarised approach sounds sensible, but I need details. Take me through the details.'

Mehmet shrugged. 'Why not? All this assumes, of course, that you can prove beyond a shadow of doubt that your technology works. You can do that?'

'Yes—both physically and theoretically.'

'Well then, it seems to me the key to penetrating the market will be to agree on the maximum price that may be charged for the power generator,' Mehmet began. 'We agree that $100,000 is out of the question as a selling price?'

'Of course. There would be no purpose in offering something no one can afford. That is the precise source of my concern.'

'Whatever these generators of yours eventually sell for, the customer will need to save up, or borrow money from a bank or buy one on hire purchase. The price will need to be low enough to enable him to repay that borrowing, including interest, within a maximum of three years.'

'Why three years? Why not, say, ten?'

'Because the average person does not think long term. They want instantaneous gratification. If they cannot get that, they will not do anything at all. We might be able to stretch it to five years, but three is the target.'

'That seems like a very cynical view, but if you are adamant ...'

Mehmet nodded. 'Would you agree, that if the monthly instalment required to buy the equipment is no higher than their previous monthly cost of electricity, including the operating cost, then the average family might be quite happy to buy it?'

Yehuda nodded. 'Yes. But now I must accuse you of being the theoretician. I cannot see how such a low price would be possible.'

'The bonus will be that at the end of the three years, when the generator is fully paid off, the monthly cost of electricity to the purchasers will fall quite sharply relative to what they are paying now.'

'Yes, yes. That is an unequivocal fact. It will cost virtually nothing other than repairs and maintenance and a maybe $50 every quarter for consumables.'

'Good. Based on that statement and based on the fact that, in the US, the average family pays around, say, $1,000 a year for electricity, the equipment should not be sold for more than $3,000. That will need to include a modest royalty payment to the inventor.'

'But that is substantially less than the $100,000 we have been talking about. Even as an academic I can see the chasm of impracticality in your logic.'

'The inventor of the jet aeroplane engine faced a similar problem to yours. And just as you have proven the feasibility of your energy technology by producing a working prototype of a power generator—so did the Englishman, Whittle. The United States Government actively facilitated the commercialisation of Whittle's jet engine—which is now being manufactured, for profit, by companies like Pratt and Whitney and Rolls Royce around the world.'

'But lead me through the practicalities,' Yehuda asked. 'Precisely how would this experience with the jet engine be applied to our energy generator?'

'The US Government—or any other government for that matter— would call for competitive tenders by private enterprise, just as it did in

1941 when it commissioned Bell Aircraft Corporation to build a jet fighter, and General Electric to build the jet engines for it,' Mehmet said. 'Stage one would be to generate the final design and more sophisticated prototypes. They might appoint maybe five or six organizations all over the world to come up with a design under your guidance. Through this tender process, the best engineering brains in the world would apply their minds to generating a commercial design—just as the best engineering brains in World War II applied their minds to perfecting the jet engine. My guess is that the cost of doing that would not exceed perhaps $10 million per company, or a total of, say $50 million. To put this number into perspective, it would probably be less than a third of the money spent on advertising by a Presidential hopeful in the US elections.'

'How long will that stage take?'

'The De Havilland Comet was launched in 1949. Of course, it has been improved since those days but, within eight years, the various competing organizations had developed working models usable on a larger scale. My guess—based on what you have told me about your technology, and based on the fact that you already have over twenty years of research and experimentation under your belt—is that your commercial design could be perfected within two years. That will give the government the courage to place the opening order.'

Yehuda's brow began to unfurrow. 'So the government risks $50 million on developing a design from my prototype. But how will that help? Will the cost of a generator be brought down as part of this design process so individual units can sell for $3,000?'

'No.'

Yehuda got up out of his chair and made his way to the constantly simmering urn of water on the table behind him. Without asking Mehmet, he filled two cups with boiling water and absent-mindedly spooned in the instant coffee. He stared at the wall in front of him reached for the sugar bowl, missed, and knocked it over. Sugar spilled all over the tabletop. He scraped a couple of spoonfuls off the table and decanted them into the two cups. He left the rest of the sugar where it had landed and shuffled across to Mehmet to hand him his cup. Then he sat himself down again, took a sip and grimaced as it burned his tongue.

'So we are just spinning wheels? Still back where we started?'

'No.' Mehmet was having fun. It wasn't often that he was in a position where he could mess with Yehuda's mind. Usually it was the other way around.

Predictably, Yehuda was less patient and less sanguine to be on the receiving end. 'Explain!' he demanded.

'Does the principle make sense to you that the more you do something, the better you get at doing it? You become more efficient?'

His reply was crotchety. 'Of course, practise makes perfect. Even a child knows that.'

'Would it surprise you to discover that we are now able to quantify exactly how much better you get?'

Yehuda looked surprised. He cocked his head to one side. 'Frankly, yes.'

'Think of the electronic calculator. It was before I was born, but the first electronic calculator was produced some time in the 1960s and carried a price of a couple of hundred dollars.'

'So?'

'So a calculator with exactly the same functionality can be bought in any supermarket today for less than $5. It is one fortieth of the price after forty years of inflation. As the manufacturers gain experience, they learn to save costs. As the volumes of production output rise, the unit costs fall.'

'You say the rate of this fall can be quantified? We can know this in advance?'

'The original understanding of this fact also arose out of World War II. In this particular case it came from the aircraft manufacturing industry. A linkage was discovered between what we now refer to as the accumulated volume of production and the unit costs of production.'

Yehuda waited for Mehmet to continue.

'At first they were not able to quantify the answer exactly but in the years to come, the principle was tested across several industries. After a couple of decades it was discovered—by The Boston Consulting Group, if my memory serves me correctly—that every time accumulated output doubles over its previous total, unit costs fall by around eighteen percent in real dollars, after adjusting for inflation.'

'By double, you mean 1, 2, 4, 8, 16, 32, 64 and so on?'

'In simple terms, yes. If the first one costs $100,000 then the second one will cost $82,000 and the fourth one will cost eighty-two percent of that and so on.'

Yehuda lunged at this simple problem of mathematics. He grabbed a pen and paper and began jotting down numbers. It took him all of two minutes to come up with the answer.

'Without the benefit of a $5 calculator, I estimate that if we start off with our first generator costing $100,000, then the 262,144th generator will have a unit cost of $2,810 based on the relationship you gave me, and it can be sold at a profit at a price of $3,000.' He was beaming. 'How sure are you of this relationship?'

'Pretty sure. Just think in terms of personal computers, by way of another example. A few years ago you had to pay $5,000 for a fairly slow machine. Now you can get a much faster one with a much larger storage and processing capacity for around $1,000. It appears to be a law that works across all industries. That's why the price of motor cars doesn't rise in proportion to inflation, if at all.'

'Hmmm.' Yehuda lapsed back into doing what he did best. He thought. He doodled some more on the paper for a few minutes. Mehmet watched and, as he did so, he saw the older man's smile slowing growing broader until Yehuda looked up with a look of joy on his face.

'By my calculations, and assuming your formula is correct, the US Government could place an order for 524,000 units to be paid for on a "cost plus" basis. If they sell every single unit for $3,000 they will incur a loss of $182 million on the first 131,000 units, but make a profit of $207 million on the next 393,000 units. Thereafter, any organization which produces this equipment will be able to make a fairly comfortable profit by selling the generators for $3,000 each directly to the public. The price would likely fall further as the volumes of output reach large numbers.'

After a few seconds, he added. 'And we shouldn't lose sight of the fact that, from the perspective of the buyers, every single one of these

$3,000 generators would have paid for itself within three years out of electricity cost savings. Effectively, they would cost nothing.'

Mehmet scratched his cheek and noticed that the itch was coming from a five o'clock shadow. It was getting late. 'What I still find amazing though is that it doesn't seem possible that one of these generators could have such low operating costs.'

'You will understand after I have explained the technology to you. I am planning to do that some time next week—perhaps next Wednesday evening,' Yehuda answered.

At length, Mehmet raised his eyes to look directly at his friend. 'Assuming you are correct, why are you only thinking about the US Government? Surely, once the design has been perfected, every government in the world would be a potential contender to participate. Even the cashed up oil producing nations might be interested, given that they are running out of oil. As you have told me yourself on many occasions, energy and water are not "products". Without them civilization will not survive.' He got out of his chair and walked to the window.

Yehuda nodded his head vigorously. 'Correct.'

Mehmet stood gazing through the venetian blind at the narrowed view of the world outside. 'Well, that being the case, this technology should be made available to every government in the world. Within a few years of commencement of production, most ordinary people throughout the world could have easy access to it—even in Third World countries. If profits are made by private enterprise along the way, then that will be fine. But private enterprise should not be allowed to control the technology—to determine who may or may not have access to it, and at whatever rapacious price they choose to charge. Otherwise we will land up in exactly the same place as today—where the oil industry is holding all of humanity to ransom.' He turned to face Yehuda, his hands clasped loosely behind his back.

'My reason is simply this. If you add another $50 million for other costs such as marketing to the $50 million research and development costs, and to the $180 odd million losses in the early stages of production, the total investment required will be somewhere near $280 million to $300 million. How many governments in the world have access to that kind of money?'

'All of them, I would imagine,' Mehmet replied. 'It might sound like a lot of money to you, but it's not all that much more than is required to build a couple of nuclear reactors. In any event, according to your numbers they will likely get it all back within three to five years. They could issue short term government bonds to finance it. Ultimately, your problem will be to convince a government, any government,' he waved his hands in the air, 'that the technology is sensible. It is the first $50 million for prototype design that is the real risk.'

'But all anyone needs to do is watch the machine working, and measure energy input and energy output to determine its efficiency. It's hard to argue with that.'

'I'm afraid that may be a naïve view. It is almost inevitable that you will come up against the "not invented here" syndrome. Jealousy, prejudice and other personal agendas are likely to get in the way of other physicists or engineers endorsing this technology. The real risk is that the technology may fail to get a widespread sign-off by the professional engineering community for reasons relating to nothing other than ego and prejudice. They will claim that you are employing sleight of hand tactics and are cheating on the results.'

The expression on Yehuda's face had become contemplative. He seemed to be looking through Mehmet, rather than at him.

'If the technology is introduced sensibly and credibly, we will get people's attention. People tend to listen to creative solutions when their backs are against the wall. '

'And how will you get people to listen?' Mehmet asked, ever the practical one.

Yehuda smiled. He felt back in control again. 'You just leave that to me.'

'IT ALL SEEMS so normal from up here,' Tara observed, sweeping her arm in an arc around her and towards the horizon. Her softly spoken words mixed with the deep throated rumble of the inboard motor.

Patrick didn't register. He sat with his eyes closed, clenching and unclenching his teeth.

Tara saw the tell-tale thought sign and didn't press her point. She was content to just sit back and study his face. Was he still pre-occupied with what they had seen the turtles do? It had certainly been a memorable and thought provoking day.

Patrick leant forward at last, looking down the side of the boat's hull into the calm waters of the bay gently slapping against the vessel as it churned and rocked its way steadily forwards. After a while, he looked up to the sky. The yellow-orange late afternoon sun was sinking towards the horizon, and a couple of inquisitive gulls were circling hopefully above.

Tara followed his gaze towards the coastline to the south-west. The sun's rays glinted like morse code off the window of a fishing vessel bobbing in the distance. Patrick shook his head, a little like a dog shaking its wet body, then without saying a word, stood up and wandered towards the pilot.

Just-call-me-Charlie evinced no curiosity. He merely glanced at Patrick to acknowledge his awareness and returned his gaze forward.

'Charlie, Tara and I just saw four turtles swimming like blind men staggering around. They looked to us like they'd lost their magnetic directional finding ability.'

'Is that right?' Charlie's gaze didn't waiver.

Patrick found himself having to stifle his irritation. Could Charlie have sounded less interested? Naah. That would probably have required some effort. Well, maybe he was being a tad judgmental. Maybe he just didn't like the way the guy had ogled Tara. Try again.

'Yep. We shone the strobe light on Tara's wrist compass and it was spinning. Something happened down there.'

'Didn't notice anything up here.'

Aha. Progress.

'Ever experienced any of these magnetic anomalies yourself?'

'What do you mean "magnetic anomalies"?'

'You know, Bermuda Triangle type stuff.'

Charlie turned to face Patrick, his eyes showing a mixture of disbelief and humour. 'Old wives' tales, s'far as I'm concerned. The turtles were probably just havin' some fun. They do that sometimes y'know.'

'They do?'

Charlie laughed before answering. 'Yeah. Saw one butting his head against our boat once, like he was trying to get us to change course. He was like, "Hey! Keep outta my space." He got us all laughing at him like he was a clown or sumthin'. It was like he was playing with us. Eventually he musta got dazed because he swam off like a drunk guy trying to walk in a straight line.'

'You never heard of missing planes or boats?' Patrick asked.

Charlie grinned. 'You're kidding me, right? No one believes in that stuff anymore, or Santa Claus, or the Tooth Fairy.'

Patrick gave up.

Just-call-me-Charlie dropped Tara and Patrick back to the wharf, accepted the payment for the additional dive and turned his back before they had even stepped from the boat.

Later, at around the same time that Yehuda and Mehmet were eating their vegetarian meal on the opposite side of the island, Patrick and Tara strolled along the beach barefoot, hand in hand, away from l'Hôtel Atlantis towards La Plage de Coson where Beatrix and Josefina were preparing for their barbecue, and where Aurelio was also setting up for the evening's party.

The shimmering sun was sinking to the horizon. With a surge of emotion, Tara turned to hug Patrick tightly. If he had been predisposed to look for it, he would have seen the love in her eyes. 'Let's just sit for a few minutes. I want to bask in this unforgettable experience.'

Patrick settled himself as comfortably as he could with his back resting against a palm tree growing at the edge of the beach. Tara seated herself between his legs, her torso resting against his chest. She leant back, letting her eyelids droop so that the roughly woven carpet of sand in front of her became blurred. It was the colour of birchwood as it stretched away to join up with the ragged edge of an indigo ocean. The sounds of the rolling waves seemed to come from far off to her right. To her left, in the west, the orange hue of the disappearing sun in the darkening sky reflected off the wispy clouds suspended in the lighter blue sky, high above the northern horizon.

She realised Patrick's mind was not on the romance of the sunset as his fingers stroked the curve of her breast. She moved slightly towards him, enabling him to slip his right hand into the opening of her dress. She felt the warmth of his fingers as he gently caressed her. Her heart fluttered, perhaps in excitement, perhaps with the guilty possibility that someone might be watching. Her eyes scanned the beach; they were almost certainly alone. She allowed herself a sigh of contentment and twisted her head to reach up to his, kissing him on the lips, before turning her attention back to the majesty of the sunset. What more could a girl ask for?

She felt his breath on her neck as he bent to continue kissing her. She felt something enticingly hard press up against her, in the small of her back. An intuitive understanding of what had been causing his earlier inexplicable preoccupation with her modesty flashed across her mind. It had been a week since La Romana and they hadn't touched one another since then. She decided that it would be better to distract him rather than encourage him at this point in time.

'Those turtles seemed to be extraordinarily sensitive to that magnetic anomaly this afternoon, don't you think?'

'Hmmm.'

She persisted. 'Come on Patrick. We've got to join the others for dinner. Wait until after the party, then I'll ...'

'Promise?'

'More of a threat, really. You've been lording it over me the whole day. It'll be payback time.'

He smiled. 'You can't frighten me, beautiful lady. I'll take you on with one of my hands tied behind your back, any day of the week.'

'Hey guy,' she responded, in a flat tone that demanded his attention, 'I'm being serious here. We came to the Samana Peninsular because it's close to the edge of the Bermuda Triangle. We found a magnetic anomaly. What do you want to do about it?'

Patrick did not respond immediately. It took him a few seconds to react. She was mildly surprised when he grasped her under the armpits and she found herself rising up in the air. He stood where he had been seated, arms wrapped around her.

'You up to flying into the Triangle tomorrow?' he asked.

She considered his question; it would be inappropriate to respond flippantly. 'I think so, but there's no rush to decide. Let me think about it for a couple of hours. In the meantime, they'll be wondering what happened to us. We'd better get going.'

Tara pointed to the roof of the beach shelter in the distance. It had been draped with strings of fairy lights.

'They look like tiny fireflies sitting in a row.'

'Aurelio certainly seems to have taken his responsibilities seriously,' Patrick observed as they came closer. 'It looks like he's even connected a sound system up to that small generator over there.'

By way of marking out a dance area, Aurelio had also planted rows of bamboo lamp stands and, already, flames were flickering tentatively in the zephyr breeze of the early evening.

They were still about fifty yards away, but could see Josefina busying herself, scuttling between an open kettle barbecue and a trestle table that had been covered with a blue-and-white check gingham cloth.

'Look, they've already got a barbecue going,' Patrick said close to Tara's ear. 'Let's go see how the fire's doing.' As they reached the barbecue, it became obvious that the charcoal must have been lit well over an hour before, maybe even two. The embers were burning low. 'Seems like we're almost ready to start cooking.'

Tara looked around. There were no chairs in sight. Whoever wanted to eat would pile up their plate at the food-laden table and then go and find somewhere to sit on the beach. Then she noticed a tartan blanket had been laid out at the edge of the beach, away from the water, under the fronds of the towering palm trees. Beatrix and Aurelio, though, were nowhere to be seen.

'Hi Josefina. You'll be joining us to eat?' Tara asked.

'Señora, I will eat, but it ees too uncomfortable for a fat person like me to sit on the ground. I will eat standing at the table, and that will also make it easy for me to cook and to dish up for all of you.'

'Fair enough,' Patrick said, not wanting to subject Josefina to any more embarrassment. 'Where are the youngsters?'

Tara, who was standing slightly behind Patrick, punched him on his thigh. 'You're definitely not fat Josefina. What gave you that idea?' she asked. 'Asshole,' she whispered to Patrick through closed teeth.

Josefina pretended not to have registered Patrick's insult, or Tara's reaction to it, but smiled conspiratorially at Tara before she turned to answer Patrick. 'Señor Patrick, where would a jong man be, who ees organizing a party? He has gone to fetch more beer in case we run out.' She gestured at what looked like a half dozen cases of beer already piled up, and to a plastic tub filled with a mountain of ice. There were more beers and cans of soft drinks below the surface. 'And where would a jong girl be who has jost bought new clothes that cost a week's salary and has spent two hours in the beauty parlour? She has been in front of the mirror for an hour, making herself even more beautiful.' Josefina did a little preening wiggle and turned to Tara. 'You should see her!' Her hands went to her cheeks and she looked blissfully heavenwards. You have made Beatrix a very happy jong lady today, señora. All the men are going to be chasing her tonight. Aurelio, he will have to watch out.' Her words were accompanied by a grin that belied her warning.

'Did you carry all this heavy stuff from the house on your own?' Tara asked, a note of concern in her voice.

'No, señora. Aurelio does what I tell him. It ees he and one of his friends who brought all this from the house. And it has been very helpful to have the quad bike Señor Patrick,' she said graciously.

'I see that Aurelio got hold of a generator. Why'd he do that? I thought he was just going to pay the guitar.'

'When he saw how Beatrix is looking, I think he will only play hees guitar for a short while,' she said with a smile. 'He has a friend, Edwin, who is a disc jockey at the Syroz Bar on Saturday nights. Edwin will play merengue and bachata music, but I think Aurelio has arranged for more bachata music because Señora Tara has asked for that.' She looked knowingly at Tara. There was clearly a subplot, which went straight over Patrick's head. Tara caught it immediately.

'Uh huh.' she said. So Beatrix had made a hit.

In front of Patrick, Josefina pretended not to understand.

Josefina led them past the barbecue into the shelter. 'When we have finished eating, we will clear thees table, and Edwin can play his music here. Aurelio has put some speakers on the roof here,' she said, pointing. 'Also, he has arranged for a jong friend to play the drums while he is playing the guitar. When they are finished, this boy—his name is Rogelio—he will be barman for the night and Aurelio will pay him $5. That ees a lot of money for a boy of twelve years old.'

'How many people has Aurelio invited?' Tara asked, and saw a look of concern flit across Josefina's face.

'He has invited twenty people, señora, but I am worried maybe fifty will arrive.'

'No worries, Josefina,' Patrick said, soothingly. 'We're far from any other houses. The more the merrier. The party will end when the beer is finished. Maybe we can all let our hair down and have a fun time.'

Josefina favoured him with a look of gratitude, and moved to hustle them away to sit down on the blanket. 'I have made some tapas to start. You and the señora might like a beer with some tapas while you are waiting for the others.'

Not five minutes later, Aurelio returned with Beatrix who, as Tara had anticipated, looked exquisite. Patrick looked at her appreciatively. She wore a simple white dress with soft white shoes, the whites contrasted against her coffee-with-cream skin. Her carefully cut and coiffed shiny black hair framed her high-cheekboned face, now lightly made-up to fashion magazine standards. She even wore an elegant necklace, which Josefina must have lent her. It was either a hand-me-down or might have been borrowed from the villa owner's collection. With her tall and willowy body, Beatrix now looked as though she would be at home on any catwalk. By contrast, Aurelio looked decidedly uncomposed. Patrick smiled inwardly. The word 'decomposed' popped into his head. The little bugger had suddenly realised that the sheila he'd been treating with such condescension was world class. At least he didn't have to worry about Aurelio ogling Tara anymore.

Like a sergeant major, Josefina took charge. She instructed Beatrix to don an apron, take off her shoes and help her with the food. She ordered Aurelio to check that everything else was shipshape before either of them was allowed to sit and eat.

Patrick decided to take Tara's mind off what was happening around her by dipping into his bottomless pit of jokes. 'I've got this great story to tell Yehuda, but I need to run it by you first. I don't want to get myself into hot water again.'

She smiled in response. How did he even remember all the jokes and stories?

Aurelio was practising on his guitar in the background and already it was obvious that he was very good. The tapas were delicious. Tara had already had two. The beer was having the effect of relaxing her. She was feeling great.

'Go ahead, why don't you?'

'It's about this Jewish bachelor by the name of Yehuda,' he began.

Tara rolled her eyes. Oh my God, why did he always lead with his chin like that? But the immediate reality was that clearly, Yehuda couldn't hear Patrick from the other end of the island. She might as well humour him. She gestured with a flick of her hand for him to continue, but was careful to give him a non-committal smile.

'Yehuda had been involved in a traffic accident,' Patrick began. 'This twenty-ton IH horse and semi-trailer had shot a stop sign and creamed his car, which was now a write-off. It was a few weeks later. He was in court being cross-examined by a high powered lawyer for the trucking company.

"Didn't you say, at the scene of the accident, 'I'm fine'?" asks the lawyer. Yehuda looks at him.'

Patrick changed his voice to mimic the professor's. ' "Well, you see, this is what happened. I just put my little dog Esther into the car ..."

Then the lawyer interrupts him.'

Patrick changed his voice again, to sound pompous. ' "I didn't ask you for details," says the lawyer. Just answer the question. Did you not say, at the scene of the accident 'I'm fine'?"

"Well," says Yehuda, once again—like he never heard the lawyer—"it was like this, my little dog Esther was in the car with me, and we were driving down the road ..." ' '

Bubbles of laughter began to well up inside Tara. She could see that her man was enjoying this. What the hell? But, by the way he was drawing it out she could also see it was going take some time. She signalled him to stop and got up to fetch a second beer for them both. She returned after a few seconds and gestured that he might continue. Patrick was a study in equanimity, as if he was used to his audience meandering around during intermission.

'Where was I? Oh yes. Now the lawyer is starting to get a bit riled. He interrupts Yehuda and turns to the judge. "Judge," he says, filled with self-righteousness. "I am trying to establish the fact that, at the scene of the accident, this man told the highway patrolman who later arrived on the scene that he was just fine. Now, several weeks later, he's trying to sue my client for damages. I believe he is a fraud. Please direct him to stop all this prevarication and to simply answer the question." '

Patrick paused. 'But,' he said, his raconteur's voice dripping with drama, 'by now the judge's curiosity has been piqued. "No," says the judge. "I for one would like to hear why this witness seems to think that his little dog Esther is so important to his testimony."

"Thank you, your honour," says Yehuda. "Well," he says, "It's like this. I had just loaded my sweet little Esther into the car and was driving down the main road when this huge truck and its semi-trailer ran a stop sign and rammed my car in the side. Me, I was thrown out of the car into a ditch on one side of the road. My little Esther was thrown into another ditch on the other side of the road. It was terrible." ' Patrick paused to wipe his forehead theatrically with the back of his hand, to show just how terrible it was.

' "Then," Yehuda said, continuing his testimony, "I heard my little Esther crying in pain. She was whining pitifully. She was moaning and crying. It was just too, too terrible. I knew she was in very bad shape, but so was I. I couldn't move to help her. I just lay there, also in pain, hoping and praying that someone would come to help us."

He looks up to see if the judge is still listening. "Your honour," he says, "my prayers were answered when this highway patrolman stops to see what's going on. He can see me just lying there quietly, and he can hear my poor little Esther crying and suffering and whining, and he goes across the road to see what he can do. Your honour, the highway patrolman takes one look at my little Esther lying there suffering, and he takes out his service revolver and shoots her dead—point blank—right between the eyes! Then he comes across the road to see me, your honour. He still has his revolver in his hand. He looks at me and he asks me, 'How you holding up buddy?' "Judge," Yehuda asks. "Tell me. What would *you* have answered?" '

Tara laughed long and loudly. 'Oh Patrick,' she said eventually, 'it's clear to me that in future I'm going to have to censor all your jokes. You *may not* tell that joke to Yehuda. You haven't the faintest idea about social sensibilities. Even my father wouldn't have told a joke like that. Don't you understand that's an *entre nous* joke?'

'What's an *entre nous* joke?'

'It's an ethnic joke that one guy tells to other people in the same ethnic group. I understand that it might just as easily have been an Italian or a Newfie, but you don't tell that kind of joke across cultures … ahh what's the use,' she said, trailing off. 'You're just going to have to rely on your natural charm to dig yourself out of the shit.'

'Duhh! She loves me,' Patrick said like a punch drunk ex prize fighter. 'She tinks I got natural choim.' Tara laughed again, this time, without the admonishment in her voice.

As if on cue, Beatrix came up to them—apronless, shoeless and exceedingly beauteous, Patrick observed. He was sober, but he was mellow.

'Señor Patrick and Señorita Tara,' she said, 'Josefina has asked me to tell you that the dinner ees ready. Please to come to the table to help yourselves.'

The strains of music from Aurelio's guitar wafted off across the water—doubtless to be heard a few kilometres away through the still night.

The meal was everything both of them had hoped for.

'That was probably the best tasting, most succulent lobster I've ever eaten in my life,' Patrick said afterwards as he and Tara stood at the edge of the calm Atlantic Ocean. 'That dipping sauce of Josefina's was incredible.' They stared at the moonlit runway, enjoying the caress of the warm water as it gently lapped over their bare feet. Tara stood with her back to him, his arms wrapped around her. It seemed his hands easily encircled her tiny waist. The two were swaying as one, in time to the music.

Tara didn't respond. She was lost in the moment.

'Don't tell me that you didn't enjoy that meal,' he said.

'It was magnificent. I'll probably remember it for the rest of my life.'

'Try to curb your enthusiasm.' As he said the words, he realised that the time for humour had passed. Subtly, the mood of the evening had changed.

'I was just thinking. I think we should go.'

'What do you mean go? The evening hasn't even started yet!'

'No, Patrick, I mean tomorrow. I'm just loving the way you're holding me at this moment. It feels so right … so safe with you. I think you and I should fly into the Triangle early tomorrow morning, and we should give Aurelio and Beatrix the opportunity to discover one another. In any event, it seems to me that Aurelio needs some space to work out his true feelings for her. She fancies him. Did you know that?'

'What do you mean, "Did I know that"? How the hell would I know that? How do *you* know that? You only just met her this morning.'

'It's a girl thing.'

He was silent for a few moments. 'Are you sure?'

'Sure about Beatrix and Aurelio?' There was an edge of mischief in her voice.

'Now who's conducting two conversations at once?' Is split person-ality syndrome catchy? No, I meant, are you sure about tomorrow?'

'You came half way across the world for this opportunity. I'm a very experienced pilot. Here we are, having just today seen the type of anomaly you came here to investigate. We're spending the weekend together. We have the use of the mine's King Air. Aurelio and Beatrix couldn't care less about us right at this minute. All the vectors line up. I say let's do it.'

'We'll need a relatively early night,' he said, rather dubiously.

'That's a problem for you? You've got a perpetual hard-on and you feel obliged to avoid going to bed early with me? Your poor, poor man.'

'Oookaaay! When you put it like that, let's go.'

'No so fast Roy Rogers. We can't just ride off into the sunset here. It's barely nine o'clock. I say we make a show of dancing for an hour or so, maybe an hour and a half, and then make a dignified retreat when the party is in full swing. We can explain to them that we've had a full day and we're wanting to fly out early tomorrow on business, and that we'll be back tomorrow night. My guess is they'll be happy to hear it. What do you say?"

"You're the captain, captain. For now, why don't you let Uncle Patrick lead you a merry dance".

Already, around twenty people had arrived, including a second guitarist. Among the guests was Rogelio, the kid who had waved to Beatrix as he and his brother pedalled past on their pushbike earlier that morning. As it turned out, Rogelio played a mean bongo, and Aurelio and he were warming up nicely. Aurelio had quickly obliged when Tara asked him if he would play some bachata music. It was a way of getting the evening started. As if to reassure Tara that he hadn't wasted her money, Aurelio quickly explained that bachata music was usually played by two guitarists and a drummer. He also explained that bachata was for ordinary Dominican people, and it took Tara all of thirty seconds to work out why when the dancers started—it was 'dirty dancing' to the power n—not the kind of dancing that would be encouraged in middle-to-upper class America, or in middle-to-upper class society anywhere else for that matter.

Aurelio had asked two couples to demonstrate so that Patrick and Tara could learn. After a few minutes, Patrick ventured an observation. 'It looks like the cha cha to me, but instead of one and two and three, four–five it goes one and two and three, and kick. It's more of a four beat rhythm.'

'Seems to me that we are going to need hip joints that are really well oiled,' Tara said, noting that the swaying of the hips was very similar to the merengue in concept, but that the partners seemed joined at their swaying groins when they were dancing face to face; or the male partner was boring into his female partner when she faced away from him. The only thing that prevented them from actually doing anything 'naughty' on the dance floor was that last kick on the fourth beat. Sometimes it was accompanied by the female arching her back in mock ecstasy. Sometimes she curled her leg around his hip, or he curled his leg around her hip. At other times, one partner suggestively penetrated the private space between the other's legs, thrusting one leg deeply beyond the partner's splayed feet.

'Shit,' Patrick whispered, 'talk about space invaders. If you thought that the merengue was suggestive, this is positively obscene.'

Tara shrugged one shoulder enticingly. 'When in Rome …' and led him into the centre of the area bounded by the bamboo lamps—the space intended for the dancers. Immediately, an expectant hush fell over the small crowd of onlookers. Aurelio, strummed an opening chord. The second guitarist joined in, backed up by Rogelio, on his bongos. Tara briefly wondered what his mother might think of all this.

Patrick led her as though doing the cha cha, but held her very close and counted softly in her ear, 'one and two and three and kick. One and two and three and kick.' On the first four-count he moved left to right, on the second, right to left. After the second shuffle, Tara's hips found their rhythm and at the end of each kick count, she started to curl her leg around Patrick's hip, like a pole dancer. First a left leg curl, then one and two and three and right leg curl. She seemed oblivious to the fact that by lifting her leg like that she was exposing herself—sometimes, all the way up to her scantily covered crotch. The men in the audience watched silently.

Despite his mixed feelings about what Tara was doing, it wasn't long before Patrick's own hip swaying found its rhythm, and the two dancers were swaying in unison. After a minute or so, he started to twirl Tara as though he had been practising all his life. Emboldened, Tara began to end some moves with her back arched, throwing her head far back, her mouth slightly open. The crowd clapped to the music, encouraging them. The ice had been broken. The 'dance floor' filled. Soon, bodies were writhing across the sandy floor. Only Josefina looked on disapprovingly. After maybe a minute or two, her judgemental mood was extinguished as one of the men on the sidelines dragged her onto the floor. It took only a few moments before she too abandoned herself to the music. She was, after all, Dominican.

When at last Patrick and Tara took their dance-floor mood back to the villa, they were barely missed.

'Do the guys at your work know what you do in your spare time?' Patrick asked. They had showered and were lying, cool and naked on top of the bed. 'More to the point, does your little old mother in Connecticut know how flagrantly you flaunt your body in front of strange men?'

'Don't be so hard on yourself … you're not all that strange.'

Patrick was feeling an array of conflicting emotions. There was lust. Tara had really turned him on during the evening. There was a growing love. There was irritation. There was a hint of protective jealousy. Some residual anger. Even a tinge of lingering discomfort at their exhibitionism on the dance floor. None of this was in his conscious mind. He just knew he was feeling scratchy.

'I'm not kidding. How can you reconcile this with your blue-suit day job, and the epaulets on your shoulders and your senior pilot's cap? They just don't gel.' He needed to lash out at something.

'I'm comfortable in my skin, and I understand that there's a time and a place for everything,' Tara said.

'Too trite,' he grumped.

'Seriously, I believe that the human body is a finely tuned machine. We have appetites. We have drives. There are times when it's appropriate to suppress those physical appetites and drives, and there are times when it's appropriate to satisfy them. Too much satisfaction leads to physical debauchery. Too little, leads to mental debauchery. For example, there's nothing inherently wrong with the nakedness of the human body. It just depends on the circumstances.'

All the while she had been talking to him Tara had been stroking him with the back of her fingers. Her touch sent electric charges through his skin. She ran her fingernails lightly up the insides of his thighs. He needed her all over again.

'And sex just happens to be one of those drives?' he managed to ask.

'You behaved like a real shit today, and my guess is you weren't even aware of it. Your preoccupation with my modesty was way out of line, but I finally figured it out—we haven't touched each other for a whole week, and your body chemistry is way out of whack. Mine probably is too, for that matter.'

Who the hell did she think she was? But the behaviour of his body belied this angry thought. He had grown so hard he was aching.

As if sensing his thoughts, Tara turned on her back, drawing him with her. 'Fuck. Stop talking.'

Just like that? No preliminaries? But he couldn't help himself. Almost instantaneously his body usurped the normal functioning of his mind. He felt the electrical build-up reaching exquisitely painful proportions. His anger made him self-centred about what he was doing.

His conscious mind had switched off. In the constant war between body and mind, Patrick's body had won this round, hands down.

For her part, none of this came as a surprise. She had, after all, been consciously contributing to it. She knew he would be better off when he came to understand the three-dimensional nature of love making, preferably sooner rather than later.

It had been her father, of all people, who had explained that physical sex is only one dimension of the three dimensions of love making—the other two being cerebral and spiritual. He had said, wisely, that there was no hope in hell that any man could achieve sexual satisfaction by playing the field. 'All that serves to achieve is that it stimulates the manufacture of yet more testosterone. You show me a guy who boasts about being a virile cocksman, and I'll show you a testosterone junky.'

As a starting point, she would need to un-dam Patrick's dammed-up river of testosterone so that he could once again start thinking straight.

Within minutes Patrick shuddered as the electrical tension discharged from his body. Gradually, his mind took its rightful ascendant position in the hierarchy of his life; he looked down at Tara with remorse. 'I'm sorry. God, Tara, I'm sorry.'

She stroked his forehead and his upper arms trying to convey the empathy she felt. He closed his eyes and within moments she felt his body relax as the feel-good endorphins lulled him into sleep.

She was wide awake and frustrated. She showered again, then took herself outside to the balcony. She sat there, naked and alone, her knees drawn up to her chin and gazed up into her beloved sky, a sky that stretched out beyond the confines of any worldly issues. A sigh escaped from somewhere deep within her. Testosterone had a lot to answer for.

Her thoughts began to range. There was Professor Rosenberg: fate had decreed that he remain single, and she guessed he had compensated for that by immersing himself in other subjects that would occupy his thoughts and expand his soul. Then there was Mehmet, and the unlikely alliance between him and Yehuda. There was a wisdom that these two men exuded, both of them so connected to the same unitary God in their own quirky ways.

She thought of the clash of civilizations among the descendants of Abraham, and how it was probably their imbalanced attitudes towards sex that gave rise to either a damming or a raging of the rivers of testosterone within the males of these societies. A surfeit of testosterone seemed to become toxically poisonous, in particular, among the over-sexed, excessively competitive political and business leaders in the world, and that was probably the root cause of most clashes of human will.

She thought of her late dad, and his infectious sense of humour, his wisdom, his humility of soul, and she found her cheeks wet before she even realised she was crying for him. God how she missed that man.

Finally, her thoughts came full circle to Patrick, asleep on the bed not ten feet away. No. It wasn't the idea of love that she was in love with. It was this particular man. He was far from being a uni-dimensional human. He had layers to his personality: strength, courage, conviction. He had laughter in his soul.

With that, she padded back inside the room, and lay down beside him. He stirred, still half asleep. She shifted her body on the bed. This time it was her turn. Through half closed eyes she saw him smile in growing awareness of her. She felt the strength of his hands respond to her. And the electric charge as he gently assumed control. She started to lose herself, to experience that floating feeling. He needed to prove himself to her. This time ... she was achingly prepared for him.

CHAPTER 35

'HI SAMBUCCA.' THE two softly spoken words spilled over the edges of the mobile phone's mouthpiece and eddied off into the crisp predawn darkness. A couple of hundred metres away, the foamy whisper of a sea breathed its quiet response ... sssshhhh.

'Who's speaking please?' There was just a hint of an echo and a heartbeat's delay before the clipped query reached Patrick's eardrum 10,000 odd miles away.

'Oooh! That hurts, sister. How long has it been? Less than two weeks? And you've forgotten me already?' Patrick was leaning over the balustrade of the balcony, his shoulders slightly hunched, his voice low enough not to disturb Tara, who was still sleeping in the darkness of the bedroom behind him.

'That's my Patrick. Attack is the best form of defence. You flew off into the wild blue yonder and just dropped off the radar screen. No "arrived safe" phone call. No "Hi Sam, I was worried about how are you coping at the bank given our last conversation?" No nothing.'

'Hah huh.' His laugh was quiet, almost conspiratorial. 'I'm prepared to bet that whatever crisis you were facing two weeks ago has been resolved and that today you're facing a new one. That's the life you chose Sam, but okay. How are you coping at the bank?'

'Don't ask.'

'Bad as that?'

'It's not getting any better. Why are you whispering like that? Normally the further the distance, the louder you seem to shout.'

'It's almost 5 a.m. this side. I had to get up early to get you at home after work. What's the time there? It should be around 8 p.m.'

'Yes …'

'So talk to me Sam,' Patrick interrupted. 'What's happening? Have you been having a life outside the bank? Doing any socialising?'

Samantha's voice perked up noticeably. 'As a matter of fact, I've been keeping myself very busy. After you left, I thought about us and came to the conclusion that you and I are probably going to be just mates till hell freezes over.'

'So what have you been doing?' Patrick responded, possibly a bit too quickly.

'Well, Melissa threw an impromptu party last Saturday night. She invited about thirty people and I met someone there.'

'Boy or girl?'

Sam's laughter sounded heartfelt. 'What is it about you that pushes my happy button? Listen, Patrick, I haven't got much time. William's coming to pick me up in ten. We're heading out for a late dinner.'

'William? As in Prince William? Most Williams I know are called Bill. What's he drive, this William? A Rolls?'

'Aston Martin, actually. William Chelmsford. He's head of a multinational IT software business. Made a megabuck fortune by listing on Nasdaq a few years ago. And you're still whispering, Patrick. Are the walls so thin that you're worried about the neighbours?'

'Yeah, well you're not the only one who gets invited to parties. I met Tara last Wednesday at a restaurant, and it's been a riot. One day I'll fill you in on the details.'

'Tara? Lovely name. 'Is she Irish or Indian?'

'American. Came out here on holiday. She's a pilot and she's going to fly us into the Bermuda Triangle in a couple of hours. I think I may be onto something, Sam.' There was rising enthusiasm in his voice. 'Tara introduced me to a professor of physics she met recently and it turned out that he has been developing an electromagnetic energy technology. Been at it for over twenty years. It's very powerful …'

'Who are you talking to?' The husky question sounded more curious than challenging. He swivelled to find Tara yawning behind him, hair tousled, the back of her left hand softly rubbing the sleep from her eye, as her right hand caressed rather than scratched the porcelain skin on her right cheek.

His heart lifted. *My God you're beautiful.* 'Just hang on a second Sam.' He covered the mouthpiece. It's a banker friend in Australia. I wanted to ask her advice on how we might help Yehuda get his technology past the research stage.'

'Her?'

Patrick held up a finger. 'Sam? You still there?'

'I'm still here. But I'm running out of time. 'What happened? Did you just get caught *in flagrante delicto*?' The words, laced with merriment, were almost shouted—as if to ensure that Tara could also hear them.

Patrick ignored the jibe. 'I hope your Mr Chelmsford understands just how lucky a bastard he was to have found you.' His *non sequitur* was also intended for two pairs of ears. 'I'll be as quick as I can Sam. The reason I called is I need to ask your advice on something. Thumbnail sketch. This professor's technology—how can we get it from working prototype into the market place?'

'You want me to answer that with Tara listening in the background, and with William on his way up to collect me for a dinner date, and me not yet properly dressed to go out? Do you want to hang while I go into the bathroom? Maybe I can tell you while I'm brushing my teeth.'

'It would make a great ventriloquist's act,' he conceded. 'Thumbnail sketch, Sam. Core issues. What do I have to look for?'

'Okay. Look, let me think about this over the next few days but, assuming he has a prototype that works, and assuming it's some kind of a machine, and assuming he's got the ability to patent his Intellectual Property, then the main question will revolve around technical risk. Does the thing, whatever it is, actually do what he claims for it? Very often these "gee whiz" inventions start to unravel when a critical outsider comes at them coldly and unemotionally. Inventors often tend to fall in love with their brain babies and then they become blind to the blemishes. You need references that weren't written by the guy's mother.'

'All right. I hear you. And if it does what he claims?'

'That's what I want to think about. Now put Tara on please. I'm gonna do you a favour that you'll thank me for later.'

'Hang on.' He held the phone out to Tara. 'Sam wants to talk to you.'

'Me?'

She took the phone. 'Hello? This is Tara Geoffrey.'

'Hi Tara. This is Samantha Alexander. I see you've met Peter Pan. He's a rough diamond, but the emphasis is on diamond. When you unwrap the crumpled brown paper packaging, I thought you should know that what's inside is top drawer quality.'

'How long have you and Patrick known one another?'

'Since we were kids. Patrick can be a bit gauche when it comes to social niceties. I didn't want you to get the wrong impression about us. We were an item once, and at the time I had hoped it might lead somewhere, but it never did. Now we're just good mates.'

Tara laughed. 'Gauche? Tell me about it. Last week he invited me to a dinner party and neglected to inform me that it was formal. The hostess wore a designer outfit and I was dressed for an outdoor barbecue.'

'Sounds like our Patrick. I'd love to meet up with you one day and compare notes.'

'Me too. By the sounds of it you can give me some good pointers.'

'Yeah. A few. Fly safely. I've got to run. I'm being picked up for dinner in about five minutes. Give him a kiss for me. Tell him I'll do some research on how to commercialise the professor's technology.'

'Will do. Go well Samantha. I look forward to meeting you sometime.'

She pressed the red button to ring off.

'Smart lady that,' she said, handing the phone back to Patrick. 'Good friend too, by the sounds of it. If she hadn't asked to speak to me you might have found yourself having to do some fast talking.'

She basked momentarily in Patrick's confused expression, laughed happily, and walked purposefully back into the bedroom. 'Come on Peter Pan. We had better get dressed and have ourselves some breakfast. There's a long day ahead.'

CHAPTER 36

PATRICK AND TARA watched the glow of the awakening sun edge tentatively over the horizon's coverlet. They were just finishing breakfast on the covered patio downstairs. Not a single cloud disturbed the tranquillity of a cerulean dawn sky. It would be a perfect day for flying.

Patrick gathered the breakfast dishes and headed for the kitchen while Tara filed an early flight plan with Santo Domingo International. It would take them from El Portillo Airport across Great Inagua west of the Turks and Caicos Islands, then past Flamingo Cay and William Island in the Bahamas to Bimini. From there, they would veer north-east, heading for Bermuda, and then double back to El Portillo. The course was calculated to take them roughly along the perimeter of the Triangle.

At an altitude of 30,000 to 35,000 feet, cruising comfortably at 265 miles an hour, the King Air B200 would have a range of 2,500 miles. Tara decided to allow for slightly slower speed and less efficient fuel consumption. If she could get away with it, she was planning to fly at a lower altitude of around 12,000 feet for part of the way. She wanted to fly through thicker atmosphere to check the levels of turbulence. By her reckoning the entire distance of around 2,350 nautical miles would still only take them approximately ten hours including a half hour refuelling stop at South Bimini. They would pick up something to eat there. With this in mind they were flying light, with no carry-on luggage except her handbag and a bottle of water each.

'We're probably going to use around 550 gallons of fuel, all up,' she told Patrick as they climbed aboard the plane. 'That's going to cost the mine in the region of $2,500. Do you have the clearance for this?'

'It took a bit of persuading, but I guess I'm still the blue-eyed boy given the great publicity the mine got out of last Tuesday's caper. In any event, this is not just a joy ride.'

When they were settling in to their seats she noticed him winding up the old-fashioned wristwatch he was wearing. He held his ear to the watchface as he wound it. She shook her head, smiling. There was a little boy in every grown man, but she probably could love this one. She turned her attention to the plane.

Tara went methodically through her checklist and taxied the plane into position facing away from the rising sun. She stood on the brakes as she gunned the engines. At precisely 7.00 a.m. she called—by force of habit—'brakes off.' The plane shot forward. Although the runway was shorter than normal, her experience let her handle it almost with her eyes closed. Within less than a minute she was banking towards South Bimini.

'This is November-nine-one-nine-six-Quebec, taking off from runway 27 at Mike-Delta-Papa-Oscar for a straight-out departure, destination Mike-Yankee-Bravo-Sierra,' she said into her microphone, giving the call sign of the B200 and the initials of both the departure airport and the destination airport. 'ETA South Bimini is ten hundred hours local time.'

When they reached 300 feet she pulled up the landing gear. They were already climbing at the rate of 3,000 feet a minute. She had resolved to level out at 5,000 feet for half an hour so that they could take a visual on their surroundings.

'November-nine-one-nine-six-Quebec, set your squawk frequency at two, three, one, seven,' came the voice from air traffic control at Santo Domingo International. This was the transponder frequency by which her flight would be tracked by various traffic controllers across their entire journey.

Tara set the frequency as instructed. She ran her eye along the instrument panel from left to right and down as though reading a book. Everything seemed normal. The GPS monitor was located in the console at hip level between the pilot and co-pilot seats. By habit, she cross-checked its reading with that on the magnetic compass on the panel in front of her. 'Everything normal,' she said aloud.

At 5,000 feet she levelled out, felt the resonating whine of the turbines at a comfortable 16,500 RPM and fine-tuned her hearing so that she would pick up any subtle change that might arise. 'Feels fine,' she muttered, but allowed herself to start relaxing only after she had set the autopilot. The pitch of the props would be automatically adjusted by the B200's hydraulic systems, but it never hurt to be on top of things. Just to make absolutely sure, she double-checked that the prop RPMs were the expected 2,450. They were.

The sun's rays ricocheted off the mirror-like surface of the turquoise sea. Patrick relaxed into his seat feeling an inner contentment and at peace with the world. He looked out of the window at the surface directly below and pointed excitedly at a small herd of manatees grazing on the shallow sea bed. 'Did you know that they're related to our dugongs in Australia?'

'Aah, but did you know the elephant is their next closest relative?' Tara asked.

'They look more like a cross between a walrus and a hippopotamus.'

'I hear there are about two-and-a-half thousand of them living around Florida; most of them with scars on their backs from boat propellers.'

'So that must mean our dugongs are related to elephants.' He smiled at the thought of a walrupotamus or an elegong. It brought to mind a schoolboy joke about the hippocrocamouse. His mind kept making idle connections. 'Ever wonder about the English language and collective nouns?' he mused. 'Like why do we call it a pod of dolphins, and a congregation of crocodiles, and a parliament of owls?'

'I wouldn't have a clue. Speaking of dolphins, look at that school over there.' She was ribbing him, but he looked. Sure enough, there was a group of them cavorting in the water.

They chatted about nothing for a while. Patrick took a swig of water from his bottle and replaced it in the holder behind the console. Tara declined his offer.

Far in the distance, they saw a sailboat—probably a forty-footer—its spinnaker billowing majestically in the early morning breeze. To their right, an island grew larger on the horizon.

'That's the Turks and Caicos Islands,' Tara said. 'Up ahead is Great Inagua Island.' He could just make out a darkish discolouration of the sea ahead of them on the horizon.

Tara began the climb to the prearranged level of 12,000 feet.

'There won't be much to look at until we get to the cays where the water colour should change from deep cobalt blue to a blend of robin's egg blue and turquoise,' she said. 'Then we could see to the bottom again if we were flying lower—but it will be too dangerous to do that as we approach the busier air lanes. Anyway, precisely what are we looking for?'

'Frankly, I have no idea. From what I've read, some of the anomalies in and around the Bermuda Triangle have occurred above the really deep trenches. If you look at a map, you'll see that the so called "tongue of the ocean" starts just east of Williams Island, and then the trench snakes due north from there, past Nassau towards Manhattan Island and New York. After we refuel in South Bimini I thought we might follow it for a short detour before heading directly for Bermuda. Maybe you can turn when we get in line with the border of Georgia and South Carolina.'

'Why not? It's a beautiful day. You can tell me all about the other girlfriends you've had in your young life, but before you do that, I'd better clear your plan with the sheriff's office in case they send out a posse after us.'

Patrick waited the few seconds she needed just then to allow her to concentrate on her flying. 'A gentleman never kisses and tells,' he said. 'In any event, what do you mean by other girlfriends? Does this mean we're officially an item now?'

'Are you getting all coy on me? We've known each other since last Wednesday night—that's nine days. So far we've had dinner together twice and coffee twice. We've had the most amazing sex ever, *twice*. We've been to a fancy dinner party with strangers where I've never been so embarrassed in my life. We've learned to dance two of the most erotic dances of the Caribbean. We've been scuba diving, and now we're chasing your very expensive rainbows together.'

'Oh. So this isn't just a casual holiday fling of yours?' He was deadpan, baiting her.

'I've invited you to Thanksgiving dinner to meet my family. Is that your idea of a fling?' Her voice rose just noticeably. She was rising to the bait.

'Ask me anything except about my girlfriends, anything at all,' he said, relenting. 'My life is an open book. I want you to read it cover to cover.'

'Yeah, right. But only the expurgated version.' Nevertheless, part of her was happy to hear him talk like this. 'Tell you what. Why don't you tell me more about this environmental energy that's got you so worked up?'

'It might bore you.'

'If it does, I'll send you to play outside.'

'What do you know about Michael Faraday, James Clerk Maxwell and Nikola Tesla?' he asked.

'About as much as I know about your girlfriends ... or lack of them.'

'Okay, okay. Well, here we go then. In the late 1700s a guy by the name of Charles Coulomb was able to demonstrate how two electrical charges repel each other the way like-poles of a magnet do.' His words came out rather quickly 'This was a clue that led two other people in the early 1800s to discover that an electric current produces a magnetic field. Their names were Hans Christian Oersted and Andre-Marie Ampere.'

'Would he be related to Hans Christian Andersen?'

'Hey! Do you want to hear this or not?'

'Sorry Maassah.'

He got the message—lay off the heavy stuff.

'Michael Faraday was also born in the late 1700s. He had very little schooling, but he liked chemistry and he had a mentor—a guy by the name of Humphrey Davy—and they worked together to precipitate chemicals from solutions. They were using a technique called electrolysis, which basically involves passing an electric current through a chemical solution.'

'They saw some sort of linkage between electricity and magnetism?'

'Yes. Faraday grew to understand electricity better than most. One of his ideas was that since an electric current could cause a magnetic field, the reverse should also be true. A magnetic field should be able to produce an electric current.'

'Smart cookie.'

'Smart enough, given that this idea led to the principle of induction which made possible the dynamo or generator. As a result of his experiments, Faraday was able to express the electric current induced in the wire in terms of the number of lines of force that are cut by the wire, but most scientists of the day rejected this idea, until a guy by the name of James Clerk Maxell came along.'

'More dolphins,' Tara said pointing into the distance.

'Look, two babies with them … what do you call them—pups, calves?' Even this far away they drew his immediate interest. What would Samantha say to that? Now he was the one cooing over babies.

'Yes, you were saying … and then along ca-ame Ja-a-ames,' Tara sang, pulling his mind back into the cockpit.

Patrick had the good sense not to react. He continued as if she was just the chorus for his own song.

'Maxwell—James Maxwell.' He said the name in his best James Bond voice. 'He was the opposite of Faraday; educated first at Edinburgh University and then at Cambridge, and a star at mathematics. When he applied his mind to Faraday's ideas, he was able to quantify Faraday's concept of lines of force in mathematical format. This led to some formalised theories of electromagnetism which, in turn, led to modern field theory.'

Tara listened attentively. In spite of her banter she was genuinely interested. In no time South Bimini came into view and chatter with the tower took over. Time flew faster than the B200. They landed for refuelling. She supervised the intake, while he went to get them something to eat. It was around 11 o'clock when they were airborne once again. Because of traffic congestion, Tara had decided to play it a bit safer this time and had obtained permission to fly at 20,000 feet.

When they were at their cruising altitude, he took up the narrative where he had left off.

'Maxwell's greatest impact was his formulation of what came to be known as Maxwell's Equations. One of these equations predicts that magnetic waves will travel at the speed of light, and this led him to propose that light is therefore a form of electromagnetic radiation. He was also able to demonstrate that electric and magnetic forces are two complementary aspects of electromagnetic radiation.'

Tara nodded. In her mind she could hear echoes of her original conversation with Yehuda.

'An important point that Maxwell made at the time was that magnetic waves were undetectable by mechanical means.' Patrick's voice rose slightly in emphasis. He looked so earnest. She had trouble reconciling him with the dancer, lover and jester of the previous night.

'I'm confused,' she said.

He looked at her as if waiting to see whether this was another attempt to get him to lighten up.

'Here, have a sandwich,' he countered.

'If magnetic waves could only be inferred by mathematical modelling or by their electrical effect, then what was it that led you to believe that electromagnetic energy in the environment might be capable of being harnessed as an alternative to fossil fuels? I assume that's what's driving you.'

'Yes. That is what's driving me,' he said, his mouth half full. 'The answer is that it was a coincidence of two seemingly unrelated pieces of information. You heard me talking to Yehuda the other day about the biblical Ark of the Covenant, and how some scientists now believe that it was a rudimentary electrical capacitor and that it was used to scavenge electricity from the environment? Some people call this electricity the "telluric current".'

'Yes, I remember that.'

'Well, that was the second piece of information. When I read about that, I remembered something unusual about a guy by the name of Nikola Tesla who I first heard about when I was studying engineering.'

'Coming up to Flamingo Cay and William Island.'

'I'd like to holiday in the Bahamas one day, wouldn't you? All that turquoise and sky blue sea, beautiful beaches …'

'Playground of the rich and infamous,' she said, avoiding his question. Did he mean 'me holiday' or 'us holiday'? Instead, she brought him back to his favourite topic. 'Tesla …' she prodded.

'Tesla was the guy who was credited with having developed alternating current electricity when everyone else at the time was focussing on direct current generation. He developed the first alternating current induction motor and it was this invention that would eventually allow transmission of alternating current electricity over long distances.'

'Sounds like quite a guy.'

'Yep. Unfortunately, he had no commercial sense. He died impoverished.'

'So what's the connection between Tesla and your view that environmental energy can be harnessed?'

'My first gut understanding of the possibility was when I read that he had managed to light vacuum tubes wirelessly. You know, the good old fluorescent light? He's the guy who invented it. That told me that usable energy did not have to travel through any conduit.'

It seemed no time before Bermuda came into view up ahead of them. Tara banked the plane and reset its course, one that would eventually take them east of Cockburn Town in the Turks and Caicos Islands and back to Samana. They had been cruising at around 250 miles per hour. Their ETA back at El Portillo Airport was 4.30 p.m. local time.

Patrick's mind drifted. He was remembering his own childhood, when he and his mates ran under the overhead electric pylons in the field near his home. They'd wave fluorescent light bulbs in the air under the high power electric cables and the bulbs would light up. It was a source of joyful entertainment to a bunch of nine-year-olds. He would have drifted off further had Tara's voice not interrupted his thoughts.

'So, given what you already knew, you assumed that the Ark of the Covenant was able to do the same thing, only with electromagnetic energy floating around naturally in the environment. So far it all sounds reasonable to me ... as a hypothesis at least,' she said, 'although I'm no expert.'

'No one is. That's the whole point. We're looking at relatively unexplored territory—largely because we don't yet understand the mechanical processes involved. We know the what, but we don't yet understand the how.'

'Yet?'

'Yup, but it may be closer than we think. I read a copy of an old newspaper article published in the *New York Sun* as long ago as 1934. Basically, it reported that Tesla had announced some sort of peace ray. He claimed to have invented a beam of matter travelling at high velocity. He was seventy-eight years old at the time, and he was describing what sounded like a sort of death ray that we read about in science fiction books.'

'So what's the connection between that and environmental energy? I still can't connect the dots.'

'Although Tesla never actually delivered on the promise, he must have thought that he understood the mechanical processes of electro-magnetism. His ray relied on concentrating beams of artificially created energy. There was subsequent speculation that he had invented a sort of miniaturised, AC powered, particle accelerator, and there was a photo-graph of him using it to light a gunpowder fuse from quite a distance away.'

'Something like a laser beam?'

'Yes, but not quite the same. What grabbed my imagination was that if he had devised a way of harnessing man-made energy and concen-trating it, then it's a short step in logic to think in terms of harnessing relatively weak environmental energy and concentrating it. It seemed to me that that may have been what the Ark of the Covenant was designed to do.'

'But I thought a particle accelerator accelerates particles rather than energy.'

'Good point, but when they collide they give off energy. And Einstein taught us that energy and matter are interchangeable, so it might be possible that, at the margin, particles become pure energy. Think of light. Sometimes it's a wave of energy and sometimes it's a particle.'

'All right. Let's just accept the proposition. How would he have achieved this concentration?'

'No one knows for sure. I have read one argument that speculates the use of what is known as a Fresnel lens to concentrate and focus a longi-tudinal wave.'

Tara looked perplexed.

'A Fresnel lens is what they use in lighthouse lights. It has a stepped design that starts out thick at the perimeter of the lens and ends up relatively thin at the centre. This stepped design causes light waves to cascade down the steps from the perimeter towards the centre of the lens and in the process it amplifies the relatively weak light, by concentrating it into a narrow and powerful beam. So … by the same logic, it may be possible to amplify relatively weak energy by concentrating it through an energetic version of a Fresnel lens. I became convinced that it must be possible to somehow scavenge energy from the environment and then concentrate it, similar to the way Tesla's peace ray was being concentrated. That's why I asked the professor to investigate what he could about the Ark of the … Whoa, what was that?' Patrick suddenly felt his stomach leap into his mouth as the safety harness bit into his shoulders.

Tara did not reply. She bit her lip in concentration, her hands on the joystick; her knuckles white with tension. She watched the altimeter's numbers twirling faster than she had ever seen.

'We're losing altitude!' she exclaimed. 'It's happening too fast for me to estimate our rate of descent! We've dropped 2,500 feet … 3,000 feet … 4,000 feet!'

Less than fifteen seconds had elapsed. The propellers were screaming. The rev counters were in the red zone. Tara pulled back on the throttle until the engines sounded normal to her. She didn't have the luxury of time to remain focussed on the rev counters. She was too preoccupied with the fact that the artificial horizon was way off the horizontal. In simple terms, the plane's left wing was pointing towards the ground or, in this case, towards the sea's surface. She had flicked off the automatic pilot to assume manual control. Her focus of attention was on getting the plane to fly level again, which she managed to do. Sweat had broken out on her upper lip and on her forehead.

Patrick felt an enormous pressure on his buttocks as a giant unseen hand pushed him viciously back into his seat. He vaguely felt a reduction of tension in the harness on his shoulders followed by a sharp pain on his forehead. His hand whipped up to grab at the sore spot where he felt wetness. 'What the …' He looked at his fingers. Blood! How had that gotten there? He was securely strapped in. Surely he couldn't have hit his head on the ceiling?

Tara gunned the engines again to get traction. 'We're going up again,' she said. 'Hold on.' She managed to steal a glance at the weather radar. Nothing.

'We've hit clear weather turbulence,' she shouted.

She flicked the microphone switch. 'Pan! Pan! Pan!' She called. She was expecting the message to be monitored by New York flight control.

'This is November-nine-one-nine-six-Quebec. We are encountering severe air turbulence from Bermuda to El Portillo. My co-ordinates are …' She looked down at the GPS. Its glass had cracked. The screen was blank. 'GPS inoperative,' she said. 'Estimate 110 nautical miles heading from Bermuda. ETA local time 16.40 hours.'

Again, the rev counters were in the red. Now she kept an obsessive eye on them. If the engines overheated and blew she would have to ditch. She throttled down for a second time. She checked the inlet turbine temperature. Close to red line! Her pilot instincts were reacting faster than her eyes.

The plane seemed to go into free-fall again. The altimeter showed 18,000 … 17,000 … 16,000 … 15,000 feet. She didn't see it, but Patrick was watching it. Five seconds. 'My God!' It stopped revolving. Tara gunned the engines, hoping to hell that the automatic pitch would kick in so as to adjust the propellers' revs. She needed as much bite as they could muster.

She pulled back on the joystick. 'Patrick!' she shouted over the screaming engines. 'The water bottles have been thrown out of their holders. My GPS monitor is smashed. It must have been one of the bottles. Find them and hold onto them! I don't want anything else broken.'

It must have been one of the bottles that had hit him on the forehead as the plane rose thousands of feet in a few seconds immediately after it had originally fallen through the sky. He saw one bottle rolling around at his feet. He grabbed it.

The plane was climbing furiously under Tara's control. 15,000 …

16,000 … 17,000. It took a minute or two to get back to 20,000 feet where Tara levelled out. She braced herself for more. Nothing. She started to breathe again.

'I found one bottle,' Patrick said, happy to have something to concentrate on. 'I can't see the other.'

'Find it!' she commanded. 'Don't get out of your seat. Leave your harness on.' She wasn't taking any more chances.

He craned his neck to see. He caught a glimpse of movement. 'It's under your seat.'

She reached down to grab it. 'Hold onto it!' she ordered as she passed it to him.

'Where did that come from?' she asked.

'What?'

She was pointing dead ahead. It seemed to Patrick like a disk shaped cloud.

'What is it?'

'It looks like a lenticular cloud.' She checked the weather radar again. Still nothing!

'Shit!'

He heard her voice penetrating his subconscious. He had been thinking about the bottles and how much force must have been involved for the bottle to smash the GPS. His head was throbbing.

'What now?'

She was looking at the instruments. His eyes followed her gaze. The instruments were going haywire!

'The static air system seems to be on the blink,' she shouted. 'My vertical air speed indicator's gone. The artificial horizon indicator's gone.' Three seconds passed. 'Now the compass is spinning, and we've got no GPS, *and* the VOR's spinning.'

'What the hell is a VOR?' He probably shouldn't even be talking, but he couldn't help himself.

'It shows the direction of the destination beacon at El Portillo. Without a compass and GPS and VOR I've got no way of knowing what direction we're headed.'

Instinctively, Tara looked through the windscreen to get a glimpse of the horizon. She had to keep the plane flying level. All around them were clouds. All she could see were clouds. They had come out of nowhere. It couldn't have been more than five minutes since she first saw that lone lenticular cloud. No horizon. She looked up. The clouds tunnelled up for miles. She could see blue sky in the distance, but it was too high to think of climbing. Maybe 60,000 feet. Impossible!

'We're in deep doo doo!' Tara shouted as her instincts took over. She had vaguely registered that the engines were making varying sounds which implied that the plane was probably porpoising in the air. Tightening her grip on the joystick, she pulled the B200 into what she intended to be a left-handed 360 degree steep turn. She was searching for a gap in the clouds so that she could get a glimpse of the horizon. Without it, she couldn't fly level.

But her instincts had been too quick. The loop had taken them off course. Damn! Without her instruments she had no idea when the loop would be completed. They could land up facing in any direction, and then there was still the problem of flying horizontally.

'Patrick! What happened to those bottles?'

'I've got them here in my hands.'

'Hold one up so I can see it. I need to check the meniscus of the water.'

'That's my girl!' Brilliant—gravity would hold the meniscus level. He held the bottle so that its top was facing directly towards the ceiling.

Watching it ferociously the seasoned pilot adjusted the plane's angle until the meniscus was at right angles to the bottle's wall. 'At least we're flying level,' she said.

'Good thinking. Now what?'

Suddenly Patrick saw the colour leave her face. Tara felt herself go ice cold. She was experiencing something she had never experienced in all her years of flying. The engines were screaming. She glanced at the inlet turbine temperature gauge again. It was in the red danger zone. The RPM gauge was also red lining. But that wasn't the problem. What? Something was off centre but her mind hadn't yet grasped it. What could it be? The automatic pitch adjustment couldn't have been working. She throttled back to slow the engines. Still, her instincts were screaming. What? What? Think girl! Her heart was pounding like a trip hammer. She felt primordial terror welling up inside her.

Without knowing why, she opened the window next to her. She should have heard the sound of the rushing wind.

Nothing. No wind.

She looked back at her instrument panel. Nothing. Totally dead. No sign of life on any instrument. All of them dead. Every single one!

She looked wide-eyed at Patrick. It took him all of three seconds to intuit what was bothering her. They looked at each other. She leaned forward.

'May Day! May Day! May Day!' she called. 'This is November-nine-one-nine-six-Quebec. We are in serious trouble. We have lost all instrumentation. I am thinking of ditching into the sea. Last known position: one hour out of Bermuda on heading 215. May Day! May Day! May Day!'

Nothing! The radio was dead too. Only the sound of the engines and her pounding heart told her that she was alive and that this was no nightmare.

It was surreal. She remembered the old bar room joke amongst pilots. 'I've run out of air speed, altitude and ideas all at the same time.' What made her think of that? Then she understood. *And* visibility. She couldn't see more than ten feet ahead. She was having difficulty breathing but it was not for lack of oxygen. Her windpipe was constricted in fear.

'Holy cow!' Patrick shouted.

He was looking out of his side window. He couldn't see the wing tip. It was as if the wing had been amputated at its elbow—if it had an elbow.

'It's an optical illusion,' he heard her say. 'The fog has closed in on us.'

'What are you talking about? How can there be a fog 20,000 feet up?' he demanded. 'How far above sea level are we?'

'I haven't the faintest idea.'

He couldn't help himself. He was programmed that way. The words just popped out of his mouth. 'Thank God. For a second there I was expecting you to tell me you haven't got the foggiest.'

She wasn't listening. She was staring at the water bottle. It couldn't be. The meniscus seemed to be dead flat. It also seemed to be higher in the bottle than she remembered. She grabbed the bottle out of his hand to turn it on its side. The meniscus didn't move.

'What the hell!' Patrick couldn't believe his eyes. 'No gravity. That's impossible!'

Something made him look out of the side window on the pilot's side. Once again he couldn't believe his eyes. Although the fog was closing in, he could still see the propeller spinning. The pointed spinner seemed to be trembling like wobbly jelly. 'Switch off the engines!' he screamed in a voice that made her jump, but she reacted immediately to do as he commanded. The propeller slowed. The wobbling stopped. The fog closed in. They couldn't see one inch out of any of the windows. Everything was a yellowish grey. No, that wasn't it. It was more of an eerie yellowish luminescence with no discernable light source.

Dead silence. No wind. No motor. No radio, No sound except the pounding of their hearts and the hissing of their fearful breathing.

'We're going to die,' Tara said in a tremulous voice. 'I'm sorry, Patrick. I'm sorry.' She reached for his hand.

'No we're not,' he answered. 'You switched off the engine just in time. We're still in one piece and we're not moving.' Any explanations seemed too far-fetched.

They sat in silence. Tara was still holding her bottle. Patrick put his back in its holder. Absent-mindedly, he wound his watch and looked at it. It showed 2.15 p.m. He looked closer. The second hand was no longer moving. The watch had stopped. 'What's your time?'

Tara looked. The face of her battery-powered watch was blank. The battery had been drained. 'It's dead.'

A thought struck her. 'Patrick. If this ever clears up, how am I going to start the engines again if the batteries have drained?'

'I've got a hunch that won't be a problem. We only just switched off the engines. They will have been re-charging the starter motor batteries right up until that point. Your instruments went on the blink long ago.'

They sat there in silence. Each wrapped in their own thoughts. Time passed. They couldn't gauge how long. Except for their beating hearts there were no reference points. Eventually Patrick spoke.

'Tara, I don't know if we're ever going to get out of this alive, so I'm just going to tell you what's on my mind.'

'Yes?'

'I don't know how you feel about me, but in nine days flat I've fallen in love with you. I need to know how you feel.'

'You dumb bozo,' she answered. 'I'm head over heels crazy about you. Can't you tell?'

'Well, the thing is, I don't know you well enough to be able to tell.'

In spite of their dire predicament, she laughed. 'It's your sense of humour that won me over. You make me want to laugh all the time. I love it and I love you.'

'If we get out of this, I want to get married as soon as possible after our families have met.'

'Is this a proposal?' she asked.

'Why don't we invite my parents to meet your family at Thanksgiving in Hartford?'

They planned their life in surreal detail. Yet, there was no real conviction. It was almost as if it helped pass the time, helped take their minds off their imminent deaths.

'I always thought I'd have a white wedding.'

'Not me ... too *Miami Vice*. Black tux maybe.'

'Bridesmaids?' she asked idly.

'Naah, don't think I have any woman friends who'd believe me that I'd be getting married. Could probably scare up a best man. I'd like to stay on in Santo Domingo though—at least for a while.'

'I'll hand in my notice a month before Thanksgiving,' she said.

Patrick looked at his watch for the umpty-umpth time. How the hell could a fully wound mechanical watch stop? They had been trapped in whatever it was they were trapped in, for who knows how long?

Just as suddenly as the fog had descended, it now started to lift. Instead of a luminescent greyish yellow fog, they saw blackness.

Tara was the first to react. 'Where are we … what is this—night?' she asked.

Patrick felt his stomach rising again.

'We're in free fall!' they shouted in unison.

Tara's instincts quickly took over. She leaned forward to go through what she expected would be the motions of starting the engines. To the intense surprise of both of them, the engines turned over and caught. The instrument panel lights came on again. The artificial horizon and the magnetic compass were working.

The pilot in her assumed control.

'Altitude 5,000 feet and rising. RPM 2,000 and rising. Air speed ninety knots and rising.' They were way off course but the B200's downward spiral had been arrested. She had managed to pull it level, then into a steep rise. Slowly, deliberately, she manoeuvred the plane back onto a heading of 215 degrees.

'This is November-nine-one-nine-six-Quebec. Can anyone read me?'

'November-nine-one-nine-six-Quebec this is Santo Domingo International. What happened to you? You went off the radar.'

It was almost five o'clock on Patrick's watch when they landed at El Portillo. The gas tanks were a third full. Local time, they found out when they finally stepped onto the grass was 12 p.m.—midnight. Seven hours were unaccounted for, vanished into the electronic fog.

'You wanted to find out just how awesomely powerful environmental energy can be?' Tara asked. 'Maybe now we know.'

CHAPTER 37

'YOU ARE LUCKY to be alive,' Mehmet said.

He and Yehuda had been listening intently as Patrick and Tara recounted their frightening experiences of the day before. Yehuda had asked them to spare no details. Tara peered at him through the dense fog of blue pipe smoke as he concentrated. It was almost as dense as yesterday's electronic fog.

It was Sunday evening. The four were sitting in the professor's study—Yehuda and Mehmet in their usual chairs, Tara and Patrick on the threadbare settee below the two colourful Haitian paintings. Brown ringed cups, long ago drained of coffee, sat on the large old coffee table in the centre of the room.

While the scientist in Yehuda was enthralled by the detail of their experiences, Mehmet seemed genuinely concerned. He turned to face Patrick. 'What possessed you to take such a risk if you already knew from Tara's dive compass that the likelihood of magnetic anomalies was high?'

'It was precisely *because* the compass went haywire that we decided to go,' Patrick answered. 'Tara is an experienced pilot. She was happy to fly into the Triangle, and I was happy to put myself in her capable hands. As it turned out, she happens to be a brilliant pilot.' He looked at her and smiled.

'Yes, but …' There was a look of consternation on Mehmet's face. Patrick cut him short with the wave of his hand in the air. 'You're worrying for no reason, Mehmet. Here we are, safe and sound.'

Yehuda seemed more bemused than concerned. He leaned forward, put down his pipe, reached for a sweet and noisily unwrapped it. Belatedly, he offered the bag around. 'I'm trying to cut down on my smoking.'

Mehmet continued to look concerned. Patrick tried to explain further. 'I told you at our meeting the other night about my interest in the subject of electricity,' he said, his cheek bulging with the sweet Yehuda had just given him. 'More accurately, I've been interested in whether the energy that occurs naturally in the environment might be capable of being harnessed. As a matter of fact, one reason I accepted the appointment at the nickel mine here was that the Bermuda Triangle is one of twelve similar triangular regions on the face of the planet where electromagnetic anomalies abound. I wanted to get some first hand experience in the most famous of these locations. Tara and I were expecting to find evidence of anomalies. When her compass started spinning, we both saw it as an ideal opportunity to investigate further.'

'Twelve?' Tara blurted out.

'But you could have died,' Mehmet protested. 'Did you not even contemplate that possibility?'

Tara was not to be ignored. Their experience was behind her. They had survived. She had no interest in woulda, coulda, shoulda discussion. 'Twelve!' she insisted. 'Why didn't you tell me that before?'

'If I had, would it have changed your decision to fly into the Triangle?'

'Probably not, I was just as curious as you were to investigate—but twelve? How come I've never heard about the other eleven?'

'My guess is that you have heard of some of them. It's just that you've never connected the dots. Most people don't because two of the twelve are located over the poles, and eight are located over the oceans. You've probably heard of the Devil's Triangle in the Sea of Japan, for example. Both of the land locations are in relatively inaccessible areas: one is in the Sahara Desert in Algeria, and the other is bounded on one side by the Indus River on the border of Pakistan and India.

Yehuda wagged his finger in the air. 'Strictly speaking, the anomalies in all of these regions are probably the result of interactions of varying wavelengths of electromagnetic energy in the environment, but the concept is still too vague to have been the subject of serious study by academics. It is believed by some that when waves of electromagnetic energy travelling in one direction collide head-on with others, you get a kind of turbulence.' He cupped one hand in the air and brought it sharply up against the vertical palm of his other hand. 'It's very difficult to isolate and measure or predict the effects of this turbulence. As far as we can tell, this is why the anomalies seem to occur randomly, and for some unknown reason it seems to be amplified over the twelve regions Patrick referred to.'

The group looked at Yehuda expectantly, waiting to hear what else he might have to say.

'To my knowledge,' he continued, his eyes sweeping the three listeners, 'the only man who has persistently investigated this particular aspect of energetic anomalies over a long period has been a Canadian by the name of John Hutchison. But even he admits he has no clear under-standing of the science behind the phenomena that you and Tara experienced yesterday. Most physicists who have seen Hutchison's labo-ratory—myself included—have walked away scratching their heads. All I can say for certain is that by pure accident, originally flowing from the way Hutchison had laid out the equipment in his laboratory at home, he caused various wavelengths of electromagnetic energy to collide or intersect. Over the years, he has managed to replicate in the laboratory every single experience you had yesterday—including the yellowish grey electronic fog and the levitation of objects as the forces of gravity appeared to have been neutralised. There is even a series of photographs on his website showing the liquid contents of a plastic cup levitating out of the cup.'[x]

He paused, cocked his head and raised his eyebrows in a manner that invited comment, but there was none forthcoming.

'I have also personally seen how a steel table knife in his laboratory was merged and embedded into a slab of aluminium metal without the shape of either object having been in the slightest distorted. And, no, it wasn't a Uri Geller trick or sleight of hand. If I may say, Tara, you acted with exceptional presence of mind when you decided to switch off the engines at the point you did. That action probably saved your lives because, from what you have described, the physical properties of the propeller spinners were changing at atomic level. They would probably have disintegrated.'

'That was Patrick's doing,' Tara said, grasping his hand in affection.

Yehuda kept his eyes above their linked hands. His smile seemed mildly uncomfortable.

'Ah yes,' Patrick responded, 'but it was your idea to use the bottle of water to keep us flying level. That was a stroke of genius.' Patrick dragged his attention back to Yehuda. 'You seem disinclined to attribute the Bermuda Triangle's energy—or that of any of the other eleven regions, for that matter—to harnessable environmental energy.' Tara could hear the disappointment in his voice. 'If what we experienced yesterday was as a result of electromagnetic turbulence, does that mean I've been looking in the wrong direction … that I've been wasting my time these past months?'

'As it happens, I believe that you may have stumbled onto something important—as have I. In your case it relates to the Ark of the Covenant. In my case it has to do with the embedding of that steel knife in the aluminium block. There seems to be a linkage …'

All three looked at him expectantly, waiting for him to continue. Instead, Yehuda's gaze was riveted on the wall, at a point slightly above Patrick and Tara's heads. Patrick turned to find out what had grabbed his attention, but all he could see were the two Haitian paintings. Yehuda picked up his pipe, got up out of his chair and took a few steps towards the paintings. He held the pipe in his mouth with one hand; his other hand was plunged deep inside his trouser pocket. He stood slightly to the left of the paintings, his head slightly tilted as though examining them for flaws, or perhaps checking their horizontal alignment. Who could tell?

Mehmet's voice broke softly into the silence. 'My suggestion is that you help yourselves to fresh cups of coffee. What you are witnessing is Yehuda with his brain engaged in some inner thought process. Don't worry about it. When he has resolved whatever has been concerning him, he will come back down to earth. But it may take a few minutes.'

As if this kind of thing happened to her every day of the week, Tara rose from her seat, skirting the motionless Yehuda, and did exactly as Mehmet had suggested. 'Do you also want a fresh cup of this very unusual coffee?' she asked him. Her voice, too, was low in deference to Yehuda's meditations. Mehmet stood up, looked sideways at Patrick, silently inviting him to do likewise.

'You guys seem to have had a life altering experience,' Mehmet observed as Tara fiddled with the spout on the urn.

'You have no idea, mate,' Patrick responded. 'We lost seven hours. How can we explain that to anyone? At best they would think were hallucinating, at worst they would think we were nuts.'

'Do you feel any different?'

'Physically? No. Mentally? I don't think either of us will ever be the same again.'

'How do you feel Tara?'

'I suppose, if I had to reduce it to a single word, I would say I feel "humbled". There's so much we don't understand.'

Mehmet opened his mouth as if to speak, hesitated, then said, 'Do you think you might have come into direct contact with Allah?'

'I'm afraid that my mind doesn't have that frame of reference,' Tara answered. 'All I can say is that, if there are any scientists out there who genuinely believe they have a tight handle on everything that goes on in this universe of ours, then they are probably either supremely arrogant or they're delusional.' She picked up an antique looking brown can embellished with faded decorations and shook it gently. There was a satisfying rattle from within. She undid the lid, then held the can out to Mehmet and Patrick. Mehmet shook his head. Patrick helped himself to a biscuit from its depths.

'I understand some scientists argue adamantly that there are no such things as electromagnetic anomalies in the Bermuda Triangle,' she continued. 'They refer to it as fictional fantasy. They can't explain what we went through, so they deny anything untoward happens. Well, I can tell you that it was no fantasy, and we definitely lived through it just as we described—as have several others. To me, the attitude of those nay-sayer scientists is just as dogmatic as anything a religious person might be accused of by anyone in the scientific community. Excuse me for putting it that way, Mehmet.'

'No offence taken. I understand you have a different frame of reference, so let me put it another way then. Are you prepared to concede the possibility that man will never understand fully that which Allah has created?'

'I would prefer to be more optimistic than that,' Tara replied. 'If we ever do reach the threshold of understanding everything there is to know, then we will have become "like God". I guess under those circumstances we will have entered the Messianic Age that religions have been expecting.'

A voice behind them joined in. 'If you're right, when the physicists have finally cracked the so called "theory of everything", then the Age of Aquarius will be upon us.' The three looked towards the sound of the voice. Yehuda had rejoined them. 'Are you prepared to think in those terms?' He took a chocolate biscuit from the open can, broke it carefully in half, then bit into it before continuing. 'Given your frame of mind, Tara, I think it may be appropriate for us to address some biblical matters once again. Perhaps, given your experience yesterday, you will have more of an open mind regarding possibilities.'

'My mind has never been closed, Yehuda, but I suspect I might have a lot more empathy with your and Mehmet's frame of reference than before yesterday's experiences. To be honest, I think we *are* closer to being on the same wavelength.'

Yehuda smiled. 'Interesting choice of word, don't you think, under the circumstances?' He headed back to his chair, with the others following his lead. 'It was your original question regarding the Ark of the Covenant that allowed me to open my mind to possibilities,' Yehuda said addressing himself to Patrick. 'And I want to thank you for that. Let me explain.' He took his pipe, knocked it against the side of the ashtray then laid it carefully on the coffee table next to the bag of sweets, then focussed his full attention on his guests.

'At the core of human progress is the need to keep an open mind. You asked me to research the Ark of the Covenant, Patrick, which I did.

My witnessing the steel knife embedded in the aluminium block allowed me to keep an open mind on the possibility that otherwise well known substances might have different physical properties under different circumstances. That, in turn, let me imagine possible physical explanations for some of the apparently mystical references to the Ark of the Covenant in the *Torah*, the *Old Testament*.' He turned to Tara. 'I mustn't assume that you must already know what the Ark of the Covenant is exactly so let me pre-empt this by telling you a little about it.'

Tara smiled her appreciation at him. She assumed that Patrick had some knowledge of it because of his interest in the subject, and Mehmet must be aware of it too, so Yehuda had just come to her rescue.

'Perhaps you know that the Ark of the Covenant was a box-like container made of gold, which was decorated with cherubs of pure gold mounted on its solid gold lid. It had a wooden inner box that fitted snugly inside. The Ark was very heavy, and its weight was supported on wooden poles that ran lengthwise and protruded front and back. It was carried around on these poles by a group of men specially chosen from a group known as the Levites.'

Tara nodded. This much she vaguely knew.

Yehuda continued. 'According to tradition, two sparks came out from between the two cherubs on the lid, and these sparks killed all the serpents and scorpions, and burned the thorns of plants in the desert through which the children of Israel were wandering. The smoke from the burning plants gave off a sweet fragrance.'

Then he had read a number of the Biblical references to them from the book of Samuel, which told how the Philistines—who had stolen the Ark from the Hebrews—took it to several places in their country. At each place misfortune befell them. They had put it in the Temple of Dagon, at a place called Ashdod, and the next morning the statue of Dagon was found lying prostrate in front of the Ark; and after being replaced, the statue was again found the next day lying on the floor, but this time broken in pieces.

He read to them how Uzzah had died when he put his hand out to steady the Ark after the oxen had shaken it. 'In the wording of the *Bible*,'

Yehuda said, '*God in His anger smote Uzzah for his error in touching the Ark.* Superstitious minds in days gone by, reading what I have just read to you, might have attributed some mystical powers to the Ark. I now believe there may have been a more practical physical explanation.'

Tara glanced at the others. Mehmet sat relaxed in his chair; the muscles in Patrick's clenched jaw were pronounced, but both men looked expectantly at Yehuda.

'When all of this and other similar information is read together, it seems quite possible that Patrick's instincts may have been correct: that the Ark of the Covenant was scavenging telluric current from the environment, and was somehow storing an electrical charge. If this was so, the slightest tremor might have caused some or even all of the stored electricity to have been discharged.'

'But how?' Patrick asked.

'This is where I believe, it gets particularly interesting. As you suspected when you first raised this matter with me, the principles at work here would have been virtually identical to that of a modern day electrical capacitor. Electric current passed into the inner body of the Ark via the wings of the cherubim, which acted as electrodes. There it was stored as an electric charge, and when the accumulated charge reached a critical point, it was discharged. The sparks being given off between the two cherubim would have been consistent with such a discharge of electricity, but we should remember that the Ark of the Covenant was made out of gold and timber. It weighed tons—as opposed to the few grams that a capacitor typically weighs. So it would have been exceptionally powerful, also exceptionally dangerous. A high voltage bolt of electricity discharged from a capacitor this size would certainly have been life threateningly destructive.'

'Interesting.' Patrick scratched his chin and sat forward in his chair. He looked across at Tara and Mehmet. 'Gold is a very efficient *conductor* of electricity, whilst wood is a highly effective *insulator* of electricity. Capacitors also typically have conductive metal electrodes leading into and out of their bodies. They are ceramic and are an effective insulator. I agree, the extended wings of the two solid gold cherubs mounted on the solid gold lid of the Ark could have acted as electrodes, and the wooden box might have done the same job as the ceramic housing of the capacitor.' He turned back to Yehuda. 'But it doesn't answer the question as to how the telluric current was scavenged or, more importantly, how the electric charge was stored inside the timber box.'

'Can someone please explain to me what is telluric current?' asked Mehmet who was no longer sitting back relaxed in his chair.

Yehuda held up his hands at the questioners. 'One thing at a time. Patrick, Mehmet, bear with me please.'

He paused to unwrap another sweet. This time, he was so absorbed in his thought processes that it didn't occurred to him to offer them to his guests. Tara wondered what it might be like to have such powers of concentration. Or maybe it wasn't his powers of concentration. Could it be that he lived alone and didn't have to worry about anyone else? She felt a pang of sadness.

'In simplistic, layman terms,' Yehuda continued, 'think of what happens when you connect two copper wires to the electrodes of a battery and then join the wires to, say, a light bulb to create a circuit. In fact, two things happen. The first is that additional electrons are pumped into one of the wires by the battery, at a pressure which is dependent on the battery's voltage. Electrons begin to flow as they move from the orbit of one copper atom inside the wire to the next. As part of this flow, if a circuit has been created, electrons begin to exit the opposite end of that wire and into the light bulb's filament, like flowing water exits a hosepipe. This whole process happens at the speed of light. The second thing that happens is that an electromagnetic field forms around the copper wire through which the electrons are flowing—again at the speed of light.' He paused. 'Do we all accept that?'

Clearly, this particular professor was not one to allow his students to drift off or fall behind. They all nodded obediently.

'Good, good,' he said. 'Now, there are three things we need to think about when we talk about electricity. The first is the number of electrons that are shifted. This is called an electrical charge and is measured in coulombs. The second is the current or rate of flow—which is measured in amperes. The third is pressure, which is measured in volts.

'Finally, when thinking about electricity, it's also important to understand that it is not necessarily the electrical charge itself that is dangerous, but the rate of flow of that charge and the pressure behind it. In your own body, for example, you already have electrical charges floating around. When you get an electric shock, it is either because you are causing the existing charge to flow too quickly through your body, or you are introducing an additional charge at a voltage pressure which your body was not designed to handle.'

He waited for a moment to gauge that they were following what he was saying. Satisfied, he continued.

'Now, Mehmet, let's turn to your question. "Telluric" is derived from the Latin word *tellus*, Mother Earth. And "current", in terms of what I have just told you, implies a flow of negatively charged electrons. So, specifically, telluric current is a flow of negatively charged electrons induced to flow through the Earth's crust and also through the atmosphere close to the Earth's surface. This happens as a result of the collision between solar winds and the earth's magnetic field in the ionosphere. You may have heard of the Aurora Borealis and Aurora Australis, the so-called polar lights?'

'Of course,' Mehmet answered, 'but I've never really thought about them in terms of electrons flowing through the Earth's crust and the atmosphere.'

'The Auroras are caused by collision between the earth's magnetic field and large numbers of electrically charged particles ejected by the sun,' Yehuda explained.

Tara's hand reached across Yehuda to the packet of sweets.

'The borealis lights are exaggerated versions of what happens all over the planet,' he continued without seeming to have noticed her action. 'Closer to the Earth's surface, the potential pressure gradients caused by telluric currents are of the order of 0.2 to 1000 volts per metre. You may remember that, from time to time, when there are eruptions on the sun's surface we experience electrical anomalies here on Earth. For example, in 1989, the voltage of Quebec's power grid began to fluctuate wildly. Seconds later, the lights went out across the entire province and some millions of people were without electricity for nine hours. That was a direct consequence of a massive solar storm at the time. In simple terms, there was a surge in telluric current and its associated voltage.'

'But if we have all this telluric current in our environment,' asked Mehmet, why is it that no one has ever worked out a way of harnessing it?'

'Oh, many have tried. The problem up until now has been that the technologies have been very rough and ready. The cost would have been prohibitive relative to the benefits.'

There was silence in the room as Yehuda stopped talking. He reached for his copy of the *Old Testament* on the side-table near him. He turned their attention back to Patrick's original question by reading to them from the Book of Numbers, about how the staff of Moses' brother Aaron—when it was placed within the Tabernacle in close proximity to the Ark of the Covenant—*was budded, and brought forth buds, and blossomed and yielded almonds*. Finally, he recounted a story about how, when King Solomon brought the Ark into the Temple, all the golden trees in the Temple were filled with moisture and produced abundant fruit, to the great profit and enjoyment of the priestly gild.

'So apart from people attributing mystical powers to the Ark, what you're talking about now is nature … biology,' Patrick observed. 'Are you suggesting that the Ark's technology had more than one aspect to it?'

'Yes. By recounting those various passages, I am inviting you to consider that they all point to the conclusion—or more accurately, the hypothesis—that the vibrational wavelengths of energy given off by the Ark very possibly did have a biologically stimulative effect.'

He glanced up to see the confusion on Tara's face.

'Tara, everything will become clearer when we finally turn our attention to how the Ark might have scavenged and stored its electrons or electrical charge. For the moment, I want you to consider if there is any other evidence in nature that might corroborate this hypothesis. By way of illustration, has any one of you here this evening heard of a place called Findhorn, in Scotland?'

'Yes,' Tara answered, 'as a matter of fact … something about their crop production?'

'What have you heard?'

'Well, I don't want to destroy the momentum of your argument.'

'No, no, it's very relevant,' Yehuda reassured her.

'Well, Findhorn is in a fairly inhospitable area of Scotland. Its soil is stony and not particularly rich in nutrients, and yet the produce cultivated there is remarkable for its size and quality. I remember speculation that the reason lies in the unusual energetic fields within the area. It seems that Findhorn is located smack on top of one of the Earth's magnetic ley lines.'

'Bravo. And now,' he continued, 'there are two more mental seeds I would like to plant first. These have nothing whatever to do with Patrick's question, but may explain one of your experiences in the Bermuda Triangle yesterday.' He paused, pointedly shifting his gaze first from Tara, to Patrick, and then to Mehmet.

'There are also various biblical references to the fact that the Ark of the Covenant was where God communicated with Moses and the High Priests. Allow me to quote from Exodus, Chapter 25 verse 22.'

Patrick thought fleetingly that it was odd how a professor of physics should be so interested in the *Bible* given the apparently opposing stances of science and religion. Perhaps he was a bit like Sir Isaac Newton who was deeply committed to the goal of reconciling the 'what' of religion with the 'how' of science.

Yehuda polished his glasses on his sleeve. He put them back on and peered at the text in front of him. '*And there I will meet with thee and I will commune with thee from above the mercy seat, from between the two cherubim which are upon the Ark of the testimony, of all things which I will give thee in commandment unto the children of Israel.*'

At that point, he paused, but held one finger in the air to inhibit any interruptions. 'In letting your imaginations soar, I will ask you to focus on the possibility that the various electromagnetic anomalies you experienced yesterday may well have placed you in a different time dimension. That is the only physical explanation I can imagine to

account for your lost seven hours. I can offer no further sensible specu-
lations, but I urge you to keep your minds open to the possibility. So, if
that could happen to you, it might also have been that the Ark offered a
portal to a different dimension. The problem is that we know so little
about this subject that it must be relegated to the realms of fiction for
the time being. I raise the issue merely to give you some idea of the Ark's
awesome capacity, and you should understand that the idea is not outrageous from the perspective of theoretical physics.'

A thought flitted quickly through Patrick's mind how oddly he
would be regarded by his fellow engineers if he postulated such an
explanation for their time lapse in the B200. He found Yehuda's idea
intriguing but saw no purpose in pursuing it any further this evening.
'You said there was a second mental seed?' he prompted. 'I take it that
this seed introduces a fourth aspect?'

'The fourth aspect revolves around the Ark of the Covenant's ability
to store energy, and this may be exceptionally important from the
perspective of modern day needs. My research has brought me to the
conclusion that one of the items stored inside it might have been an
exotic form of a conventional precious metal. In its exotic form it might
also have been used as a raw material in the manufacture of the
capstones of the Egyptian pyramids and obelisks. If my understanding of
this material is correct, the capstones which covered the peaks of these
structures may have facilitated the ability of these structures to artificially energise the lands surrounding them in a similar way to that in
which the land in Findhorn is naturally energised—but perhaps far
more effectively.'

After making this last statement, it seemed to Patrick that Yehuda's
face had a smug look on it, as if this was a subject that he would be
prepared to debate, but he ducked the opportunity. Instead he said, 'But
we still need to know how you think the Ark of the Covenant might
have scavenged and stored the telluric current. You've told us the "what"
but not the "how".'

Yehuda glanced at his watch and saw the reason for Patrick's im-
patience. 'Let me take you all out of your misery, but I also have another

and equally important subject to discuss with you, and perhaps we can reconvene on Wednesday for that. In the meantime—'

'I'm sorry,' Patrick interjected, 'but Tara and I have arrangements on that night. It's a special event, which we wouldn't like to miss. Could we postpone our meeting until Thursday?'

Yehuda looked at Mehmet, who obligingly shrugged his acceptance.

'Thursday night it is. Then I will explain the workings and possible applications of the electromagnetic technology, which I have been attempting to validate during the past twenty years. But shall we continue with your "what" and "how"?' he asked.

Patrick gestured to Yehuda, palm upwards, inviting him to continue.

'The other day, Patrick, you mentioned Sir Laurence Gardner as the author of a book you had read. My research into his work kept giving rise to references to a material that was being described as "non metallic gold". This reminded me of the subject of alchemy and how one of the world's most brilliant physicists—Sir Isaac Newton—tried to unravel the mysteries of gold. He devoted nearly a third of his life to this task he had set himself, locked away on his own, in secret.'

'Do you recall too,' Patrick said, 'it was Isaac Newton who put the world onto the gold standard?' *It's a pity Samantha couldn't be here. She would have found this interesting.* 'And that he retired from the field of physics to become Master of the Royal Mint in England—in charge of all the gold in Great Britain. He certainly seemed to have an extraordinary interest in the subject.'

Yehuda nodded. 'Yes. As a physicist myself, I had often wondered how a man of such giant intellect—a man referred to by some as the father of modern day physics, and who was also as passionate about the *Bible* and its secrets as I am—could have had such a fixation on how to turn base metals into gold. The *Bible* is quite clear that the silver shekel was the accepted currency in the days of Moses and Aaron. From my perspective, the only reason that I could think of would be his interest in its physical properties.'

'Sounds to me like putting a wolf into the hen house, having him in charge of the Royal Mint,' said Tara with a stifled giggle.

'I cannot bring myself to even imagine that Newton had any interest in gold as money,' Yehuda responded. 'He was a bachelor—like me—and had no need of wealth. What did he discover about gold? I think he came to understand gold's *real* value to humanity and that he wanted to ensure all of Britain's gold would be held in a central repository.'

'He had two nervous breakdowns, didn't he?' Patrick interjected. 'Did you ever think he might have been mentally unstable?'

Yehuda turned his gaze to rest on Patrick. 'To be honest, it did strike me as a possibility—although they were thought to have been caused by mercury poisoning. But I finally asked myself the question the other day as a result of your original inquiry—and I thank you for that—what if Newton was not trying to turn base metals into gold? What if he was trying to turn gold into something else?'

'What would be the point? What's more valuable than gold?' Tara asked.

Yehuda seemed to savour the moment. He did not answer immediately. Instead, he spent an irritating couple of minutes straightening his *Old Testament* on the sidetable and stacking the empty coffee cups in front of him.

Patrick was tired and mildly irritated. *No wonder Yehuda was a bachelor.* When Yehuda finally looked up, it was with a glimmer of amusement in his eye. 'I suspect it might have been one of the four items stored within the Ark of the Covenant. I suspect that Isaac Newton was trying to turn gold into what the *Torah* referred to as "manna".' He sat back, and looked about him, enjoying the drama of the moment.

None of the other three spoke. Patrick looked at Tara then at Yehuda. *How on earth did he reach that conclusion?*

'The four items,' Yehuda continued, with the faintest hint of a satisfied smile, 'were Aaron's staff, which continued to sprout inside the Ark, the stone tablets of the law, a golden jar, and a white powder known as manna that was stored within the jar.'

'Manna ... the food the children of Israel ate in the desert?' Tara asked.

'Indeed it was, but it was not only that. When I first started researching the Ark of the Covenant from a scientific perspective, thanks to you Patrick, I came across various references to non-metallic gold. This piqued my curiosity, so I did a search of patent records and discovered a British patent referring to transition elements that had been lodged in the name of DR Hudson in 1989.[xi] To cut a long story short, one research finding led to another and I finally discovered that the exotic materials referred to by Mr Hudson occur in atomic micro-clusters. In particular, the gold micro-clusters now referred to as "Ormus M-State Gold Powder", except that the powder is not gold in colour. It is snow white. And it is also edible. And it tastes like bread.'

'The manna?' Tara asked.

'You're getting ahead of me. But, yes, it was partially for these reasons that I began to suspect that the Ormus M-State gold powder and manna may have been one and the same.'

Suddenly, Yehuda's listeners were wide-awake again.

'Perhaps more importantly, the powder was found to be an electrical superconductor.'

'A more powerful conductor?' Tara asked.

'In layman's terms, a superconductor is a material through which electrons will travel with no loss of voltage.'

'But the powder inside the gold jar couldn't have been in the form of wire,' Patrick objected.

'Correct, and it is for that reason that I took pains earlier to differentiate between an electric charge and an electric current. The superconductive M-State Ormus Gold Powder is apparently able to *store* extraordinarily large electrical charges—so much so, that when exposed to the Earth's magnetic field it loses almost forty-five percent of its mass … its weight. To quote Mr Hudson, "Your hand has sufficient amperage that, if passed under the tube [in which the powder is stored] the material *floats*, it is that sensitive to magnetic fields".'

Mehmet threw his head back contemplatively and looked at the ceiling. Patrick's jaw muscles clenched and unclenched. Tara, alone, was motionless among them.

'It is not well known, but in an ancient Hebrew recounting of the events of this era there was a rather strange reference to the fact that the

Levites were carried by the Ark as it hovered. At face value, this makes no sense at all because it implies that the Ark was defying the laws of gravity,' Yehuda said. 'Remember the Ark must have weighed tons and the manna inside that jar could not have weighed more than a couple of kilograms. This fact gives some insight as to how powerful the technology must have been.'

'Well,' said Patrick, 'I will grant you that this is absolutely fascinating in itself, but the question arises as to how the charge was converted into a current? As you said earlier, the input voltage of the telluric current is very low. The output voltage of the Ark of the Covenant must have been way in excess of this. Even if the super-conductive manna could store and build up a charge of electrons—or coulombs, to be more technically correct—how would it have been possible to deliver them at a voltage in excess of the input? And surely the amperage must also have been enormous?'

'I suspect that it has to do with the fact that if you have two or more circuits in series, the voltage adds up. And if current was being pumped in again and again, then the voltage pressure would build up to a massive potential. Sadly, I cannot prove it to you without significant experimentation. I have too few facts available to me.'

'You say the Ark of the Covenant was so dangerous to be around,' Mehmet said, looking to the ceiling. 'Would the electrical discharges of the Ark have been capable of being managed?'

'Conceptually, I see no problem with that,' Yehuda answered. He rose from his chair and reached towards Patrick and clasped his hand warmly in his own.

'I want to thank you for originally drawing this to my attention. If all of what I have told you tonight can be scientifically validated, then it may help explain our collective and, perhaps instinctive, reactions to why we regard gold as a valuable mineral—as currency, as jewellery—and perhaps even why Sir Isaac Newton put Great Britain on a gold standard.'

'Well, I don't know about that,' Patrick said, 'but I do know that if what you have told us about the Ark of the Covenant and how it might have worked can be validated then it will also validate the idea that energy can indeed be scavenged from the environment. And that will begin to raise some serious questions about whether the laws of thermodynamics are as rigid as some scientists would argue.'

Tara and Mehmet had no idea what Patrick was on about, but they were just too tired to ask. It would have to wait for another day. Yehuda, on the other hand, looked knowingly at him, winked and chuckled.

CHAPTER 38

'T HE WESTERNER IN me wouldn't quite let me admit to Yehuda that the special event we were going to was a cock fight,' Patrick admitted to Tara on Wednesday night as they made their way into a large wooden building alongside men, women and even children. Patrick and Tara had chosen to sit in the front row behind a low wooden wall that separated the spectators from the sawdust ring. Tara was already beginning to question the wisdom of their seating. There was a smell of death in the air. The arena was packed and strumming with anticipation.

Suddenly, the crowd, which had been noisily placing bets backwards and forwards across the room, fell quiet as two handlers—the *galleros*—entered the ring. The only sound was the writhing and straining of the cocks in their canvas bags. Nothing and no one else moved.

The first rooster was lifted from its carry bag. Tara's eyes were fixed on the three elongated toes that splayed outwards like limb extensions from both his feet. Each of his toes culminated in a wicked looking razor-sharp claw. His gelatinous crimson comb stood straight up—protruding defiantly from an aggressively angled head atop a column-like neck. Long white feathers swept majestically back across his upper body like a lion's mane. A few speckled brown feathers showed like stippled drops of dried blood under the white of his chest and wings.

The bird struggled to free itself from the hands of his captor. His crimson wattles jerked defiantly with every turn of its head while a murderous eye glared with crazed hatred at anyone and anything in its line of sight.

'His name's El Diablo,' Patrick told Tara. 'Last month he reputedly despatched six opponents in the same evening within one hour.'

The second rooster, publicised as Azul because of the blue identifying band around its leg, was pure white with a bright red comb and wattles. His curved beak snapped in time with the forward jerking movements of his lunging head. He strained his head to peck at the *gallero's* hands.

'Here comes a third bird—a *mona*. They use it to taunt the two fighting cocks,' Patrick explained.

'Looks like they're succeeding. Both of them look on the verge of an apoplectic fit.'

'At least the two fighters look around the same size and fighting weight,' Patrick observed. He could not remember ever having seen such diabolical anger and naked aggression in the eyes of any living creature. 'You've got to wonder if both birds are temporarily insane with all that testosterone induced venom.'

The two *galleros* stood facing each other a few feet apart when, at some unseen signal, all other onlookers and handlers withdrew from the fifteen-foot circular cockpit.

'Good grief … look at the artificial spurs on the back of their legs,' Tara said in a horrified whisper.

In unison, the two *galleros* released their champions—flinging them at each other. The two birds collided in mid air, squawking ferociously amid a wild flutter of adrenalin fuelled wings and flailing legs and beaks.

'Oh-oh, first blood,' Patrick said in a loud whisper as the birds fell back to earth. El Diablo had managed to gouge Azul at the base of its neck, and blood had started to ooze onto its white feathers. The noise in the room rose to a cacophony. Bets were still being shouted across the room with increasing urgency.

Patrick translated from the shouted Spanish all around them.

'One hundred pesos on El Diablo.'

'Fifty pesos on Azul.'

'Kill the Azul.'

'You can get him Azul. He's not so tough.'

Tara was torn between revulsion and fascination. She had placed a hundred peso bet on El Diablo. Not to be outdone, Patrick pointedly bet ten times than amount on Azul.

The men were thirsty for blood. Tara, on the other hand, feeling Azul's pain, was regretting being here. It was akin to watching a boxing match—except in this case the boxers would have been wearing spiked knuckle dusters instead of padded gloves. Why was she here? She didn't even like boxing matches.

The crowd roared. Immediately on landing, Azul had done the unexpected. Instead of cringing or running, he had lunged at El Diablo gouging him with his beak—right in the eye socket. The blob of mucous-like substance came free of its housing, trailing connective tissue and blood behind it. Tara felt queasy. A shiver ran over the surface of her skin as she looked quickly away. Patrick, impassioned, was on his feet, raucously cheering Azul on.

El Diablo seemed to react more in anger than in pain. Instinctively, the tough old gladiator lunged for the weak spot, the point of injury where his opponent must surely be feeling pain. His beak disappeared beneath the surface of the white neck feathers. El Diablo's head whipped from side to side as he wrenched at his opponent's already wounded skin.

Blood spurted from the wound. Azul squawked and flapped vainly trying to distance himself. A stain of red spread below his shoulder. Testosterone boosted adrenalin rushed to his rescue as Azul swung a leg viciously across El Diablo's head digging a deep gash on the same side from which the eye had been gouged.

The wound seemed to drive El Diablo to a greater crazed anger. He pounced on his opponent from behind, his claws gripping into the other's shoulders. Azul tottered under his weight.

Suddenly, El Diablo swivelled downwards, in a kamikaze dive, his feet still clamped in place. It let him to pivot downwards until his comb was pointing to the ground and he was looking upwards at Azul's belly. He lunged upwards, sinking his beak deep into Azul's underbelly, but his own was exposed in the process. Azul did exactly the same, the difference being that the move came more fluently to him.

Neither bird let go. They toppled onto the floor, wings flapping, feathers fluttering. Horrible shrill squawking noises emanated from the melee.

Patrick shouted 'Go Azul! Go Azul!' Tara hid her eyes.

Suddenly it was over.

Blood was spattered across the ring. Both birds lay still on the floor. The crowd was silent. How could this be? Was there to be no winner?

Then Azul's body moved jerkily. His wings moved—a tremble more than a flutter. A rising 'ooh' swept through the crowd—a mixture of anxiety touched with hope for victory. The bird flapped and squirmed, then in a flutter of loose feathers managed to extricate himself from the motionless debris that was El Diablo. A roar of excitement and victory rose up as Azul staggered away. He toppled drunkenly, then rose again. The cheers of the winning punters rose to a crescendo.

Tara could only glance sideways at the wreckage. She felt sickened. What had been the point? Azul would surely never return to his former prowess, never strut the stage again.

Patrick was triumphant. This was the stuff of legends. He had won 5,000 pesos—around $150.

'I'll wait for you outside,' Tara said. She wanted nothing more than to get out of this revolting palace of death. How could she have even considered being an audience to this? Tears of anguish welled in her eyes. She parted the crowd before her with the stiff-elbowed determination of a footballer heading for his goal line. The sea of jostling people blurred around her.

Outside, she made for the leeside of the building, away from the flow of the crowd. She leant against the wall and took a deep breath, then another. She shuddered. Then all of a sudden she was shivering, hugging herself. She turned her body to the wooden building to hide her sudden sobs.

Why was she reacting this way? She held her own on a daily basis with testosterone addled males. She had been sickened by the fighting cocks, but what had dismayed her even more—what had triggered her sobs—was Patrick's enthusiastic crowd participation. He was suddenly alien to her. How could this caring, gentle man also be so aggressively bloodthirsty? How little she knew him.

For some reason she thought of her father. What would he have done? She could almost hear his voice in her head. He would have said that all men are built this way. If Patrick hadn't gotten so worked up he wouldn't have been normal. She didn't like the thought, but it calmed her.

By the time Patrick found her fifteen minutes later, he had collected his winnings and his victorious euphoria had been overtaken by concern for the missing Tara.

He saw her tears. 'I was worried ... are you all right?' He stroked her hair, then put a protective arm around her shoulder. When she nodded, the buoyancy of his mood resurfaced. It was like her dad had told her.

In the car home, she remained subdued, her demeanour contrasting starkly with his banter and good humour. He could not help but notice. 'I read an article a couple of years ago about how they measured the testosterone levels of a soccer team immediately before each game, and compared it with their normal readings.'

'Oh?' She kept her eyes downcast. Her tone was indifferent.

'Seems that home games gave rise to a much higher testosterone surge than away games, but the levels were always raised. It's a natural aggression mechanism. The increase was more exaggerated when the team was defending its own turf. The goalkeeper's levels rose the highest. They're the body's mechanism for facilitating territorial defence. In fact, the more of a threat the visiting opposition team was perceived to be, the higher the testosterone surge of the home team. If memory serves, it was forty percent higher for moderate competition and sixty-seven percent higher before a bitter rival match.'

'Probably explains why the *galleros* use the *mona*,' she offered listlessly.

'I can understand you might be upset, but ... what's really bothering you?'

'What happens to the testosterone after the event?'

'I don't understand.'

'The fight's over. One cock is dead. The other survived. How does the survivor get rid of the surplus testosterone that surged as a result of what he was exposed to? Does he stay violent? Does he remain sexually aggressive towards females? Does he remain belligerent to males?'

'What's your point?'

'Take your soccer team whose testosterone levels surged so high. What happens to those levels after the soccer match? Do their wives and girlfriends cop it or do they just go on a drunken binge at the pub and get into bar fights? Do the soccer fans' wives experience the same problems?'

'What do you mean "cop it"?' Tara could sense a new tension in his body. 'If it makes the guys more virile and demanding, their women folk are likely to benefit aren't they?' Patrick asked.

'You men think that love is all about whipping it in, whipping it out and wiping it,' she retorted. 'What's the Australian man's idea of foreplay again—"Brace yourself Sheila". Have I got it right?'

At first he said nothing. There was both hurt and surprise on his face. Hurt, because he had been genuine in his caring and giving; surprised, because she was not really making any sense. What more could he have done, for God's sake?

'That's unfair, Tara. I was under the impression that you really enjoyed our times together. "The best sex ever," you said.'

She was silent for several moments, then gave a deep, wobbly sigh. 'I'm sorry Patrick. It really was beautiful … mind blowingly fantastic in fact.'

'But?'

'There's more to love than physical sex, however artful or erotic or caring it might be. Even as love, it was great, but I want us to soar.'

'Then teach me how to make you happy.' It was all he could muster.

She managed a smile. 'Let's go and have a light meal, and then back to your place.'

The shrimp dinner had mellowed them both. The bottle of Californian white had helped.

They were seated on the couch in his lounge room. 'Why don't you put on that Mozart CD?' Tara suggested.

'D'you want a drink?'

'What I really want is a shower to clean away the day … cleanse my aura.' But I could do with a cognac.'

'Hennessy okay?'

'Yup. You got a spare towel and T-shirt?'

'What do you want first?'

'Towel and shirt. I'll enjoy my drink while you're showering. I can chill out listening to the music.'

Patrick's T-shirt was long enough on her to wear as a nightshirt and, after their showers, he joined her on the couch and lay with his head in her lap. The music played softly in the background.

'My dad was a very wise man,' Tara said.

'Hmmm?' He raised his eyes to her. She was looking straight ahead.

'Amongst the many pieces of advice he gave me when I decided to go head-to-head with the men was that feminism is okay, but you gotta let guys be guys and gals be gals 'cos that's how the good Lord made us.'

'What does that mean?' He stroked her arm which lay relaxed across his chest.

'The male body produces up to twenty times as much testosterone as the female body. That's a fact, and no one can change that. Sensitive new age guys and metrosexuals are all very well, but not if they get emasculated in the process.'

'So, you want us to have the testosterone, but you don't want us to let it show. Is that it?'

'Don't be obtuse. His advice to me was that a husband and wife should be friends, and hopefully best friends. His testosterone should be channelled to drive the partnership. Her oestrogen should be channelled to nurture it. That way they'll be a team working towards a common goal.'

'Sounds like good advice, but it raises a couple of questions.'

'Such as?'

'First, how can a woman compete in the commercial world if you're going to have to behave like a schizophrenic? In competitive situations, women's bodies also produce testosterone, or didn't you know that?'

'That one's easy,' Tara answered. 'I suspect it's only small amounts of testosterone in women, but I don't think it matters. I don't look at what I'm doing as competition. It's a profession, and I conduct myself professionally. We need to work smart. We need to sidestep the "women are from Venus, men are from Mars" paradigm, and to compete on the basis of intellect, where we are undoubtedly equals. Beating our chests is not a productive activity. I'm happy to leave that to the guys.'

'Fair enough. The second question is harder, though. How can a husband and wife be best friends if he enjoys the rough and tumble of life and she aspires to the emotionally satisfying stuff?'

She twirled a lock of his hair absent-mindedly around her fingers. The look in her eyes seemed far away from the room.

'By making a point of talking to each other at the end of every single day; by setting aside time to do stuff that both can enjoy, like going to movies or concerts or dinners or just sitting in the same room and reading a book; by laughing together—loudly and often; by sharing our recreational time fairly, with some for each other and some for outside interests; by doing thoughtful things for each other from time to time; by working at the relationship rather than taking each other for granted; by touching one another just for the pleasure of conveying tactile affection and with no ulterior motive.'

'The way you rolled that off the tongue, you have obviously given this a lot of thought.'

'Naah. Just telling you how my father treated my mother. I really loved that guy. He had his head screwed on right and we laughed a lot.' All the while, Tara had been stroking Patrick's forehead, his chest, his arms, his belly and his hair. He found it both soothing and comforting. She bent down to kiss him on the lips—warmly and softly. He could sense her feelings through it. It was nurturing. He felt his own love for her growing.

He shifted so that he was lying on his side. Now he could stroke the length of her thigh down to the back of her knee. His fingers traced the inside of her thigh but she gently slapped his hand away. Their bodies were not yet in sync. Her unspoken message was that this was still talking time.

'What about sports, and other guy stuff?'

'Sure. Guys have gotta be guys. But the whole point is to share the time fairly. I've got no problems with separate boy and girl stuff, but we should make time to share our thoughts.'

'That could work for me,' he said. 'So what do you want to talk about? Football? Surfing?'

'Tell me about Australia.'

'I guess the most important thing for me is the space and the distances,' he said softly. 'Australia's about the same size as the US but everyone seems to want to live along the coastline ...'

Somewhere along the way they had switched places. He was sitting upright on the opposite end of the couch, her head now in his lap. He was the one doing the talking. From time to time he ran his fingers through her hair. He marvelled at the silky softness of the skin on her arms and face. Occasionally, the palm of his hand glided gently over the fabric across her belly and upwards over the curve of her breasts. Her nipples were soft.

The room was only indirectly lit by the lamp in the next room. Her features were barely visible. He could see that her T-shirt had crept tantalisingly up her thighs, but the shadow hid the detail. He stopped talking. The music had long since ceased playing. He could hear the slow throbbing of his own heart and the smooth, rhythmic flow of her breathing. He brought his face towards hers to see if she was sleeping. The soft light of the room was reflected in her eyes. He brushed his lips gently over her forehead, across her face towards her slightly parted lips. For a few seconds he allowed them to dwell on the satin of her cheeks. Was his mind playing tricks? He could have sworn he heard kitten purrings in his ear.

'Hmmm.' The sound came from the back of her throat. 'What's that gorgeous smell?' She snuggled her face into his neck.

'It's my cologne,' he murmured as his hand crept under her T-shirt.

For long minutes they kissed, their tongues gently exploring the insides of one another's mouths, their lips cushioning against each other. Patrick felt his lower lip being gently tugged. He felt a tiny electric shockwave travelling down his stomach. He reached down, picked her up and carried her into the bedroom where the covers of the queen sized bed had been pulled back.

As he gently laid her down, he pulled her T-shirt up. She lifted her arms allowing him to take it all the way off. He kicked off his shorts.

Instinctively, their bodies rolled towards one another until her breasts were softly flattened just below his ribcage. He pulled the bedclothes to cover them both, wrapping his arms around her warm torso, with his cheek touching her forehead. Her arms locked around him as she sighed in contentment. There was no urgency to their movements. His erection was full and proud, but it was patiently nestling, warmed by her soft belly, waiting for what it would have known would be a far more blissful experience than their previous couplings, if it indeed had a mind of its own.

Patrick smiled as he remembered the old joke, about how God had endowed man with two heads, but only enough blood supply to operate one at a time. It seemed to him that both of his were flying on automatic pilot at the moment.

Her hands were stroking him—from his shoulders all the way down his back, over the curve of his buttock to the back of his thighs. He took her left ear in the cup of his right hand, gently pushing her head back to kiss her—first on the neck in the soft spot where her windpipe ended, then on the earlobe and then full on the lips. Their mouths continued to explore.

The night watched silently as time stood still. Their souls wove together, merging, absorbing, subsuming.

CHAPTER 39

THE EXPRESSION 'TIGHT and needy' popped into Tara's mind as she and Patrick walked into the library at Yehuda's home. She tended to think in spoonerisms when she was happy.

Yehuda's neat and tidy appearance flowed from his having had his hair cut and—she glanced furtively at him to confirm her suspicion—even his eyebrows were trimmed. His clothes were pressed and clean. He was freshly shaven. There was no sign of the briar pipe that often served to fuel his distraction. Even his bifocals had a certain sparkle about them. The evening was obviously important. He was about to put his trust in two relative strangers—to share the results of over twenty years of research.

Somehow, Mehmet also looked different. He was as relaxed as always, but there seemed to be a subtle shift in his energy, as if he had opened himself up to embrace a change in their relationships. Of course, it was possible that she was just projecting her own feelings.

'Coffee?' Yehuda asked. He was standing half facing them, his hand on the tap of the urn. She knew that coffee, in his language, was really a kindly euphemism. Yehuda's unusual brew was about as far removed from a barista's espresso as brackish, stagnant river water was from the clear waters of a bubbling alpine brook. Nevertheless, in her current frame of mind, Tara really couldn't have cared less. Neither, it seemed, could anyone else. Within five minutes they were all seated, each nursing a mug of steaming hot, chicory-adulterated instant coffee.

'Patrick and Tara,' Yehuda began. He cleared his throat. For some reason he seemed a little nervous. 'The primary purpose of this evening's get-together is for me to introduce to you the electromagnetic energy technology which I have been investigating and testing for some years. In fact, I first tried to patent it twenty-seven years ago—'

'You say, "tried". Does that mean the Patent Office rejected you? And even after that, you've worked on it for most of your working life?' Tara asked in disbelief.

'Well, we're honoured you would share it with us,' Patrick said, wanting to give Tara's ankle a nudge but unable to do so without being obvious.

'Yes. That is precisely what I have been doing.'

'Why, for God's sake?'

'Because at that time my ideas had yet to be proven from a scientific perspective, as opposed to a technical perspective.'

'But that was twenty-seven years ago,' Tara protested. 'Surely someone would have validated the underlying assumption in the interim?'

'Someone did. I did.' He allowed himself a small smile. 'After developing the technology and the prototypes, and testing each and every stage, I now know that it does exactly what I predicted it would do, and why.'

Patrick took a deep breath. 'Okay Yehuda. You've got the floor on this one, and I must say, at the very least, you need to be congratulated on your persistence.'

Yehuda smiled. 'The world moves very slowly when it comes to paradigm shifts in thinking. In fact, even today, very few mainstream physicists would take this technology seriously. It is highly unorthodox, and at face value—as the Patent Office concluded—it appears to fly in the face of at least one of the laws of thermodynamics. It appears to have a greater energy output than input.'

'Appears?'

Yehuda laughed at some private amusement. 'I knew even before you and I met that we would get on well, Patrick. Yes, the operative word is "appears". In fact, I modestly think I might have discovered something that could help explain several phenomena that physicists have been wrestling with for years.'

'That's one hell of a sweeping statement.'

Patrick clenched both hands around his crossed knee; then, as another thought seemed to occur to him, he hugged his arms lightly to his chest; still not satisfied, he slowly placed one hand firmly on his mouth, all the while frowning. He projected an odd mixture of confusion, concern and, possibly, scepticism—unaware that both Yehuda and Tara were closely observing his face and body language.

Tara was surprised by his reactions. Patrick had come halfway around the world to pursue an intuitive whim. Why wasn't he being more open minded?

'I think it's important for you to hear me out,' Tara heard Yehuda continue. 'I need to give you all a high level overview of a particular cutting edge issue in the field of physics. You need to appreciate that, in the area of environmental energy, our knowledge base is far from complete.'

Yehuda saw Tara look at him questioningly. 'That's not to say our current knowledge base is inaccurate, merely that it's incomplete. For example, have either of you heard about a concept known as dark energy?'

'Do you mean dark as in evil—like the black-clad Darth Vader in *Star Wars*?' Tara asked, with a hint of a smile.

Mehmet's smile was enigmatic. Yehuda had confided in him on this project before. He sat patiently in his wingchair. The others looked at Yehuda blankly.

'No, no. I mean dark as in "invisible" or "physically undetectable". Nowadays, physicists believe our universe is made up of roughly seventy percent dark energy, twenty-five percent dark matter and five percent ordinary matter.'

'I won't even pretend to know what that means,' Tara said with a resigned sigh.

'It means that we can only physically see five percent of what makes up our universe. The other ninety-five percent is made up of matter or energy that theoretically exists, but we can't prove it, except by mathematics. By implication, it must be there, because if it wasn't we wouldn't be able to explain some observable phenomena.'

'Perhaps it would be better if you explained in layman's terms.' Mehmet suggested.

Yehuda looked at Mehmet for a few seconds, then nodded slowly. 'A major discovery in astrophysics in the late 1990s was that our universe is expanding at an accelerating rate. Let me just go back a step to explain.' He leant forward to reach for a pencil at the far end of the coffee table. 'Now, you will agree that in order to create movement, it requires work … an action?' He swivelled the pencil between his thumb and forefinger. 'And that work requires energy?' He pointed at his fingers. 'And that, therefore, movement requires energy?'

Patrick and Tara nodded, their eyes on Yehuda.

'So, your understanding of this linkage between energy and movement will make it very easy to understand the simple idea that I now want to share with you, that in order for the universe to be expanding at an accelerating rate, there must be an increasing amount of energy being applied to facilitate this. Can you agree with that?'

'Well, from your explanation it's self-evident, but—'

'But if the first law of thermodynamics is true,' Yehuda interrupted, 'where is this ever increasing amount of energy coming from?' He spread his upward palms at shoulder height and pulled a comically mystified face. 'This law states that the total energy of a system and its surroundings remains constant. It follows that either the additional energy must be coming from outside our universe, or there is more energy within our universe than we had previously understood. It happens that physicists cannot agree on the answer with any degree of certainty. My point is, if people—physicists—tell you it is impossible for any motor to have a greater energy output than input, they would be forced to reject their own observations that the universe is expanding at an accelerating rate—which it clearly is. There must be an explanation that complies with the first law of thermodynamics. It's just that they haven't understood that explanation yet.'

'So you're saying your technology does not contravene the laws of thermodynamics?' Patrick asked.

'That is exactly what I am saying.'

'But that doesn't make any sense. Where would the additional energy come from? From another parallel universe?' Patrick's nose wrinkled to show his confusion. The Dominican expression was contagious.

Yehuda laughed softly. 'Nothing quite so weird and wonderful. In fact, the explanation lies in precisely what you understood intuitively would one day be possible. Yes, my energy machine generates what we physicists refer to as over-unity energy. But it does this by scavenging already existing energy—of a type that is ubiquitously trembling in our environment and which is also contained inside all atoms. It's called "light" energy, or electromagnetic energy. Remember when we discussed the entire spectrum of electromagnetic energy being referred to as "light", Tara, because it travels at the speed of light?'

Tara pulled at her lower lip as she thought back. Patrick shrugged amicably and settled back into his seat on the settee. 'I'm happy to keep listening.'

Yehuda merely nodded. 'Now, getting back to the dark energy in the universe; it also has another name. It is sometimes referred to as zero point energy. The two names flow from two different ways of looking at the same thing.' He dropped his pencil back on the coffee table and it rolled slowly away from him.

'Zero point energy is defined as the energy that exists in any system where the temperature of that system is zero. It is the energy that remains when all other energy is removed from the system. For example, if you cool helium gas to zero point it still remains liquid. What keeps the helium in its liquid state—and what prevents it from turning into a solid—is the zero point energy.'

Yehuda stopped talking then, but he held up one finger to indicate that he hadn't yet made his point.

'Theory says,' he continued after a few seconds, 'that the universe is made up of a very large number of smaller systems, each of which has a finite amount of zero point energy. But—and here's one problem the physicists are wrestling with—when we add up all the theoretical zero point energy, the resulting number is so large that the accompanying gravitational forces would cause space to curve back in on itself. Our universe would very quickly revert to the single point of matter that existed immediately preceding the Big Bang. But the fact is this is not happening, and no physicist can explain why. The top-down view of dark energy does not reconcile with the bottom-up view of zero point energy and, again, no physicist can explain why.'

Yehuda looked across at Tara. She looked back intently at him, her brow furrowed in concentration.

'And, the reason I am telling you this is that it demonstrates how little we know about the energy that is present in every nook and cranny of our universe. So, for physicists or the Patent Office to reject something they don't yet understand is facile. And, finally, understanding why my technology works—just as I have done on a small scale—represents a cutting edge discovery in the field of physics in general.

'But what makes you think we'll understand you?' Patrick asked.

'I am going to try to explain it in layman's terms as far as is possible. I will simplify it, and I think you will understand it well enough to know that, if I am correct, you'll see we have a means of lifting humanity to a new level in its evolutionary journey.'

Patrick raised his eyebrows and cocked his head to one side. He glanced at Tara who looked back at him, but still she said nothing. 'Okay,' he responded. 'You've certainly got our undivided attention.'

'In simple English,' Yehuda began, 'I discovered a process by which matter could be converted into energy in a manner that is consistent with Einstein's equation of $e = mc^2$, but without any fancy nuclear power generation paraphernalia or any radioactive fallout. I may be the first man in history to understand the underlying physical process of electromagnetism.' Yehuda smiled self-effacingly, drew a deep breath and let it out again in a long, tension-releasing sigh. 'I was sitting in this very chair one day, when I asked myself the question, "*Why* are electrons within an atom negatively charged, and *why* are protons positively charged, and *why* do neutrons have no detectable electrical charge?" '

'I assume you came up with a hypothesis?' Patrick asked.

'Mmm, yes.' He turned to Tara. 'Do you remember at our first meeting when I was so insistent that you understood the concept of light being either a wave or a particle, and that the name of that particle is a photon, which is a tiny package of energy that appears to have no mass?'

'Yesss ...' Tara nodded, but with a dubious expression on her face.

'It's not strictly correct, but I want you to keep that little photon in mind as I'm talking. In simple terms, I asked myself a what-if question. "What if that photon is always *spinning* at the speed of light?" I postulated that the photon might, in reality, be a spinning mass-energy particle, and I thought of that mass-energy phenomenon as the ultimate building block from which all electrons, protons and neutrons are made. I imagined these particles are always simultaneously both mass and energy and the observer would describe them according to the physical circumstances, depending on the direction of spin relative to the viewer.' Yehuda paused, looked over the top of his bifocals and smiled. 'Sorry, for what you might call the techno-babble but sometimes there is no way around it.'

Tara glanced first at Mehmet and then at Patrick. She was amused to see that the expression on Patrick's face was transparently reflecting her own emotions. This was either the stuff of madness or of genius and he, too, wasn't yet quite sure which. But she took comfort from Mehmet's expression of comfortable equanimity.

'Okay, so where did this reasoning lead you?' Patrick asked.

Yehuda slid his glasses back up to the bridge of his nose with one finger. 'It led me to the conclusion that, when you pass an electric current through a copper wire, infinitesimally small, spinning photons—point-like particles of mass-energy—are transferred out of the copper wire and into the magnetic field lines surrounding it. I built a machine that was able to harvest the kinetic energy in those spinning photons.'

'But I thought that photons have no mass.'

'They *appear* to have no mass. It depends on their direction of spin.'

Patrick's face lit up. 'Both Isaac Newton and James Clerk-Maxwell anticipated that, one day, we would come to understand it—the physical process which underlies electromagnetism—but until this minute I never knew that anyone had. Are you ... are you absolutely sure?'

'That is what I have spent the last twenty or so years validating,' Yehuda answered calmly. 'All I *can* say is that the probability of error in this logic is vanishingly small because my results have consistently met my expectations.'

'But if you are correct, why didn't you fight the Patent Office's ruling?' Tara asked.

Yehuda patted his pocket absent-mindedly, shifted his position in his chair, then squared his shoulders as if readying himself for the next part of his revelation. He seemed to have either forgotten Tara's question, or not to have heard it.

'The important physical property I focussed on was that the photons were very likely rotating or spinning at the speed of light, like sub-atomic sized spherical gyroscopes, and always moving in some rotational direction at the speed of light.'

Tara was tempted to repeat her question, but instead let him continue.

'I wondered whether its direction of rotation would impact on its electrical charge. For example, if it was rotating anticlockwise—from east to west—it would have a negative charge and be perceived as an electron which has almost no mass. If it was rotating clockwise—from west to east—it would have a positive charge and be perceived as a proton, which has both a charge and a perceived mass. And if it was rotating north–south or south–north it might have a neutral charge and be perceived as a neutron. It also struck me that if it had no detectable energetic charge, it might instead have what we perceive to be mass, but with subtly different properties.'

'Such as the potential for *negative* mass, as you once explained to me,' Mehmet unexpectedly broke in. 'And if the Ancients had worked out a way to influence the direction of spin, it might explain how the enormous monoliths could have been levitated into place.'[xii]

'Whoa, this is getting way ahead of me. Can we go back to why they must be spinning at the speed of light?' Tara asked.

'Because James Clerk Maxwell's equations proved that all electro-magnetic energy travels at the speed of light. It's the way all of nature is designed.'

Patrick's jaw muscles were working furiously.

'Sometimes these particles would be seen as the energy within a substance, and sometimes they would be seen to contribute to the mass of that substance.'

'Just like light is sometimes a wave and sometimes a particle,' Tara commented.

'Hmmm,' Patrick mused. 'If that's so, it also explains why, when electrons from a battery are injected into a copper wire at one end, other electrons exit the other end of the copper wire at the speed of light. It's not that the electrons themselves are injected at the speed of light, it's that the electrons—photons which are spinning anticlockwise—are already and perpetually spinning at that speed.'

'I want you to imagine just two of these spinning point-like particles,' Yehuda continued. 'If it will help you, think in terms of two gear sprockets with teeth. Imagine that one is spinning clockwise at the speed of light, and the other is spinning anticlockwise at the speed of light. What do you think might happen if they come together?'

'They'd mesh together like gears in a mechanical Swiss watch,' Patrick, the engineer, ventured. 'They would be attracted in the same way that opposite magnetic poles attract.'

'And, by the same reasoning,' Yehuda continued 'if they were both spinning in the same direction, they would repel each other—just as two, like-magnetic poles repel. He paused.

'I think I see where this is going,' Patrick said. 'If some of these mass-energy particles are repelling others, then some would be bumped forward and some would even be bumped outside the confines of the copper and form a magnetic force around the wire, and rejoin the wire further down its length—a bit like a tributary rejoins a flowing river.'

In her mind's eye, Tara could see the lines of iron filings being formed around the bar magnet of her schooldays. She shrugged. Why not mass-energy particles? It all seemed feasible.

'Good, good, you see where I am leading,' Yehuda said. I now want to focus on Einstein's famous equation, $e = mc^2$. What I am almost sure you do not know, is that this was not how Einstein first wrote the equation.'

'You'd be right. I didn't know that.'

'Albert Einstein's first paper on the subject stated that, "If a body gives off energy '*l*' in the form of radiation, its mass will diminish by l/c^2." '[xiii]

Tara pulled a face, too late hoping that Yehuda would not see it.

'Would you like to take a short break?' Yehuda asked.

'Let's keep going,' Tara suggested. 'If I find that I'm not following, I can just tune out and then tune back in again later when it seems appropriate. But why did he use the letter "*l*" and not the letter "e"?'

'Because, my dear, Einstein was thinking in terms of *light* energy. Because that is how Isaac Newton had framed it. Newton said, and I can even quote it to you, *The changing of bodies into light, and light into bodies, is very comfortable in the course of nature, which seems delighted with transmutations.* And that is what led me to make the connection with light. If it was spinning photons being bumped outside the confines of the atomic domains of the copper wire to form up in magnetic grid lines, then the copper wire might be losing microscopic amounts of its mass in accordance with Einstein's original expectation. Therefore, photons must have mass under certain circumstances.' There was the sound of finality in his voice, as if he was completing the argument.

Tara felt her thought processes scrambled, and sat back in her chair, resigned to being a passive listener.

'So,' Patrick conjectured, 'applying this reasoning, it must be possible to somehow harness the kinetic energy in the spinning photons in the tributary before they have time to return to the original confines of their atomic domains within the copper "wire—before the tributary rejoins the main river, so to speak. In the process, it becomes usable energy?'

'Exactly right, Yehuda answered with enthusiasm. 'You've got it!'

'But how could it be harnessed?' Tara asked.

'The answer to your question is very simple. I took a copper wire several miles long, and wound it into a coil. I then connected one end of the wire to a DC battery—a Direct Current battery. That caused the photons to start flowing both down the wire and through the tributary or, more precisely, that facilitated a transfer of photons beyond the original atomic domains of the copper atoms within the wire. Are you with me on that?"

'Mmm.' Tara bobbed her head non-committally.

'Then, by switching the polarity of the battery, the photons moved in the opposite direction and collided with those still approaching from the original direction. At the point of impact, the combined speed was trending towards twice the speed of light, which Patrick, because of his engineering background, will understand is very significant. A side benefit was that some of the photons that had left the battery re-entered it, thereby re-charging the battery. It follows that it was the mass of the protons and/or neutrons, or both, that must have been converted into energy.'

Patrick whistled in response. 'That's brilliant.'

Tara was less impressed. 'You lost me,' she said. 'Yehuda, can you please explain precisely how you harnessed the energy?'

'The magnetic fields around the wire—pulsing first in one direction and then in the other—cause a fixed magnet to rotate around an axle and a rotating flywheel was able to transfer electromagnetic energy into mechanical energy.'

Patrick slumped back into his seat on the worn settee. 'And the first law of thermodynamics remains intact.'

'Correct.'

Patrick stared at the ceiling. 'The copper wire loses infinitesimally small amounts of mass which convert to usable energy, and the batteries remain charged. Well I never!'

'It turns out that, after all these years, there are also others who are beginning to discover the secrets of over-unity energy production,' Yehuda added, by way of an afterthought. 'However, unlike my technology, they are attempting to scavenge the energy that pulsates in the environment—the energy that is not confined within atoms of matter.'[xiv]

'One final matter before we wrap up for the evening, Yehuda—and please excuse the choice of the word *matter*,' Patrick said with a hint of mischief in his voice.

'Yes?'

'With this invention, people will become less dependent on the power grids, and we'll all enjoy the bonus of a reduction in greenhouse gas emissions.'

'A very significant reduction,' Yehuda responded. 'So it doesn't matter whether the IPCC scientist are right or wrong. We will all land up with both what we want and what we need—a low cost means of coping with climate change and with peak oil. Having said this, we should be pushing for its adoption as a matter of urgency.'

CHAPTER 40

'CAN YOU REMEMBER the best breakfast you ever had?'

'Huh?'

'You were a million miles away. I thought it might be nice if we exchanged a few pleasantries.'

'Was I? Sorry about that.'

It was early Saturday morning and the first time Patrick and Tara had seen one another since he had dropped her off at the hotel two nights ago. Patrick's work commitments had overtaken him until now, and Tara could see something was still preoccupying his thoughts. They were sitting in the sunshine at the sidewalk café outside her hotel, enjoying a leisurely breakfast. The early morning traffic droned in the background and, across the road, Columbus Park and the Cathedral of Santa Maria beyond seemed to sparkle in the early sun, as if enthusiastically greeting the new day. Or perhaps it was just the reflections off the remains of the dawn dew.

'Look.' Tara pointed to a large flock of birds circling high above the statue of Columbus just visible beyond the foliage of the park's trees. The Great Admiral, frozen in time, seemed to be pointing at them too. 'I'll bet that little old lady over there is the attraction.'

Even from the distance they could see her begin to scatter crumbs or little bits of bread, throwing them with gusto in a wide arc around herself.

'Is she allowed to do that?' Patrick asked, a look of feigned concern on his face.

'I suspect she's reached a stage in her life where she couldn't care less, one way or another,' Tara responded. 'To her, life is simple. Look at how deliberate her actions are.' She rested her hand on his forearm.

'Probably been doing it for years. And yes, I can remember the best breakfast … other than this one.' Patrick covered her hand with his and blew her an impish kiss. He grinned. 'Is this going to be another one of those multiple simultaneous conversation days?'

'Not if you feel you can't handle more than two at a time. I wouldn't want you to strain your brain. Poor little thing, it's been working so hard lately.'

Patrick's eyes crinkled at the corners. *Oh-oh*, she knew this sign. He leaned back, disengaged their touches in the process, and lifted his glass of orange juice in salute before taking a sip. 'Mmm, ambrosia … There's a little Italian restaurant on the northern beaches in Sydney that I go to from time to time. I once had a breakfast there when everything just came together. The chef must have been inspired. I've been going back there for years, and I keep ordering the same dish. They've never been able to replicate it exactly.'

'Were you alone? Tell me more about this breakfast of yours.'

'I can still taste it. Eggs lightly scrambled with fresh basil and spinach, still juicy and infused with fresh parmesan, but it was not just the food …'

Tara wondered whether she wanted to hear what was coming.

'What made it so special that particular day were a couple of dolphins cavorting in the waves within a hundred metres of where we were sitting. They were surfing, and when they caught a good wave they'd ride it halfway to shore and then flip backwards high into the air behind it, as if to say, "Wow! Did ya see how I caught that one?"'

'We?'

'Listen. I know I'm a bit of a recluse, but I'm not in the habit of eating breakfast alone in a restaurant ten kilometres from where I live.' He paused. 'There must have been at least twenty other patrons there.'

With that, he bent down to pick up what looked like an old rolled-up newspaper that he'd unceremoniously tossed to the ground next to his chair when they'd arrived. At the time she hadn't paid it much mind. Maybe he had just folded it badly after reading it. He handed it to her. 'Open it gently. I took a lot of trouble to steal that.'

On closer inspection, she saw that the paper had been rolled into a cone shape, folded over and sealed with a piece of sticky tape at the top. The tape looked just as used as the newspaper, as if it had stuck to itself and then been separated.

'Steal it or seal it?'

Patrick had certainly taken very little trouble to wrap whatever it was that was inside, if there *was* anything inside. It weighed hardly anything at all. 'What on earth is it?'

'Should I get the bill?' he asked.

'*Check*, not bill. A bill is what a duck uses instead of a mouth. No. They'll put it on my tab. Let me put it another way. Were you part of this twenty patron group, or were you there with someone—like we are today?'

'Come on, Tara. A *tab* is something you pull open to get at the beer inside its can. And there could never be any situation that even comes close to like we are today. You're absolutely unique.' He couldn't resist a mischievous smile.

'You're never going to tell me, are you?'

'No. Now why don't you just open that? I went to great stealth to get that newspaper for you.'

Tara moved the empty plates, cups and glasses to one side to clear a space in front of her. She laid the cone of newspaper down, gently prised off the crumpled tape and lifted the flap. The newspaper unfurled to reveal a long, leafy stem, at the top of which was a deep red rose, its petals just opening.

Wordlessly, she looked up at Patrick and drew in a long, slow breath.

'My blossoming love for you has turned me into a criminal,' he said in response to the look on her face. 'I could go to jail for stealing this, but it will have been worth it, just to see the way you're looking at me now. Whenever I look into your eyes I see the blue amber that drew us together in the first place.'

Tara looked away from him and focussed intently on the flower. She caressed the petals with her fingertips, but said nothing.

'Too cheesy?' he asked with a hint of nervousness.

Without saying a word, she pushed her chair back, walked over to him, lifted his face between the palms of her hands and kissed him warmly on the lips. 'I'm going upstairs to my room to put this into a glass of water,' she said, with a distinct catch in her voice. 'I want it to live forever. And when I get back, perhaps you and I can wander across to watch the little old lady feed the birds.'

'Okay, but after that I want to go into the cathedral. I hear the acoustics are great inside.'

'Yeah. It couldn't possibly have anything to do with Yehuda and Mehmet's view of creation, could it? It's exquisitely beautiful, and its perfume is indescribable. Thank you, Patrick.'

By the time Tara had returned, the old lady and the birds had left. Patrick draped his arm across her shoulder as they walked up to the Great Admiral's statue.

I wonder what he's pointing at?'

'Probably telling us that the birds went that-away,' Patrick responded. 'Look. Even the little guy on the plinth below him is pointing.'

'Naah. They're both pointing north-west, probably to Nueba Yol,' Tara speculated. She was remembering her conversation with Aurelio when they had seen the monument on the way to Santiago, and she wondered why the grass always seemed greener on the other side. Hispaniola was as close to paradise as it was possible to get—magical things had been happening to her ever since she had first decided to vacation here.

They ambled slowly towards the series of arches at the side of what looked like just another old building from the outside. 'Did you know that this is the oldest cathedral in the Americas?' Patrick asked. 'The Vatican apparently wanted it to be a beacon for Christianity in those days, a sort of a launch pad for proselytising the pagans. It's around 500 years old.'

'Do you want to go inside? Maybe we can offer a small prayer of thanks for everything that's happened in our lives over the past couple of weeks. Phew! Now that's something I wouldn't have thought I'd say a few weeks ago.'

'Do you think the God of the Catholics will listen to us non-prac-tising Protestants?' he countered, the mischief surfacing once again. 'I assume that's what you are?'

In answer, she withdrew her arm from around his waist and dug her elbow into his ribs. 'Come on you! Let's go find the main entrance. And I doubt if Jesus would care one way or another which denomination we were, if we happened to be walking into a church.'

They had walked around the block to Archbishop Merino Street to approach the building's main entrance. A row of concrete boundary fence posts with darkly green pointed tips greeted them—the produce of generations of mould. A decrepit old bell tower, home for two age-worn bronze bells, stood behind the dubious protection of an outer wall that had been slowly succumbing to corrosion.

'Looks about as solid as a sugar cube after you've licked it.' Patrick knocked his knuckles against the stone then poked at the crumbling edge.

'Vandal!' She tapped him on the shoulder. 'That piece of stone may have lasted days if not weeks without your helping it to its grave.'

They walked through the outer gate. A black pathway led away from them and towards the cathedral's entrance. 'Seems to me that these lines of black slate have been laid to look like a lighthouse,' Patrick observed. 'Look there.' He pointed to a white-filled circle about two-thirds down its length. 'The white spot could be a lighthouse light—a beacon—and the criss-crossing black lines are light beams emanating from it.'

'Maybe you should tell Yehuda about your newly discovered dark light,' Tara said and chuckled. Frankly, I think you've got an overactive imagination. It's just a pathway leading to a door.'

'Maybe. But look at that entrance and all the statues in the alcoves, the carvings and the friezes. A lot of thought and effort went into this building. It could stand anywhere in Europe. It was obviously built by master craftsmen.'

'The doors are open, but it looks pitch black inside,' Tara said. 'Do you think it's open to the public?'

'I'm sure it is. And I'm equally sure that you're going to be surprised by just how bright it really is inside. If this building was built in the way the European cathedrals were built, I'm sure we're going to find vaulted ceilings and gothic arches and stained glass windows. All those things are designed to enhance and reflect light. That's probably also why the acoustics are so good. I'm told cathedrals are designed so that you can hear the ring of truth bouncing off their ceilings and walls.'

'Let's check it out,' she said, clasping his fingers in hers. She was surprised to feel the dampness in his palm. Clammy hands … Why?

They crossed the threshold into the instant silence of the interior.

'My God,' Tara whispered, 'you were right. Look how bright it is. It's almost like daylight inside. Where's the light coming from?'

'Let's sit at one of these benches,' Patrick suggested, pointing to the first of a row of solid mahogany pews. 'I want to get the feel of the place.'

They sat quietly for some time, absorbing the ambience of the cathedral. Towards the front, a backpacker stood in the aisle taking photographs. About a dozen pews ahead, a couple, knelt with heads bowed, oblivious to their surroundings. Off to one side, a man sat in quiet contemplation. A woman who had been kneeling in prayer further down the aisle crossed herself, stood up and walked with an air of serenity towards the door behind them.

'You can almost hear the silence,' Tara whispered. 'I thought you said that sound carried inside this building.'

'I did,' he whispered in return, 'and so does silence. Why don't we test it? I'll say something and you see if you can hear what I'm saying. I'll sit here and you go forward—say five rows at a time. If you can hear me just nod your head.'

She nodded.

He laughed, trying to suppress the sound. 'Not yet, you twit.'

'Ha ha.'

She moved five pews forward, sat down, turned to face him, gave him a thumbs up, and turned away to face the front again.

'Ring of truth,' he said, quietly and distinctly.

She heard the words clearly, nodded and got up to repeat the process. A further five pews ahead …

'Ring of truth.'

A couple of heads turned inquisitively as Patrick and Tara continued with their experiment until, eventually, he joined her at the front pew.

'Clear as a bell,' she whispered. 'All the way to the front. It's incredible.'

Without saying anything, he drew a deep breath and let it out in what might have been a sigh. He sat with his gaze fixed straight ahead at a statue of the Virgin Mary with the baby Jesus in her arms. Then he allowed his gaze to wander upwards to the stained glass light reflected on the arches in the vaulted ceiling.

He turned to face her. 'You up for another experiment? I want you to close your eyes. Just nod again like last time when you hear me, but this time I'm going to whisper.'

'Okay.' She closed her eyes. She heard him shuffle, as if he was getting up to walk away.

After what seemed like thirty seconds, she heard his whisper. 'Ring of truth.'

She nodded. Amazingly, it seemed as if he hadn't moved. Where was he?

Another thirty seconds went by. 'You can open your eyes now,' he whispered.

As she did so, she discovered that he hadn't in fact moved away at all. He sat with his body turned to face her. His two arms extended towards her, one hand clenching the other and supporting a closed fist, palm upwards. She looked down, just as he opened his clenched fingers. 'Ring of truth.' This time the words were said out loud, and they had a note of finality about them.

She looked down at an exquisite gold ring that clasped a blue amber in a squat tubular setting. The amber seemed to float above the gold.

Tara reached out to take it from his hand, her fingers trembling ever so slightly. It was heavier, more solid, than she expected, as if the gold had been cast as an ingot around the amber. It was exactly what she would have chosen herself.

She lifted it into a shaft of light to look at it more intently, and drew a sharp breath. She knew this particular stone. It was the one she had seen at Señor Fernadez' store. But how? Speechless, she just looked at Patrick.

'What's wrong?' Patrick asked, a look of concern on his face.

'Let's go outside,' she said. The manner in which she said it made him feel even more insecure.

He followed her into the blazing sunlight.

'What is it?'

She didn't respond. Instead, she put on the ring, held it up to the light and inspected it from different angles.

Then, with her eyes moist with emotion, she threw her arms around his neck and hugged him. Finally she kissed him fully on the mouth with a long, lingering kiss.

'I absolutely love this ring, and I'm learning to adore you,' she said. 'There's something about your style that's just a bit out of left field so that you often take me by total surprise. I had no idea what was coming there.'

He grinned, his sense of centeredness returning. 'Phew! For a minute there you had me going. I thought I had blown something. What took you so long to react?'

'Patrick, that's not just any old piece of blue amber. That particular piece is the very one I was inspecting at Señor Fernandez's store. How in God's name did you come to choose that particular stone?'

'Aha! That's for me to know and you to find out.'

'Not this time buster. This doesn't involve any other women. This is just you and me. I want to know how exactly how you did it.'

Patrick smiled with mock resignation. 'Teamwork. Yehuda asked Gerardo to ask Aurelio where you had bought the amber gifts for your family. Aurelio took me and the committee of Yehuda and Mehmet to meet with Señor Fernandez. We pumped him about what he had shown you and he told me that you had looked at this particular stone.'

'What the hell made him remember that? I looked at many stones.'

'Ah, but this particular stone seemed to draw your attention. Señor Fernandez overheard you say that you wished some stranger would give it to you. He thought you were some crazy *gringa* to say a thing like that—especially out loud.'

She remembered the incident. 'He misheard me. I was talking about "some strange man". You remember … the family joke? Strange as in "unusual" as opposed to strange as in "weird"?'

'Aaah. So I did good?'

'Perfect. I absolutely love it. But why did you need a committee, and when did you guys find the time?'

'I just wanted reassurance by the locals that I wasn't being ripped off. We went on Tuesday. I bought it there and then, and then went on my own have the ring designed by the jeweller that Señor Fernandez recommended. Aurelio took me. It was delivered yesterday.'

'And all this time I thought you were slaving over a hot computer.'

'That too. I was up until midnight last night clearing the decks. I'm taking another ten days off. Unpaid leave. You are taking me to meet your mum and your family next week, and then you and I are going to meet my parents in Australia. That way, everyone will feel at home when we meet over Thanksgiving dinner.'

'You seem pretty cocksure of yourself.'

'Oh? Are you going to give me any arguments?'

'Hmmm. Now that I think about it …'

'Tell me, who else knew about this?' she asked by way of an after-thought.

'Samantha.'

'What!?'

'I phoned Sam to speak about Yehuda and the financial prospects for his technology, but she wanted to know about you and wouldn't have a bar of it until she got what she wanted. I only told her because she prised it out of me. How do women know these things? I don't know … it used to be a man's world.'

'What did she say?'

'Not now … I don't want to talk about Yehuda or Sam, or Mehmet or Aurelio. Just you and me.'

CHAPTER 41

TARA MANAGED TO leave the subject of Samantha's reaction unsaid until the next morning. She and Patrick were wandering in the direction of the retail precinct. It was late morning, and they were in no particular hurry to do anything. Their meeting with Yehuda and Mehmet was only scheduled for four o'clock.

'So, what did Samantha say?' Tara asked.

'In a word? Joyful. Apparently, William has been pushing her to accept his proposal of marriage and she saw this as a sign. She tells me they've got a lot in common, and they're getting on like a house on fire. But, you know bankers. The glass is always half empty. She was worried that it was all too good to be true. Now she reckons that if you and I are prepared to reach for the brass ring, then why not her and William?'

'Brass? My man gave me a brass ring?'

'Rest assured, light of my life, and fire of my loins. Except for that beautiful little piece of blue amber, that thar ring is solid gold. Given what Yehuda has been discovering about the real value of gold, I thought we might as well have an insurance policy. If Aaron's staff could bud when it was close to all that gold, then maybe you could bud, if you know what I mean?'

Tara laughed that tinkling laugh he had come to love. 'Now, there's something we need to talk about, buddy. Though I do feel a'blossoming all over.'

'Blooming marvellous.'

Their light-heartedness continued for another couple of minutes before Tara abruptly changed the subject. 'Tell me, what did Samantha say about Yehuda's technology?'

'You and I have just sealed a lifetime guarantee romance deal and now you want to talk about Yehuda's technology?' he asked, incredulously. 'Won't we get enough of that tonight?'

'Give me an overview. Just the highlights. I want us to be on the same page before tonight. Yehuda's not just being polite by inviting us along. He wants something, and I want to be prepared.'

Patrick sighed resignedly. 'Okay, but can I keep it short, please?'

'Shorter, the better.'

'Sam was going on about technical risk. You know, "Does Yehuda's technology do what he claims?" I told her that the only way we could test it properly would be to measure the wattage of both the energy in and the energy out, and that we would also have to devise a means of testing the batteries before and after. If we can validate more watts out than in—or even, less energy out than energy in with no reduction of battery life—then we had better take his technology damned seriously.'

'Okay. Let's assume this could be done, and the results are positive, then what?'

'Which watt?'

'What …?' It took Tara a couple of seconds to work it out, and she punched him playfully on the arm. 'We're not going to do one of those "Who's on first" numbers now.'

He shrugged. 'Okay. You know how bankers think. If their left ear's itchy then they scratch it with their right hand extended over their head. She thinks some sort of ownership structure based in a tax haven like the Cayman, or Cooke, or Jersey Islands. And she was talking about a board of directors that will be skewed towards ethics as opposed to profitability. Apparently the current financial problems in the world are really spooking her and some of her more honest colleagues, and "ethics" is now the new buzzword. She's thinking about a board consisting of leaders of the world's major religions, and the inventor, and a couple of Nobel prize winners from the sciences and humanities, and maybe one or two very successful businessmen who don't need any more money. Definitely no ex-politicians.'

'She's thinking of a not-for-profit? I can't believe that.'

'Not really. She concedes that the inventor should earn a modest royalty, but she's arguing that all other profits should flow to fund infra-structure in poorer countries. I agree with her, by the way. If agricultural production is going to have to shift to the poorer countries, then they are going to need infrastructure.'

'A banker talking against private enterprise?'

'Mmm, I never said that. Samantha knows which way is up. She's still hot for private enterprise, but she doesn't see energy as a "product".' Patrick emphasised the word by drawing inverted commas in the air. 'Energy drives the world's economy. It's too important to allow anyone with a vested interest to control its source. That's how we got into the shit we're in, and we need to learn from that. The Jersey Island company will license the technology to private enterprise manufacturers who will compete in the normal world on a for-profit basis, but the Jersey Island company will ensure that there's always plenty of competition. The amounts for license fees will be a trade-off on how much to rob Peter to pay Paul—given that profits will flow to build infrastructure. The arrangements need to be structured to be transparent, so that no money can possibly cling to sticky outstretched hands along the way. No skim-ming, period. That needs to be publicly validated on an annual basis by third parties whose necks are terminally on the chopping block.'

'What about the money to finance it?'

'Strangely, she didn't see that as a problem. She reckons that one or more of the charitable foundations like Doorways or Mansfield or Goodwill could spring to pay for the technical testing and, maybe even for the prototype design. Given the linkage between science and religion, she thought that Mansfield might be particularly interested. Fifty million dollars is not all that much in the grand scheme of things. Thereafter, she sees it as a structuring problem. Every government in the world would probably throw money at it if it can be proven that there's no longer a technical risk. Can we stop talking about this now please?'

Tara nodded thoughtfully, and turned to face Patrick. 'Yes. I've got the picture.' Then, she grabbed his hand, tugged on it so that he lowered his head towards her, and she kissed him affectionately on the cheek. 'Thanks. Now we can enjoy the rest of the day.' She grinned at him. 'See how easily pleased I am?'

CHAPTER 42

'WHAT A WONDERFUL day on which to end my vacation. The engagement ring is gorgeous. I just love it, and I loved the way gave it to me yesterday. The weather's perfect, our lunch was exquisite, and you had me laughing so hard, my sides were hurting. Are you going to be like this all our lives, or are you just trying to impress me now?'

Patrick and Tara strolled contentedly, hand in hand, under the mottled canopy of shade spread by the closely packed row of old trees on Avenida Independencia. They were two blocks away from Yehuda's house. The late afternoon sunshine was still strong enough to penetrate the gaps in the overhead foliage, and the patterns on the sidewalk would have raised the spirits of even an unromantic soul. In Tara's case, she was floating on air whilst Patrick had a grin that seemed permanently plastered on his face.

'It's not *my* doing. You seem to have a knack for pushing my buttons. I've merely been reacting to the opportunities you create. Think about it. *You* chose to throw yourself at me in the restaurant. *You* chose to pursue the blue amber. *You* chose to make contact with Yehuda. *You* chose to stay at a hotel across the way from the cathedral. Do you expect me to believe that all the opportunities you create are just coincidences? It's like you're one step ahead of the curve all the time.'

'Yeah, I do seem to be plugged in lately, don't I? But it never used to be this way. *You* being super-hero and getting into the newspaper; *you* rendez-vousing with Mehmet in the restaurant where I threw myself at you ...'

'Well perhaps it's the hairy finger of fate?'

It was at that point that they arrived outside Yehuda's home to discover Yehuda and Mehmet on the porch, both sitting in wicker chairs. They waved, then rose to greet the newcomers.

'Welcome Tara and Patrick,' Yehuda said, extending his hands towards them. 'Have you enjoyed your day so far?'

'It's been amazing,' Tara answered.

'Come and sit with us on the porch, or should we go inside?'

'Porch is good,' Patrick answered. 'How about you?'

'Fine with me.'

'Coffee? Mehmet and I have just finished our second cup, so we won't join you. Frankly, I don't know what he sees in that coffee of mine, but he seems to be happy to drink a lot of it.'

Mehmet looked at Yehuda in surprise but had no chance to comment.

'No thank you. We've just eaten.' Tara had to stop herself from adding the words, "Thank God". She didn't think she could stomach Yehuda's coffee right then.

Both men offered Tara their chairs. Patrick seated himself on the low front wall of the porch, while Tara insisted on sitting on a stool that looked as though it might have doubled as a basking place for a favoured cat. She looked around her. 'Do you know, Yehuda, I've never paid attention to the outside of your house before. Except for the red corrugated iron roof, it looks like a typical Dominican Republic home, painted in buttercup yellow and pastel green as it is. I particularly like the old wrought iron fence and gate. Have you owned it a long time?'

'Thank you Tara. Yes, I have only known two homes in my lifetime. I painted it these colours because I'm attracted to happy colours. That's also why I bought those paintings which are hanging in my study. Colour brings me joy.'

'Speaking of joy, I believe congratulations are in order,' Mehmet said, an uncharacteristically impish grin on his face. 'Tara, Yehuda and I would like to present you with a gift of our appreciation. If it had not been for you, we would not all be sitting here. Perhaps you would consider it a sort of engagement present from the two of us.'

'That's very kind of you and Yehuda, Mehmet, but we have much to thank you both for too.'

'Don't worry about that.' Yehuda interjected. 'We should tell you, Tara, 'that we have an ulterior motive. The gift is not altogether unrelated to the discussions we have been having.' He reached for a small brown paper parcel and handed it to her.

'I'm dying of curiosity. What is it?' There was no sticky tape holding the parcel together, but the corners had been creased with origami-like precision and were folded in on themselves. She undid the package carefully.

In its folds lay a necklet of two amber teardrops—one blue, one honey—joined together in a perfect circle bounded by a band of solid gold, similar in a way to the setting of her ring. Inside the main body of the blue amber, a tiny circular eyepiece of honey amber had been embedded, and the opposite had been done in the main body of the honey amber. The pendant was threaded with a beautiful gold chain.

'This is breathtakingly beautiful,' Tara said in an awed voice. 'It's amazing. Patrick, a Yin-Yang of honey amber and blue amber. Where did you get this?'

'Yehuda and I had it made especially for you.' Mehmet said, the pleasure showing on his face. 'I have to admit we cheated a little. You will know that both of us went with Patrick when he selected your ring. Señor Fernadez advised us on your taste and on the choice of amber, and on the selection of the jeweller. You can see that it required some skill to be able to make this piece and we are very happy with the result.'

'Not half as happy as I am,' Tara replied. It's exquisite.' On an impulse she stood, took the two steps to Yehuda and hugged him. He had no time to rise from his chair and bent towards her, stiffly hugging her and patting her avuncularly on the back. Oh dear, Mehmet's culture did not look well upon contact between men and women like this. *Now what should she do?* He came to her rescue, extending both his hands to her in a warm and friendly handshake. 'Thank you Mehmet, thank you.'

She turned to Patrick. 'Did you know about this?'

'Of course! The Three Musketeers collaborated. Yehuda and Mehmet wanted it to match the ring, although they tell me this piece is highly significant from their perspective. That's why they wanted the gift to be from them.'

'I'm dying to hear.'

'Yehuda cleared his throat. 'Mehmet, would you like to explain?'

'Certainly. You are aware that Yehuda and I are close friends. In fact, we are more than close friends, we are collaborators. Between us we have been searching for clues in the annals of history that might help to defuse the tensions in our world today. Of course, Yehuda has also been passionately evaluating his electromagnetic technology, but in our spare time we meet regularly in our attempts to reconcile the three Abrahamic religions, but in particular the Judeo–Christian viewpoint with the Islamic viewpoint.'

'I was obviously aware that Yehuda is Jewish and that you are Muslim, and I was aware that you are friends, but I must admit I hadn't delved much more deeply than that.'

'If you are prepared to accept some linkage between these various cultures, however tenuous, there seems to be a possibility that there may be a common cultural point of origin across nearly 4.5 billion of Earth's current population—as distinct from a commonality of DNA. Yehuda and I have identified some interesting crossover points.'

'What has all this got to do with this Yin-Yang?' Tara asked.

'If we slice through the mists of time, and ignore the splinter groups that have emerged since the beginning days, then it becomes reasonably clear that—for want of a better description—the "yellow skinned" races of the world also have their own common point of cultural origin. The cultural views and values of these people were originally encapsulated in a document call the *I-Ching*. In English, the name means the "Book of Changes" and this book—which has been evolving over the aeons—is a record of Taoist philosophies and cosmological understanding. It was reputed to have originated at some time between 2800 and 2737 BCE, a mere 350 odd years after the Abrahamic civilizations began to emerge—at least what can be traced back to the Harappa in the Indus Valley. I suspect that if we look hard enough, we will probably find that it dates back to a similar common point. It appears that at that particular point in history something extraordinary happened across the planet.'

'So you think there was a link there too?'

'There is no evidence of such a link, but Yehuda and I have a partic-ular mindset. We are prepared to assume that all have their perspectives, each adding to the combined knowledge of humanity. Together, all the knowledge possessed by all the religions, philosophies and scientific disciplines of the world represent the combined truth. Its not an either–or situation. It is all. Likewise, it's not a question of science or religion. Both science and religion contribute to truth.'

'So what role does the *I-Ching* play?'

'If you add this Taoist body of knowledge,' Yehuda interjected, 'we are now contemplating commonalities in the combined views of nearly 6 billion of the 6.5 people in the world. With the remainder being mainly categorised as religiously non-aligned Africans—interestingly, whose ancestors are of course believed to be the forefathers of all of us, from a DNA perspective. The few remaining tribal Africans represent some of those amongst us who are able to live in harmony with nature. And from them, too, we can all learn something from their version of the truth.'

'We are getting side tracked, Yehuda,' Mehmet gently chided, 'and there is much to discuss today. Tara is leaving for the US tomorrow.'

'Sorry. Go on, go on.'

'All right then,' Mehmet continued, 'any attempt to discuss the *I-Ching* in the space of ten minutes would have the effect of trivialising it. What we need to focus on is that at the very epicentre of Taoist philosophy is the concept of Yin and Yang—which is an energetic concept. That is, it refers to energy, which is Yehuda's field of expertise. Perhaps, after all, Yehuda you should take over from here.'

'Thank you, yes. The Tao philosophy does not comment on the existence or non-existence of God. Rather it sidesteps the question by accepting that the origin of the universe is too difficult a concept for the human mind to grasp. It starts from the base proposition that in the beginning there was nothing—Wu Chi, symbolised by an empty circle. Then, out of nothingness emerges two complementary energetic forces, the Yin and the Yang."

'So far, I am following.'

'In very simplistic terms, the Tao philosophy believes that all of creation is formed from the interaction of these two energetic forces of Yin and Yang. The whole point of this discussion is that Yin and Yang are seen by Taoists as forces that are continuously changing from Yin into Yang, and vice versa. They are spinning in a sort of a vortex, and out of that vortex emerges all of creation. That is a philosophical concept articulated around 5,000 years ago.'

Patrick's jaw clenched. 'Aah! James Clerk Maxwell's molecular vortices in the ether! Your mass-energy spinning photons which join together to form atoms.' Patrick stared at Yehuda.

'Yes,' Mehmet said, 'the *I-Ching* has been storing that particular nugget of knowledge for all of humanity through the millennia, just as the various Abrahamic testaments have been storing their secrets, and just as the ancient Hindu and Sanskrit texts have been storing theirs— waiting patiently, silently, inscrutably for the day when all of humanity will grow up to attain the wisdom we need to look past all the dogma.'

'It may interest you to know,' Yehuda broke in, 'that the Jewish kabbalistic belief regarding the origin of the Universe has some similarities with the Wu Chi concept too. *First, there was nothing, and out of nothing came something.* The kabbalists also view that "nothing" as a circle, and they view that "something" as the supernal light of God—or energy of God—that was injected into the circle, given that we now know that light and energy and matter are all closely related.'

Given the way he was feeling, Patrick had probably never been quite as gob-smacked in his entire life. 'The elusive Theory of Everything. It's there—I can feel it in our grasp.' His eyes were wide open, but he was not looking at any of them.

'Sadly, the biggest obstacle to human progress,' Mehmet continued, 'is ego … good, old fashioned, Neanderthal ego. When scientists scoff at the religions, they reflect their own levels of ignorance; when the various religions scoff at each other, they entrench a focus on their petty differences rather than their important commonalities. The pure truth is that each interest group—whether of religion, science, culture, gender—

has something of value to offer this planet, something for the greater benefit of us all … if only we could see beyond our differences, our vested interests and greed, our egos.'

'*E pluribus unum,*' Tara said as much to herself. 'Out of many, one.'

'Interesting you say that,' Yehuda responded with a wry smile. 'The country that was once the pariah of the community of nations on this planet, South Africa, originally had a motto which is perhaps even more meaningful. *Ex unitate vires*: out of unity, strength. These concepts of unity are not new. What will be new in the dawning of the New Age of Enlightenment—or the Messianic Age, or the Age of Aquarius, or however one wants to describe it—will be a deep understanding in our souls of the true meaning of this concept of co-operation, towards extending the hand of friendship, to which, previously, we paid nothing but lip service.'

Mehmet stood. 'Let's go inside. I think this might be a good time to tell Patrick and Tara of your plan of action.'

CHAPTER 43

YEHUDA HAD OFFERED coffee all round and had been declined all round. Patrick saw a bottle standing on the table next to the urn, and had asked for a scotch instead. A small, insulated bucket with ice cubes stood next to it, as if in waiting. Yehuda might yet turn out to be a drinking partner. 'Cheers,' he said to no one in particular. Mehmet, of course, didn't drink alcohol; Yehuda was preoccupied with ordering his thoughts; and Tara seemed disinclined to want to move out of her zone of composure. She seemed to Patrick to be happy to just go with the flow.

'Mehmet and I calculated that after eight million personal energy generators, or PEGs—as I like to call my invention—have been produced, the selling price could be brought down to $1,000 per generator. That covers one tenth of the total number of households in the USA, and at that price these generators could be supplied to Third World countries. In turn, the generators would give those countries access to water that needs to be pumped from underground, and lead to the opening of small cottage industries—all without any carbon emissions at all.'

'How long would it take to gear up to produce eight million of these generators?' Patrick asked.

'Let's say three to five years after the prototypes have been finalised, if private enterprise really applied itself to the task on a world-wide basis.'

'Well, if global cooling came along, I guess we'd be prepared,' Patrick said with a smile that turned up one corner of his mouth.

'Or, even if it didn't, we would still have a way of reducing the carbon dioxide emissions in our environment,' Yehuda countered.

'Could the PEG be adapted to be a drive train for a motor car?' Tara asked.

'Possibly, but my view is that our top priority should be to reduce our reliance on overhead power cables, and as a matter of urgency. In time, the PEG might be adapted to charge a bank of batteries in an electric car, but we should not get sidetracked from the primary objective to produce electricity. The car manufacturers are already travelling in the right direction targeting hybrid and battery operated cars.'

'But what will we do about peak oil?' Tara queried. 'If the world is running out of oil, how will we keep providing gasoline to all the tens of millions of existing cars that are still driving around on the roads?'

'Ah yes, Tara, but we are not yet running out of coal, and that brings me to the Fischer Tropsch technology that I wanted to talk to you about. Some people call it FT technology. It has been around since World War II and it holds no secrets. The plants are expensive to build from scratch but, depending on the price of coal, the FT process can be used to produce synthetic diesel from coal for around $45 to $50 a barrel. That's around half the current world price of crude oil. And we will have a wonderful window of opportunity to go into large scale production—at least in the United States to begin with.'

'But if they're so expensive to build, where is the window of opportunity coming from?' Tara asked.

'If industry has geared up to produce millions of PEGs, then coal-fired power plants all over the country, will become redundant. They can be adapted to produce FT diesel.'

'Won't it be complicated to convert them?' Patrick asked.

'To the contrary, it will be relatively easy,' Yehuda responded. And it will also be relatively inexpensive from an incremental perspective. There is a huge existing investment in coal mining and in the transportation of coal to these power plants. These investments have already been made and it would be foolish just to abandon them. The plants can be phased out slowly, as the population of internal combustion cars is replaced over time by new technology.'

'Is there enough coal to keep us going?' Tara asked

'Absolutely—well, 150 years of coal— compared to, roughly, forty years of oil left at current consumption levels. The transition will be relatively painless. In the process, because the PEGs will have facilitated a migration from Tesla's distributed electricity model, carbon dioxide emissions will contract sharply. Remember that up to twenty-five percent of the coal currently burned to produce electricity is wasted because of friction heat loss in the copper cables. If you think in terms of coal and oil together being described in terms of equivalent barrels of oil, the total number of equivalent barrels of oil consumed will fall dramatically because of the introduction of the PEGs.'

Tara smiled inwardly, but was careful not to let it show. He was making it sound so easy.

'Those countries which will suffer the most painful consequences of all of this are the ones that currently rely on the sale of oil to finance their economies. Many are Islamic countries, which will need to think very carefully about the folly of supporting terrorism in the future if they wish to be embraced by the world community and be afforded unrestricted access to the new energy technologies. Their economies can flourish for other reasons, which I will go into later. There will be no need for threats or cajoling.'

'All this is dependent, though, on whether your electromagnetic power generation technology actually works,' Patrick could not help saying.

'You need have no concerns in that area. It is only a matter of time. A working prototype of the PEG is available for inspection right now.'

'And, ironically,' Mehmet added, 'time will become our friend in the medium term. If the price of synthetically produced gasoline falls back to where it was when oil was at $45 a barrel, it will have a highly stimulatory effect on the world economy—quite apart from the incremental wealth generated by producing tens of millions of PEGs, many of which will be used to drive a brand new set of industries that will grow up around the new energy technology. For example, if the world's poorer nations can be empowered in this way, they will start to trade more actively both internally and externally, and the wealth will spread both deeply and broadly.'

Tara had been watching Yehuda intently as he was delivering his ideas. She was looking for signs that he was dealing from the "passion" pack rather than the "logic" pack. Credit to him, he seemed to be quite calm in his arguments. Mehmet looked as though he had heard it all before. She smiled to herself. Patrick and she were probably fresh meat. No. That was too unkind. So far, nothing Yehuda had said sounded off-the-wall. The problem was practicality. What did he expect to do about all this? Could the vision of one man sitting in his library at home on a tiny island in the Caribbean ever be realised? And then she remembered Samantha. It's not what you know, but who. The real power of bankers is not their money, it's their networks. At her level in the bank, Samantha must be *very* well connected. Mmm. Maybe she should keep an open mind.

'I hear you on all this,' Patrick interjected 'but it still doesn't address the question of economic priorities. In the foreseeable future, the rich will stay rich and the poor will stay poor. Merely handing out these PEGs to the inhabitants of the poorer nations is not going to get them to generate production output. They won't have the skills. The world economy still needs to grow while they are acquiring these skills. What will drive the growth in the meantime?'

'I think you are being too pessimistic,' Yehuda responded. 'The process will have started. We will not be handing out canned fish. We will be empowering people to fish for themselves. But I agree with you. Other things must happen too.'

'As soon as we have put these matters in train, humanity's top priority will be to address the need to reclaim a potable grade of water from the oceans.' There was an enthusiasm in Mehmet's voice. 'And we will need to do that as quickly as possible—which, in itself, can be very stimulatory from an economic perspective.'

'Yes, but that's a two-edged sword,' Patrick protested. 'We'll also need to significantly increase the farm yields per hectare if climate dictates that there'll be less arable land. And we'll probably need to use land in what are now arid areas, and much of that land is low quality and lacking in nutrients.'

Tara's eyes went from one speaker to the next. It was like watching two tennis players warming up for a game. First one would hit the ball over the net, and then the other would return it. "Sproing … thwack … sproing … thwack. It reminded Tara of the night she had first met Patrick. He seemed to be in his element when he was processing information deftly and creatively. She wondered briefly what it would be like for their children to have an engineer and a pilot for parents. What would their world look like if Yehuda's plans were implemented?

Yehuda's voice penetrated her reverie. 'You're quite right, of course. And that is precisely where the poorer nations are located. In the longer term, we will need to bring on-stream what is now arid land in the Middle East and Africa north of the equator, which will need to be irrigated with desalinated water.'

'The oil producing countries,' Tara observed, her scepticism rising.

'Exactly right. They should become the food bowls of the Northern Hemisphere, and land reclaimed in the Australian outback will likely service the Southern Hemisphere.'

She had a flash of insight how a bachelor such as Yehuda could avoid becoming bored and lonely. The guy's mind was so full that there wasn't any space for personal worries and self doubts. He certainly seemed to have thought it through, but she wasn't sure just how in touch with the real world he might be.

'How can we achieve that?' she asked. 'Much of the land in the Middle East is nothing but low nutrient desert dunes, won't it be very energy intensive and very expensive to reclaim sea water?'

'The short answer is that "everything is possible". We have the water desalination technology, but there have always been two inhibiting factors. One has been the cost of the energy to power the desalination plants.' He allowed himself a small, satisfied smile. 'With my technology, the cost per kilojoule of energy will fall to a peppercorn level.'

'Do they have the technical expertise to reclaim the land?' Tara found herself spiralling into a series of questions and answers. She couldn't help herself. If Mehmet would only join in, maybe they could play a set of doubles.

'Ha.' Yehuda responded patiently, 'who on this planet has the most expertise in land reclamation if not the Israelis, although, admittedly, their knowledge is more skewed to reclaiming malaria infested marsh-lands than deserts?'

'Are you crazy?' This time the outburst came from Patrick. He couldn't help himself either. 'Do you expect anyone to embrace the idea that the Israelis will willingly help the Arabs to green the Middle East?'

'Why not? In our hearts, the Jews don't hate the Arabs.'

Tara raised an eyebrow sceptically.

'If it's a win–win outcome, I'm sure the Israelis will be only too happy to lend a helping hand. Don't forget that there are seven million people living in that tiny postage stamp of a country. If we take a twenty-five to fifty year view, one consequence of turning the Middle East and North Africa into a breadbasket to the world will be that population pressures and tensions within Israel will likely abate. The Middle East will become a Garden of Eden, and the Israelis, who are technology oriented, will more willingly share their technology and their technical expertise if the ultimate outcome is peace. History has shown time and again that those who were once enemies will become friends again.'

'But you are ignoring the fact that the Arabs and the Jews barely talk to each other,' Tara broke in. 'And when they do it's just going through the motions to keep the US or the EU or the UN off their backs.'

The professor smiled, glancing at Mehmet as he did so. Something about his smile told Patrick that the two had something else up their sleeves which they were keeping to themselves for the time being. His suspicions were heightened when Yehuda chose to ignore Tara's last comment completely.

Instead, he said, 'We were talking about constraints in water desali-nation. I would like to address the question of capacity now, if you don't mind.'

She shrugged, sighed in resignation and waved one hand in acceptance. 'Okay.' Every muscle in her face and body screamed a lack of conviction.

'The capacity issue is not so much related to the absolute number of litres of water, but rather to how many litres need to be reclaimed to do the required job. For example, if it might have required, say 100,000 litres a day to irrigate a particular area of land, but we can somehow double the yield per hectare of that land, then the effective desalination capacity requirements—and cost of water—will be halved. How could that be facilitated?

Instantly, Patrick's entire demeanour changed. 'Gold! The Ormus M-State white-powder gold of the Ark of the Covenant.' A wry smile spread across his face. 'Applied in the very same geographic region of the world where Moses and the Children of Israel wandered for forty years. What beautiful, ironic synergy.'

Yehuda laughed in response. 'I see your sense of irony is alive and well. And if, on top of the benefits of the white-powder gold, we can reduce the cost per kilojoule of energy, the costs of bringing these regions to biological life will fall even further.'

'And suddenly we have a whole new ballgame.' Patrick nodded in understanding.

'We should not get carried away, though. The PEGs will represent a practical, small-to-medium scale stopgap measure for water desalination. To extract large quantities of potable grade water from the oceans will require very powerful technology, possibly nuclear fusion technology. But, in the short-to-medium term we will not need exceptionally large quantities of water because the power of the white-powder gold can be harnessed relatively quickly.'

'And thanks to Sir Isaac Newton's far sightedness, most of the world's store of gold is sitting in central repositories.' Patrick stood suddenly, thrust his hands in his pockets and energetically paced the room. 'Can I ask you to backtrack for a second please? Could solar power be used in the warmer climates to reclaim seawater? Does it deliver sufficient amperage?'

This time, Yehuda rewarded him with a broad smile. 'By your asking that question I can see that you are very close to a full understanding of the possibilities, but the reality is that solar power will have a far more important application. In the hot sun of the desert, it may be used to very efficiently scavenge solar energy and convert it into electricity ...

which will be stored in the superconductive, micro-cluster white-powder gold.' He paused.

In the short time Tara had known him, she had learned to read the signs. This was one of his dramatic pauses. What else could he possibly have left to reveal?

'And now,' Yehuda continued, 'we need to change gears. I would like to reveal something I have only recently discovered, thanks to my pouring over the religious tomes since Patrick pointed me in that direction.'

'What if we all took a short break?' Mehmet said. He frowned, stood and walked out of the room.

CHAPTER 44

PATRICK AND TARA had walked out onto Yehuda's porch. Mehmet had disappeared and Yehuda had walked off after him. 'What was that all about?' Patrick asked without expecting an answer. 'Yehuda was about to impart something especially important, got himself all psyched up ... and Mehmet walks out.'

Tara responded with a smile. 'For my part I could handle a few minutes break. I wouldn't mind a real coffee and something deliciously sweet and non-fattening.'

'Well, let's go back in and see if we can raid Yehuda's bikkie tin—if not his coffee jar.'

Tara smiled at him affectionately. 'You and I are going to need synchronising, my man. In the US it's a cookie jar and a coffee can.'

He hugged her in response. 'Let that be the biggest problem in our lives.'

They walked back inside to see Mehmet and Yehuda were back in their usual chairs in the library.

'Would anyone like some coffee before we start?' Mehmet asked.

Patrick and Tara looked at him in surprise.

'How about you, Patrick?'

'No thanks. I've just had a scotch.'

'That was an hour ago. 'What about you, Tara?'

'We had coffee at lunchtime.'

'That was around four hours ago. Yehuda, that leaves you. Would you like some coffee? '

'I'll be happy to join you, if you would like a cup, Mehmet.'

'But why would you do that? If I remember correctly, your exact words when Tara and Patrick arrived here from their lunch were, "I don't know what he sees in that coffee of mine". Why would you drink this coffee if you can't understand why *I* drink it? It is clear now that you don't enjoy your own coffee.'

'Because you like it.'

'Have I ever actually told you that I like your coffee, Yehuda?'

'But you always seem so happy to share a cup with me whenever I suggest it.'

'Apparently for the same reason that you have just agreed to join me. I was merely being friendly. Patrick, would you please confirm that when you and I met the other night I explained in great detail how I go about making real Turkish coffee in my home? I take my coffee very seriously. It's a labour of love.'

Patrick laughed. 'That's quite true, Yehuda. It's a ritual for him. Clearly, your ersatz coffee has been serving to stoke the fires of his passion for his own coffee. I don't want to hurt your feelings, but I can now see why Mehmet is so passionate about that subject. Yours must be the just about the most revolting I've ever tasted.'

'Patrick!' Tara admonished. 'You can't say things like that! It's hurtful.'

'Why should it be hurtful?' Yehuda asked. 'I didn't grow the damned stuff. I agree with Patrick. The coffee is terrible.'

'Then why do you keep buying it?' Mehmet asked.

'I thought you liked it.'

'Which brings me back to the original point. In all the years you and I have known each other, and in the years you and I have been drinking this beautiful looking, richly coloured, dark liquid, I am prepared to bet that you that I have never once said I liked its taste.'

'But why didn't you tell me you didn't like it?' Yehuda pressed.

'Why didn't *you* tell me *you* didn't like it?' Mehmet countered.

'How many years have you guys known each other?' Tara asked.

'That's an easy one to answer,' Yehuda responded. We met in 1997, three years before I introduced him to the Eagle Mines. We have been meeting regularly ever since his appointment as its agent.'

'You've both been drinking this witch's brew for seven years?' Patrick asked throwing his hands in the air in mock horror.

'Yes. It's been seven lean years,' Yehuda said in the same tone.

The four looked at each other as shocked smiles turned into broad grins then laughter. It was a full minute, before Tara managed to ask, 'You wouldn't happen to have a teabag lying around, would you Yehuda?'

'I can do better than that my dear,' he said and walked out of the door and into his kitchen, where they heard a cupboard door being opened and then slammed shut again. Within thirty seconds, Yehuda walked back in carrying a multi-cup espresso machine.

'I hide this in the kitchen every time, just before you come to visit me, Mehmet. I bought it as a sixty-fifth birthday present for myself some years ago. Who would like a cup of genuine, mild, slow roasted, espresso coffee? It's blended for me by a friend in the coffee roasting business who uses mainly Nuevo Mondo Arabica beans that are shade grown right here on the island. It has a full-bodied, earthy taste, but he blends them with another Arabica variety which he brings in from Kenya to give it smoothness. I believe he also adds just a small proportion of Robusta beans, which he imports from an organic farming estate in the high country of India. The Robusta serves to give the final product a slight citrussy bite.'

'When you put it like that, I'll have two cups please,' Mehmet said, giving rise to another round of laughter. 'And that leads me to the reason I called for a break.' This time it was his turn to head towards the kitchen. He returned in a moment holding aloft a plate with a fresh cream-cake.

'In Turkish we call this *taze kremali pasta*. A little something to celebrate the engagement. I'd left it in Yehuda's fridge and it needed to come to room temperature before I served it.'

Patrick and Tara exchanged secret glances.

'It becomes self-evident that clear, precise, truthful and unambiguous communication between two parties is necessary to avoid misunderstandings,' Mehmet said when they were all once again comfortably seated, each nursing a cup of freshly brewed, coffee and finishing off the slices of Mehmet's dessert.

'Mmmm *dlshious*,' Tara said, finishing off a last mouthful.

'A true Turkish delight,' Patrick said. 'And do you know the difference between a Turkish delight and an Englishman's delight—'

'Stop. Stop. You're turning into my father!' Tara put her hands to her head in mock horror. 'You two and your jokes.'

Mehmet smiled; he'd heard it all before.

Yehuda seemed to be in deep contemplation. He was staring at the paintings behind the settee. 'Wha ...?' he said, after a few seconds of silence. 'Oh. Yes.' He cleared his throat. 'Actually, I agree with Mehmet. As it happens, I have made an important discovery which will hopefully lead to more open and honest communication in the world, so why don't I just wrap up this discussion we've been having on how the white-powder gold may have worked to stimulate crop yields?'

The others nodded their agreement.

'If we read between the lines of the biblical stories I related to you earlier,' he began, 'the Ark of the Covenant seems to have been sufficiently powerful—with maybe only a couple of kilograms of manna inside the golden jar—to have delivered bolts of electrical energy that were so powerful they were able to destroy the fortification walls of the city of Jericho. The story of the trumpets is apocryphal. The sound of trumpets does not make walls fall down. There must have been a weapon of some sort and the probabilities favour that the weapon was the Ark of the Covenant. I ask you, once again, to allow your imaginations to soar with mine. Imagine how powerful the energy would be that was scavenged and stored in, say, a ton of that material.'

'But what would you do with a weapon of such destructive capability?' Tara demanded.

'You are holding the telescope the wrong way around, my dear,' Yehuda responded gently. 'Knowing what we now know about this technology we can understand that one of the purposes of the Egyptian pyramids may have been to energise the surrounding lands, which were irrigated by water drawn from the Nile.'

'You'll have to explain that. So far, I've heard nothing which could even remotely point to that conclusion.' Her voice was tinged with exasperation.

'Bear in mind the budding of Aaron's staff. Then, remember too, that it is known the pyramids were built with what we have come to refer to as capstones covering their pointed peaks. Reading Sir Lawrence Gardner's work, it appears that those capstones were made from a highly conductive gold-glass substance that incorporated the white-powder gold. The pyramids are so large that the capstones must have contained enormous quantities of this powder—which would have been scavenging massive amounts of telluric energy. Whether, now, the energy should be scavenged in the manner of the Ark of the Covenant, or whether we can more effectively apply solar energy technology for that purpose remains to be seen, but the end result will hopefully remain the same. Also, we may not need to build such large edifices—which, in my view, were deliberately left for posterity. The same principle could be applied by a large number of smaller energy conduits dotted throughout the lands. What is important here is a principle regarding how electricity behaves, which was made famous by …'

'Benjamin Franklin!' Patrick suddenly interjected and rising to his feet. His voice was higher pitched, excited.

'Yes, my friend,' Yehuda said grinning with the pride of a teacher whose student had finally put two and two together, 'Benjamin Franklin.'

Mehmet had a puzzled expression on his face. 'What about him? Please bear mind that some of us in this room are neither engineers nor professors.'

'Do you remember the story about Franklin's experience with the kite in the thunderstorm?' Patrick paced in a small circle. 'How the lightning struck the metal key that was tied to the string near the kite as it was flying in the air—and the electricity ran down the string to earth?'

'Yes,' Mehmet responded. 'Vaguely, only vaguely. It is not a history I learnt at school.'

'The pyramids would have worked in essentially the same way. The capstones would have scavenged telluric energy, and the electric charge that built up in the white-powder gold would have been converted into enormously large electric currents that flowed down the sides of the pyramids, thereby energising the surrounding land for some distance.'

'It's a phenomenon known as Ohm's Law,' Yehuda joined in. 'In the absence of resistance, a steady increase in voltage gives rise to a linear rise in current. The current running down to earth along the sides of the pyramids would have been vibrating at a biologically stimulative wavelength.'

Tara looked at him, her eyes screwed up to reflect the intensity of her thinking. 'The village … er, er … Findhorn!' she exclaimed, then laughed out aloud. Finally, she understood. She felt as if they had been reconstructing a 500-piece jigsaw puzzle, and she could finally see where the few remaining pieces would fit.

Yehuda smiled. 'Yes, Findhorn, where the nutrient level in the soil is poor but the crop yields are exceptional because the village sits on a magnetic ley line. Of course, the key lies in the superconductive nature and other physical characteristics of this white-powder gold material. My guess is that if the world pools and concentrates its brainpower, the technology can be under small scale trial within a couple of years, and large scale application within maybe five years. It can be used to stimulate crop yields. Irrigation will be by means of desalinated potable quality water using existing water micro-filtration technology, powered by existing energy technologies as augmented or replaced by the low cost PEGs.'

Once again, Yehuda's smile was enigmatic.

Tara smiled, ruefully. She hoped the substance in those water pipes would be less hallucinogenic than what Yehuda must have been smoking in his little briar pipe. Speaking of which, where was that pipe? He hadn't lit it even once since their arrival.

'Patrick and Tara,' Yehuda continued, 'the fact is that the ancient religions have pre-empted science, and science is now catching up. It is now an undeniable fact that the "what" of religion and the "how" of science are converging. This is a very humbling development for all concerned.'

CHAPTER 45

'**I** BELIEVE THAT the key to defusing the clash of civilizations, which has been raging since time immemorial, may lie in Yehuda's ersatz coffee,' Mehmet said, his eyes glinting with a touch of humour.

'You think that the clash of civilizations boils down to a breakdown in communications?' Tara asked, arching her eyebrow at Mehmet.

'There is not a shadow of doubt about it, in either my mind … or Yehuda's,' Mehmet responded. 'Let me illustrate the importance of clear communication by showing you a particular passage from the *Holy Qur'an*, written in Arabic.*ᵛˣ* It appears twice. Once in Surah 2:62 and then repeated in Surah 5:69.' He picked up a piece of paper which had been lying on the top of the pile on one side of the large coffee table, and laid it face up on the opposite end of the table so that Patrick and Tara could see it.

'I don't expect you to understand what this says, so I will translate it for you. What it says, precisely, is this:

Those who believe, and those who are Jews, and Christians, and Sabians and who believe in Allah and the Last Day, and work righteousness, shall have their reward with their Lord; on them shall be no fear, nor shall they grieve.'

'That doesn't seem too momentous, or am I missing something?' Patrick asked.

'There are those who would twist the precise meaning of these words to serve their own ends. It happens that the Sabians were a group of people who had lived for around 1,100 years near to where our Prophet Muhammad lived in those days, peace be upon him. To all intents and purposes, the Sabians no longer exist. What is important is that whilst the passage is clear that Jews, Christians and Sabians *who believe in God, and the Last Day, and work righteousness [sic] shall have their reward*, there are those who argue that the words "those who believe" should be interpreted to mean, "those who believe in the *Holy Qur'an*, and only those who believe in the *Holy Qur'an*".'

Mehmet turned to Yehuda. 'Tell me, do you believe in the one Almighty Creator; do you believe that there will be an end of days, similar to the Christian belief; and do you believe that you conduct yourself righteously?'

'I think that I can honestly answer "yes" to all three and, I imagine, so can everyone else in this room if they were really pressed.'

Mehmet turned to Patrick and Tara. He raised his hands in front of him, as through gripping a large unseen globe. 'Do you both believe that the universe must have had some external consciousness brought to bear in its creation, or are you prepared to embrace the statistically random event that some scientists argue was the ultimate cause of our existence?'

They looked at one another and shrugged. 'I can't speak for Tara, but I was brought up as a Christian. And even though I hadn't set foot in a church for years until yesterday, I would agree that there must be a Creator, or a God, or "the Force" if you're a *Star Wars* fan, or however else you want to describe the universal intelligence. The probability that a universe of such exquisite physical precision could have evolved from a mere statistical accident is so remote that I can't even begin to imagine how it might be true. And, yes, I agree there will probably be an end of days from the perspective of humanity, and yes, I do try to conduct my affairs with integrity.'

As her man was speaking, the image of the perfect rose he had given her drifted into her mind. 'That about sums me up too,' Tara agreed.

'So the problem does not lie in the words of the *Holy Qur'an*,' Mehmet continued, moving his hands to the horizontal as though holding a book. 'It lies in how some people choose to interpret those words which might have had some ambiguity if they were read out of context.'

'But as you say, it seems self-evident from the wording what was intended—so why bring it up?' Patrick asked.

'Because the so-called jihad that is being fought is justified in the minds of those extremists on the basis that anyone who is not a Muslim is a non-believer. That argument, as we have just illustrated, is clearly and unambiguously untrue.'

'But it doesn't change the fact that, as far as I am concerned, the Arabs hate the Jews, and vice versa, notwithstanding Yehuda's earlier protestation.' She turned to face him. 'With all due respect, no one is going to buy into the idea that the Arabs and the Jews are just going to bury the hatchet—unless it's in each other's heads.'

'Both Yehuda and I substantially agree with you,' Mehmet persisted, 'but we also both believe that we have finally come to understand why it is so. And if we are correct, then the position is very likely reversible. It revolves around communication and the meaning of words.'

'Well I, for one, am at least prepared to hear the guys out,' Patrick offered. What's the downside?'

Tara shrugged. 'Okay by me. I'll listen to anything you have to say— even if it's got a five percent chance of working. The alternative's not particularly appealing.'

'Well, now,' Yehuda said, 'that is probably my cue to enter the fray because I am the Jew amongst the four of us, and the question that needs to be asked is whether or not we Jews might have done anything in the shadowy mists of history to cause the animosity in the first place. After all, it takes two sides to have a disagreement.'

'Like the Jewish occupation of Israel.' Tara said with a hint of defiance in her voice.

'And before that, the proposition that Abraham's younger son, stole the birthright of his older brother?' Patrick added.

'The birthright is the historical point of contention, but it would seem the facts are far more subtle. When you examine the actual words of the source documents you see two things: first, that God's original covenant—as reported in the *Torah*—was with Abraham personally and not in respect of either of his sons. The second thing is that, in the *Holy Qur'an*'s recounting of the story of Abraham about to sacrifice his son on the mountain, in Surah 37:100–102, the identity of the son was not specified. The issue revolves around Surah 37:107 which states, from memory, *We ransomed (Ishmael) by substituting an animal sacrifice.* In the original text, the name of Ishmael was not specified in that Surah either. It was put in later in brackets by someone who must have taken a so-called executive decision. It was certainly not the Angel of God or Muhammad who put it there later.' One corner of Yehuda's mouth twitched upwards at his little joke. 'It was put there by an ordinary person, however learned he might have been.'

Tara glanced at Mehmet to gauge his reaction. She saw that he was sitting quietly and stroking the bridge of his nose with his thumb and forefinger. There was no outward sign that he disagreed with anything Yehuda had said.

'The next point is that, in the *Torah*, God made subsequent covenants with Isaac and Jacob wherein He promised that a particular geographic region—Canaan—would be reserved specifically for Isaac and Jacob's descendants. He made the same covenant with Moses. Although the Hadith talks about chasing *pagans* out of the Arabian peninsular, Muhammad never challenged God's covenants with any of these three God-fearing individuals. So, if you read the original documents, you see that Abraham took no decisions at all to favour one son over another.'

Yehuda paused, but his body language indicated that he still had something more to say. He shifted in is seat, and scratched his head as if it helped him arrange the thoughts in his mind.

'And, finally, Isaac and Jacob also behaved in accordance with God's covenants with them personally. Moses was specifically instructed to lead the children of Israel to the "promised" land and there can be no doubt that the land of Canaan was promised to the children of Jacob, who later became known as Israel.'

Tara looked at Patrick. She saw his eyes meet hers then look away again. Surely he must be thinking the same as her. This was like splitting the hairs on the hairs on the hairs. The events being spoken about had happened over 3,500 years earlier. The real world had moved on. Hadn't it? Tara shrugged, and turned back to face Yehuda.

'Of course,' the professor continued, 'it might be argued by some that the *Torah* contains references which are at best inaccurate and at worst lies, and it cannot be denied that inaccuracies are possible. But there are so many references and cross references in the *Torah* to God's testaments with Isaac and Jacob that you'd have to conclude any error could only be the result of large scale skulduggery. That would cast doubt on the entire Book, and even the Prophet Muhammad himself did not try to do that. Broadly speaking, he accepted the truth of the *Torah*. Mehmet, this is your area of expertise. In how many places does the *Holy Qur'an* specifically acknowledge that the *Torah* represents the truth as given by God Himself to Moses?'

'From memory, I think at least six, perhaps more.'[xvi]

'So,' Yehuda said with a smile, 'it would follow that at least six separate references in the *Holy Qur'an* to the truth of the *Torah* were false. That would cast doubt on the truth of the *Holy Qur'an* itself. Are we prepared to do that? Are the jihadists prepared to do that? If so, who gave them the authority to do that? Are the jihadists infidels that they do not believe what the *Holy Qur'an* itself so clearly states?'

'I agree with Yehuda's logic,' Mehmet interjected. 'We are forced to either accept that both the *Torah* and the *Holy Qur'an* are true, or to reject them both as false. For example, Surah 3:3 states, *And He sent down to you this scripture, truthfully, confirming all previous scriptures, and He sent down the Torah and the Gospel.*' Mehmet emphasised the word "confirming". 'No Imam or other religious leader in this world has the authority to put his own interpretation on those clear and unambiguous words.'

'This all sounds highly convoluted to me,' Patrick said a little wearily. 'And there are other possibilities, given that the *Holy Qur'an* didn't exist at the time of either Moses or Jesus, and—if my memory serves—the *Torah* was actually committed to writing hundreds of years before Muhammad was born and it hasn't changed since. So how can anyone claim that it was falsified later? Nevertheless, let's say for the sake of argument that we accept both the *Old Testament* and the *Holy Qur'an* as being true. In the next breath you're going to point out an error in the *Old Testament*, which might have given rise to the clash of civilizations. How would that be possible if you've just got through telling us that the *Old Testament* is true?'

Yehuda laughed. 'There is indeed an error but it is not an error in the *Torah* itself. It is another example of an error of human interpretation of what is written there. Have a look at these three sentences all with the identical consonants.'

With that, he took a second piece of paper from the same pile on which the one with the Arabic writing had been lying and turned it to face Tara and Patrick in the same way that Mehmet had done earlier.

וְהוּא יִהְיֶה פֶּרֶא אָדָם יָדוֹ בַכֹּל וְיַד כֹּל בּוֹ

GENESIS CHAPTER 16 VERSE 12 (WITHOUT VOWELS)

וְהוּא יִהְיֶה פֶּרֶא אָדָם יָדוֹ בַכֹּל וְיַד כֹּל בּוֹ

GENESIS CHAPTER 16 VERSE 12 (WITH TRADITIONALLY ACCEPTED VOWELS)

וְהוּא יִהְיֶה פֶּרֶא אָדָם יָדוֹ בַכֹּל וְיַד כֹּל בּוֹ

GENESIS CHAPTER 16 VERSE 12 (WITH VOWELS PLACED MORE ACCURATELY, IN LINE WITH PRECEDING CONTEXT)

Tara was the first to react. 'Yehuda, as neither Patrick nor I can read what you've just put in front of us, I'm not sure what you are hoping to achieve here.'

Yehuda inclined his head towards her with a little smile of acknowledgement. 'What I have put in front of you is the identical sentence, written in Hebrew three times.[xvii] The first is in the exact form as it appears in the *Torah*. You will notice it has no dots or dashes.'

'Okay, Patrick said, 'but I can't see any difference between numbers two and three. The dots and dashes look identical.'

'No they don't,' Tara exclaimed. Look at the seventh word in the sentence. Its got a little dot hanging in the air to the left of the third letter, and it's got no little dots underneath that same letter.'

'Its like playing spot-the-five-differences.' Patrick peered at the paper then said with a chuckle in his voice, 'Any other differences?'

'That is the only one,' Yehuda said, 'except of course that Hebrew is read from right to left, so it is not the seventh word from the left, but the third word from the right, and it is not the third letter in the word, but the first letter.'

'Well, yes, okay,' Patrick agreed. 'What does it all mean?'

Those little dots and dashes are the vowels, and the *Torah* does not have vowels. The vowels were inserted afterwards by the rabbis who interpreted where they should go, based on the guidance of a document called the *Masoretic Text*, which began to be widely distributed around the time of Muhammad. Importantly, the *Masoretic Text* had some anomalies in it, relative to the earlier *Septuagint* which was the Greek translation of the *Torah* that was made in the third and second centuries BCE. With that one little change of the vowel, in terms of the rules of Hebrew grammar, the sentence takes on an entirely different meaning.

'Okay,' Tara said 'I'll buy. What do sentences two and three mean?

Yehuda sat back in his chair, and stared over their heads for a moment or two, looking at his happily colourful pictures behind them. Then he cleared his throat and smiled.

'Both sentences refer to Ishmael, among whose progeny were the Quraysh tribe, the direct ancestors of the Prophet Muhammad. The Muslims believe that Abraham and Ishmael together rebuilt the Ka'aba, which is the shrine that stands today in Mecca. They believe that the original Ka'aba had been built by Adam, and that it had been washed away in Noah's flood. Ishmael is therefore a very important figure in Islam.

'With that in mind, the first sentence translates to mean, *he shall be a wild ass of a man; his hand shall be against every man and every man's hand against him*. However, just by changing those little dots around one single letter, the sentence translates to mean, *he will be a fruitful man; his hand shall be with everyone, and every man's hand shall be with him*.' He paused. 'And it just so happens, that in the context of the surrounding ideas, the second interpretation would make more sense. For example, two paragraphs earlier in the *Torah*, in Genesis 16:10, the Angel of God delivers

God's message to Hagar, Ishmael's mother that, *I will greatly multiply thy seed, that it shall not be numbered for multitude.* By describing Ishmael as a fruitful man, the Angel of God would merely be reinforcing what he had already told Hagar about the multiplicity of her descendants.'

'I take it that the "wild ass" description is the one that is generally used,' Tara noted, 'otherwise we wouldn't be having this conversation.'

'Correct.'

'Touchy lot. Surely that wouldn't cause centuries of hatred?' she asked.

'Tara,' Patrick responded, 'the second translation basically says that the father of all Islam, the guy who helped build the holiest shrine in all of Islam, was a nice guy who everyone liked, and the first translation basically says he was an obnoxious man who was prone to violence and who got everyone offside. Let's get real here. I can see where Yehuda and Mehmet are coming from. How would you feel if someone spoke about your late father that way?'

'Well yes, I guess I would be pretty darned upset. My old man was a great guy. He never had an enemy in the world. Everybody loved him. He had a wonderful sense of humour. But I'm not going to hold a grudge for the rest of my life and kill whoever said it.'

'Okay, now you and I are not particularly religious, but it would be as offensive as Muslims denigrating Jesus for all time. Put yourself in Mehmet's shoes. I've noticed that every time he mentions the Prophet Muhammad's name, he uses the words, "peace be upon him".' He turned to Mehmet. 'Am I right? Would that description of Ishmael being a wild ass of a man be taken seriously by most observant Muslims who are generally respectful towards their forebears? Does it upset you?'

'Because of my Sufi training, I am more tolerant to insults than most, but I would imagine that there will be large numbers of people who would regard that description as extremely disrespectful—especially if they had their own historical reasons to believe it to be untrue.'

'So you think the real problem may be the perceived attitude of disrespect of the Jews towards the Muslims that reverberates down through the ages?' Tara asked, turning to face Yehuda. 'You don't think it was related to the birthright issue at all?'

'I didn't say that, Tara. I'm sure the birthright issue rankles with many, but the practical reality is that the birthright issue did not have any real consequences to Ishmael. The land that Jacob inherited was promised to him by God Himself in the *Torah* that the *Holy Qur'an* specifically validates at least six times. The Muslims would need to go to a far higher authority than the Jews to redress that particular issue.'

'So sue Allah,' Patrick said, laughing.

'It's not a laughing matter, Patrick,' Mehmet said severely.

'Sorry, Mehmet, I didn't mean you any disrespect.' Patrick paused, although not for long. 'But come on guys, again let's get real here. Let's assume you're right Yehuda. Let's assume that the real issue is that the Muslims are programmed in their genes to be congenitally upset at the disrespectful way their highly respected forebear was regarded by the Jews, who were the descendants of his younger brother. And let's agree that if that assumption is right, then the irritation regarding an otherwise meaningless birthright in practical terms was exaggerated out of all proportion. What can be done about it now?'

'It's not for me to prescribe a course of action, but this particular issue does have a precedent.'

Both Tara and Patrick looked surprised. Tara was the first to recover. 'Precedent?'

'Yes. For centuries, the Jews were very upset because the Christian *Bible* blamed us for the death of their Lord, Jesus Christ. This was something to which we took strong exception given that crucifixion was a peculiarly Roman practice, and given that whatever Jesus was doing he was certainly not breaking any Jewish laws that would warrant His execution. Even His last supper in this life was a celebration of the traditional Jewish Passover. Eventually, the Holy See moved to redress the error in the *New Testament.*'

'You mean, the Catholics apologised to the Jews?' Patrick looked confounded.

'Yes, I vaguely remember hearing about that—Pope John XXIII,' Tara said nodding her head. 'Didn't he also take out reference to "perfidious Jews" from the Good Friday prayer too?'

Out of the corner of his eye, Patrick saw Mehmet nodding. 'The question needs to be posed,' Mehmet said, 'as to whether it might be appropriate for the Jews to apologise to the Muslims in respect of this particular matter. No one is saying that the *Torah* is faulty. What appears to have happened, is that the rabbis in ancient times may have applied an incorrect interpretation to what was recorded in the *Torah*.'

Tara looked at Yehuda for his reaction. Yehuda returned her gaze for a long moment before replying. 'It would certainly be the next most significant olive branch ever offered between the descendants of Abraham,' he said, quietly and firmly. 'Frankly, if a gesture of such magnitude did not give rise to a good faith response in which all parties gathered around the negotiating table, then I can't see what will.'

'And what if the Muslim extremists do not accept the apology?' Patrick queried. 'Where will that leave the rest of humanity—including those Muslims who are peace loving and who may be predisposed to accept it?'

Mehmet cleared his throat. He smiled and turned to face Patrick. 'Do you know the original meaning of the word "infidel"?'

'I think so. It meant one who is an unbeliever in God.'

'Correct. And the *Holy Qur'an* is quite specific, not only that the *Torah* is true, but also that those who repent and demonstrate their belief in God, and live righteously should be left to live in peace. It would follow by the commandment of Allah Himself, via the Angel Gabriel, that any Muslim who did not accept such an apology would be classified as an infidel; and the *Holy Qur'an* is also quite specific regarding the obligations and responsibilities of Muslims in respect of the treatment of infidels.'

'Are you serious about this? You're telling us that devout Muslims would be bound to take action against the extremists?'

'Of course. I am myself a devout and peace-loving Muslim. There would be no question in my mind as to the significance of such an apology, or, for that matter, of the lack of bona fides of anyone who refused to accept it.'

Tara opened her mouth to say something, but words escaped her. Patrick's jaw was clenched. No one spoke. Eventually, Yehuda broke the silence.

'There is a verse in the *Torah*, or the *Old Testament*, or the Book—whichever you wish to call it—which all adherents of Abrahamic religions believe to be true,' he began. 'Genesis 33:18 opens with the words, *And Jacob came in peace to the city of Shechem.* Our sages tell us that he was at peace within himself, because the rift between him and his brother Esau had been healed. Our sages tell us that only when brothers are at peace with each other can they find peace within themselves. The time has come for the family of man to become whole again.'

Mehmet nodded several times, his eyes closed in thought. He rose from his chair and, almost as though speaking to himself, he said.

'My quest here is done.'

YEHUDA DID NOT see Mehmet after that day. Mehmet did not explain why. Yehuda heard he had returned to the monastery for a time. Perhaps, after all, there was no need to explain.

Tara and Patrick had met with Samantha Alexander, the new country head of Union Banking Corporation in Australia. She had been impressed with the vision and depth of evidence Professor Rosenberg had been able to send her afterwards, and she had guided him on how to present it to the Mansfield Foundation. It was amazing what doors her new title opened for her. Perhaps, after all, she could manipulate some good in the world of finance, even as its structures continued to disintegrate.

CNN reported that the world's most elusive and most wanted terrorist had travelled at considerable personal risk to the great monastery to meet with its new spiritual leader, the successor to Baba Amyn. There are some who whisper that he is the great leader of men ... the great hope.

EARTH

I see a new Earth;
An Earth that is alive–glowing with the care of man;
Man grown wise and free.

The influence of different civilizations flows evenly around;
Races and nations and sexes understand each other,
Endue each other with life.

Invisible threads of sympathy cover the earth;
Science and religion, art and industry, are one in truth;
The motive of every act is love.

Frank Townshend[xviii]

AUTHOR'S NOTE ON
ELECTROMAGNETIC ENERGY

1. THE TECHNOLOGY AS IT IS DESCRIBED IN
BEYOND NEANDERTHAL

The details of the electromagnetic technology described in the novel have been simplified to facilitate greater ease of understanding of the underlying principles by people with a limited scientific background, and have been fictionalised and adapted to suit the storyline.

They are based on the author's broad understanding of the workings of a prototype motor generator invented by Mr Joseph Newman, who submitted his first patent application to the US Patent Office on March 22, 1979. It took the Patent Office until January 1982 to reject the application, on the grounds that the Newman Energy Machine breached the laws of thermodynamics.

Mr Newman fought this ruling in court. Federal District Judge Thomas Jackson, who heard the case, appointed a special master to evaluate Newman's machine. The man he appointed was Mr William Schuyler Jr, a former commissioner of the US Patent Office. Mr Schuyler investigated and concluded the invention worked. He went so far as to recommend that a patent be granted, but Judge Jackson took the unheard of approach of refusing to accept the recommendation of his own expert appointee. Instead, he sent the issue back to the Patent Office for more study. What followed appears as a circus of obfuscation over a period of some years. The patent was never granted, although patents have been subsequently granted in more than half a dozen other countries.

The author has been in communication with one of Mr Newman's associates, Mr Evan Soulé Jr, who has been extremely helpful in his attempts to educate the author, for which I am most grateful.

Following is an extract of a note from Mr Soulé to the author, written on March 28, 2008:

> It is Joseph Newman's understanding that an electron (as other subatomic particles) is composed of large numbers of gyroscopic massergies; order of magnitude: in the millions.
>
> As far as the 'direction of spin' goes: all gyroscopic massergies simply 'spin'—they don't inherently spin in one 'direction' or the other. Since they are constantly moving in SOME direction, their orientation with respect to OTHER gyroscopic massergies changes and thus, by consequence, their 'direction' of spin appears to change; but in actuality it does not ... inherently. If, say, a given gyroscopic massergy spins clockwise, and if it were to move in a different orientation relative to either the frame of reference of an observer OR another gyroscopic massergy, it would then APPEAR to have counter-clockwise spin. However, that gyroscopic massergy does not [suddenly] stop spinning and then suddenly start spinning in the opposite direction. That does not happen. It simply spins ... period. At the speed of light. Then, its subsequent movement relative to other gyroscopic massergies gives the mechanical effect of it spinning in a direction opposite to that direction it was originally spinning in. But remember, inherently it never stops and 'changes' direction.
>
> [For example:] Say a given GM is spinning clockwise. If it were to flip over, it would then appear to the outside observer to now be spinning counter-clockwise. But inherently that particular GM never 'changed' direction of spin—it simply flipped its position 180 degrees.
>
> The degree-angle at which GMs merge (angles which can vary from 0 to 360 degrees and anything between) results in the creation of the various types of mass that can be observed or detected. Some degree angles, however, are more mechanically stable than others ... thus some type of mass—such as atoms of lead—are more inherently mechanically stable than other co-joined angles, such as atoms of plutonium.

Both atoms of lead and atoms of plutonium consist of the same
GMs ... but their angles of gyroscopic intersection are quite different.

The description in the novel of how these spinning mass-energy particles (gyroscopic massergies) are bumped out of their atomic domains as electricity begins to flow through a copper wire is substantially as it has been described by Mr Soulé to the author in other communications.

2. THE IMPORTANCE OF ELECTROMAGNETIC ENERGY TECHNOLOGY IN GENERAL

It is a natural human trait that no-one wishes to be seen as foolish. It is primarily for this reason that thought paradigms change slowly at the level of society.

As these words are being written, there is debate raging regarding climate change. Most scientists acknowledge that there is a linkage between man-made carbon dioxide emissions and global warming. The majority of scientists are now convinced that this linkage is a cause-and-effect linkage. Some believe greenhouse gases are exacerbating a trend to global warming which has been caused by the sun's unusually high sunspot activity within its eleven year cycle over the past seventy years or so. Of these, some believe that we may be approaching the end of a cycle of warming and that the Earth may—from 2012 onwards—enter a period of global cooling. Some argue that the issues are not necessarily mutually exclusive.

Beyond Neanderthal was predicated on a 'what-if' question. 'What if the global cooling scientists are correct?'

If they are correct, then one implication will likely be that the Earth's cloud cover will increase and thereby impede the rays of our sun from reaching the planet's surface. This poses a potential threat to the effectiveness of solar power technology which is being proposed by many scientists as a sensible alternative to fossil fuels—which, indeed it is.

Another implication may be that Nikola Tesla's model of centrally produced electricity, which is delivered to remote points of consumption by overhead cable, will come under threat because the grids will be vulnerable to power outages. For example, in January and February 2008, China experienced a 'wild winter storm' the ultimate cost of which was estimated at around $23 billion, and well over a million people went without electricity because of power outages. (http://www.usatoday.com/weather/storms/winter/2008-02-01-china-snow_N.htm; March 29, 2008).

With all this in mind, and with the notion of 'peak oil' also looming, the question that needs to be asked is whether there is an energy technology that might be used, which:

- does not give off carbon emissions? (assuming the global warming scientists are correct);
- is not dependent on the whims of the climate? (assuming the global cooling scientists are correct);
- does not substitute one form of pollution for another? (such as nuclear fission technology would do);
- has the capacity to replace oil as an economic driver in that it can create significant job opportunities in downstream industries within the economy?

The conceptual answer to this question is, yes. Technologies which claim to scavenge electromagnetic energy from the environment may offer this possibility, *provided* their claims are capable of being validated.

Unfortunately, this brings us back to the very first sentence above: 'It is a natural human trait that no one wishes to be seen as foolish.' The fact is that the underlying concept of the various electromagnetic energy technologies appears to breach the first law of thermodynamics and, possibly, also the second law which states that everything in the environment is trending towards maximum entropy. In layman's language, 'entropy' is the tendency for all matter and energy in the universe to devolve towards a state of inert uniformity. (This may be better understood from the example that a hot cup of coffee left on a table will go cold, but a cold cup of coffee will not become hot.)

The argument of the mainstream scientists goes something like this: 'Because the low entropy energy forms in the environment dissipate over time, there can be no practical way of scavenging this type of energy from a maximum entropy pool.' In light of this argument, and again given the opening sentence above, it is likely that few mainstream scientists will be predisposed to investigate any over-unity claims with any degree of enthusiasm.

Having said all of this, there is one clear path forward: Theories and arguments aside, if any protagonist of any technology which purports to produce over-unity energy can produce *third party verifiable* evidence that either (1) the measured energy output is in fact greater than the measured energy input, or (2) the measured energy output is less than or equal to the measured energy output, but the batteries which have been providing the source of energy input have not been depleted—then there can be no rational basis for any mainstream scientist to continue arguing against the technology.

Beyond Neanderthal was also predicated on another 'what-if' question. What if the protagonists of over-unity energy production are correct?

The author does not have a scientific background, and it follows that others, better qualified than he, should be investigating the various technologies on offer.

So far, the author has identified the following (non mainstream) alternatives which seem to warrant serious and disciplined investigation:

- The white powder gold, patented by Mr David Hudson—with specific reference to its ability to store electricity without reliance on chemical reactions (which may allow it to be coupled to solar power as a storage technology); and with specific reference to its linkage with DNA and the possibility of significantly improving agricultural crop yields. (http://www.lyghtforce.com/WhiteGold/hudson1.html; and http://www.lyghtforce.com/WhiteGold/hudson2.html; March 29, 2009)

- The Newman Energy Machine, patented by Mr Joseph Newman (http://video.google.com/videoplay?docid=1610087835473512086&hl=en;

http://video.google.com/videoplay?docid=4290794214864470920;
http://video.google.com/videoplay?docid=874167984066336720;
March 29, 2008)

- The 'Genie', a technology being developed by Magnetic Power Inc
(http://magneticpowerinc.com/exec.html; March 29, 2008)
- The 'Perepiteia Generator', invented by Mr Thane Heins
(http://youtube.com/watch?v=ogLeKTlLy5E&feature=related;
March 29, 2008)
- The concepts of Mr Tom Bearden, who is author of Energy from the
Vacuum (http://cheniere.org/; March 29, 2008)
- Sterling Energy Systems (an interesting variation of conventional
solar energy) (http://www.stirlingenergy.com/default.asp; March 29,
2008).

Brian Bloom
Sydney, Australia, April 4, 2008.

BIBLIOGRAPHY

Best, Robert M, *Noah's Ark and the Ziusudra Epic*, Enlin Press, 1999

Cremo, Michael A, and Thompson, Richard L, *The Hidden History of the Human Race*, Bhaktivedanta Book Publishing, 1999

Dawkins, Richard, *The God Delusion*, Bantam Press, 2006

de Blij, Harm, *Why Geography Matters*, Oxford University Press, 2005

Diamond, Jared, *Guns Germs and Steel*, WW Norton & Company, 1999

Dolan, David, *Israel in Crisis*, Fleming H Revell, Baker Book House, 2001

Dunn, Christopher, *The Giza Power Plant*, Bear & Company, 1998

Emoto, Masaru, *The Hidden Messages in Water*, Beyond Words Publishing Inc, 2004

Fagan, Brian, *The Little Ice Age*, Basic Books, 2002

Feiler, Bruce, *Abraham: A Journey to Heart of Three Faiths*, Harper Collins, 2002

Gardner, Laurence, *The Shadow of Solomon*, Harper Element, 2005

Griffin, G Edward, *The Creature from Jekyll Island*, American Media, 2003

Hatcher Childress, David, *Technology of the Gods*, Adventures Unlimited Press, 2000

Lindsey, Hal, *The Everlasting Hatred*, Oracle House, 2002

Maimonides (Rambam), *Mishneh Torah: The Book of Judges*, Moznaim Publishing Corp, 2001

Morrison, Reg, *The Spirit in the Gene*, Cornell University Press, 1999

Peters, Joan, *From Time Immemorial*, Harper & Rowe, 1984

Price, Randall, *Searching for the Ark of the Covenant*, Harvest House, 2005

Sacks, Jonathan, *The Dignity of Difference*, Continuum, 2002

Schlemmer, Phyllis V, *The Only Planet of Choice*, Gateway, 1993

Scott, Ernest, *The People of the Secret*, The Octagon Press, 1983

Townshend, Frank, *Earth*, George Allen & Unwin Ltd, 1929

Vatsyayana, Mallanaga *The Illustrated Kama Sutra* (trans. Sir Richard Burton, FF Arbuthnot) Hamlyn (Octopus Publishing), 1996

Weiner, Norbert, *The Human use of Human Beings*, Houghton Mifflin Co, 1954

Wucker, Michele, *Why the Cocks Fight*, Hill and Wang, 1999

ENDNOTES

i See reproduction of maps at www.beyondneanderthal.com.au.

ii Psalm 90:4; 2 Peter, 3.8; Surah 32:5. All three refer to the distance the moon travels in 1,000 years as it orbits the earth, but the computation is facilitated by the wording of the *Holy Qur'an*, which is more explicit and gives meaning to the other two. That distance, adjusted for the fact that the moon is slowly drifting away from the earth's gravitational pull (implied average 0.96 cm per year over its 4.25 billion year life), and divided by the number of seconds in a day, gives rise to an accurate quantification of the speed of light, namely 299,796 kilometres per second.

iii Source: *The Giza Power Plant*, Christopher Dunn, Bear & Company, 1998.

iv Source: *The Hidden History of the Human Race*, Cremo and Thompson, Bhaktiveda Publishing, 1999.

v A new direction of research has led to a focus on digging out deletions or duplications of code among relatively long sequences of individual DNA, and then to a comparison of these so-called 'copy number vari-ations' (or CNVs) across a range of volunteers of different ancestry. The researchers were astonished to locate 1,447 CNVs in nearly 2,900 genes, or around one eighth of the human genetic code.
http://www.abc.net.au/science/news/stories/2006/1795367.htm; November 23 2006.

vi Source: *The Hidden History of the Human Race*, ibid.

vii *The Hidden Messages in Water*, Masaru Emoto, Beyond Words Publishing Inc, 2004

viii *Noah's Ark and the Ziusudra Epic*, Robert M Best, Enlil Press, 1999. After reading this book, the author contacted Mr Best, whose reply was: 'My focus was on Mesopotamia and I did not research Mayan, Hindu, or other ancient civilizations. If 3113 BCE has some significance in your theory, it is a coincidence.'

ix Reproduced with permission of Richard C Duncan, PhD.

x http://www.americanantigravity.com/hutchison.html, March 29 2008.

xi Patent #GB2219995.

xii http://en.wikipedia.org/wiki/Coral_Castle; March 22 2008.

xiii http://www.fourmilab.ch/etexts/einstein/E_mc2/www/; April 23, 2008.

xiv See Author's Note.

xv Based on an analysis by Dr Ken Biegeleisen, www.ark-of-salvation.org

xvi Surahs 3:3, 3:65, 3:93, 5:44, 5:66, 5:68.

xvii Based on analysis by Dr Ken Biegeleisen, www.ark-of-salvation.org/wild_ass_200.htm, April 23, 2008.

xviii Source: *Earth*, Frank Townshend, George Allen & Unwin Ltd, 1929.

ABOUT THE AUTHOR

Brian Bloom was born and educated in South Africa and migrated to Australia in 1987. He originally trained on the stock market as a port-folio manager and, after a stint as a corporate planning officer for a large industrial conglomerate, he bought an insolvent manufacturing business which he nursed back to financial health.

One day in the early months of 1984, he found himself in a heated discussion—over a game of snooker—on the likely direction of the gold price. Out of this emerged a three-part book entitled *Stock Market Magic*. A copy of the book landed on the desk of the editor of the finance section of the *Sunday Star*, who contacted Brian and invited him to become a contributing columnist. The column, headed 'Albert Tells How' was based on the sage advice of a 300-year-old Swiss gnome who liked to raid Brian's fridge late at night and was willing to share his finan-cial expertise to assist Brian (and thousands of businessmen and women like him) to muddle through the savage recession of the 1980s.

Brian was then approached by a leading South African stockbroker to write a twice-monthly report on interest rate movements and, within a year, a nationwide poll of financial institutions voted him the number two financial writer in that space in the country. (He hadn't quit his day job yet but knew he wanted to keep writing.)

Then a reader of the 'Albert' columns drew Brian's attention to an article that had appeared in the May 1985 edition of *New Scientist*, which demonstrated three things: firstly, that 'peak oil' was just around the corner; secondly, that the mathematical model which forecast this was based on a set of equations originally developed in the 1920s to model biological growth. (It had proved that the Earth's ecology is really just one large and integrated biological entity.) Thirdly, it showed that the world economy pulsed to a fifty-five to sixty-five year beat that was ultimately driven by the emergence of new energy paradigms.

Here was a business opportunity of the future and it all made enough sense for Brian to want to position himself as a venture capitalist to help finance newly emerging alternative energy technologies. He sold up everything in South Africa and joined Citicorp in Australia where he quickly rose to the rank of Vice President.

But the new energy opportunities that should have come through didn't, and Brian started to wonder why. In 1991, he moved to greener pastures, and has been a strategic adviser to fast growing small businesses ever since.

By 1999 the Nasdaq was running out of control. The artificially low value of gold at the time—and the obvious Central Bank interference in its market price—put gold back on the radar screens. Brian had concluded that the USA was heading for serious economic trouble and he wanted to know if others were picking up on what he was seeing. Everything he read in the traditional media seemed to be shaded by some form of editorialising so he began contributing a column to first one, then two and then three and four internet blogs. What he found was an entire subculture of people who, like him, were becoming deeply concerned about the lack of ethics being displayed in big business and politics.

Fearing that he was seeing the death rattle of ethics in business and politics, he decided that someone needed to write something about this to reach a broader segment of the community. Sometime in 2005, the idea for *Beyond Neanderthal* was born.

Several technologies are unveiled in *Beyond Neanderthal* that have not yet seen the light of day in the world of commerce. They hold the hope that we might look forward to a brave new future but, this time around, in an ethical world, which is how it should be.